OPERATION SEAL ISLAND

Gordon Henderson

AUP UK
Terrestrial And Universal
Publications

Published in the United Kingdom

TAUP UK
Sheerness
Kent

enquiries@taup.uk

Prologue

Gregori's troubles started one Monday morning just after his first coffee of the day. His office telephone rang and he picked it up without speaking.

'Comrade Deputy Director?' Somebody on the other end of the line asked.

Gregori recognised the voice immediately. It belonged to Yuri Sikorsky, who was secretary to the Director of the Soviet Atomic Energy Institute. 'Yes,' his single word reply was as cold as ice. *Who else did you expect to hear on the end of my phone, cretin?* He was tempted to ask, but he kept quiet. Such sarcasm would be lost on Sikorsky.

'You are to report to the Director immediately,' the secretary's soft voice said. He did not add 'or else,' but there was a distinct threat in his tone that made the unspoken message clear enough.

'Tell him I will be along just as soon as I have finished my coffee,' Gregori replied defiantly, before realising he was talking to himself. Sikorsky had hung up on him. He stared at the silent telephone and swore quietly. 'You little shit! Someday you're going to regret talking to me like that,' he threatened aloud, 'and that day will be soon.'

Gregori violently pushed aside his coffee mug, upsetting it in the process, spilling dregs across his already badly stained desk top. He cursed again, this time louder and with vehemence.

He heaved his heavy body upright with such force that his chair shot back on its castors, squealing across the linoleum covered floor like a wounded animal. It clattered into the cream painted wall behind him, spraying the floor with specks of loose paint.

Gregori stomped irritably over to the window and stared out through his thick lensed spectacles. Although the blanket of snow that had covered Moscow since mid-October had started to thaw with the advent of spring, the city's waning winter beauty had been rejuvenated temporarily by an overnight snow shower.

1

At roof level the city sparkled brilliant white in the morning sunshine. However, down at street level the new covering of snow had already lost its virgin whiteness. The vehicles that sped along Lenin Street were spraying only oily black slush over any pedestrian who wandered too close to the kerbside. On the flat roof of the building opposite, the dowdy green overalls worn by a number of men from the Moscow City Council's works department stood out boldly against the bright white background. They stood in a line manhandling a long roll of canvas onto a low parapet from which a shower of fine snow fluttered down to the pavement far below as it was disturbed by the efforts of the men.

One man, presumably the team leader, stood to one side urging his comrades forward with waves of his left hand, while his right hand was clenched tightly round a vodka bottle from which he stole the occasional swig.

Eventually the men managed to manoeuvre the roll over the edge of the parapet and in unison they let it slide from their grasp. The canvas fell down the face of the grey stone building until suddenly its fall was broken as securing ropes that were attached tightened. It unrolled to reveal a banner on which was written in large Cyrillic letters the message: The 65th Glorious Year!

The banner was part of the upcoming May Day celebrations and was a sure sign that spring really had arrived and summer was on its way.

Gregori's thoughts returned to Sikorsky and the plans he had laid that were calculated to bring an end to the secretary's career. *I screwed the bastard once and now I am going to finish him off,* he thought with a smile that was so tight it did nothing to lighten his dour features.

He pulled at his face in an absent minded way, kneading the flesh of his heavy jowls between thumb and forefinger. He recalled with relish how he had scuppered Sikorsky's ambitions to become secretary to the Chairman of the Academy of Sciences, of which the Atomic Energy Institute was a part. It would have been a prestigious promotion for him.

Under normal circumstances Sikorsky's application for the important position would probably have been a shoe-in. It was endorsed personally by the Director of the Institute, Boris Braun, who was keen to have one of his own protégés in a position of influence inside the Academy Chairman's office.

But the pair had not reckoned with Gregori's opposition.

Gregori hated Braun, whose position as Director he had held before being demoted to Deputy Director following one of the frequent upheavals at the top of the Communist Party. He was convinced his successor had connived behind the scenes to have him demoted so he could take his place as top dog in the Institute.

Sikorsky's job application gave Gregori a golden opportunity to even the score with his boss and he came out in open opposition to the secretary's promotion. With that decision, the battle lines were drawn in what was to become a long running departmental feud.

Of course Boris Braun should have carried the day. He and his deputy director had powerful friends, and their respective influence was fairly evenly matched, but his higher rank carried enough extra clout to swing the decision Sikorsky's way.

That was until Gregori pulled a master stroke.

It had been simple. Gregori was friendly with an under-secretary in the office of Leonid Brezhnev, who was General Secretary of the Central Committee of the Communist Party of the Soviet Union and Chairman of the Presidium of the Supreme Soviet of the Soviet Union. Gregori encouraged his friend to apply for the post in which Sikorski was interested.

At first the under-secretary was reluctant to apply for the job because he thought his chances of winning such an excellent promotion were slim. However, Gregori persuaded his friend to put his name forward by promising to sponsor him and suggesting a strategy that would give him the edge over all his rivals.

The very next day, following his mentor's advice, the under-secretary mentioned casually that he was interested in the post at the Academy to Leonid Brezhnev, who immediately offered his endorsement.

As soon as news of Brezhnev's support was relayed to Gregori, he had a quiet word with a couple of members of the selection panel. He explained that the Party Leader was keen for his under-secretary to get the job and he didn't have to spell out the advantages of keeping the Chairman of the Presidium happy. They knew the way the system worked.

The upshot was that Gregori's friend was promoted to the Academy of Sciences. It left Yuri Sikorsky very disappointed; Boris Braun very angry; Gregori very happy; and the atmosphere at the top of the Atomic Energy Institute very sour.

The bitterness had taken root and covert warfare had opened up between Gregori and Braun. Yuri Sikorsky took an active and enthusiastic part in the regular office political skirmishes. He acted as the Director's eyes and ears, in addition to being a skilled agent provocateur on his boss's behalf, which is why Gregori had the secretary in his sights again.

In a locked drawer of his office desk he had stored away graphic photographs showing Sikorsky and his male lover. When the time was right, those photographs would be handed over to the Academy's Security Committee. Not only would the secretary's career be finished, but hopefully he would be heading for a Siberian prison camp. Then he would turn his fire on Boris Braun.

Gregori stared out of his office window and sighed heavily. Unfortunately none of the workmen had bothered to check that the ropes securing the banner to the parapet rail were properly fastened and now the banner was sliding down the side of the building, with gathering speed, towards Lenin Street.

He was not surprised, because once the workmen had finished manhandling the banner over the side of the parapet they clustered round their team leader, who still held the bottle of vodka in his hand. A second bottle had appeared from another man's pocket and soon they were all taking turns to swig from one or other of the two bottles.

Gregori closed his eyes and shook his head in despair. It was 65 years since the Glorious Revolution and this was what the Motherland's workforce had become: lazy, incompetent, indifferent and drunk.

He turned away from the window and headed for the door. Briefly he considered contacting the head of Moscow City Council's works department to report the leader of the team, but he quickly abandoned that idea. It would be a waste of time and effort, because workplace drunkenness was rife in the city, even amongst managers and deputies.

The Atomic Energy Institute was a department within the Academy of Sciences and was housed in the same multi storey building. Gregori, as Deputy Director of the Institute, was entitled to an office on the fifth floor. However, the Director's office was two floors higher and that rankled with Gregori. When he knocked on Braun's door he didn't wait for an invitation to enter, instead he pushed open the door and marched briskly into the office.

To add insult to injury, as well as Braun's office being on a higher floor, it was much larger than Gregori's. However, apart from a square of fawn rug, which hid a small area of the cheap linoleum that covered most of the floors in the building, the office was decorated in a similar fashion to his own.

There was the same standard cream paint flaking off the walls and the same cheap portraits showing the same party leaders. On one wall was a larger portrait that was slightly better framed than the all the others. It was a photograph of the Communist Party Leader, Leonid Brezhnev.

Positioned in front of the portrait was a simple desk and behind it was Boris Braun. To one side of the desk sat his trusty secretary, Yuri Sikorsky, who Gregori thought looked even smugger than usual.

Sikorsky had a small round face, with generous lips, seemingly pursed in a permanent kiss. He wore metal rimmed glasses through which blinked a pair of blue eyes that were as weak as his smooth chin. His hair was grey and cropped short above a pair of pointed ears, giving him the appearance of a short sighted pixie.

Gregori looked at the secretary and remembered again the photographs that were stored safely in his desk drawer. The photographs had been taken by a series of hidden cameras placed in the secretary's apartment on his orders and showed two naked men crouched on a carpeted floor in an illegal act of sodomy. One of the men had cropped grey hair and was unmistakably Yuri Sikorsky. The second man was younger with curly blonde hair, who he guessed was a rent boy.

'Come in, my dear friend,' Braun said heartily, with no sign of irony or sarcasm in his voice, despite his deputy already being halfway across his office. 'So how is it with you, Gregori Evseyevich?'

The Director's question was innocent enough and delivered in pleasant tone, but it was accompanied by an unsettling, wolf-like smile that set alarm bells ringing in Gregori's head. He narrowed his eyes and answered with an unsmiling non-committal grunt. He stared at Braun and tried to find any clues that might be hidden in his face, which contrasted starkly with that of Sikorsky.

The Director's face was gaunt, with hollowed cheeks and a high bony forehead. He had a grey, pallid tinge to his skin, which was accentuated by the film of talcum powder that he rubbed into his long pointed chin to cover the dark shadow that Gregori knew required frequent shaving.

Like his underling the Director wore spectacles, but the eyes behind the lenses were deep-brown, strong, intelligent and hard. They were hungry eyes that were forever sizing up their prey and accentuated the lupine smile created by the man's long chin.

Braun leant back in his padded, executive style chair. 'And how is that little librarian you keep tucked away in that downtown flat?' He asked with a knowing wink.

Refusing to rise to the bait Gregori did not respond to Braun's question, in silence he lowered himself onto the uncomfortable hard backed chair that was positioned in front of the Director's desk. He wondered how Braun had found out about Zia. He glanced at Sikorsky who made a point of avoiding eye contact with him. That was answer enough.

Braun did not push the subject, instead he asked: 'Would you like coffee, Gregori Evseyevich?'

Gregori shook his head.

'As you wish.' Braun said and turned to Sikorsky. 'The Comrade Deputy Director does not appear to be thirsty, Yuri, but I would like a cup.'

Sikorsky stood and walked silently over to a side table on which stood a metal coffee percolator. He poured a cup of thick black coffee, added three spoonful's of sugar, stirred it briskly then placed it on the desk in front of his boss before resuming his seat.

Braun picked up the cup and blew on the surface of the coffee to cool it, before taking a delicate sip. He nodded in satisfaction and returned the cup to its saucer. 'Now, down to business,' he said, pulling a buff coloured file from the wire tray that stood on the corner of his desk. He opened the file and looked up at his deputy. 'The Chairman has an urgent project he wants us to tackle…'

'What project?' Gregori interrupted eagerly, suddenly very interested. He was keen to be involved in such a project, because if the Chairman of the Academy of Sciences wanted urgent work undertaken there could be kudos to be won for those involved.

Braun held up a hand. 'Patience, Gregori Evseyevich, patience!' He took a photograph from the file and flicked it towards his deputy.

Gregori almost missed the photograph as it scudded across

the desk top and slipped over the edge, but he managed to catch it before it fluttered to the floor. He studied the low resolution photo, which was in black and white and of poor quality.

The photo looked as if it had been blown up from one of a series taken from a satellite run. It depicted an island, the surface of which was charred black and was devoid of life. Even at the great height from which the photograph had been taken, there was little doubt the island had been struck by some great disaster. Gutted by what must have been a tremendously hot fire, the island had been left sterile and dead.

Gregori looked up and raised a thick, questioning eyebrow.

'In your opinion, comrade scientist, would a nuclear explosion have caused such damage?' Braun asked. He rested his arms on the desktop and leaned forward, looking intently at his deputy as he waited for an answer.

The Director's hands were big and as bony as his forehead. They looked clumsy and too large to be controlled by the thin white wrists that poked out from the sleeves of his navy-blue serge suit jacket. Slowly, one by one, he interwove the long fingers of his left hand with those of his right, until both were joined in a white barrier across the centre of his desk.

Gregori studied the photograph again and squinted through his thick lenses to view it more closely. He thought he could detect debris on the island's surface and in its centre a depression, possibly a crater. It was not much to go on.

He shook his head slowly. 'It could be,' he said with a shrug, 'but it is very difficult to determine with any degree of certainty if a nuclear device has been detonated on that island using only the evidence of a photograph.' He paused and for several seconds he was lost in his own thoughts. When he did resume talking, it was almost to himself. 'Yes, it's certainly possible the damage was caused by a small nuclear device,' he mused. 'However, to be certain I would need evidence of radioactive debris, or perhaps air acoustic measurements,' he paused again. He looked up with a frown creasing his pock marked face. 'Have you collected any such evidence?' He asked.

Braun shook his head.

'Are you telling me no tests have yet been carried out?' Gregori was genuinely surprised.

'It has not been possible,' the Director replied with a little self-deprecating shrug. 'That satellite photograph was only taken a couple of days ago.'

With a disapproving shake of his head Gregori continued to study the photograph before he spoke again. There would be times when he wished someone had cut out his tongue before he spoke but nobody cut out his tongue and the fateful words came out loud and clear: 'Well, we won't know for certain what caused the damage to the surface of the island until you do send somebody to the island,' again he paused briefly. 'And those tests must be carried out without any further delay, or the evidence might be contaminated.'

'Is that your considered opinion, Comrade Deputy Director?' Boris Braun interjected quickly and formally.

Gregori looked up just as Braun lowered his hands and leaned forward even further, his long chin thrust out like the antenna of an insect searching for weaknesses in his victim. 'It certainly is, Comrade Director,' he replied equally formally. He looked into his superior's hard eyes and thought he saw a glint of triumph. Only then did he begin to suspect that something was amiss.

'That is an excellent evaluation, comrade, with which I fully concur. You are right, I must send somebody to the island immediately,' Braun said and his lupine smile returned.

Gregori stared at the Director who stared back, still smiling. He switched his gaze to Sikorsky, who looked knowingly at him before lowering his eyes again.

'And you will be pleased to know that the Chairman shares our view,' Braun went on. 'He wants to find out exactly what happened on that island.' His smile widened. 'That, Gregori Evseyevich, is the urgent project we have been set. I have been instructed to send somebody to investigate whether a nuclear device was exploded on the island.'

'Where is this island?' Gregori asked warily, finally realising that he might have fallen into a trap of his own making.

'The South Atlantic.'

'The South Atlantic?' Gregori repeated dully. 'Who?' He asked, suddenly no longer so keen to take on the project.

Braun reminded Gregori of a cat playing with a mouse he is about to kill.

'You mean who exploded the bomb?' Braun asked. 'I believe it was...'

Gregori knew Braun was toying with him and he fought to control his anger.

8

'…the South Africans,' Braun was saying. 'They have the…'

'No!' Gregori snapped as he lost the battle with his temper. 'You know very well what I mean.' He clenched his fists. 'Who is to carry out the tests?' He asked Braun, but when he looked over at Sikorsky he knew the answer.

The secretary ran a pink tongue across his pursed lips like a snake and his blue eyes shone out from behind his spectacles. He stared at Gregori and a barely concealed satisfied smirk spread across his face.

'I am sorry, my friend,' Braun said, although he looked neither apologetic nor friendly. 'It was not my decision. It was the Chairman himself who instructed me to send you to undertake this very important task.'

So the trap was sprung.

'How will I get to the island?' Gregori asked, his stomach sinking as he contemplated what lay ahead of him. 'Will it be by ship?' He added hopefully, at least that way he would be able to escape the constraints of his cabin by going on deck.

'Part of the way,' Braun said with a smile.

'Which part?' Gregori asked. 'And what of the rest of the journey?'

'You will fly from Moscow to Angola,' Braun explained. 'There you will transfer to a ship from our Antarctic fleet that will then take you most of the way to the island.'

'But you know I have a big problem with flying,' Gregori protested. 'It's in my file. Why can't I travel to Angola by ship?' He asked, wanting to plead, but being stopped by his pride.

'Surely that is obvious, my dear Gregori Evseyevich. As you rightly point out the tests must be carried out as soon as possible and it would take far too long to travel by sea. Sorry, but you will have to take the plane to Angola,' Braun said in a voice that stopped well short of being sympathetic.

'But the last time I flew I came close to having a nervous breakdown and that was only a flight from Moscow to Leningrad.'

Braun shrugged. 'I am sure you will be okay, comrade,' he said, his face impassive. 'After all, you did survive your previous flight, did you not?'

Gregori was not deceived by Braun's lack of expression, because the cruel glint in his eyes gave the game away. The Director was enjoying sticking the knife into him. Suddenly something else struck him. 'You said the ship would take me most of the way to the island.' He said. 'What does that mean?'

'Think it through, comrade,' Braun replied. 'If a ship flying a Soviet flag sailed close to the island the South Africans would intercept it immediately. So the plan is for our ship to anchor up well away from the island, in international waters, and transport you the rest of the way by helicopter.'

'By helicopter?' Gregori was even more appalled at the prospect of travelling in a small cockpit, than he was sitting for hours in the cabin during the much longer Aeroflot flight to Angola.

'Yes, you should be able to get to the island, collect your samples and return with them to the ship before the South Africans have time to send an aircraft from the mainland, which is hundreds of kilometres away.'

Gregori half rose to his feet and his face flushed. 'You can't send me!' He protested angrily.

'It is not me sending you, comrade. As I explained, your orders come from the Chairman.'

'I won't go!'

Braun raised an eyebrow. 'You won't go, Comrade Zamyatin? Is that what you want me to tell the Chairman?'

'But why me?' Gregori asked as he slumped back in his chair. 'Those tests could be carried out by the Institute's most junior nuclear physicist. It doesn't need me to go traipsing halfway round the world.'

For a moment the Director said nothing, he simply leaned across the desk, took the photograph from Gregori's hand and looked at it for what seemed an age. Eventually he replaced the photo into the file and closed its covers with a finality that spoke a thousand words.

'You do yourself an injustice, Gregori Evseyevich,' Boris Braun said softly as he rebuilt the wall of white fingers. 'It is true that a more junior member of staff could carry out the tests, but that is not the point, is it?' He paused and looked at Gregori steadily, a teasing smile flickered across his lips.

'So what is the point?' Gregori asked.

'Time is of the essence in this project,' Braun said. 'For the mission to be successful the tests on the island have to be carried out as quickly as possible. You said that yourself, comrade. You are our most experienced scientist. Not only will you be able to complete those tests quicker than anybody else in the Institute...'

'Rubbish!' Gregori's brought his fist crashing down on the

Director's desk. 'I could name half a dozen other people in the Institute who could complete the task as quickly as me.'

The wall of bony fingers crumbled and collapsed into two separate hands that settled comfortably and serenely on top of the buff file. Apparently quite untroubled by Gregori's outburst Braun continued his sentence without a pause: '...but, perhaps more importantly, you will be able to analyse the results of those tests immediately.' His tone had not altered, but suddenly a perceptible bite had been added to its evenness.

'We need to know as quickly as possible not only whether a nuclear device has been exploded, but also the type of device, its size and how advanced is the technology behind it. I told the Chairman that you are the best nuclear physicist we have, comrade. That is why it has to be you who visits the island.' Boris Braun must have known that Gregori was not convinced, but he showed no sign of caring.

'But you can't send me,' Gregori pleaded, forgetting all about his pride in his desperation. His heavy, scarred face had lost the infusion of colour brought on by his anger and was now a pasty grey. 'What about my illness?' He whined.

'Illness?' The Director feigned puzzlement, then a dawning of understanding swept across his thin face. 'Oh, you mean the minor problem you have with claustrophobia?'

'Minor problem!' Gregori spluttered. 'But you have seen the doctor's report. I have acute claustrophobia.' He spelt the word out: 'A.C.U.T.E. Do you hear? Acute. Have you any idea what that means?'

Braun shrugged his shoulders again, but said nothing.

'It's all in my medical file,' Gregori went on. 'The doctor warned about what could happen if I am cooped up in a small space for too long. He said that the long term effects could be disastrous for my mental health.' His voice rose another couple of octaves. 'You cannot make me go.'

Braun waved a little expression of apology with his big hands. 'Sadly it is out of my hands, comrade. As I have explained already, your orders came from the very top. I am sure the Chairman will have been briefed about your health problems and would no doubt have taken them into consideration. But he specifically asked that you be sent.' He smiled again. 'We must all be prepared to make sacrifices sometimes, Gregori Evseyevich.'

Gregori shook his head defiantly. 'Niet!' He retorted. 'Not

11

even the Chairman of the Academy of Sciences can ask that of me. I will not do it. I will appeal to the Central Committee. I will appeal to...'

The Director cut him off with another wave of his hand and smiled again. 'Who mentioned the Chairman of the Academy?' He raised an eyebrow. 'I am sorry, comrade, perhaps I misled you,' he said. 'It is the Chairman of the Presidium of the Supreme Soviet, Comrade General Secretary Brezhnev, who has requested you be given the honour of serving the Motherland in her hour of need.'

That is when it all fell into place for Gregori. As he looked into Braun's hard eyes he realised he had fallen into a well-planned trap, his fate was sealed and there was no way out for him.

It was common knowledge that Brezhnev was dying and his potential successors were already jockeying for position. There were two front runners; Yuri Andropov, who was head of the KGB, and Konstantin Chernenko, second only to Brezhnev in the Communist Party hierarchy.

Brezhnev was covertly lobbying hard for his close friend Chernenko to succeed him. Boris Braun was also pushing for Chernenko, but more openly. Gregori, on the other hand, was actively supporting Yuri Andropov.

It was quite obvious to Gregori that sending him to the South Atlantic was a ruse to take him out of play and ensure Chernenko had one less enemy to worry about. He wondered how many other of the KGB boss's allies were being side-lined in a similar way.

Gregori closed his eyes and felt like weeping. He dreaded the journey with which he was now confronted and felt frustrated yet there was no way out for him. If the powerful Yuri Andropov had been outmanoeuvred by his enemies in the Party, what hope did he have of defying them?

He was trapped.

The following days found Gregori fighting a battle that can only be appreciated by those who themselves have suffered from acute claustrophobia. His morbid dread of confined spaces deadened his brain, killed his spirit and left his body weak and listless. He became increasingly depressed and mentally unstable.

Gregori's rising terror began when he was cooped up in the cabin of the Yakovlev Yak-42D aircraft that flew him from Moscow to Angola. Because of the inevitable Aeroflot delays, including a six hour re-fuelling stopover in Addis Ababa, during which passengers were not permitted to leave the plane, the anticipated ten hour journey eventually stretched across eighteen long-long hours.

Two hours into the flight Gregori took a couple of tranquillisers, but they had no immediate effect. They did nothing to ease the anxiety that preyed on his mind, making him imagine that the plane's fuselage was slowly contracting about his head. Nor did the pills stop the irritation he felt about the way he was being robbed of much needed air by his fellow passengers. It included the KGB agent who had been assigned to guard him and whose only positive attribute was that he spoke very little.

He wanted to shout at them. They were stupid people all of them. Rough handed peasants and black savages, who filled the seats with their fat backsides and polluted the air with their inane, unconcerned chatter. Did they not understand what was happening? Could they not see he was suffocating? Being smothered to death by their very presence?

But, just as Gregori felt he could take no more, the tranquillisers finally kicked in and he slept, but there was no real escape. Even in sleep he had nightmares that were destined to recur time and again over the next few days. There could be no escape from his torment, because his tormentor was merciless, unyielding and unbeatable. It was his own tortured mind.

When the Yak-42D landed at Quatro de Fevereiro Airport in Luanda, after the long flight across Africa from Ethiopia to Angola, a helicopter was already waiting for Gregori and his KGB travelling companion. No sooner was he free from the hell of the narrow fuselage of the airliner, than he was imprisoned once again, this time in the even smaller confines of the helicopter's cockpit. The journey to the Akademik Krylov took only ten minutes, but it did nothing to improve his mental state.

The ship was an expeditionary oceanographic research vessel that was working in the area and as soon as the scientist was on board she set sail for the South Atlantic. Soon after the ship started her journey south, Gregori suffered his first bout of sea-sickness. The attack was prolonged and debilitating to such an extent he was unable to leave his tiny cabin for most of the voyage.

Gregori thought those few days during which he was confined to his cabin were a living nightmare, little did he know that fate had something infinitely worse in store for him. Soon he would exchange one type of prison for another and be pushed ever closer towards insanity.

The South Atlantic

Tuesday April 6th 1982
Alexei Borodin

Somewhere in the vast expanse of a South Atlantic Ocean that stretches from the scorching hot coastline of Equatorial Africa to the icy wastelands of the Antarctic a ship lay at anchor. Her rust stained hull rolled lazily with the gentle swell of azure seas that mirrored the clear blue skies above.

It was a warm day and quiet with the silence broken only by the occasional flapping of the grimy red flag. It flew from the mast at the ship's stern as it was ruffled by the wind that blew in from the south-west.

It was only a light wind, little more than a breeze, and the white folds it nipped and tucked into the water's surface barely scarred the ocean's surface. Every so often the breeze summoned up enough extra energy to unfurl the flag, at which time a dirty white hammer and sickle emblem was revealed in the centre of the faded red material.

At the bow of the ship the name Akademik Krylov was painted in large white Cyrillic letters that were difficult to read because of the red ferrous streaks with which they were badly stained.

Suddenly the tranquillity of the day was broken as Alexei's Kamov Ka-26 helicopter rose from the ship's heli-pad with a clatter of rotor blades that hacked uneven chunks from the morning air. As the ungainly craft quickly gained height he banked sharply left and headed in a southerly direction.

Alexei tried to settle his long, lean frame more comfortably into his seat, but the back of his neck was tight with tension. He was twenty-two years of age and had only recently qualified for his pilot's wings. This tour of duty with the Akademik Krylov was his first seaborne assignment and most times when he took off from the ship he felt the same thrill as he had on his very first solo flight.

Flying was everything to Alexei. It was his escape. The endless open skies offered him a taste of freedom that had been denied him all his life.

14

During those precious moments when he was airborne in his hoody, as the Kamov helicopters were affectionately known by the pilots who flew them, he was able to pretend that he was in control of his own destiny.

He could imagine that he had escaped from the all-pervasive, suffocating state bureaucracy that had nurtured him from birth and against which his youthful optimism was beginning to rebel.

Of course, there was no question of any real rebellion. Alexei understood that any hint of dissent would lead to recriminations, not only against him, but also members of his family.

Like many Soviet citizens Alexei suspected that he was being watched by government spies. Whether or not that was true, he was careful to keep his festering dissatisfaction to himself. He did not even discuss his views with his closest friends, because one or other of them might be tempted to report him to the authorities.

Alexei knew that he was probably being paranoid, but he lived by the rule that it was better to be safe than sorry. He had heard stories of people who had spoken out against the government, only to disappear soon after. He did not want the same thing happening to him.

Alexei was pragmatic enough to recognise his day-dreams for what they were. The bitter truth was that even in the air he was still controlled by the strict discipline imposed on him by the state apparatus that dictated his every move. But knowing there was no escape from the system with which he had grown up, did not stifle his longing for more freedom. Neither did it dilute the pleasure he usually felt whenever the twin rotors of the hoody lifted him off the Akademik Krylov on another flight.

But this flight was different. Alexei felt no pleasure or thrill, because on this occasion he was not alone. Today he had unwelcome company. Not for the first time he felt a twinge of unease as he remembered again the two men who sat in the helicopter's passenger seats, both of whom exuded an ill-disguised hostility that he found intimidating.

Suddenly a premonition of disaster sent a shiver down Alexei's spine and deepened his sense of unease. He clenched the helicopter's joy-stick tightly and the feeling of impending doom quickly disappeared, although the disquiet about his passengers remained.

A couple of days earlier Alexei had been assigned to collect the two men from Quatro de Fevereiro Airport in Luanda and fly them to where the Akademik Krylov lay at anchor several kilometres off the Angolan coast. He soon discovered that both his passengers had personalities as appealing as a vacation in Siberia.

The first newcomer was a short, stockily built, middle-aged man who was dressed in an obviously expensive well cut suit. It probably had been purchased from some smart shop in the West, but now looked as if it had come from a cheap magaziny on Moscow's Herzen Street.

The man was going bald and what remained of his straight black hair was plastered across the dome of his skull with strongly scented pomade. He had bushy eyebrows that were knitted together permanently into a fierce scowl that accentuated the dour expression on his pock-mark ravaged face, the square shape of which hinted at Ukrainian roots. He had a large fleshy nose, on which were perched a pair of heavy framed spectacles with thick lenses.

Alexei had been told that the man was an important scientist, but he did not know his name, nor had he asked. It was enough that everyone aboard the ship, from the captain down, treated the newcomer with a deference that was reserved for members of the powerful Communist Party elite that ran the Soviet Union. Now the Ukrainian sat in the passenger seat next to him and gazed out of the cockpit window with his face a picture of misery.

Alexei glanced at the scientist and saw that his body was pressed hard against the cockpit door as if he derived strength and comfort from the solidity of the aluminium frame. At the same time he noticed the door catch was not fastened properly and momentarily he had a vision of the door sliding open allowing the Ukrainian to tumble out.

Briefly Alexei imagined what would happen as the man's bulky body hit the surface of the sea and that vivid image cheered him up, but the feeling of cheerfulness soon passed. With a guilty sigh he leaned across and pushed the catch fully home.

He made a mental note to speak to the ship's mechanics about the door when he returned to the ship. The catch had been playing up for some time and he had submitted at least two written requisition notes for it to be fixed. Alexei sighed loudly; it was symptomatic of the incompetence of his ground crew that he was not surprised that his requests had been ignored.

Alexei was not surprised also when the Ukrainian did not thank him and instead continued to stare moodily out of the window. That too was how the system worked; the political elite took preferential treatment for granted. It was their right to be protected from even the smallest danger.

The Kamov Ka-26 was usually able to carry six passengers, but Alexei's hoody had been fitted temporarily with a special cargo pod. It was designed to carry just one additional passenger, leaving the rest of the space free for cargo. That seat was positioned directly behind Alexei and it was occupied by the second newcomer, who, if anything was even less appealing that the scientist.

The man was tall and as thin as a rake. Younger than his companion, he had a mean, sallow face and the cold eyes of a cobra. His lips were thin scratches round his mouth, his nose was long and carried on its end an almost permanent dewdrop. An aroma of long dried perspiration had impregnated his cheap shabby clothes. When Alexei had collected the men from Luanda this smell, mingled with that of the Ukrainian's pomade, had filled the hoody's cockpit with a pungency that still lingered.

His two passengers were surrounded by the unmistakeable aura of Soviet officialdom that was a manifestation of the transparent protection bestowed on those who were members of the upper tier of the Communist Party's machinery of power. That privileged position gave the men a power that Alexei recognised, feared and accepted as a normal part of life in a communist state.

As a small boy, he lived in the squalid, overcrowded tenements of downtown Moscow. The naturally shy and sensitive Alexei had developed a stammer and a tic that pulled at the corner of his mouth whenever he became excited or was nervous.

He had conquered his speech impediment, but his facial affliction remained and now his mouth twitched regularly as the thought weighed heavily on his mind that his passengers were dangerous men who it would be best not to upset.

Like Alexei, his two passengers were dressed from head to foot in protective clothing. It included a helmet, protruding from the back of which was an air-pipe connected to a multiple cylinder oxygen tank that was stored just behind the front passenger seat.

The Ukrainian had told Alexei nothing about the operation they were on, which was another symptom of the secretive society in which they both lived. Everything was always on a need to know basis, and all Alexei needed to know was that he was expected to fly his passengers to an unnamed island destination for which he had only a map reference.

17

Alexei could only guess at the reason why the scientist had insisted they all wear protective clothing. They would be forty minutes into their flight before he received his first hint as to the answer, although at first he made no connection when it did arrive.

He glanced down at the helicopter's control panel and his feeling of unease deepened when he saw the needles of his navigation instruments sweeping back and forth across their dials like tiny windscreen wipers.

He tapped the compass sharply with a white gloved knuckle, but there was no discernible improvement. He did not bother checking the other navigation instruments because he guessed the result would be the same.

With tuts of annoyance Alexei switched on his radio handset to inform the Akademik Krylov of his predicament and seek advice. He half hoped Captain Gorchakov would order him to abort the mission and return to the ship, but this hope was soon dashed when the only sound he received from the radio was a high pitched whistle.

Alexei touched the Ukrainian scientist's arm to attract his attention and pointed to the control panel. The man seemed unconcerned, he simply glanced at the dials on the navigation instruments and with a wave of his hand indicated they should continue on their way.

Alexei's first thought when he noticed the erratic way in which his instruments were behaving was that the ship's mechanics had screwed up yet again. It was a distinct possibility, considering the way in which they had failed to repair the latch on the passenger door when asked. But now it dawned on him that the problem might have something to do with them having to wear protective suits. But what was it?

And this was just one more question to add to all the others that had been nagging him. Why, for instance, had Captain Gorchakov not moved the ship closer to their destination? Why was Alexei ferrying his two passengers to an island in the middle of nowhere? Who were these sinister men anyway?

What was the purpose of all the scientific equipment that was stored in the hoody's pod? And what was the cargo they would be bringing back from the island?

Alexi decided that with so many unanswered questions it was no wonder that he felt so uneasy, but he consoled himself with the thought that his situation could not get any worse.

Gregori Zamyatin

Gregori stared down at the scorched surface of the island as the helicopter hovered like a hungry buzzard looking for a carcass on which to feast. The close-up view he was now given of the devastated area simply reinforced the opinion he had formed the moment the helicopter's instrument went haywire. There was little doubt in his mind that if the South Africans hadn't exploded an atomic device on the island, then somebody else had. He pointed with his finger to indicate to the pilot that he should land.

The helicopter went down amidst a swirling cloud of ash, swept up from the island's surface by the down draught produced by its powerful coaxial rotor system. A stiffening breeze snatched ash and blew it out to sea where it was deposited as a black scum across the water. As the twin rotors slowed, then clattered noisily to a standstill, more ash settled in an even layer of dust on every part of the machine.

Gregori barely waited for the rotors to stop turning before he tugged open the cockpit door. Quickly he left the suffocating confines of the helicopter and clambered out into the wonderful openness of the island, closely followed by the tall upright figure of the young pilot, whose name he neither knew, nor cared to know. They both wore a small portable oxygen cylinder on their backs.

They stood in the shadow of the helicopter, ghostlike in their white overalls. Gregori stirred up dust with the toe of a protective boot. Surrounded by that hostile and sterile environment, he felt like a fictional space traveller, tentatively testing the surface of a long dead planet, searching for sound footings before setting off to explore the interior. But there was no interior to this particular tiny burnt out planet, just a wide expanse of flat, inhospitable rock and black dust.

Now Gregori was out in the open, the panic with which he had been plagued throughout their journey from the Akademik Krylov had subsided somewhat and he began to relax.

Soon the two men were joined by the KGB agent, who had been assigned by Yuri Andropov. Ostensibly it was to protect Gregori, but probably the man had been tasked with ensuring that he was not tempted to defect, either to the West, or worse still, to the Chernenko campaign camp.

Gregori ordered the man to unload the equipment from the

helicopter, which he did without argument and with no change of expression on his mean, sallow face. Neither man asked the pilot to help with the unloading, but, the youngster did so anyway. Soon the tools, lead lined boxes and other equipment were unloaded.

Under the guidance of Gregori, the KGB agent and the pilot set to work collecting samples of rock, metal fragments and other easily moveable debris. The two men scoured the tiny island searching for suitable specimens, while the scientist stayed close to the lead boxes approving, or rejecting the various samples with which they returned.

The plan was to fill the lead boxes, load them into the helicopter and transport them to the Akademik Krylov. As an oceanographic research vessel it had six large laboratories, one of which had been hurriedly and specially fitted with the most up to date atomic testing equipment available to the Institute. It would be to that laboratory the samples would be taken and in which Gregori would undertake his tests, analyse the results and relay to Moscow his conclusions.

Alexei Borodin

Alexei and Cobra-Eyes searched for samples, which the Ukrainian scientist examined carefully to ensure they were suitable, holding each in heavily gloved hands. Totally engrossed in their task none of them noticed the bank of fog that was building up out at sea, a kilometre or so south of the island.

As the mist thickened, it moved quickly across the ocean towards the rocky atoll on which they worked. By the time the lead boxes were stored inside the hoody's storage pod an almost impenetrable blanket of sea fog engulfed men and machine.

After loading the last of the equipment into the helicopter, they clambered aboard. They were hot and uncomfortable inside their protective clothing, none more so than Alexei, who now viewed the still thickening fog with real concern.

They sat in the cramped cockpit for almost an hour, waiting for the fog to lift, but if anything it seemed to get thicker. Alexei tried to make conversation, but neither of his passengers responded. Cobra-Eyes just sat looking out of the window into the swirling misty fog, whilst the scientist said and did little except become increasingly agitated.

Eventually it was Zamyatin who broke the silence. 'We

cannot wait any longer,' he said. 'Take off.'

'That is not possible, comrade scientist.'

'Take off,' the Ukrainian repeated. 'Get this helicopter off the ground now!'

Alexei was horrified. 'But we cannot fly in such thick fog, comrade scientist.'

'Fuck the fog!'

Alexei tried to argue with Zamyatin, explaining the difficulties involved with attempting to fly the helicopter across open sea without navigation instruments. 'It is far too dangerous, comrade scientist. We would be flying blind and I have no way of knowing over how wide an area the fog bank covers. It could be hundreds of square kilometres. It would be better to remain on the island until the weather has cleared a little.'

'You idiot!' Zamyatin screamed. 'Didn't you hear me? I said get this fucking helicopter off the ground!'

'But, sir, if the fog persists we might not be able to find our way back to the Krylov before we run out of fuel,' Alexei explained patiently.

'I won't tell you again,' the scientist said, his voice cold and menacing.

'But the fuel is already very low, Comrade Zamyatin,' Alexei repeated his warning. 'If you remember you instructed the mechanics to only half fill the fuel tanks to reduce the weight to accommodate more samples.' Alexei pointed out, but he realised with frustration that his passenger was not listening to him.

However, Alexei would not give up, because he was not exaggerating the very real danger they faced should they try to take off in such thick fog. He felt duty bound to warn his passengers of the perilous risk they would be taking.

So he tried yet again.

'Comrade Scientist, I really must protest in the strongest possible terms.' Despite his mounting anger and frustration, Alexei forced himself to speak slowly and calmly. 'If you insist on ordering me to fly in this fog then you will be putting our lives in danger.' He paused to add weight to his next words.

'Comrade, when we left the Krylov we had only enough fuel to fly direct to the island and then straight back to the ship. We have a little fuel in reserve, but not much, and if we do not locate the Krylov at the first attempt, then we are in real danger of running out of fuel. Taking off in this fog would be folly. It would be suicidal.'

But Zamyatin was not listening. His heavy, pock-marked face contorted in rage as he leaned towards Alexei. 'Take off, you fucking imbecile,' he screamed, almost hysterical now.

Alexi stared at the older man and wondered how a scientist, who no doubt was highly intelligent, could not understand fully the dangers they faced. He decided the man must be consumed by some blind fear that affected his ability to think rationally.

In the hope he would help persuade his travelling companion to see sense, Alexei turned in desperation to Cobra-Eyes. 'Please explain to comrade scientist the danger we are in,' he pleaded, but his heart sank when he saw the look on the KGB agent's face.

Behind the Perspex mask of his helmet the man's expression remained hard and indifferent. He stared at Alexei for several seconds, his eyes cold and indifferent, then he pointedly turned back towards the window and once again gazed through it at the foggy outside world.

Alexei was not a stupid young man and knew when he was beaten. Getting Cobra-Eyes on his side had been his last hope. With a shake of his head he prepared for take-off.

When the helicopter finally shrugged off the shroud of sea fog Alexei's worst fears were realised. A carpet of fog stretched in every direction for as far as the eye could see. They could have been flying over the Kalahari Desert for all the water that was visible.

Alexei looked at his useless instruments grimly and this time there was desperation in the hard tap he gave the compass. It was no good because the needle still swung back and forth across the dial like a metronome. Which way should he head? He had no idea. He tapped the compass again and cursed silently to himself, but the oath helped no more than did his knuckle. Finally he took the bull by the horns and tugging the hoody's joystick to the left he banked and set a course for what he believed was a northerly direction.

It was a fatal error of judgement.

The inexperienced Alexei did not realise his mistake until they were some way from the island. The hoody's navigation instruments were still not working, but suddenly it occurred to him that the afternoon sun was slowly sinking down in the sky to his right. That's when he realised they were flying south and the Akademik Krylov was anchored somewhere behind them to the north.

Alexei immediately swung the helicopter round and headed in

the opposite direction, but it was too late. They had flown only half way back to the island when the hoody's engines spluttered several times, steadied, coughed and finally cut out. Three thousand kilos of dead weight dropped like a stone into the thick fog below.

Gregori Zamyatin

If Gregori had believed in God, then he would have described his escape completely unharmed from the helicopter crash as a "miracle". And if he had lived in the West then, no doubt, his good fortune would have been picked up by an uncensored media, for whom it would have made good copy for days.

But Gregori was a godless man, from a communist godless society, so it meant nothing more to him than a stroke of luck that he fell through the cockpit door that somehow slid open for no apparent reason. He was thrown clear just before the helicopter hit the water and exploded in a ball of fire that turned his KGB guard into charred pieces of flesh and bone.

Now he found himself in the debris covered sea, minus his protective helmet and spectacles, thanking the good fortune that had allowed him to survive the crash. But his initial feelings of relief at being alive, were soon drowned in the cold waters of the South Atlantic Ocean as he realised the deadly predicament in which he found himself. He was alone and now had to swim for his life, a task for which he was singularly ill prepared.

Gregori trod water, assisted somewhat in his efforts to stay afloat by the layer of air that was trapped inside the bulky protective overalls he wore, but it was a real struggle for him. He was a poor swimmer and his desperate efforts to doggy paddle his way to safety were hampered further by his lack of physical fitness. It was a result both of his sedentary lifestyle and a diet that had led to him being seriously overweight.

His legs were soon numb with the cold from the sea and his chest ached as he forced huge gulps of air into his protesting lungs. He was under no illusions about the danger he faced because of his physical condition. Unless he was rescued very soon, his remaining strength would seep into the cold sea and he would be finished.

Suddenly Gregori froze as he watched a dark shape move through the water towards him. He stared at it through myopic eyes, which were made even worse by the loss of his spectacles, and his stomach churned with fright. Although the object was little more than an indistinct blur, it looked to him like the triangular dorsal fin of a shark.

He screamed wildly and beat the surface of the water with his hands as he remembered that this was supposed to frighten off sharks. But his frenzied actions had no effect on the menacing shape, which drew ever closer.

Gregori closed his eyes to shut out the nightmare of the shark that he thought was approaching him, but the beast's attack never materialised. When he eventually plucked up the courage to open his eyes it was to stare into the blurred face of the young helicopter pilot, who kicked his way feebly through the water towards him.

The boy was obviously in a very bad way. He was so weak that he struggled to control properly the oblong shaped life-jacket that was keeping him afloat. The slippery dark red rubber jacket bobbed and twisted in the water and every so often it escaped his grasp. When this happened one corner of it jutted above the waves and Gregori realised this was what he had mistaken for a shark's dorsal fin.

The young pilot stopped swimming when he was within an arm's length of Gregori and stared pleadingly at him with pain filled eyes. There was a deep gash across his forehead from which blood welled, leaving the side of his face a gory mess. One of his ears had been ripped off and blood dripped down onto his shoulder, turning the arm of his white protective suit as red as the life-jacket. He tried to speak, but all that came from his mouth was a gush of life blood that spouted into the sea.

Gregori reached out a hand and managed to pull the pilot closer to him. He smiled as he put his arms round the boy's shoulders to better support him. 'Don't worry, I will help you,' he whispered into his ear, as at the same time he gently started prising the life-jacket from his weak grip.

'That's right, let go of the jacket, I will keep you afloat,' Gregori said reassuringly. 'You can trust me, my boy. Leave it to me.'

The pilot let go of his life-jacket and immediately sank lower into the water.

Gregori pulled the life-jacket over his own head and tied the straps round his waist. 'Here, boy,' Gregori said gently, 'let me help you.' He took the injured pilot's head in both hands and turned him round in the water so that he was facing away from him. Then, with a sudden twist and lunge, he pushed the young man's head under the water, tensing against an anticipated struggle that never came.

When Gregori was sure the pilot was dead he released his head and let him sink slowly beneath the waves. Then he swam away from the wreckage of the helicopter, kicking his legs with renewed vigour. He had no idea where he was going and he did not really care. He was just relieved to still be alive and afloat.

The sea fog disappeared as quickly as it had formed and as it lifted so did Gregori's spirits. He smiled to himself. Whoever or whatever was responsible for his run of good fortune, really was on his side that day. Even without his spectacles he was able to make out the massive shape of the Akademik Krylov steaming slowly towards him.

Gregori started waving his arms frantically and a short while later a dinghy was lowered over the side of the ship. Soon he felt strong, calloused hands hauling him from the sea and he was lowered onto one of the dinghy's rough wooden benches. A sailor wrapped a grey blanket round his shoulders and he felt an uncharacteristic sense of well-being towards his rescuers and when he thanked the smiling men who clustered around him, there was real warmth in his voice.

The sailors laughed and started talking amongst themselves. Gregori stiffened in shock. He did not understand a word they were saying. They were certainly not speaking Russian, so obviously did not come from the Akademik Krylov. Instead, they spoke a guttural language in which Gregori thought he could detect the odd German word.

'Hy nie Afrikaans verstaan,' one of the sailors said.

Another sailor bent down and unlatched a small cupboard positioned in the bow of the dinghy and pulled out a small round flask. He handed the flask to Gregori and spoke to him in a language he did understand. It was English.

'Here, meneer, take a sip of this,' the sailor said. 'It's good Cape Brandy,' he paused and made a great show of raising a hand to his lips and tipping it in a drinking action. 'Brandy. You understand?'

Gregori understood all right. He took a grateful sip of the brandy and sighed deeply in appreciation. He had no idea of the nationality of his rescuers, but he hoped they were not American. He dreaded the humiliation and embarrassment that would be heaped on his head if he was delivered back into the safety of the

Motherland courtesy of the Yankees.

But Gregori had not been rescued by the Americans. However, if he had known then of the torment that awaited him over the coming weeks, he might well have wished he had been picked up by his country's arch enemies. 'Who are you?' He asked in his heavily accented English.

The sailor who had given Gregori the brandy smiled down at him. 'I'm Chief Petty Officer Coetzee of the South African Navy,' the man replied. 'Our ship is the Hertzog.' He paused and frowned slightly. 'But more to the point, meneer, who the hell are you?'

David Statton

Wednesday April 14th 1982: Allington, Kent, England

It was a warm spring day. Down by the River Medway most of the tables lining the forecourt of the waterfront public house were occupied by female workers from the nearby Kent County Council offices drinking wine from long stemmed glasses. Clustered round the tables were male office workers, some drinking dark brown real ale from pint tankards, whilst others sipped lager straight from the neck of a bottle.

The women wore skimpy tops and were pretending that summer had arrived, while their male counterparts wore cheap suits and open neck shirts with enough buttons undone to reveal an assortment of chest hair and gold-plated chains.

On the water, boats of various size and degrees of smartness were moored in a long, bobbing convoy. Some vessels had paintwork that dazzled white in the bright sunshine, while others had hulls displaying a patchwork of dull red primer where they were being prepared for the forthcoming season.

The River Medway started life deep in the Sussex Weald. It was born clear, clean and full of hope for a healthy life, knowing nothing of the poisonous industrial waste that waited down-river to pollute its waters before being discharged into the Thames Estuary.

Unaware of its ultimate fate the river meandered through the beautiful Kent countryside until it widened and bisected the industrial Medway towns in the north-east of the county. It was here that it collected most of the pollution that was eventually disgorged into the sea off the south coast of the Isle of Grain.

The Medway was navigable up-river as far as Tonbridge, right in the heart of the Kentish farmlands. Its slow winding progress was interrupted only by the occasional, well maintained lock, which assisted the passage of the numerous boats that explore the lower reaches of the river all year round.

There were seven locks in total, dotted between Tonbridge and Maidstone. One of them, at Allington, was located close to the riverside public house. At the lock a young man was heaving on the long wooden arm that operates the lock's sluice gates. His loud grunts of exertion, interspersed with the occasional curse, could be heard above the sound of rushing water.

Away from the river a silver Ford Cortina turned into the access road to the pub's car park. It slowed briefly to let a second car pass in the narrow road and then it accelerated, bouncing over the speed humps that were positioned at regular intervals along the way.

Moored alongside the pub floated a luxury cabin cruiser; all port-holes, chrome rails and radio antennae. On the craft's deck a ruddy faced man was cleaning a brass bell that hung from a stainless steel bracket fixed to the roof of the wheelhouse. The man was immaculately dressed in a well cut blazer, cravat, cream slacks and white deck-shoes. Set carefully on his head at a jaunty angle he wore a navy corduroy cap.

Up at the lock the youth had finally succeeded in opening the sluice gates and as the water in the lock rose a small motor boat came slowly into view. Behind the wheel stood a second youth, dressed in a black leather jacket and sporting a bright orange Mohican haircut.

The man in the corduroy cap broke off from burnishing his bell long enough to remonstrate with the owner of a scruffy dog that was relieving itself against the cabin cruiser's gleaming hull. The dog's owner seemed unconcerned by the loud complaints being directed at him and his pet seemed to care even less.

In a field on the other side of the river several archers stood in a perfect line as if imitating English longbow men at the Battle of Agincourt. With a smooth synchronised movement they fitted arrows to bows, pulled their strings taut and with a volley of feathered shafts let the French have it right between the eyes. The twangs of the high tension bow strings, and the thuds as the aluminium arrows hit the round straw targets, drifted across the still surface of the river almost simultaneously.

By the time the archers had fitted fresh arrows to their bows the small motor boat had finished navigating out of the lock and had arrived at the pub's moorings. Now the two youths who crewed her were attempting to manoeuvre the little craft into a space astern of Corduroy Cap's cruiser.

In the car park two men got out of the Ford Cortina. They were both tall and built like men who never have sand kicked in their faces. One of the men slipped a hand into the front of his loud check sports jacket as if checking to ensure his wallet was intact, then they walked across the car park and disappeared from sight behind the pub.

Corduroy Cap had switched his attention from the unrepentant dog owner and instead was viewing with horror the erratic progress of the motor boat as it manoeuvred into the space behind his own vessel.

Suddenly he let out a cry of alarm and leapt down the short flight of steps leading to the wheelhouse with anger deepening the redness of his face. He snatched up a long boat hook from the deck of his cruiser and speared at the smaller boat in a desperate attempt to prevent it from colliding with his own craft.

The two men from the Ford Cortina had reached the forecourt of the pub. They stopped and looked around as if to get their bearings. The taller of the men noticed Corduroy Cap's confrontation with the punks and a wide smile split his face. His colleague touched his arm and pointed towards the metal footbridge linking the lock to the river bank.

I waved and the taller man returned it with a genial smile, before he and his colleague headed my way. As they climbed the steps leading to the footbridge, I saw the shorter man check the inside pocket of his sports jacket again.

'Hey, Dave!' The tall man said as he strode towards me, his smile widening into a grin. 'Is that really you? Jeez, man, I didn't recognise you. Howya doin' ol' buddy? Long-time-no-see.' He shoved a huge hand my way. 'You've gotten old,' he added bluntly, never one to beat about the bush.

'Probably because I've been waiting so long for you,' I complained sourly, ignoring his outstretched hand. I had no desire to have Hank Graham repeat his trick of crushing the bones of my hand with one mighty squeeze. Anyway, I was not ready to be mollified by his Yankee charm just yet. 'You're late.' I looked pointedly at my wristwatch. 'I told Rogers one o'clock. So where is he?'

Hank Graham said nothing. I guessed he was deciding which way to play it.

The sound of angry voices drifted over from the pub forecourt.

'…you stupid oafs…'

'…fuck off you old fart…'

'…caused a great deal of damage…'

'…what damage?'

'…damn yobs…'

'…up yours…'

'…you need a good dose of discipline…'

'…you need a dose of clap…'

'…I'll teach you a lesson…'

'…come on then granddad. Garn, you're all fucking mouth…'

'…I'll show you…'

The two youths from the motor boat were dancing about on the pub forecourt in front of the cabin cruiser, teasing Corduroy Cap, egging him on and spoiling for a fight.

The man's ruddy face was almost purple now with rage. He stabbed the air with his long boat hook, using it like a fighting lance.

The youth with the Mohican haircut edged towards the cruiser, sparring with the end of the boat hook, trying to catch hold of it as it was stabbed at him.

'Come on, Hank, we're wasting time,' Graham's companion said. 'We have to get back.'

'Who's he?' I asked, nodding my head towards the shorter man.

'My partner,' Hank replied. 'Joe Welensky.' He turned to his colleague. 'Joe this is Dave Statton.'

Welensky nodded a couple of times in my general direction, but he might just as well have been greeting the metal girder behind my head. He flashed a quarter of an inch of plastic tooth at me in a cold smile. Satisfied a couple of seconds was long enough for me to admire the wonderful workmanship of American dentistry, he shut his perfect false teeth back into their thick lipped box.

If that smile was cold, then the look in Welensky's eyes was even colder. He did not like me and it showed. But this only mirrored my feelings towards him. I hated him on sight and the hostile stare with which I studied him did not even try to be discreet.

Although Welensky was slightly shorter than the six feet three inches tall Graham, he was beefier and by the look of the hard bulges that stretched his tight fitting sports jacket, the extra weight was all muscle.

His face was deeply tanned and his fleshy nose was a fair match for his thick lips. He wore his hair short, razor cut to the military style favoured by the US marines. His hair was almost the same dark brown as the evasive eyes that refused to meet the challenge of my own steady gaze. On his feet he wore expensive black shoes with fashionable leather tassels.

I sized Joe Welensky up in one go; all brawn, but no backbone. He was the kind of man who is a loyal friend when you are on the way up, but who is more than happy to join the communal kicking when you are on the way down. Not a man I would like watching my back in a fight.

Perhaps I was being unfair to Welensky, after all I knew nothing about him. Perhaps he was a dependable, honourable, likeable, genuine all round nice guy, but I wouldn't have bet too much of my hard earned money on it.

I looked at Hank Graham, who was watching me sizing up Welensky with a wry smile on his face. He winked at me, his eyes twinkling. I guessed he shared my assessment of his colleague. 'So, where's Rogers?' I asked again.

'I'm sorry, pal,' he replied with a shrug. 'He ain't coming.' He held up a hand to pre-empt any complaint I might have. 'But don't worry, we have it all worked out. Okay?' He looked at me hopefully, appealing to my better nature. He was playing it exactly the right way and he knew it.

I smiled at him. Hank Graham was one of life's nice guys and you could not stay annoyed at him for long. But that was not to say he had won and he knew that as well. 'So what's the story?' I asked.

Before Hank could reply, a shout of triumph rent the air. The orange haired punk had succeeded in grabbing the end of the boat hook and a tug of war had begun between him and Corduroy Cap. Each time he pulled the long pole the youth let out a whoop of excitement.

Suddenly the older man's foot slipped and he was yanked off balance. As he fell forward he caught his knee against the chrome rail of the cruiser's deck and toppled overboard, letting go the boat hook.

The youth, caught off balance himself by the release of the pole, fell over backwards, landing in a heap on the forecourt. Somehow Corduroy managed to land on top of the youth and soon the pair was rolling on the ground in a scuffling dog-fight.

The second youth joined in the fight. He was dressed in faded blue jeans, hitched up by a pair of bright red braces, worn above a dirty white T-shirt. The jeans were skin tight and short in the leg, barely reaching the top of the Dr Marten boots he used to kick out wildly at the fighting pair, seemingly unconcerned on whose body his kicks landed.

'The story Hank?'

'It's no big deal, Dave,' Hank said, returning his attention to me. 'The man couldn't make the meet so he asked us to take you to him.'

I sighed. 'Why couldn't he make it?'

Hank shrugged and looked uncomfortable. 'Does it matter, Dave?'

'Yes, it matters. It matters very much.' I suspected Rogers had sent his two subordinates to collect me simply to assert his authority. He wanted to remind me that he was a deputy director of the American Central Intelligence Agency and was the one who called the shots. As it happens I needed any work that Rogers might offer, so I'd made up my mind already to accompany the two agents, but I wasn't going to make it easy for them, or their boss.

Hank sighed and for a moment I felt sorry for him. Some people, Welensky and Rogers included, I disliked on sight, others I felt an immediate affinity with. Hank was one such person. Although I don't know why I got on with him so well, because he epitomised the type of man of which I generally steer clear. He was typical of the sort of extrovert who wears T-shirts emblazoned with obscene slogans emblazoned and is hurt when you get upset if they put salt in your coffee and sugar in your petrol tank as a prank. A real pain in the arse.

I first met Hank one New Year's Eve, at a time when I was still working for Section 2F of the Department for Covert Operations, a secret unit of British Intelligence. I was on a six months secondment working with the CIA.

Hank was standing naked in the middle of a busy New York precinct house, exuberantly drunk while police officers took Polaroid photographs of his generous undercarriage. Graham explained that he wanted to give his ex-girlfriend something to remind her of what she was missing.

We laughed a lot that night. I got drunk and Hank got drunker. We grew pretty close during the time I was stationed in the United States, but, as is the way of such friendships, we lost contact as soon as we drifted our own separate ways.

But Hank Graham, for all his man's man bonhomie, was nobody's fool. Lying just beneath the good-natured surface was a ruthlessness that made him stop at nothing to get his own way. He also had his fair share of toughness, selfishness, slyness and unscrupulousness. All in all he was well suited for the CIA, of which he was an agent.

'He had an important appointment...' Hank started to explain, then seeing the cynical look on my face let his voice tail off.

'With his hairdresser or his manicurist?' I asked.

Hank did not answer but the knowing twinkle in his eyes and the deadpan expression on his face spoke volumes. Whatever Rogers was doing, it was probably not work related.

In many ways Hank Graham's face was like viewing a negative photograph of Joe Welensky. They had the same severely cropped hair style, the same round face, the same thick lips and the same fleshy nose. But where Welensky was dark, Hank was light. He had fair hair, a pale face and pale blue eyes, which, unlike his partner's, refused to be bowed into submission by my own.

'Where is he, Hank?' I asked, dropping the edge from my voice.

'We're staying at a hotel up by the airport. He's there,' he replied with a grin, perhaps relieved at the change in my tone.

I stared silently at the forecourt of the pub, making a point. I was determined to keep the two CIA agents waiting for my decision. No doubt my reaction would be reported back to Rogers and it was all part of the negotiating process that would start when I actually got to meet with him.

A couple of the male office workers had broken away from their group and were edging hesitantly towards the fracas, seemingly in two minds as to what to do next. They were rescued from the dilemma of deciding whether to go to the aid of Corduroy Cap by the appearance of the pub landlord who, assessing the situation at a glance, took action that was immediate, economical and effective.

He strode across the forecourt and with his left hand grabbed the kicking youth by his red braces and pulled him backwards, while with his right he landed him one short, sharp punch to the kidneys. The young man crumpled like a deflated balloon as the landlord released his grip on his braces.

Next the landlord bent down and grabbed the orange Mohican comb of the second youth. He yanked sharply and a piercing scream of pain reverberated round the forecourt as the youth was pulled bodily to his feet, making him loosen his grip on

Corduroy Cap in the process.

Still holding the youth's hair in one hand the landlord took him by the seat of the pants with his other. With a single beautifully co-ordinated movement he swivelled and marched the punk across the forecourt to the water's edge where he dumped him into his motor boat.

The youth with the red braces was just easing himself to his feet and when he saw the landlord heading his way he made a dash to join his mate in the little vessel.

The landlord untied the boat's ropes from the squat mooring posts and threw them aboard. He picked up the discarded boat hook and pushed the motor boat away from the forecourt until it caught the current and started to drift. 'Okay,' he shouted. 'If I ever see you back 'ere again you can expect trouble. Geddit?'

The young men got it alright. Hurriedly they started the engine of the motor boat and headed upstream looking for a safer berth.

The landlord helped Corduroy Cap to his feet and they walked across the forecourt together and disappeared into the lounge bar.

I turned back to Hank Graham and was about to agree to go with him to the hotel when Welensky elbowed him aside and thrust a pointed finger into my chest.

'Alright, I've had enough of your bullshit, Statton. You're coming with us so why don't you just cut out all this crap.'

'Oh, shit!' Hank murmured.

I glanced at him and saw him look heavenward and roll his eyes. Then I turned my attention to Welensky. I smiled and looked down at his finger. 'If you want to lose those pretty false teeth of yours, then I suggest you leave that finger exactly where it is.' I said it quietly, but I saw the finger waver and then withdraw. 'Now, Welensky, when I spoke to your boss on the telephone and set up this meeting where did we agree to meet?'

Welensky glared at me but did not reply.

I answered my own question: 'We agreed to meet here.' I paused and spread my hands wide. 'Look around you. Can you see Rogers anywhere?'

'I don't give a fuck for all that shit,' Welensky retorted angrily. 'All I know is that when Rogers says fetch, we fetch. Is that understood?'

I smiled again. 'Oh, I understand alright, but it leaves you with a problem does it not?'

Welensky looked at me blankly and shrugged. Hank Graham just groaned.

'No? Well it is this. I am not going to let you "fetch me", as you put it. If Rogers wants to talk to me then he knows where to find me. I'm booked into the pub until tomorrow morning so he has got,' I paused and looked at my watch, 'twenty-four hours in which to contact me. Now, piss off back to your master and give him that message.'

That is when he came for me. 'Come on, Hank. Let's take this limey son of a bitch.'

But Graham stayed where he was. He smiled wryly as he watched his partner draw back a massive fist and let fly.

It is surprising how long you have in such situations when you are prepared. I watched the fist as it sped towards my face and at the very last moment I ducked and twisted out of the way. I didn't see his fist hit the metal girder, but I certainly heard the crack of bone and his cry of pain. I didn't even have to hit him. Joe Welensky would not be throwing any more punches that day.

I turned to Graham. 'I'm sorry, Hank, but I can't come with you now.'

He shrugged and grinned. He understood me better than I had thought.

'If Rogers still wants to see me I will be here until this time tomorrow. Okay?'

Hank nodded and I saw a warning light in his eyes. I turned in time to see Welensky's good hand slide under his jacket, but I knew he wasn't really checking his wallet. 'If your hand so much as touches that gun I will break your arm,' I warned him.

Hank moved to his partner's side and touched his arm in warning. 'He'll do it, Joe,' he said.

The CIA agent had more confidence in me than I did myself. I had no idea what I would have done had Welensky actually removed his pistol from his shoulder holster. Tough words are easier than tough action.

'Let it go. I warned you to stay cool,' Hank went on, 'and Rogers said to treat him gently, remember?' These last words had some effect on Welensky because all he shot at me were looks of hate. 'Come on, Joe. Let's get you to a doctor.'

Welensky looked down at his already swollen hand and nodded. Then he turned to me and said: 'Someday I'm gonna get you on your own, Statton, and when I do…' He let the threat hang in mid-air, but waved a clenched fist in my face to replace the missing words.

By three o'clock the sun was dressed in a black shroud of rain laden clouds. In the chill of the dark, overcast afternoon, the earlier pretence by the office workers that summer had arrived was shown up to be nothing more than an optimistic charade.

The westerly spring breeze on which the rain clouds had hitched a lift from the Irish Sea, had strengthened into a cold wind that quickly blew the skimpy topped secretaries back to their typewriters. The male office workers buttoned up their shirts and returned to their desks where they would shuffle paper and watch the clock until it was time to go home.

Across the river the English bowmen had decided their conquest of France could wait for a warmer day. They stored away their straw targets beneath black polythene sheets and packed their archery equipment into the boots of their cars in readiness for a tactical withdrawal.

I decided to join the exodus. I left the seat I had found on the forecourt and headed inside the pub where I found the lounge bar almost deserted. A waitress with short legs, wearing an even shorter blue overall, was clearing away the debris left over from lunch.

She leisurely piled dirty plates and glasses onto a rickety chrome trolley that looked ready to collapse under the weight, but the trolley stood up to the challenge. Eventually the waitress wheeled it noisily towards the kitchen.

The only other two people left in the lounge bar were standing at the far end of the room. The red faced man in the corduroy cap was leaning on the long teak bar chatting to the landlord who had rescued him from the two youths.

The lounge bar was fitted out like an annexe to the Maritime Museum. Hanging on a frieze round the artificial wood panelled walls were sepia photographs depicting the glory of the British Navy. They were taken when the Admiralty could not make up its mind whether steam was a dirty word or the greatest boost to naval power since the invention of the sextant. Evidence of their final decision was that photographs of stumpy funnelled ironsides outnumbered those of billowing sailed windjammers by a ratio of three to one.

Displayed at regular intervals beneath the row of blackened-wood frames were various objects connected with the sea including life jackets, lifebuoys, seafaring charts with exotic place names marked in Old English script, barometers and other nautical instruments.

I tapped the glass of one massive barometer that hung beside the lounge's wide lattice window and it immediately registered "Rain". Looking out of the window at a sky that was darkening by the minute I was not inclined to argue with the instrument's prediction.

I smiled at the landlord as he wandered up the length of the bar to serve me. He was short, stocky and running to fat and the baggy green jumper he wore was fighting a losing battle to cover his enormous pot-belly, but don't get the idea that his weight was a sign of weakness. His broad shoulders and strong muscular arms bore witness to his strength, as had his action on the waterfront earlier that day.

He had wild curly hair and beneath matted eyebrows, which were criss-crossed with tiny scars, was set a pair of eyes that sparkled with good humour. His nose had been knocked into a flattened crookedness by innumerable fist fights and the redness this punishment had inflicted on it had been deepened to an almost purple hue by extensive sampling of his own alcoholic wares.

At one time the landlord had been a not very successful professional boxer who scraped a living fighting bouts in the many small private boxing clubs that were dotted round the East End of London. When he eventually realised he was never going to be another Henry Cooper, he hung up his boxing gloves just in time to save his brain (if not his face) from being scrambled. Instead, he settled for a life managing public houses.

Unfortunately for the landlord's nose, the fights did not end with his change of career. The only difference was that now he was out of the ring he was not paid for the numerous bare knuckle fights in which he found himself involved.

Born within the sound of Bow Bells, the landlord was a true Cockney with a wicked sense of humour, a fearless nature, a fiery temper and a heart of untarnished gold. If he liked you, then you were a friend for life. If he disliked you, then you crossed him at your peril.

Happily I fell into the first category. Billy Neal and I had been friends for many years.

'Looks like rain, Billy,' I said motioning towards the window.

'Bleeding weather,' he moaned. 'When I woke up this morning and saw that lovely sun I thought for one minute that we'd seen the end of the sodding winter. Fat chance. Is yours a pint, Dave?' Billy asked, then unselfconsciously scratched his crotch as he waited for my reply.

I shook my head. 'No thanks, I'll have something more warming. A double scotch I think and one for yourself.'

'Cheers, Dave, I don't mind if I do. You're a real gent. Now let me see, you prefer Teacher's don't you?'

I nodded and smiled. 'Yes, and make sure it's the pukka stuff, Billy.'

The landlord looked at me with open-faced innocence. 'I don't know what you're talking about,' he protested in a low voice. Expertly he measured out the whisky from a bottle of Teacher's. He slid the rim of each glass across the bottom of the optic with a delicate twist of his hand, ensuring every last drop of the amber coloured liquid was captured.

'All the best,' I said, raising the glass to my mouth, I tipped half the amount down my throat and straight into my stomach where it lay generating its own heat. I began to feel warmer immediately. It was good stuff. 'Okay, Billy. That's the real McCoy.'

'No it ain't. It's Teacher's like it says on the bottle.' He grinned at his own joke. 'Look, Dave, I'd never do the dirty on you. You're a mate. Anyway, I left the booze well alone this week.' He paused and tapped the side of his squashed nose with a stubby finger. 'I can't be doing switching the good stuff with cheap hooky stuff at the minute 'cos I'm expecting a visit from the brewery geezer any day.' He winked. 'Know what I mean?'

I smiled. I knew exactly what he meant. Based on the premise that most customers could not tell the difference between one whisky and another, it was common practice among some pub tenant-landlords to replace the whisky in proprietary brand bottles with a cheaper non-proprietary alternative. Although this practice produced some nice undeclared profit for the landlord, it was frowned on by the breweries who owned the pubs.

'How's your son?' I asked.

'He's a chief superintendent now, Dave,' he said. 'Youngest super in the Met,' he added proudly. 'Bright boy. Don't know where he gets it from. Probably his mum, God rest her soul.'

There was a clatter of plates from the kitchen.

'Stupid cow!' Billy shouted at the kitchen door, before turning back to me. 'If the stupid bitch has broken anything she can bleeding well pay to replace it.' He knocked back his scotch and appeared to quickly forget his clumsy waitress. 'Your visitors turned up alright then, Dave?'

I nodded and wondered how Billy knew about Graham and Welensky. I certainly had not told him about my planned meeting with Rogers.

He grinned at me. 'I might not be as bright as my boy, but I ain't stupid, Dave.' His grin became broader. 'And the Good Lord gave me a pretty sharp pair of eyes. Truth is I see you up on the bridge with them when I come out to drag them two yobs off Major Carsons over there.'

I looked down the bar at the man in the corduroy cap. He seemed no worse for having had his confrontation with the two youths. The only sign remaining from his fight was the wet stain on the crown of his hat where it had scudded across the forecourt and landed in a pool of spilt beer. The cap now lay on the bar and Carsons saw me looking at the stain. He picked up his cap and sidled along to join us carrying a half filled glass in his other hand.

'Beer,' he explained, touching the stain tenderly as if it were a bruise. 'My cap fell off and landed in it.'

'Are you alright?'

His already ram-rod straight back seemed to stiffen more while he studied me with rheumy eyes as if I was mad. 'Alright?' He snapped. 'Of course I am alright. Take more than a couple of young punkhawallahs…'

'They're called punks, Major,' Billy corrected him with a smile.

'Punks, punkhawallahs, whatever, I don't care what the morons are called. It will take more than a couple of yobs like them to get the better of me. What?' He shook his head in disgust. 'My, God! What is this wonderful country of ours coming to? All those punkhawallahs need a damn good thrashing if you ask me.'

Carsons glared at Billy as if daring him to disagree, but the landlord diplomatically nodded his head in agreement. Carsons turned to me and held out a pink hand. 'We haven't actually been introduced, old boy.' He said it like I had just committed some social gaffe. 'Carsons is the name. Major Percival Carsons, retired.' He smiled but never explained whether he was a retired major or a retired Percival Carsons. It was something I was to wonder about often over the next few weeks.

He was a perfect caricature of the type of colonial army officer, so beloved by film makers, who sits on a mosquito infested veranda, with a large drink in his hand, complaining about the sun setting on the British Empire. Meanwhile, his neglected wife is being laid by half the members of his officers' mess and most of their household servants. I had met a number of such men in Africa and Asia, so I knew they existed, but Carsons was something else again.

His head was trimmed with silver hair, cut in a severe short back and sides. His face, naturally flushed, was spotted brown by continual exposure to the hot sun. Beneath a long, thin nose he wore a bristly grey moustache, which every so often he stroked with a pink little finger, as if checking it was still in place. His light blue eyes stared out from behind heavy bags that told of endless late, boozy nights. Now he was closer to me I could see that his dark blue cravat was decorated with Mercury, the emblem of the Royal Corps of Signals.

I accepted his outstretched hand and returned his surprisingly firm handshake. 'Dave Statton,' I introduced myself, resisting the temptation to add that I was temporarily retired due to the lack of suitable employment.

'Major Carsons reckons your visitors were Yanks, Dave.' Billy said. 'Ain't that right, Major?'

Carsons sniffed loudly and finished off in one gulp what looked like a gin and tonic. 'Quite right, William. That is exactly what I said. Well, Statton? Come on, out with it. Am I right?'

'Was it that obvious?'

'Ha!' Carsons snorted. 'There you are, William. Didn't I tell you they looked like bloody Yanks?' He slapped the bar in triumph. 'I can tell a Yank a mile off.'

I drained my glass and invited the two men to join me for another drink. I did not have to insist because they both accepted immediately.

'Do I get the impression, Major, you don't care overly for our Transatlantic cousins?'

My question was all Carsons needed to have another rant. He cleared his throat and spent the next twenty minutes telling me exactly what he thought of America, its people, its culture, its way of life and its armed forces. None of his comments was complimentary.

'But of course,' he said eventually, 'I wouldn't want you to get the wrong impression. I don't dislike all Americans, in fact some of my best friends are Yanks.' He took a sip of his gin and tonic. 'And please do not think I was criticising your friends, whoever they were.'

'No offence taken, Major. They weren't what I would describe as friends, more associates.'

'Aaah!' Billy murmured knowingly. He scratched his crotch again thoughtfully before saying: 'Actually, when I see them come trooping back this way after they'd met with you,' he paused, looking at me with knowing eyes, 'one of them looked a bit down in the mouth. He seemed to have hurt his hand, if you get me drift.'

I said nothing but my smile was comment enough for Billy.

He smashed his right fist into the open palm of his left hand. 'Good for you, Dave!' He cried picking up his glass and raising it in a salute. 'If they come back looking for a punch up, just give me a yell and I'll sort those American bastards out for you.'

I laughed and raised my own glass to him. 'Thanks for the offer, Billy, but I hope it won't be necessary. I think that if they come back it will be in peace,' I said this with more confidence than I felt.

I wondered briefly if Hank Graham and Joe Welensky would actually return the next day. It was possible I had burnt my boats when I refused to go with them so I had no right or reason to be optimistic, because Gavin Rogers was not renowned for his patience. Of course, if they did turn up at the pub it would show the CIA deputy director needed me more than I needed him and that would certainly improve my negotiating position.

However, because of something Hank had said to Welensky, I was more confident than perhaps I had a right to be. 'Rogers said to treat him gently,' he had said. That did not sound like the Gavin Rogers I knew and I was intrigued about why he was so concerned about my feelings. Could it be that he wanted me more badly than I could ever have imagined? If so, why? Suddenly I realised that Carsons had asked me a question. 'I beg your pardon?' I apologised.

'I said, don't you agree?'

'I'm sorry, Major, I didn't catch your question. My mind was elsewhere.'

'I was saying that I blame the increase in violence on the Yanks,' he repeated patiently. 'It's the fault of all those trashy films they churn out. Don't you agree?'

I gave a non-committal shrug. I shared his view about the quality of some films being released at that time. However, I'd take a lot of convincing that British film makers were in any way inferior to their American counterparts when it came to producing rubbish movies.

'First it was drugs and long hair, then muggings and punkhawallahs, now it's the bloody blacks rioting. Where's it all going to end?' He paused briefly to finish his gin and tonic. 'Another one?' He asked.

'Why not?' I accepted his offer of a drink without pointing out that it was British pop groups, led by the Beatles from Liverpool, who started the cult of long hair. Neither did I mention that the birthplace of punk music was London, not New York.

'Where was I?' He asked. 'Oh, yes. The blacks. Did you watch the riots on television? They are animals, sir. Nothing but animals. I feel ashamed that Brixton is in our country. It's about time the Government stopped shilly-shallying about and sent in the troops to sort the young thugs out.' Carsons was getting up a real head of steam now.

'The police simply cannot cope. They haven't the experience you see. They need to send in the Paras to sort them out.' He sipped his drink, swilling it around in his mouth as if to gargle away a nasty taste. 'If I had my way I would send them all back to where they came from.'

'Leave it out, Major!' Billy exclaimed, his face was serious, but his eyes sparkled with amusement. 'We have enough black faces in London already.'

Carsons looked at the landlord blankly. 'I don't follow you, William,' he said with a frown.

'Oh, it's nothing, Major,' Billy said with a wink my way. 'I was just being a bit facetious, like. Know what I mean?'

'No! I do not know what you mean. Explain yourself, man.'

'Well, it's like this. You said you wanted to send them all back to where they come from. But many of those black people were born in our country, weren't they? In London and wherever. They're like British, ain't they?'

'British, William!' Carsons exclaimed incredulously. 'Don't be ridiculous. How on earth can they be British? Listen, because somebody is born here does not make them belong here does it? I mean to say, man, just consider lions and tigers. Some of them are born in our zoos. Agreed? Well, you can't say that they really belong in our country, can you? I mean to say, you don't see lions prowling round Epping Forest do you?'

'But…'

'No "buts", William. Do you or do you not see lions in Epping Forest?'

'But…'

'William. Answer the question!'

'I suppose not, Major.'

Major Carsons sat back on his stool satisfied. He had made his point.

Billy retired hurt. He wandered over to where the waitress with the short skirt and several other members of day time staff were just leaving through a side door and the evening shift was starting to arrive.

The Major and I were both staying overnight in the cosy little bedrooms on the first floor of the pub. We sat at the bar and talked for a couple of hours, although it would be nearer the truth to say that Carsons pontificated and I listened.

Major Percival Carsons in full flow made awesome listening. He had very set ideas on every conceivable subject. Ideas so extreme that at times they were frankly farcical. It soon became apparent that if Carsons positioned his chair any further to the right on the political stage it would topple over the edge.

But I was not convinced. Major Percival Carsons (Rtd), with his rheumy eyes, impeccably cut clothes, Royal Signals cravat and ultra-extreme right wing views, was just too much of reactionary parody to be true.

In addition, nothing Carsons had said during his long conversation with me had even hinted as to why he had been following me for the past two days.

When I eventually got to my bedroom, the rain that had been threatening all afternoon had finally arrived and was bucketing down. It hammered against the window of my bedroom like a swarm of demented locusts on a kamikaze mission.

Already the heavy downpour had produced miniature lakes in the window box that was screwed to the ledge outside. There were no flowers in the box, just a few small straggly clumps of chickweed that had been uprooted by the force of the rain.

I tugged at the heavy embroidered curtains until I had drawn them together and shut out the dismal scene. The room, which had become gloomy with the arrival of the rain, was plunged into darkness. I switched on the lamp standard that stood in one corner and a warm, subdued light spread across the nineteen fifties style wallpaper that was covered with pastel coloured flowers that could have been of any variety or none.

The bedroom was tiny, yet comfortable in that cosy, homely way that the large hotel chains have never been able to replicate. There was no television, radio, piped music, room service, sanitised toilet seat, advertising brochures, Picasso prints or Gideon's Bible, but then who wanted them?

I settled for the sturdy wooden bed (with its clean sheets, plump goose down pillows and thick old-fashioned patchwork quilt), the narrow two door wardrobe, two comfortable armchairs, the lamp standard, and, on the narrow inside window sill, a half-dead house-plant.

I opened the door in answer to the quiet, but firm, knock.

Gavin Rogers told Hank Graham and Joe Welensky, to wait for him downstairs. The two agents disappeared, leaving behind a wink from Hank and an ugly scowl from Welensky that was designed to remind me he still had a score to settle. I smiled when I saw the plaster cast on his right hand.

At five foot seven tall the CIA deputy director was no midget, but he did not have to duck as he made his way into my bedroom through the ridiculously low doorway. It had probably bruised more than one forehead in its time.

He closed the door behind him, turned round, looked intently at me and smiled. It was the kind of smile that I suspected had been recommended by some management institute as the best way to get recalcitrant subordinates back on side.

'Apologies, David.' He showed me the palm of one well-manicured hand as he spoke. In his other hand he carried a black briefcase. 'Sorry I couldn't make our meet as planned, but I was pretty tied up with an important telephone call from the States.' He smiled again and sat down in the armchair opposite my own and put the briefcase on the floor at his side. His voice was pure Ivy League, although there was a hint of Radcliffe College in there somewhere. He looked around the bedroom before asking: 'Where's the john?'

'At the end of the corridor. Do you want to use it?'

Rogers shook his head. 'I can wait,' he said as he settled

himself more comfortably into his armchair. It looked as if he intended to stay for a while. 'You certainly managed to get Joe Welensky wound up, David,' he continued. 'What the hell happened between you two? Was it really necessary to break his hand?'

'Who said it was me that broke his hand?'

'Well he didn't catch it in his goddam fly. So, what happened?'

'Didn't he tell you?'

He shook his head and shrugged. 'He wasn't very communicative.'

'I bet he wasn't.' I smiled. 'He tried to beat up a metal footbridge.'

Rogers frowned and I could see he was debating whether to pursue the matter but evidently he decided to drop the subject because he went on to say: 'What the hell! That's all in the past and it was my own fault. I should have known you would refuse to come with them to my hotel. You were always a stubborn son-of-a-bitch, Statton.'

I noticed he had abandoned first name terms, but he threw me another of his institute-management style smiles to compensate.

I threw that insincere smile right back at him and decided it was time to see how far I could push him. His very presence in my room hinted at the strength of my hand, but it would be good to see if I held a straight flush or a full house.

'And you, Rogers, always were an arrogant, pompous, arse-licking, back-stabber.'

I saw a flash of anger in his eyes and his smile disappeared for a split-second before breeding came to his rescue and he managed to force half of it back onto his face. He made no move to leave and that spoke volumes.

'So, now we know exactly where we stand,' I went on, 'perhaps we can talk business.'

The American had the dapperness that short, trim men seem able to achieve effortlessly. He was one hundred and one percent solid class, from the 22 carat gold pin that held together the two wings of his Brooks Brothers shirt, down to his neat Gucci shoes. I had never seen him anything other than immaculately dressed, even when wearing casual clothes. He always reminded me of one of those handsome male models on the pages of mail order catalogues who are photographed fiddling around with the engines of vintage cars while wearing spotless, well fitted clothes.

Already well into his forties, Rogers looked barely older than thirty. His unlined face had perfectly proportioned features and was fringed with hair worn in a youthful, modern style. However, a dab of grey on his dark brown temples hinted at his true age and gave him an even more distinguished look. He had been lusted over by most of the hostesses on the Washington cocktail-circuit, all of whom had been left disappointed.

Wendy Wandell once wrote of him:

"Handsome man about town Gavin Rogers II is said to be the target of just separated Mandy-Ann Scriblier, wife of Senator Mark Scriblier, however, Mandy-Ann is unlikely to succeed where so many other women have failed. Confirmed bachelor, Rogers, has in the past taken the fancy of many beautiful women, but has always resisted their charms. Not long ago Rogers formed a close relationship with Alan Blake Jnr, son of Senator Alan Blake of Colorado, who it is said, was not amused."

'Yes,' Rogers said, straightening his already perfectly aligned club tie, 'let's talk business.' He paused and then asked: 'What do you know about nuclear fission?'

I raised an eyebrow at him. 'In relation to what?'

'In relation to South Africa.'

I shook my head. 'Not a lot. I know that the French are building a nuclear power station northwest of Cape Town, which I believe is due to open in a couple of years.'

'That's the Koeberg Nuclear Power Station,' Rogers confirmed.

'And I read in the newspapers that the South Africans were supposed to have exploded a nuclear weapon a couple of years ago in... When was that? Seventy-eight? Seventy-nine?'

'Nineteen-seventy-nine.'

'But the South Africans denied the story.'

Rogers nodded.

'As I recall it caused quite a stir at the time, particularly in the United Nations.' I smiled to myself as I remembered the furore in the UN General Assembly when it was alleged that South Africa had developed its own nuclear weapon with the help of the Israelis. The South African response to the allegations had simply made matters worse; they had denied all knowledge of a nuclear weapons test. At the same time they had insisted that as a sovereign nation they had every right to develop such a weapon. 'Did the South Africans actually test a nuclear device?' I asked.

The American shook his head. 'Not in Seventy-nine.' A sudden blast of wind increased the tempo of the rain against my bedroom window to a noisy crescendo. He waited until the noise had abated before explaining: 'We planted that story, but actually there was no such explosion...'

I held up a hand to interrupt him and put a finger to my lips. I stood up and walked over to the door. Silently I turned the handle and then quickly pulled open the door. The corridor outside was empty. I frowned. I was sure I had heard footsteps. The toilet flushed in the bathroom at the end of the corridor, which seemed to address my concerns. However, I was not convinced. Somebody had been listening to our conversation, but who?

I closed the bedroom door again and wandered over to the wardrobe, opened the door and rooted around in the canvas holdall that was stored there. I pulled out a bottle of whisky and waved it in the general direction of Rogers. 'Drink? I asked.

He indicated with a thumb and forefinger that he would have a small one. I poured two fingers of scotch into one of the glasses that I had brought up from the bar and handed it to him. I poured myself a more generous measure and returned to my seat.

'You were saying?'

'I was saying that there was no nuclear explosion off the coast of South Africa in seventy-nine. The Firm started that rumour because we received reliable information that the South Africans were in the process of developing a nuclear device. We hoped that by creating an outcry they would be persuaded to cancel their programme.'

'And did they?' I asked.

Rogers sipped delicately at his scotch, then he gingerly ran the palm of his hand down the front of his trouser leg as if testing the crease for sharpness. He studied his hand as if frightened he might have cut it on the well pressed material. Satisfied there was no lasting damage to his palm he looked up and shook his head. 'No they didn't cancel. However, they did postpone their first test for three years.' He paused and looked at me with mournful eyes. 'Six weeks ago the South Africans succeeded in exploding a low level nuclear device on a small island about five hundred miles south-west of Cape Town.'

The deputy director looked like a man who owns the only strip club in town. He wakes up one morning to find that Hugh Hefner has opened up a Playboy club next door and is charging half price for admission. But then I suppose it must always be a bit of a shock for the nuclear club when an outsider threatens its cosy monopoly.

'Are you sure it was a nuclear device?'

Rogers nodded.

'No chance it was a conventional bomb?'

'No chance!' he insisted emphatically. 'It was a nuclear explosion.'

'How can you be so sure?'

He was silent for a few seconds as he took another sip of his whisky, then he sat staring down at his rain sodden shoes. He leaned down and dabbed at a shoe with his fingers, plainly upset at what he discovered. I suppose I would have felt the same way if I had a pair of Gucci shoes to ruin.

Eventually he shrugged and answered my question: 'A couple of weeks after the explosion we sent a team of experts to the island to investigate. They made tests and brought back a number of samples.'

'Didn't the South Africans try to stop you?' I asked.

He shook his head. 'It is a remote, uninhabited island and our boys were in and out before they knew we were even in the area.' He took another sip of his whisky. 'Those samples prove beyond doubt that a primitive nuclear bomb was exploded on that island.'

'How primitive was the bomb?'

'Do you know the difference between nuclear fission and nuclear fusion?'

'Only schoolboy level stuff,' I admitted. 'If memory serves me right the earlier nuclear bombs were fission, which relies on the disintegration of a uranium-235 isotope to cause a chain reaction resulting in an explosion.' I looked at Rogers. 'Am I right?'

He smiled. 'You make it all sound so easy!'

'It has been a long time since I was at school. I don't profess to be a nuclear physicist.'

'I apologise. You're doing okay. Now what about a nuclear fusion bomb?'

'I know even less about that,' I replied. 'Isn't that a thermonuclear weapon? An H-bomb?'

Rogers nodded and smiled in encouragement.

'Produced by...' I stretched my limited knowledge to the limit, 'the burning up of a hydrogen isotope.' I scratched my head. 'Isn't it called deuterium or something?' I shrugged and went on:

'Anyway, the isotope is ignited at tremendous temperatures by using a fusion device.' I puffed out my cheeks. 'And that is about the sum total of my knowledge.'

'Not bad!' Rogers clapped his hands in light applause. 'I'm impressed!' He made it sound as if I was an imbecile who had worked out how to hold a spoon properly.

'Which bomb did the South Africans test?' I asked. 'Do you know?'

'Oh, yes. It was a small fission device. The nuclear boffins estimate it was about twenty kilotons.'

'Twenty kilotons is small?'

'Yes.'

'But as I recall the bomb that was dropped on Hiroshima during the Second World War was about that size and look at the devastation it caused.'

'You're right. But by today's standards Hiroshima was a baby bomb. Consider this: one kiloton is the equivalent of one thousand tons of TNT and one megaton is the equivalent of one thousand kilotons. Then consider that some thermonuclear bombs can yield up to sixty megatons, which is the equivalent of sixty million tons of TNT in one bomb.'

'That would be some explosion!'

'Exactly. That's how we know the South African bomb was of the fission variety. If they had tested a fusion device, there would have been no goddam island left from which to collect test samples.'

'Why test a bomb now?' I asked.

'We think they did it because the World's attention is concentrated on the war you limeys are fighting with the Argentinians over the Falkland Islands.'

It made sense. With a war raging in the South Atlantic what was one more explosion? 'So, when will the South Africans be capable of producing a thermonuclear weapon?' I asked as I gave my glass another generous shot of whisky. I held the bottle out to Rogers but he shook his head.

'That is the million dollar question. If you had asked me even a week ago I would have said that under normal circumstances it would take several years for the South Africans to master the fusion technique.

'To give you some idea it took the US some seven years to move from fission to fusion. It took the Russians four years and by the time the Chinese were testing nuclear weapons in the nineteen-sixties it took them three years to make the leap from fission to fusion, but that was a remarkable achievement.'

'And the South Africans?'

Rogers frowned, perhaps upset that I had interrupted his lesson on the history of nuclear technology. 'The South Africans? That is a difficult question to answer. The best estimate is that it will take them at least five years to develop a fusion bomb, but even if they do manage that timescale they will have an even bigger problem.' He paused and held out his glass. 'Perhaps I will have another drink after all.'

I tipped another couple of fingers into his glass. 'And that problem is?' I asked.

'Having produced a bomb they would still have to deliver it to its target. Of course, they could use bombers to attack targets in Africa. However, the question that needs to be asked: Why would the South Africans want to use nuclear weapons on any other country in Africa when it has the capability of defeating those countries using conventional weapons?'

'I can't think of a reason, except that the Boers have sometimes acted on gut instinct rather than logic.'

'But let's assume they are being rational for a change. Logically, the only reason to have a nuclear arsenal would be to act as a deterrent against attacks from countries further afield.'

'Such as the Soviets?'

'Yes, if the South Africans felt threatened by the Reds…'

'As well they might,' I interrupted him.

'As well they might,' Rogers agreed. 'The only realistic deterrent would be to have a nuclear bomb that was deliverable with a long range Inter Continental Ballistic Missile – an ICBM – which could be fired from land or sea.'

'Could the South Africans do that?'

'Not at the moment and without the right help it would take some time.' Rogers stared at his shoes again as if still unable to believe the rain would dare to deface them in such a way. 'That would have been my answer a week ago,' he told his shoes. 'But now the situation has changed radically.'

'How's that?' I asked.

Seemingly fed up with talking to his shoes Rogers looked up and viewed me with his doleful brown eyes. 'Last week the Russians finally followed our lead and visited the island.'

'And?'

'For some reason known only to themselves the Reds sent along one of their top nuclear scientists and, Statton, I mean their top man.'

The CIA agent lifted his black briefcase from the floor and balanced it with one hand on the arm of his chair. He took a handkerchief from his breast pocket used it to wipe several spots of rain from the briefcase's leather surface, then, satisfied it was dry, he placed it across his knees. He opened the briefcase and took from it a buff envelope that he handed to me without explanation.

I opened the envelope and found a photograph inside. I guessed the photo was an enlarged segment from a different picture. The man's face that scowled sourly out at me from the glossy surface did so from behind a bulky overcoat covered shoulder of an unidentified figure who had obviously been the subject of the original snapshot.

'Of course, he was younger then,' Rogers explained. 'That photograph was taken almost twenty years ago when he accompanied Khrushchev to London. His name is Gregori Zamyatin. Have you heard of him?'

I studied the photograph carefully, but recognised neither the face nor the name. I shook my head.

'Don't let it bother you,' Rogers said with a smile. 'Not many people in the West will have heard of him, except perhaps members of the scientific community. Anyway, Statton, what Zamyatin does not know about nuclear fusion could be written down on the back of a five cent postage stamp. He is by any measure a scientific genius. Let me tell you a little about him.

'At twenty years of age Zamyatin joined the team headed by Igor Kurchatov who after World War Two produced the very first Soviet atomic bomb. Twenty years old, Statton. Can you imagine? Even more remarkably, such was his contribution to the nuclear programme that despite his age he was made Kurchatov's second in command.

'It was Zamyatin who first realised the significance when the number of American scientific papers being published about nuclear fission started to tail off. He put two and two together to work out that the reason was because we were starting to concentrate our efforts on nuclear fusion.

'It was Zamyatin who accompanied Kurchatov when he appeared before the Soviet State Defence Committee to plead, successfully as it turned out, for a start to be made on nuclear fusion experimentation.' Rogers sat forward on his chair and tapped the photograph that lay on my knee. 'When the Russians eventually exploded their first thermonuclear device, in August nineteen-fifty-three, Gregori Zamyatin was awarded the Red Star, which is just about the highest military honour the Soviets can award.'

Rogers tapped the photograph again, as if to add weight to his next words: 'Let me put that into perspective for you, Statton. It is almost unheard for a civilian to receive such an honour, that it should have been awarded to one so young was a true recognition of Zamyatin's value to the Soviet nuclear programme. It was a quite amazing achievement!'

He stared at me as if waiting for me to argue with him, but I said nothing because my lack of knowledge about the Russian put me in no position to disagree.

'And that was not the end of his achievements,' he went on, feeding my ignorance. 'Not only is he one of the world's pre-eminent nuclear physicists, but he is also one of its leading missile experts. Indeed, there are many in our own scientific community who maintain that the Soviet prototype ICBM would have been delayed by anything up to five years if it had not been for Zamyatin's contribution. As I said, Statton, he is a genius.'

Again he stared at me as if challenging me to argue, but I remained silent. I wondered where all this was taking us.

'Understandably, when Kurchatov died in nineteen-sixty it was Gregori Zamyatin who took over from him as Director of the Atomic Energy Institute. But for some reason he fell from grace and a couple of years ago he was demoted. Our Counter-intelligence Centre Analysis Group believes he was a victim of the Kremlin power politics with which Zamyatin has always been involved. Trouble is that he might be a genius where science is concerned, but apparently he is crap when it comes to politics.'

'So he's never going to become President?'

'Absolutely not,' Rogers replied with a chuckle. 'However, ironically he has everything needed to be a politician. For a start he is one mean son-of-a-bitch who would put the finger on his own mother if he thought it would advance his career.'

As Rogers spoke, I detected a hint of admiration in his voice. It would appear that Gregori Zamyatin was very much a man after his own heart.

'But, despite his undoubted talents, even Zamyatin found it

difficult to compete with the rest of the back stabbers at the top of the Communist Party,' Rogers went on. 'He was up against some pretty ruthless men. Mostly old timers, many of whom were survivors from the Russian Revolution, and were the men who had built the Party hierarchy to suit their own ideological ends.

'Those old boys set out the ground rules and they ruled the roost. Perhaps being a scientist Zamyatin was a bit too unworldly and those Party apparatchiks were able to chew him up for brunch. No trouble.' The admiration in Rogers' voice had turned to one of bitterness and I wondered why.

'However, despite what the ruling elite did to him, Zamyatin remains a committed Communist Party man, which might explain why he was sent to investigate the South African nuclear test. The Reds don't usually let people of his calibre out of the country, just in case they defect. They would have few worries with Zamyatin. He is a fanatical communist and his country has been good to him. He has his own apartment in Moscow, complete with mistress, and another in Leningrad. He is allocated a new car every year and he has a dacha on the Black Sea to which he has access for two months every summer.'

'So what happened to Zamyatin? Has he defected?'

Rogers shook his head as he tested the crease of his trouser leg again. 'No, but he might just as well have come over to us, because unfortunately for the Ruskies, they lost him anyway.'

'What do you mean, "lost him"?'

'Somehow the chopper in which he flew to the island crashed and before his base-ship could reach the scene of the accident and rescue him he had disappeared.'

'Perhaps He drowned.' I suggested.

'Two bodies were found. They were those of the pilot and the KGB agent who was escorting Zamyatin, but of him there was no sign.'

'Perhaps he was eaten by sharks.'

Rogers shook his head. 'No, he wasn't, but it might have been better all-round if he had been.' He said morosely.

'Who picked him up?' I asked.

'The son-of-a-bitch was picked up by the goddam South Africans.'

'Are you sure?'

'Oh, we're sure alright. Of course, the South Africans deny it. They say they have no knowledge of Zamyatin, but we know differently. We know for a fact that he was picked up by one of their ships, the Hertzog.'

'How can you be so sure?'

We have a contact in Simon's Town who was working in the harbour when the ship docked. He saw the Ruskie with his own eyes.'

'Not good news.'

'You can say that again.'

I resisted the temptation and instead kept quiet.

'So now the South Africans have the one man who could not only advance their nuclear programme by years, but could develop a long range delivery system. Just imagine the implications of that to the balance of power in the world, let alone the region.'

'But surely it would simply swing the balance of power towards the West? You don't get much more anti-communist than those hard men in Pretoria.'

'On the face of it, yes,' he paused and took a tiny sip of his whisky. 'But life isn't that simple,' he went on. 'Just think about it for a moment. There are two very good reasons to be worried. The first is how would the Ruskies react to the current South African regime having a nuke? They certainly won't sit back on their butts and do nothing. At the very least they will increase even further their spending on arms. The President would not like that at a time when he is trying to reduce our own defence spending.'

'And the second reason?'

'The second is an even more worrying scenario from our perspective. At the present time the South African government is friendly to the West, or it at least shares many of our values, but what about the long term position? No, not even that, more the medium term. Look, let's not kid ourselves. Southern Africa is in a mess with the political climate in the region changing dramatically, and not necessarily for the better.

'Now that the Rhodesian problem has been sorted, tremendous pressure is building for similar change to take place in South Africa. The country is like an unstable tinderbox. A spark in the wrong place and the whole place will be in flames.'

I nodded my agreement. I was no international expert, but I did know that South Africa was facing a big problem with its disaffected black population becoming increasingly militant. One wrong move and there could be an explosion of violence that would make the Soweto riot seem like a playground squabble.

'To be fair to the current regime, it knows it is facing a big challenge and is already taking steps to avoid a disaster. The realists in the South African National Party are starting to have a far greater influence on policy. They know that change is inevitable. Their objective is to manage that change in a way that best protects the long term future of the country's white population. But one thing is for sure, Statton. Change is coming and that change could take place sooner than you think'

Rogers paused and stared off into the middle distance, then he shook his head gently. 'Just imagine. The white, pro-West government develops an ICBM; the white pro-West government is overthrown; a radical black government takes over, almost certainly sympathetic to Moscow, and has at its disposal its own nuke. It doesn't bear thinking about.'

I did not argue with him. 'Perhaps they won't be able to persuade Zamyatin to work for them,' I said without much conviction.

'You don't really believe that, Statton, do you? They will make him co-operate, one way or another.'

I did not answer, but I knew Rogers was right. As sure as night follows day, the Russian would be persuaded to give up his secrets. One way or another. The South African Government was not renowned for being squeamish about how it interrogated prisoners and I had little doubt the scientist would co-operate. Eventually.

That's when the CIA agent let me have it. 'Statton. We want you to get Zamyatin out.'

'Why me?' I asked. 'Why not use Agency agents? You could always use those two stooges downstairs.'

Rogers shook his head. 'No can do, Statton.'

'Why not?'

'Orders.'

'Orders?'

'Yes. The Agency has been ordered to have no involvement in the operation, overtly or covertly, directly or indirectly.'

'So it's political.' It was not a question, but Rogers did not seem to notice.

'Yes, it is political. The President of the United States decreed it himself.'

'Are you telling me that Reagan wants Zamyatin left in South Africa?'

'Christ, no! He very much wants Zamyatin out of there as quickly as possible, but any attempt to remove him without permission from the South Africans will be construed as a hostile action against a friendly sovereign nation.'

'So why doesn't Reagan simply ask them to hand him over?'

'Because they are hardly likely to agree and even if they did, the President wouldn't want to ask.'

'How so?'

'Because he doesn't want to be indebted to the South Africans. If things go sour in the country as quickly as we are predicting, then it's quite possible the Government would ask for the President's help.'

'And?'

'With an election due in two years' time, such help would not be a winner amongst black voters and the President is desperate for a second term.'

'He could just say no,' I pointed out.

'Not possible. It's not his style. He would look upon it as a debt of honour and feel obliged to help.' Rogers shook his head sadly, as if unable to understand such a concept. 'So, a direct approach to the South Africans is out of the question. For the same reason the President does not want anyone involved in the operation who can be traced back to the Administration or Government agency, and that includes the Firm.'

'Particularly if there is any risk of the operation going tits up?' I asked.

'I am sure that the President has considered every eventuality,' he replied with a smile.

'No doubt Reagan would be much more sanguine about using American personnel if there was a way that Zamyatin could be lifted without detection?'

'Of course.'

'So what you are saying is that there is no guarantee of success?'

'Is there ever?' He smiled again, but it did not make me feel any better. I suspected there was a nasty surprise waiting for me just round the corner.

'And if the mission is a failure, and the shit hits the fan, Reagan doesn't want to be stood underneath without an umbrella. Is that it?'

'That's pretty smart of you, Statton. That's why we need

56

you.'

'So it's not just because I'm a Limey?'

'Well, hiring somebody who is not an American citizen does have a certain attraction,' he admitted.

'What do you want me to do?'

'We want you to put together a team and get Zamyatin out of South Africa. You can recruit as many men as you need, within reason, the only criterion is that whoever you choose must be unable to implicate the Agency should they be caught. Only you must know who is funding the operation. It needs to be strictly need-to-know only. Okay?'

I nodded my agreement, although it was not an order I was likely to obey. I would only recruit men that I could trust implicitly and they would expect me to return that trust. However, I didn't think that Rogers needed to know the truth. Anyway, it was pretty irrelevant because if the mission was a success then it would not matter, and if it failed, there was a strong possibility that we would end up dead. That was a mercenary's lot.

'You can offer each man fifty thousand US dollars and your own fee will be one hundred thousand dollars. Half of it will be paid if you agree to take the contract, with the balance payable when you hand Zamyatin over to us. The same applies to members of your team. Fifty percent up front and fifty percent on delivery.'

I poured myself another drink and found it easy to resist the temptation to smile. $100,000 was a lot of money for a single operation. However, any feeling of anticipation I might have experienced at such a big pay-day was tempered by the realisation that such a large sum would not come my way easily.

'Do you want the Russian dead or alive?' I asked.

'Very much alive,' Rogers said quickly. 'He will be no good to us dead.'

'So what are you holding back from me?'

'I don't know what you mean.'

'Don't treat me like a fool, Rogers. You said they were only interested in stopping the South Africans from using Zamyatin's knowledge. They wouldn't get much co-operation from him if he was killed. So, what gives?'

Rogers did not answer immediately. Instead he took some time to check the crease on his trousers yet again before replying: 'Well, our primary objective is to get Zamyatin out before the South Africans can use whatever information they can squeeze out of him.

However, it is very important also that we have the opportunity to question him ourselves,' he paused, as if deciding whether he could trust me with his secret.

Of course he could. I was too trustworthy for my own good.

'The truth is, Statton, we want Zamyatin very much indeed.' he went on. 'That man has locked away in his head details of the entire Soviet defence system. If we could get our hands on that information, it would give us a tremendous advantage in the event of war. God forbid. Now, what do you say? Will you take the job?'

I was certainly tempted by his offer, but didn't want him to know that straight away. 'What about expenses?' I asked.

'Unlimited.' He looked at me intently. 'And I mean that, Statton. This is the big one. We want that Russian bastard badly. You can buy any equipment you need. No penny pinching. All expenses met without argument. You have my guarantee on that.' His voice was so full of enthusiasm I half expected him to add that the future of the world as we knew it was at stake, but even he must have known that would have been stretching my credibility well beyond the limit.

The prospect of action and the money on offer excited me, but my naturally cynical nature suspected there was a catch. 'Where is Zamyatin being held?' I asked.

Rogers started talking to his shoes again. I suppose it was easier for him to avoid my eyes that way. 'In prison,' he said.

'Why am I not surprised? Which one?'

Still the CIA agent refused to look directly at me and I just knew I was going to hate the answer when it came. But for a time he was silent.

'Which prison, Rogers?' I repeated.

'The Maximum Security Prison on Robben Island.' He said it lightly, but those last two little words weighed on my mind like a five ton weight.

I stared at him silently. He must have felt my eyes burning into the top of his head because eventually he looked up. 'Are you off your rocker?' I tapped my temple with a finger. 'If Zamyatin is being held on that bloody island, it will take nothing short of the Marine Corps to get him off.'

'Sadly you cannot hire them, Statton. I think you'll find they work for the US Government.' He smiled self-depreciatingly at his own joke. Perhaps that smile had been learned also at his man-management institute. If it was, it worked no better than his win-them-over smile. They were both wasted on me.

'Very droll,' I said.

'Oh, come on. Don't be such a defeatist. I know it will be tough.'

'Tough!' I interjected with a snort of derision.

'I know it will be tough,' he repeated, ploughing on remorselessly, 'but as the television programme says, no mission is impossible. A little dangerous, I grant you, but not impossible.'

'There is one little difference, Rogers. This is not a television show. This is the real world and in the real world people get killed. A little dangerous, you say. That is the understatement of the year. Trying to get Zamyatin off Robben Island would be suicidal. Do you really believe I would be willing to risk my neck just to get some stupid Russian scientist out of prison just so you can waterboard him? If so, you need to visit a toy shop and buy some new marbles.' I pointed a thumb at the bedroom door. 'Listen, why don't you take a hike and find yourself another sucker. I still have plenty of living to do.'

Rogers smiled again. He was enjoying himself.

'You mean you don't think you can do it?' He asked.

I glared at him. 'I mean I won't do it.'

'It will be a cinch, Statton.'

'Then go do it yourself.'

'I have explained why that is not possible. Come on, I have every faith in you.'

'Faith is easy when you're sitting behind a desk.'

'Think of the money.'

'No!'

'Then think of how you will be helping our country.'

I raised an eyebrow at him. 'Our country? And which country would that be? You seem to forget that I no longer work for the British Government and you are an American.'

'OK, point taken. So what about doing your bit for world peace?'

'I said no and I meant no.'

'I don't believe you,' he said finally.

He must have been reading my mind because I didn't believe myself either. My mind was already mulling over the problems such an operation would pose, and the possible solutions. My biggest problem has always been that I like a challenge and I suspect Rogers knew it.

'Look, Statton, I know there is risk involved, but that's why we're offering top dollar for the job. After all, you are a mercenary and the money is good.'

There he had me. The money was good. Damn good.

'How long do I have to decide?'

He looked at his watch. 'How long do you want? One minute? Two minutes? Five?'

'That quickly?'

He nodded and said: 'Yes, that quickly. The situation is critical. There will be a lot of planning and time is of the essence. We need somebody in place as soon as possible. If you say no then I'll fly to Brussels tomorrow and talk to somebody else.'

I laughed. 'That will be an interesting conversation,' I said. 'There's only one man in Belgium who would have been capable of executing an operation like this. That's Eddie Le Pen and you won't get him.'

'Why not?' Rogers asked suspiciously.

'Because Le Pen was found face down in the Meuse last week.'

'There are other mercenaries in…'

'Don't worry, Rogers,' I cut him off. 'I'll do it, but don't expect Zamyatin overnight. As you pointed out an operation like this will take time to plan and I need to put together a team I can trust.'

He nodded. 'Of course, but please remember we want Zamyatin before the South African's have had time to squeeze too much information out of him. Can you deliver him to us within a month?'

I shrugged. 'I can only promise to do my best.'

'Fair enough.'

'I will need money straight away for immediate expenses. The first thing I'll need to do is visit South Africa.'

Rogers opened his briefcase again and pulled out another envelope, smaller but much thicker than the first. He handed it to me. On the front of the envelope was neatly typed: ZAGEZSEAL

I raised an eyebrow. 'I recognise the first part of the code name,' I said, pointing to the first two letters.

'How do you know about the composition of our code name?' Rogers asked sharply. 'That information is highly confidential.'

'Not as confidential as you think,' I replied. 'Don't forget I used to work for the British Government. You're not the only one with useful contacts in the right places. So don't insult my intelligence. Look, I know the first two character prefix of your code names is called a digraph and that it shows a geographic region. In this case the ZA stands for South Africa. Am I right?'

'Does it matter?'

'It does to me. It's called trust.'

Rogers thought about that for a moment and must have realised that knowing how the code name was made up would compromise neither the CIA nor the operation. 'You are right, the digraph is for South Africa.'

'Thank you. And the rest?'

'You should be able to work out the next three letters because they are Zamyatin's initials. Gregori Evseyevitch Zamyatin, as for the remainder of the code name; Seal is the English word for Robben,' Rogers explained.

'Very original.'

Rogers must have recognised the sarcasm in my voice. 'It was all I could come up with at the time,' he protested lamely.

'It was your choice?' I was surprised, CIA code names are usually generated by a separate operations team.

'Yes. The number of people involved in this operation has been kept to a bare minimum. Inside the Firm the only people in the know are Bill Casey, my immediate team and me. Outside the Firm the only people who know what is going on is the President and his Chief of Staff. As covert operations go, this one is as deep and black as a coal mine.'

I looked down at the envelope. Rogers did not have to tell me what was in it. I know what money feels like. But he told me anyway.

'There is sixty thousand dollars in the envelope. That is the first half of your fee, plus ten thousand dollars for expenses during the planning stage. Will that be enough?'

I nodded.

'Okay,' he continued, 'now for the good news. You don't have to worry about how you get Zamyatin out of South Africa. I will arrange for a submarine to collect him from a rendezvous of your choice in the Cape region. Once your plans have been laid all you need do is provide me with a time and location and I will do the rest. Agreed?'

I agreed. Who was I to argue?

Rogers gave me his Washington telephone number and we

arranged that I would contact him as soon as I had finalised a plan of action, complete with my budget for expenses. He would then arrange for the necessary funds to be made available. He asked me if I had any questions.

'Yes, why is Zamyatin being detained on Robben Island anyway? I thought the prison was for non-white use only? Why isn't he being held in somewhere like Pollsmoor Prison?'

'A good question and we're not entirely sure. We think it's because Zamyatin is so important to the South Africans they decided to waive their usual strict Apartheid rules so that they could keep him in the most secure prison in the country. Remember that nobody has ever escaped from Robben Island.'

'Thanks for reminding me.'

Rogers laughed lightly. 'It is our understanding that Zamyatin eventually will be transferred to secure accommodation that is being prepared for him at the Koeberg Nuclear Installation. Anything else?'

'Yes. Where exactly is he being held in the prison?' I asked.

He delved into his briefcase again and brought out an envelope identical to the first, from which he withdrew another photograph. It was an aerial shot that had obviously been taken from a high altitude reconnaissance plane. It showed in detail all of Robben Island.

Rogers pointed to a group of buildings in the northern half of the Island and said: 'That is the Maximum Security Prison. It was built about twenty years ago and consists of four H-block general sections here…' he tapped the photograph, '…each of which has a communal cell that can house fifty-two inmates and each of which is divided one from the other by ten feet high walls.' He paused and smiled at me. 'I think I should perhaps add that in addition to those walls there is a sixteen foot high wire fence surrounding the whole complex.'

'It gets better and better,' I murmured sourly.

Rogers smiled again. 'At one time all the prisoners were housed in those H-blocks irrespective of their status.' He tapped the photograph again. 'But about five years ago another building was added to the complex. It contains a hospital and an isolation block containing 90 single cells, which is divided into three sections that are designated A, B and C.

'Section A comprises the southern wing of the building and most of the western wing. It is used for convicted members of the

Black Consciousness Movement and Umkhonto we Sizwe.' He looked at me smugly and went on to explain: 'It is the Zulu name for Spear of the Nation, which is the armed wing of the ANC.'

'I know,' I said, hoping to burst his balloon of pomposity, but Rogers didn't seem to notice.

'The eastern wing of the block is Section B,' he went on without acknowledging my comment, 'which is used to house influential leadership figures, such as Nelson Mandela, and is better known as the Leadership Section. Sections A and B have communal rooms for eating and recreational activities and the courtyard here,' he tapped the photograph yet again, 'is used for outdoor activities including gardening. The courtyard is guarded by a raised catwalk that surrounds it.'

'What about the last section? Section C?' I asked.

'It is used for prisoners who are in solitary confinement or on starvation diet punishment. The inmates call it Khulukuthu.'

'I've never heard that name. What does it mean?'

'There is no direct translation, but it literally means throwing something spontaneously into something.' Rogers tapped the photograph rapidly several times as he went on: 'The remaining buildings are for administration, here behind the hospital, a store room, kitchens and dining hall, here, here and here to the west of the H-blocks. You will find in the envelope a detailed plan of the prison, with more information about other security arrangements, such as the location of the guard rooms.' He passed the envelope to me.

I pulled a sheet of paper from the envelope. It was a hand-drawn, large scale plan of the prison with writing on it. 'All very well,' I said, 'but you still haven't told me exactly where Zamyatin is being held.'

'I think he is being held in B wing.'

'You think?' I said, failing to keep irritation out of my voice. 'Jesus wept! It gets better by the minute. Could you explain how we are supposed to find Zamyatin if, miracle of miracles, we ever get into the prison?'

'Don't fret, Statton. By the time you contact me with the plan I will have the information you need. We have somebody working on it.'

'Why am I not reassured?'

'Don't be cynical.'

'I'm not. I'm just wise to the ways of the CIA.' I studied the photograph and plan again. 'Can I keep these?'

'Of course,' Rogers replied.

He watched me as I stood up and walked over to the wardrobe and stashed the photographs, plan and money in my canvass holdall.

'Just one other thing, Statton,' he said, his voice cold and hard.

I turned and looked at him.

'Don't forget who that money belongs to.'

'Me, I thought.'

'You know what I mean. Remember where the money came from. Don't go getting any ideas about using it to take a one way trip to some tropical destination.' He stared at me in a way he probably thought was intimidating. 'If you take a powder we will track you down and find you wherever you try to hide.'

I stared back at him. I was not intimidated. I had been threatened by far tougher people than him. Eventually he lowered his eyes.

'Don't try to play the heavy hand with me, Rogers. It's not necessary. I won't run off with your bloody money and you know it, which is why you came to me in the first place.' I walked over and opened the bedroom door. 'Now, get out of my room before people start getting the idea that I'm a faggot too.'

He stormed out of the room and left me with a look of pure poison and a door that slammed with such force it rattled the hinges. The man-management institute he attended would have been very disappointed at his loss of control.

Personally I could not have cared less. I had a much needed job in the bag and sixty thousand dollars to keep it company.

Thursday April 15th 1982

By two o'clock the following morning the rain clouds had moved north and were already dumping water on London in a futile attempt to cleanse its grimy streets. Now the sky above the waterside public house was as clear and bright as a planetarium.

In the forecourt of the pub dozens of pale yellow full moons shone in uniform reflection from the surface of the numerous puddles that had been left on the gravel by the now departed storm. The wind had dropped to a zephyr that rippled the mirror moons into distorted, dented orbs and carried on it the clean fresh smell of newly watered grass.

The only sign of life in the peaceful, moonlit spring night was a light that shone aboard the cabin cruiser owned by Major Percival Carsons. Why was he up and about at this time of the morning? Did he perhaps suspect I was planning an early departure to give him the slip? I decided it would do no harm to investigate before making my moonlight flit.

I made my way downstairs where I left a note for Billy by the cash register. Carrying my canvas holdall I made my way out of the back door and headed for the car park in which stood a handful of cars, including my own and the one I knew belonged to Carsons. I stowed my holdall in the boot of my car, locked it and headed towards the waterfront.

As I crept on tip-toe across the forecourt, the crunch of the gravel beneath my feet sounded to my ears like a cinema audience getting stuck into free rations of popcorn. I was convinced the noise would warn Carsons of my approach. However, I need not have worried, because I arrived safely at the cruiser's side without there being any sign that I had been spotted.

I stood in the shadow of the boat and decided my next move. The cabin cruiser had several portholes, each of which was covered with a red hessian curtain. I inched along the boat's hull, checking each porthole in turn, but at first I could see nothing.

When I reached the last porthole I saw the curtain had not been drawn properly and there was narrow crack at one end. By craning my neck and twisting my body like a contortionist I could just see inside the long, narrow galley.

There were two men sitting in the galley and they were in animated conversation. I could hear the occasional word but I could make no sense of it. However, the subject of their heated exchange was not difficult to work out. My ears were burning.

I had given up trying to make sense out of what the men were saying and was just easing my neck back into something akin to its normal position when I heard a slight rustling noise to my left. I pressed myself closer to the hull and froze, not daring even to breathe.

Somewhere up river an owl hooted as it searched the river bank for that night's meal. Perhaps right at that moment a water vole was peering up through the reeds hoping the bird would look elsewhere for its victim.

If there was a vole hiding from the owl then I wished it luck. As I stood motionless in the boat's shadow, I knew just what the tiny rodent felt like.

I was standing at the bow end and the noise had come from the stern. It was not repeated but I did feel the cruiser roll slightly against my chest and I guessed that somebody had climbed aboard.

I waited for a few minutes and when I eventually emerged from my shadowy hideaway it was on bare feet. I crept on tip-toes towards the car park with my shoes and socks in my hand. The forecourt was icy cold beneath my feet, but at least the gravel did not crunch.

When I reached my car I put on my socks and shoes before starting the engine. Soon I was heading for London.

At that time of the morning there was very little traffic on the M20, just the occasional vegetable lorry making its way to Covent Garden carrying produce from one or other of the Kentish farms. I drove along with only part of my mind on the road. With another part of my mind I mulled over the operation I was about to undertake and who I wanted to recruit for my team.

Yet another part of my mind considered why Gavin Rogers II and Major Percival Carsons (Rtd) were sitting in the galley of a cabin cruiser on the River Medway at two o'clock in the morning discussing me. It seemed pretty obvious that Carsons was working for Rogers, but in what capacity was he employed and why all the secrecy?

Finally, the last part of my mind was trying to work out the significance of another of the night's developments. What was the meaning of the shadowy figure of a man I had seen as I made my way silently back to my car? A man, quite unaware of my presence, who stood with an ear pressed against the cruiser's galley door and who I recognised immediately as the tall CIA agent, Hank Graham.

I thought about the noise I had heard in the corridor outside my bedroom during my meeting with Rogers and wondered whether Hank has also been eavesdropping on our conversation. If so, why?

South Africa

Wednesday April 21ˢᵗ 1982: Johannesburg,

My flight from London to Johannesburg took just under fourteen hours and it was not an enjoyable experience.

After an initial delay at Heathrow, the reason for which was never satisfactorily explained, I had to put up with inedible airline food; a Woody Allen in-flight comedy that was the least funny film I had ever seen; and inattentive cabin staff who seemed to have forgotten that their Easter holiday had finished over a week before.

It was with some relief that I eventually stepped out onto the tarmac of the runway and let the warm African breeze blow the stale, pressurised cabin air from my lungs.

I stood and watched my fellow travellers head towards the oblong glass and brick building that housed the arrival terminal at Jan Smuts International Airport. As they walked in a ragged line across the tarmac, displaying an assortment of hand luggage, a number of them scanned the spectator balcony of the terminal, perhaps looking for a wave from a waiting friend or relative.

I waited for the right moment and then joined the procession. I did not glance at the crowded spectator balcony. There would be no waves for me. I had no relatives in South Africa and all my friends were far too discreet.

Inside the high ceilinged arrival hall two young policemen inspected the new arrivals with hard, suspicious eyes. They stood at ease with their straight backs not quite resting against the wall. Despite their semi-casual stance the cops still managed to convey the impression that they were itching for an excuse to draw their service revolvers and that they knew how to fire those weapons accurately.

The policemen wore dark green safari suits, peaked caps, knee length socks, shiny black shoes, Sam Browne belts and granite like expressions. Their faces softened somewhat when they spotted the blonde girl in the see through white blouse standing behind me in the queue that shuffled slowly towards the immigration counter.

The girl smiled at the young policemen and one of them

smiled back shyly, although his colleague seemed more interested in what was contained in the girl's well filled black bra. I followed Blondie's example and gave the cops a friendly smile but they both ignored me.

I had chosen my place in the queue well.

When it was my turn to present myself at the immigration counter the gnarled old immigration officer barely glanced at my face as he thumbed quickly through and stamped my passport. Like the two cops he was far more interested in the shapely girl who was next in line. I did not wait around to check, but I suspected he was going to take far longer inspecting her documents. I took my passport from the man, slid it into my briefcase and headed for the baggage area.

I waited my turn to retrieve my large travelling bag from the luggage carousel that was already circulating baggage that had been recovered from the belly of the plane. Remarkably my bag had not been lost, stolen, damaged or pilfered. I pulled it gratefully from the conveyor belt and made my way to customs.

'Goeimore, meneer. Het u iets om te verklaar?' The customs officer asked and then repeated his question in heavily accented English. 'Good morning, sir. Have you anything to declare?'

I shook my head. I had nothing to declare.

'No firearms?'

'No,' I said with another shake of my head. I did this several more times as the customs officer insisted on reading out a list of prohibited items.

'Any magazines? Any books? Any drugs? Any pornographic or communist literature of any kind?' He studied me closely as he spoke, but I was still shaking my head. 'Any television sets?'

I stopped shaking my head. 'No television sets,' I said with a smile and wondered how many TVs the South African authorities discovered being smuggled into the country in suitcases each day. Maybe there was a ring of international television smugglers of which I was not aware.

Eventually the customs officer satisfied himself that I was not trying to smuggle any illicit goods into the country. With a grunt, which I loosely translated as a 'Dankie, meneer,' he waved me through to become a guest in the land of the free for some.

I made my way through the custom's barrier and along a short corridor towards the packed reception area. Half the population of the Witwatersrand seemed to be crammed into the jostling crowd that pressed against the metal guard rails, competing to be first to recognise their loved ones as they came through the automatic sliding doors. For the South African Government, they were the only barrier between them and a world full of liberalism and communism.

Behind the seething mass of people an army of uniformed chauffeurs waited patiently, some holding aloft small blackboards on which had been chalked the names of the people for whom they waited. Others called out names in loud voices like bookies shouting the odds at Epsom Racecourse.

None of the chauffeurs were trying to attract my attention so I ignored them and pushed my way through to the main door.

Suddenly I stopped dead as I felt something hard press into the small of my back. 'Freeze, Statton,' a voice hissed in my ear.

I didn't need to try any James Bond style heroics, because I recognised the voice immediately. 'Get your finger out of my back, Paul,' I said. 'I don't know where it's been.' I turned to face the owner of the finger. He laughed as we shook hands.

'Howzit, man! It's lekker to see you again.' He punched my arm lightly and took my bag from me. 'Come on, I have a car downstairs.'

We headed for the lift to the underground car park. On the way I commented that he looked a bit under the weather.

'Hell, Dave, you don't know the half of it,' he replied with a theatrical groan. 'Listen, when you made that crack about not knowing where my finger has been. Ach, man, I'm telling you I don't know where any part of me was last night!' He groaned again as the lift dropped quickly, leaving our stomachs a flight behind. 'Ugh! That's not nice.'

'A hangover?'

'A babelaas and a half, man.'

The lift stopped and the doors opened. We stepped out into the car park.

'It's the dark blue Chevy at the far end of this row,' Paul said leading the way. 'I'm ashamed to say that last night I was at a business dinner in the Booysens Hotel, but it turned into a real jol. I ended up legless and in very strange company.' He did not sound in any way ashamed. 'Anyway, when I woke up this morning I found myself in an apartment I have never seen in my life. By the look of the chick beside me in bed it's somewhere I won't want to see again in a hurry. She was a real dog.'

But Paul did not deceive me. I knew him too well. He had the pick of the most beautiful women in South Africa. 'No doubt a thoroughbred dog with an out-of-town husband,' I said.

The first member of my team grinned amiably back at me. It was answer enough.

Six days before my arrival in Johannesburg, when I drove back to London after my meeting with Gavin Rogers, I was already thinking about the operation. However, at that very early stage, the only thing of which I was certain was the name of my first recruit.

Later that day I made a phone call to Durban, South Africa. I knew that if I was to have any hope of success in my task then I would need the very best people in my team. People with whom I was happy to trust my life.

Paul was one such man. If it had not been for the big South African I would not have been alive to even think about the dangerous mission on which we were about to embark.

It was in late 1970 that Paul Helsdon saved my life. I had recently been forced out from my job with Section 2F of the Department for Covert Operations, made the scape-goat for an intelligence cock-up that had almost brought down the newly elected government of Ted Heath. I was dismissed without back pay or a reference. In disgust at the way I was treated, and almost penniless, I left Britain and joined up as a mercenary in the increasingly vicious war that was taking place in Laos.

I was one of the mainly European mercenaries hired by the monarchist Laotian Government to supplement the country's regular armed forces. They were in the process of flushing out the communist Pathet Lao insurgents who were infiltrating the country from northwest Vietnam.

One day we received word that a communist unit was operating out of a village near the Hou River, several miles east of where Paul and I were based. We set out with a Laotian foot patrol with orders to track down the Pathet Lao unit and wipe it out. The intelligence information we received claimed that the insurgents were ill equipped and under strength.

I should have known better than to trust Laotian military intelligence.

Our patrol was walking single file along a narrow track through the dense jungle. I was at point, leading a section of ten men. Paul brought up the rear and it was this position in the line that saved him from the worst of the ambush into which we walked.

Well aware of the danger posed by the thick, lush foliage, which provided such a perfect camouflage for potential ambushers, Paul allowed a sizeable distance to open up between himself and the penultimate member of the patrol. As soon as he heard the rattle of automatic rifle fire in front of him, he was able to fling himself into the undergrowth without being seen by the insurgents. I was not so lucky.

The attack should not have come as a surprise to any member of our patrol. You do not travel through that type of terrain without being constantly looking out for trouble. But the Pathet Lao unit was so well hidden that none of us saw any sign of its presence. When the insurgents opened fire it was with a savagery and accuracy that gave us no chance. Only half my men managed to throw themselves to the ground, the rest were cut down where they stood.

Those of us who survived the initial onslaught managed to find refuge behind what little cover was available on the jungle path. We returned fire immediately, but it was of no avail. We were firing at a bank of foliage with no visible targets. All we could do was rake the jungle with our fire and hope for the best. On the other hand our opponents knew where we were and slowly picked us off one by one until I was the only man left. At that time I didn't even know whether Paul was among my dead comrades who littered the path.

I kept up the fight until my ammunition ran out, expecting all the time to feel enemy bullets slam into my body. By then, I had reached a state of mind where I did not care either way. It was only when my own HK33 assault rifle was silent that I realised the enemy fire had already stopped.

I got to my feet, leaving my weapon on the ground, and raised my hands above my head in surrender. I had no other choice. For some reason my life had been spared, now all I could do was wait and find out why.

Slowly the insurgents emerged from the jungle, each carrying a Kalashnikov AK47, all of which were pointing at me. They stopped in a circle a couple of feet from me, their eyes cold and their aim steady. Perhaps they thought I intended trying to escape. I pushed my hands further into the air to emphasise I had no intention of attempting any such thing.

I thought about the intelligence report we had received and cursed silently. These boys looked neither ill equipped nor under strength.

Out of the corner of my eye I saw another figure emerge from the dense undergrowth at the edge of the track and push his way through the ring of insurgents. The man held a pistol that he waved in my face while screaming what sounded like insults at me in a language I did not recognise. It was certainly not one of the Laotian dialects with which I had come into contact. I guessed the newcomer was the unit commander, so he was probably Vietnamese. Not that it mattered; screamed insults sound much the same in any language.

The Pathet Laos unit took me to the village that we had been told was being used as their base. In at least that much our intelligence information had been accurate, but knowing this didn't make me feel any better.

The villagers had abandoned their homes and its only occupants were the communists who had captured me. Once we arrived at the village it soon became clear why I had not been shot like the rest of my men. The insurgents had other plans for me.

I was manhandled to the centre of the village where a fire already glowed brightly in the gathering gloom of dusk. I was pushed to the ground and my wrists and ankles were lashed to pre-prepared stakes, close enough to feel the heat of the glowing coals on my face. I tried not to think about the bayonet that the unit commander pushed into the centre of the red hot embers, nor for which part of my body the steel might be destined.

Paul timed his attack to perfection. He waited until I was surrounded by jeering men, and the Pathet Lao commander was waving the red hot bayonet in the general direction of my rear end, before he hit the camp like a one man blitzkrieg. The commies did not stand a chance.

Paul's ferocious onslaught lasted no longer than fifteen seconds. By the time it was over half the insurgents were dead, including the unit commander, and the rest were mortally wounded or had fled into the jungle leaving their weapons behind.

That was Paul Helsdon.

Paul was a man to whom I owed my life. He was a man I could trust. He also happened to be a man who was expert in armaments and explosives.

'Did you find us a suitable base in the Cape?' I asked as Paul drove the blue Chevrolet away from the airport and headed down the busy motorway towards Johannesburg.

'Ja. It's a beauty,' he replied. 'It's about twenty kilometres from Cape Town on the coast of False Bay. It's a quiet little dorpie called Clovelly located next to a small town called Fish Hoek. Have you heard of it?'

I shook my head.

'The house is fully furnished and nicely secluded. No nosey neighbours to bother us. The owners have gone overseas for six months, so to minimise suspicion I took it for all that time. Is that okay?'

'No problem.'

'I told the estate agent I was part of an international research group that was undertaking a study of marine life in False Bay.' He glanced at me and grinned. 'But as soon as I told him he would be paid the full six months' rent, up front and in cash, he lost all interest in why I wanted the house.'

'Where's the estate agent based? Is he local?'

'Ja, he has an office in Fish Hoek.'

'That's good. He'll be able to provide us with local knowledge.'

'I'm sure he'll be more than happy to help. He seemed a real cool oke. By the way, I told him he'd get his dough this week. Twenty-five hundred bucks. Will that be a problem?'

'No, we'll pay him when we collect the keys from him. Did you put down a deposit?'

'Ja, a month's rent; five hundred bucks. He said we can move in as soon as we want.'

'Okay. I'll square up with you later. When's our flight?'

'Tomorrow. I arranged the meeting you wanted for this evening and booked us on the early morning flight to Cape Town. We should arrive at about half past ten.'

'Good work,' I said.

We drove on in comfortable silence. I was pleased to be working with Paul again and I sensed he felt the same way. Although the end of the Transvaal summer was fast approaching the sun was still strong in the clear blue sky and it was hot inside the car. I wound down my window and stared out across the city.

The foundations of Johannesburg as an industrial mining town were built on the glitter of gold dust. By the early 1980's most of the gold had gone and only the dust remained. It was everywhere. It was a city of dust.

The wind blew across the Highveld. It whipped up clouds of yellow dust from the tops of the worked-out mine dumps that were dotted around the outskirts of the city and hurled it into the air where it formed a dusty haze. Eventually the dust settled, covering everything; the buildings, the streets, the cars, the parks, the trees and the people.

The city lay at the very heart of the Witwatersrand, a vast area in which plenty of gold still remained and which stretched from Randfontein in the west to Springs in the east. Jo'burg itself continued to thrive, even without the gold mines, because not only was it South Africa's largest city, but it was also its financial, commercial and industrial capital.

We drove over the Kazerne Viaduct. Across the dry, brown veld to the south I could see in the middle distance the shimmering waters of Wemmer Pan, complete with its illuminated musical fountain, replica sailing ship and historic miniature village.

I had half expected Paul to take the Heidelberg Interchange exit and head north towards Hillbrow, but he stayed on the M2.

'Where are we staying?' I asked.

He glanced over at me and flashed another of his wide grins at me. 'Unlimited expenses you said.'

I nodded.

'That's lekker, because I've booked us into the Carlton Hotel, hey.'

I looked past him at the jagged skyline of the city. There are well known landmarks in all the great cities of the world. Structures that rise above the surrounding mediocrity to tower above it. The Post Office Tower in London; the Eiffel Tower in Paris; and the Empire State Building in New York. All are imposing structures.

In Johannesburg it was the Carlton Centre that drew the eye. I could see it now. Tall and sleek, it was the tallest building anywhere in the whole continent of Africa. Thirty of the Centre's fifty floors were taken up by the magnificent 5 star Carlton Hotel. I nodded again. Yes, the Carlton would do nicely, thank you very much.

We lapsed into silence again until eventually Paul asked: 'So, Dave, what is the operation?'

I laughed. 'I wondered how long you would be able to hold your curiosity in check.'

'Five days and,' he glanced at his wristwatch, 'and forty three minutes, to be precise. Ag man, are you impressed?'

'I am impressed.'

'So now you're going to tell me what it's all about?'

I thought about that for a moment, remembering what Rogers had said about need-to-know. I understood his reasons for wanting to keep the involvement of the CIA a secret between him and me. Even the hardest man will give up information when faced with the hardest methods of interrogation and the only certain way of protecting that information is by ensuring it is restricted to as few people as possible. But I was not planning on getting interrogated myself and I was sure that Paul would feel the same way. It would be death or glory for both of us, so I told him of the events of the past couple of weeks.

I started from that first phone call during which Gavin Rogers set up our meeting in Kent, through to my early morning witnessing of the meeting between Rogers and Percival Carsons. By the time I finished Paul was grinning broadly at the prospect of some action. As he pointed out, things had been quiet on the mercenary front for far too long.

We drove on in silence until eventually Paul asked: 'Are you sure it was Hank Graham you saw spying on Rogers?'

'Well it was either him or his doppelganger,' I said.

'Perhaps Graham was just there to mind his back.'

'Perhaps,' I agreed without conviction.

There was another silence as we both mulled over the possible explanation for what I had seen that night in Allington. Neither of us had any sudden inspiration and so we dropped the subject.

'You didn't tell me how much I'm getting paid for this little jolly,' Paul said.

'Did I not?'

'No.'

I told him.

He whistled. 'Fifty thousand dollars and unlimited expenses, that's some pay-day, Dave. What's the catch?'

So I told him that too.

Paul turned to stare at me and allowed the car to drift over the white line in the middle of the road that separated the two lanes of the motorway. I pointed ahead and he realised what was happening to the car and hastily brought it back under control, but too late to prevent a series of hoots from faster moving vehicles using the outside lane.

'Sies man!' He exclaimed as he wound down his window and waved a hand in apology to the other motorists as they overtook us. 'Is Rogers mad? Robben Island!' He groaned and I could see that his visions of easy money were slowly disappearing into the dusty Jo'burg air.

'I thought I heard you call this operation a "little jolly".' I pointed out.

He glared at me, but there was no real animosity in it and this time he made sure not to take his eyes off the road too long. 'So, tell me one thing, Dave,' he said as he concentrated once more on navigating through traffic that was getting heavier as we got closer to the city centre. 'How the hell does Rogers imagine we're going to get this oke out of that hell hole? Does he expect us just to toddle up to the main gate and say: Howzit, meneer, we hope you don't mind but we've just popped over from the mainland to take Comrade Zamyatin off your hands.'

He paused to slam his fist viciously against the horn to warn off a mangy dog that wandered onto the inside lane of the motorway looking for carrion. 'And what does Rogers think those groentjies will do? Shake us by the hand, invite us in for tea and then hand the bastard over?'

'Well, as a plan I suppose it's a start.' I said deadpan.

He glared at me again, but this time there was a hint of a smile on his lips.

'Mind the traffic lights,' I warned him. He had turned off the motorway at Exit 10 and was heading towards Rissik Street. Having taken his eyes off the road again to glare at me, he had not noticed the lights on the corner of Albert and Rissik had changed to red. He slammed on the Chevy's brakes and we screeched to a halt.

'Sies, man, that's no holiday camp they're running on that bloody island. If the guards get a sniff of our approach they're liable to shoot first and ask questions later, by which time we're very unlikely to be alive to answer, hey.'

He revved the car engine as the traffic lights changed to amber and was ready to roar away with spinning wheels the second he saw green. He did not get far and he snorted in disgust as this time the Marshall Street lights caught him.

'Do you actually have a proper plan?' He asked.

I sat listening to the car's indicator light tick out a message to anybody who might be interested to learn that we were about to turn right.

'I have a provisional plan,' I replied as Paul pulled away and turned into Marshall Street. He accelerated quickly to beat the lights at both Eloff and Kruis Streets, but Von Wielligh Street saw us coming and had its red light ablaze in good time. 'But there's still an awful lot to be done. We need to research the area, decide on what equipment we need, procure it and of course recruit the team, although I do have some ideas about who else I'd like to join us.'

'So you think it's possible to get Zamyatin off Robben Island?'

I shrugged. What a question to ask.

'But you intend giving it a go?'

'Well, I don't think there's any harm in going down to the Cape to have a look see.'

'In that case, Dave, you're as mad as Rogers.' As if to emphasise his feelings, Paul thumped the car's horn again. This time it was to warn off a schoolgirl who had emerged from an OK Bazaars store and was about to step off the kerb just as the lights changed to green. He pulled away from the lights and as we drove past the girl and turned into Von Wielligh Street she thrust a middle finger in the air.

'And you,' Paul shouted over his shoulder.

We were almost at our destination. The OK Bazaars was part of the Carlton Centre and the complex's underground car-park was just around the block.

I patted Paul's shoulder. 'If it's any consolation, big feller. I agree with you!'

'About that kid?'

'No, about being as mad as Rogers.'

Mondeor, Johannesburg

Booysen's Road runs south out of the city until it eventually links up with the N1, the main highway to the Orange Free State, its capital Bloemfontein and then, nine hundred miles further south, Cape Town.

Just outside the city limits, to the west of the N1, are situated a number of black townships with names like Orlando, Moroka, Nancefield and Jabuvu. Over the years these townships have expanded until they coalesced into a single, massive and irritating sore on the body politic of white South Africa.

That the name of those townships is largely unknown outside South Africa was perhaps unsurprising, because they had achieved worldwide notoriety under their collective acronym. To the bureaucrats who administered the affairs of the million non-people who refused to disappear from the Witwatersrand communities in which most of them had been born, the towns were classified as the South West Townships, or Soweto, for short.

There is a point on the N1 where three other busy roads join it. They are the Baragwanath Road, Rifle Range Road and the Potchefstroom Road, which leads to Soweto. This road junction takes its name from the roadhouse that sits at the side of the intersection. It is called Uncle Charlie's. A short walk from the junction, across the veld to the southeast, is the nearest of Johannesburg's southern suburbs to Soweto. Its name is Mondeor.

It was my first visit to Mondeor and I soon realised that it was everything that Soweto was not. Affluent, well maintained, green landscaped, swimming pooled, electrified and almost totally white.

There were few of the grand mansions that could be found in some northern suburbs of the city. However one look at the neat houses and spacious, well-kept gardens that lined the grid system of well-lit roads was enough to demonstrate that this was no slum.

It was in one of those Mondeor residential roads that Paul and I sat in our parked car and waited for the pre-arranged all clear signal. The house outside of which we maintained our vigil was set well back from the road. Its long, sloping front garden was hemmed in by a low wall designed not so much to keep out intruders, but to keep in the large dogs that I knew roamed the garden during the day.

Luckily for us, those dogs were not allowed to patrol the garden at night. It was deemed safer for them to be inside the house, well away from any tempting poisoned meat that might be thrown over the wall by burglars.

The house was a Spanish style bungalow. Its wide, arched windows were darkened and fully protected by portcullis shaped burglar bars that were fastened to the wall with sturdy fittings. Under the eaves of the house were positioned security lights that washed the garden in bright yellow. They shimmered across the surface of a leaf littered swimming pool and turned the slowly freezing dew covered lawn into a carpet of silver tinsel.

There was no sign of life.

Attached to the left hand side of the house was a double garage while on the right hand side, but separated from it by a wide cement patio, were the servant's quarters. By South African law it was permissible for garages to be joined to a house in which white people lived. However, such a close a proximity for any black servant who happened to sleep overnight on the premises was strictly forbidden.

And it was the servant's quarters that Paul and I watched with growing impatience. We had already been parked outside the house for half an hour, since eleven o'clock that evening, and we had to wait another twenty minutes before the signal finally arrived. For a few brief seconds a small oblong of light showed in the window of the tiny outhouse, then was gone.

'Let's go,' I said, pleased to be on the move at last and able to stretch my cold limbs. Ignoring the wrought iron gates we vaulted silently over the wall and made our way quickly to the darkened servant's quarters. When we arrived, a door opened to receive us. Once we were inside, the door was closed and locked quietly.

The room was in darkness and as cold as the inside of a refrigerator. A shape, much blacker than the rest of our surroundings, flitted across the relative lightness of the window. I heard the swish of a curtain being drawn. There was the sound of something being lifted followed by several metallic clicks. Finally, there was the sound of a match being struck and the room was filled with light as a paraffin lantern was lit.

By the light of the lantern I could see a sheet of hardboard had been positioned across the window. It was held in position by four small metal catches and a garish orange curtain was pulled across on top of it, effectively preventing any light escaping into the outside world.

'Can't be too careful, baas,' a low, deep voice said.

I shook hands with the owner of the voice. 'How are you, Robert?' I too kept my voice low.

'As well as can be expected, David,' the African replied with a smile. He wore a colourful blanket round his shoulders to give him some relief from the bitter cold in his room. 'I would offer you a drink but sadly I have nothing stronger than a cup of tea. You understand?'

I understood. Black servants were not permitted to have alcohol in their living quarters. I pulled a bottle of Cape brandy from the deep pocket of my sheepskin coat and handed it to him. 'Here, this might warm you up a little.'

He took the bottle from me and nodded gratefully.

The room boasted very little furniture. There was an old kitchen table, two rickety chairs, two orange boxes, a battered chest of drawers and, in one corner of the room, a cot complete with thin mattress. The only colourful relief in the shabby little room, except for the orange curtain, was a large poster fixed to one grimy white wall. It depicted the Kaiser Chiefs, Soweto's premier soccer team.

We sat down at the table. Robert insisted that Paul and I should have the chairs, while he sat on one of the orange boxes. He produced three chipped cups from the top drawer of the dresser and into each he poured a generous measure of brandy.

Robert handed Paul and me a cup and then raised his own in a salute. 'Nkosi sikelel' iAfrika!' Robert intoned, before swallowing the liquid in a single gulp.

Paul and I kept our toast to a simple "Cheers!"

Robert nodded towards the house. 'Did you notice if there were any lights on in the house, David?' He asked as he poured himself another brandy.

'No, the house was in darkness,' I replied.

'Good, my madam must be in bed.' His eyes twinkled as he said "my madam" like that. 'I wouldn't want her to disturb our deliberations.'

'Why meet here anyway?' I asked.

'What are the other options?' Robert asked. 'Soweto?' He shook his head. 'I think not. There are far too many informers in the townships these days. Your hotel?' Again he shook his head. 'Out of the question.'

'Why?' I asked. 'Isn't the Carlton classified as an "international" hotel these days? Can't people of any colour stay there?'

Robert chuckled. 'That is true, if you have enough money. It's all part of the Boers' cosmetic exercise to convince the world they are more liberal these days. But, David, how would it look if a poor, humble gardener like Robert Dyakala was seen at such a place? Anyway, it would be difficult for me to visit you in the city during the day and at night, well, it is not wise for the likes of me to be caught in a white area after dark. It does not pay to draw attention to oneself. You understand? No, it is far better that we meet here.'

'Sies, man, how on earth do you put up with a dump like this?' Paul asked looking round the Spartan room.

'I recognise your voice,' Robert said with a friendly smile. 'You rang me to set up this meeting. Is that not so?'

Paul nodded.

'And from your accent it is quite obvious that you are South African. A white South African. So how can you ask such a question?'

I realised I had not introduced the two men. I did so and they shook hands.

'I'm sorry, Robert,' Paul said, looking slightly shamefaced. 'Of course I knew that servant's quarters weren't palaces, but I never imagined they were as bad as this. To tell the truth my parents always refused to have servants and I've kind of followed suit. I'm sure there are many whites in this country who don't realise how you people live.'

'Actually, it's not so bad,' Robert said with a smile. 'There are people in the townships living in much worse conditions. Anyway, living here is convenient. I can get into and out of Soweto quickly and easily.' He paused as he made short work of his second brandy. 'I have a permit to work and live here in a white area. That is a precious commodity.' He smiled again, the easy uncomplicated smile of the Bantu.

'Nobody suspects that Robert, the pleasant slow-witted garden boy, is one of their so-called "terrorists". I tell you, Paul, if I lived in Soweto my time would soon be up. Here in Mondeor, as long as I am careful,' he nodded towards the hardboard on the window, 'and as long as it is "yes baas" this and "no madam" that, then I am rarely bothered. And as it happens I have a very understanding employer.' He smiled, but didn't elaborate.

I found it difficult to believe that any employer was understanding enough to turn a blind eye to Robert's nefarious activities, so could only assume they were blissfully unaware of his real role. When he called himself a terrorist he was being over modest because he was not just any terrorist. Without him the effectiveness of the black armed resistance in South Africa would have been considerably diminished.

In addition to a number of other important roles in the Freedom Movement, Robert Dyakala, was quartermaster to Umkhonto we Sizwe. Any illegal firearms, explosives or other military style equipment needed in the ANC's somewhat sporadic attacks against South African government targets were obtained via the intricate network of agents Robert had put in place. Very few people knew of Robert's real work or his background, but as it happens, I was one of those who did.

Robert had described himself as "slow-witted". That was as far from the truth as you could get. That he was still free, despite the important position he held in the ANC, bore ample testimony to his intelligence and guile.

He was thirty, yet looked several years older. As he once told me, you grow up quickly in Soweto. I knew all about his background, because he had once told me about the incident that had motivated him to join the armed struggle.

Robert Dyakala was born a gentle, peace loving boy, who found himself drawn into a world of violence by events over which he had no control. He readily admitted to me that his commitment to the ideals of the ANC had been shaped by his own experience of growing up in the Meadowlands Zone 8 district of Soweto.

Before the fateful events of 1976 that changed the lives of many black South Africans, Robert was politically a moderate. He supported a slow, peaceful evolution towards the day when he and his fellow blacks would have a say in the government of their country. He believed that such change was inevitable and could be brought about with patience and peaceful protest, unlike many others of his age who thought the only way of achieving their goal was through violence and bloodshed.

When riots erupted throughout Soweto in the winter of 1976, Robert was deeply shocked by what he saw. Of course, he had heard the whispers about the uprising that was coming. He knew of the injustices that had festered for so many years in the townships, but, like many other people, he never believed anything would ever come of the words of rebellion. He had put it down to the brash rhetoric of school kids.

At first Robert tried to use what little influence he had to calm the angry young rioters, but he had contact only with his immediate Zone 8 neighbours and most of them ignored his pleas to embrace conciliation.

So Robert withdrew into a state of isolated neutrality and watched the growing carnage with a semi-detached feeling of despair and horror. It was the killing of Aunt Maggie that diverted Robert from his chosen path of pacifism to one of violence. It was a conversion that was irreversible.

Aunt Maggie was a large joyous woman whose extended family of nephews and nieces seemed to embrace half of Zone 8 and yet in reality embraced none. Nobody cared that none of her true blood relatives actually lived in the townships. She was still Aunt Maggie to everybody, young and old, and it seemed always had been. Of all her adopted nephews Robert Dyakala was her favourite. She saw in him much of the same love, gentleness and goodness with which she herself had been endowed.

Like Robert, Aunt Maggie was dismayed and horrified at the tragedy that was slowly unfolding in her community. She too abhorred the violence that daily shattered the peace she craved. She wept for the dead and injured on both sides of the escalating conflict; accepting as natural, and without anger, that her own people suffered far more casualties than did the predominantly white police force with which they clashed.

Aunt Maggie was born into an early twentieth century age where black people in South Africa were always worse off than their white counterparts. The Group Area Acts, Pass Laws and other Apartheid legislation passed after 1948, were just an extension of the unfairness and poverty imposed on her people for as long as she could remember. There had been centuries of domination by a succession of rulers, the worst of whom had often been black.

It was the nature of things and there was no point in getting angry about Apartheid. You just got on with life because at least death had always been colour blind. The sweet Lord Jesus took to his bosom all those who died as Christians, whether they were white or black.

It was late afternoon and it was clear that the evening was going to be cold. Above the thick pall of smog hanging over Soweto the sky was clear blue, crisp and darkening by the minute.

The riot squad arrived in armour-plated troop carriers at just after five o'clock to break up the large, silent crowd that had gathered outside the ruins of the burnt out school. The policemen were dressed in jungle green military style uniforms and came with dogs, guns, batons, shields, helmets and hate.

The crowd remained silent as the police poured from their vehicles. Most of the protesters were frightened kids. They were frightened of the well organised cops with their dogs, guns and batons, but even more frightened of letting their peers see their fear. They stood nervously, hands behind their backs, their sullen eyes watching as the uniformed policemen shuffled into formation in front of them.

Slowly the police moved towards the crowd. Several of the dog handlers were pulled onwards by their snarling charges. As they edged forward the less experienced cops were still adjusting their riot helmets.

Suddenly, and without warning, the silent crowd erupted. As with one arm they hurled a barrage of concealed bricks, stones and bottles at the advancing force. That's when the noise started. Chants, wails and screams from the protesters; shouts, curses and whoops of excitement from the cops. The dogs just barked, snarled and bit whichever black limb they could sink their teeth into.

One young policeman who had forgotten to lower the grille-front of his helmet was hit full in the face by an oblong wedge of concrete. He slumped to the ground as if pole-axed. Unseen by his colleagues, who were already charging at full speed towards the scattering crowd, he lay in the dusty road with blood pouring from his face.

But Aunt Maggie saw the young cop and did not ignore him. She was on her way to see a friend from her church when she saw the large crowd that had gathered on the corner of her road and arrived on the scene shortly after the police.

Aunt Maggie stood and watched in horror as the violence erupted, wringing her hands and praying that nobody would get killed. When she saw the young policeman fall, she rushed to his aid. She knelt at his side staring down at his badly gashed face. She shook her head mournfully and tried to stem the pouring blood with the material of her voluminous skirt.

Aunt Maggie looked up when she heard another burly policeman run up behind her and she held out a podgy hand to receive the help that she assumed was coming. Then, without time to register shock, her caring, tear stained face broke up under the weight of the cop's boot.

The policeman kept kicking, his eyes glazed with a killing madness, his nostrils flared, filled with the smell of blood. As he kicked, so he beat his victim with his baton at the same time. Nothing could stop the hate-fuelled orgy of violence, not even the pleadings of the dazed and bloodied young policeman. He had staggered to his feet in a futile attempt to stem the murderous attack on the woman who had tried to help him and who he saw brutally killed before his very eyes.

When Robert heard what had happened, he at first refused to believe that Aunt Maggie was dead. Even when the jolly figure did not appear in the neighbourhood for a couple of days, he managed to convince himself that there must be another explanation for her absence. After all, who would want to harm such a gentle woman? It was only when the large, cheap wooden coffin was carried shoulder high to the Zone 8 Cemetery that Robert was forced to accept the truth. Finally, he believed and was angrier than he had ever thought possible.

Robert's first reaction was to kill the first white policeman that he saw, but he was intelligent enough to realise that such action would bring about nothing more than his own death or imprisonment. At the very least it would get him noticed and some inner instinct told him it was important to stay under the radar of the police and security services.

So he controlled his anger and did not seek immediate retribution. He resolved to avenge Aunt Maggie's death by helping to overthrow the regime on whose behalf the police acted, but he could best do that by being patient. He would play the long game.

Several weeks later Robert slipped out of his home in Soweto and disappeared. Nobody noticed him going and few would have cared if they had. He left South Africa and was out of the country for three years. At one stage he surfaced in London, which is where I first met him.

He was travelling under an alias, but because of my work I was one of the few people who knew his real identity. The reason for his visit was to arrange an arms delivery to the ANC guerrillas who were fighting alongside the Patriotic Front in the war against the Smith regime in Rhodesia.

Eventually in 1979, it became apparent that the war in Rhodesia would soon be over. It was decided by the ANC that Robert should return home to help re-organise its Internal Liaison and Movements Section, which was recognised by the leadership to be shambolic, chaotic and ineffective.

Robert settled into the role of a stupid, plodding gardener. He successfully used this lowly manual position as a front that allowed him to remain undetected by the Authorities, but at the same time to fulfil his ANC role with dedication and distinction. Or so he thought.

Somewhere out in the silence of the cold suburban night an exhaust back fired, or maybe it was a gunshot. Being Johannesburg either was possible.

'So what do you want of me, David?' Robert asked as he poured more drinks.

'Weapons and explosives,' I replied.

He looked at me steadily and pulled the blanket tighter about his shoulders.

'So why come to me?' He asked. 'I can think of at least one mutual friend who could supply you with what you require.' He was talking about one of my past employers. 'Why not use him?'

'Our mutual friend would not be suitable on this occasion,' I said. 'We want the goods for use here in South Africa.' I smiled at him. 'You know only too well how difficult it is to smuggle such things into the country.'

Robert nodded.

'I've come to you,' I continued, 'because I believe you are my best chance of getting what I want. If you cannot bring them into South Africa, then nobody can.'

He nodded his agreement again.

'When will you want these munitions?' He asked.

'I'm not entirely sure, but soon,' I answered.

'What will you want?'

I shrugged. 'Sorry, but I'm not sure of that either. To be honest, the purpose of my visit tonight was to introduce you to Paul. He will be liaising with you and acting on my behalf. Is that acceptable to you?'

Robert looked at Paul and nodded.

'When I know exactly what equipment we want and when, Paul will contact you again and arrange delivery. He will also arrange any necessary payments.'

'In cash?'

'Of course,' I assured him.

'Of course,' Robert repeated with a smile. He was silent for a while as he studied my face with troubled eyes. 'David, there is a question I must ask you before agreeing to supply you with anything,' he paused.

I nodded. 'Go ahead.'

'And you will answer me honestly?'

'It depends on the question.'

He nodded his understanding. 'This operation in which you are involved, will it in any way harm our struggle?'

I thought about his question for a while. 'I have no way of knowing that,' I answered honestly. 'However, if we succeed then I promise you the South African government will not be happy. Is that a good enough answer?'

'Can you tell me what the operation is?'

'No,' I said.

Robert seemed to accept my answer. 'Okay,' he said. 'Is there anything else I can do to help you?'

'Yes,' I replied. 'I would like a contact in the Western Cape. Somebody who knows the area well. Somebody who we can trust. Do you have such a person?'

His eyes narrowed and he looked at me with interest, perhaps searching my face for clues. 'The Western Cape covers many square kilometres, in which part are you interested?'

'Oh, the coastal area from the Cape of Good Hope to Atlantis, taking in Cape Town itself and Table Bay.' I deliberately kept my answer vague.

Robert reached over and grabbed my arm. 'In that case, David, I must ask another question,' he said urgently. 'And once again I hope you will answer me honestly.'

'And once again it depends what the question is, Robert.' I smiled at him. 'But ask away.'

'Does your operation involve the Koeberg Nuclear Power Station?'

'Koeberg? No.' I said honestly.

He released my arm and sat back on his orange box. He busied himself pouring us all more drinks, but he could not hide the look of relief on his face. When he had finished he took a sip of his brandy and looked at me thoughtfully. Then he smiled. 'Robben Island,' he whispered eventually. 'Your destination is Robben Island. I am right am I not?'

I had forgotten how smart Robert was. I answered him with a shrug that I hoped was neither a denial nor an agreement.

'Okay, I would not expect you to tell me. But I will assume for now that whatever your destination you will require somebody with a knowledge of the waters off the Western Cape. Would that at least be a fair assumption?'

I nodded. I needed his help so there was no point denying it.

'You are in luck, David. I have such a man. His name is

Johan Carlse. He is a fisherman and knows the waters off Cape Town area like the back of his hand. Carlse is currently doing some work for me, but I will contact him and ask him to…' his voice trailed off and he cocked his head.

'What is…?' I started, but he stopped me with a finger to his lips.

It was silent in the little room as we looked at each other. I could hear soft footsteps now. Paul stood up and tapped my arm. I quickly slid the brandy bottle back into my pocket as Robert took two of the cups from the table and hid them behind the upturned orange box.

'Okay, kaffir,' Paul said in a loud voice as a knock came on the door. 'But just don't let me catch any girlies in here with you. Verstaan?'

'Yes, baas,' Robert said deferentially.

Paul silently unlocked the door and pulled it open. He let a look of surprise cross his face when he saw the woman who stood outside the servant's quarters. She wore a dressing gown that was open at the front to reveal a negligee that barely covered the top of her legs and on her feet were fluffy pink slippers.

'Who are you?' The woman asked as she pulled her dressing gown tighter round her generous bosom.

Paul whipped his wallet from his pocket, opened it and flashed it in front of the woman's face. 'Police,' he said as he quickly returned the wallet to his pocket.

'The police?' The woman looked at her gardener with a concerned look on her face and said in a soft voice: 'What have you been up to, Robert?'

'Nothing, Madam, I have done nothing.' The African protested his innocence, keeping his eyes firmly riveted to the woman's fluffy slippers.

The woman turned to Paul, who was easing out of the room. I followed and closed the door behind me. I tried to look like a cop.

Paul smiled at the woman. 'Don't worry, mevrou. It's only a routine visit. We're just checking passes in the area and making sure that none of these boys has a woman with them, hey.' He motioned towards Robert's room with his head. 'But he seems alright. A bit of a dommie maybe, but I take it he's no trouble. Ja?'

The woman shrugged. 'Well, we've had no trouble with him yet.' She shivered.

'You're up late, mevrou,' Paul said.

'I thought I heard a noise,' the woman's cheeks had a pink flush on them. 'My husband is away on business and I was worried for my safety,' she explained.

'I apologise if we disturbed you, mevrou. You look cold,' Paul said with a smile. 'You'd best get back to your bed.'

The woman nodded and quickly disappeared inside her house.

'Totsiens, mevrou!' Paul called after her, but the front door was already closed.

There would be no jumping over the wall on the way out, so we headed up the path towards the wrought iron gate, which squealed loudly as I opened it.

Dogs started barking inside the house behind us, although I only registered this with part of my mind, the rest was too busy pondering the mysteries of life. In particular, I was wondering whether the understanding relationship Robert had with at least one of his employers had anything to do with her nocturnal visits to his room when her husband was away. But then I have always been a cynic.

Paul and I said little on the way back to the hotel, instead we both sat deep in thought. However, at one point Paul did break the silence. 'Any idea why Robert was so interested in the Koeberg Nuclear Power Station?' he asked.

It was a very good question, for which I could think of no answer, let alone a good one.

Robert Dyakala

When his two visitors had left Robert Dyakala asked himself whether he trusted them. It was a question that troubled him. He had known David Statton for many years and on balance decided he could trust him. However, the big South African, Paul Helsdon, was an unknown quantity. He should have represented everything against which he was fighting, but Robert sensed he was different. Perhaps it was because he was not a Boer.

Robert pushed aside one of the orange boxes and using a knife he prised up a floor tile, then a second, to reveal a hole in the ground. He took a small black leather bound book from the cavity and sat down at the table. It was a diary. He opened it and began to write in a neat precise hand that would have surprised his employers, who thought he was just another illiterate black. He set out his thoughts on his meeting with the two white men.

This record keeping was a daily ritual with Robert. He knew it was a dangerous practice, but it was his insurance policy in case he ever needed to use the information to blackmail those with whom he came in contact. Anyway, he reasoned that as long as he continued to be careful, the chances of him ever being caught were slim.

Just as he finished making his notes there was a quiet knock on his door. He did not hurry. He knew who it was and knew she would wait for him. He stashed the diary away in the underground hideaway, replaced the two tiles and slid the orange box back into place. Only then did he open the door.

Carol du Toit came into the room and Robert could see from her agitation that she was desperate for sex. He took her by the hand, led her to his bed and pushed her roughly down onto the stained bed cover. He pulled open her dressing gown and saw that her nipples were already hard with excitement as they strained against the sheer nylon of her tight negligee.

He removed her clothes and ran his hands over her large breasts, then taking a hard nipple between his thumb and forefinger he squeezed it until she cried out loud. He liked hurting the white woman in this way, but his feeling of domination was blunted somewhat by the knowledge that she loved the feel of his coarse black hands on her body and the pain he inflicted on her.

Carol helped Robert take off his own clothes until he too was naked, then she grabbed his waist and pulled him down, guiding him into her body as she had on so many other occasions. She cried out again as he entered her and she felt him fill her in a way that her husband never could.

'Screw me you black bastard,' she sobbed. 'Screw me hard.'

So Robert did as she asked and when they were finished they lay in silence on the bed, their bodies glistening with sweat and sex.

'When is your husband coming back?' Robert asked casually.

'Tomorrow morning. Why?'

'I need time off work.'

'You are going away?'

'Yes.'

'Where are you going?'

'You know there are things you should not ask me.'

'When will you leave?'

'May 6th,' Robert replied.

'How long will you be gone?'

'Just a few days.'

'I will tell my husband you have to visit your home village for a family funeral.'

'My home village is Soweto.'

'Gerald doesn't know that.'

'When is your husband next away on business?' He asked.

'I think it's the Wednesday after next,' she replied. 'The day before you go away,' she added with a smile, perhaps anticipating with relish another night of sex with her gardener.

Cape Peninsula

David Statton - Thursday April 22nd 1982: Clovelly.

Our flight from Johannesburg to Cape Town took just under two hours and was far more enjoyable than my journey from London the previous day. There were no delays, no in-flight movies, no plastic food and the smiles from the two air hostesses seemed at least partially genuine, although the presence of Paul Helsdon might have contributed to that.

Paul was six feet five inches tall and the frame that filled the seat next to mine with such casual confidence was padded out with two hundred and thirty pounds of South African muscle. Dressed as he was in tight fitting faded blue jeans and a short sleeved polo shirt, most of the muscle seemed to be on show.

Paul's thick fair hair was sun bleached and hung in unruly curls over his shirt collar. He had lively, humorous blue eyes that glinted wickedly whenever he hit you with one of his expansive smiles. His face had a tan deep enough to betray his love of the outdoor life, but was not deep enough to hide the scar that joined his right cheek to his right ear.

He used women in the same cavalier way in which foreign diplomats collect and discard parking tickets. When a woman became a nuisance, or threatened his independence, he tossed her aside without compunction. In short, Paul was a woman-manipulating-male-chauvinist-pig of the first order. And yet women still lusted after him and those two air hostesses were no exception. Life is full of such ironies.

We were met in the car park of D.F. Malan Airport by an Avis hire car, a beggar and a full strength southeasterly wind. The wind was all the more unexpected because of the clear, cobalt-blue sky that had been visible through the airport's glass windows.

The southeasterly started life as an offshoot of the anti-cyclones that girdle the southern hemisphere and whirl round in an anti-clockwise direction with the spin of the Earth. This powerful air current travels from the south or southwest until it reaches the mountains that line the edge of Africa's southern coastline.

Confronted by a solid barrier of granite the wind whips round the coast in search of a gap until it eventually finds Cape

Hangklip, where it whistles into False Bay. Picking up speed as it flies across the warm waters of the Indian Ocean, the wind eventually hits land and sweeps across the Cape Flats in a haze of dust.

As we stepped out from the shelter of the arrival terminal the wind was so ferocious it momentarily stopped us in our tracks. It was all the time the beggar needed. He had been huddled against the outer wall of the terminal building, but now he shuffled towards us. He wore a bright red pullover that was visible beneath a khaki army greatcoat that was tugged open by the wind. On his feet he wore a pair of old plimsolls, without laces and with holes in the toes. In one hand he carried a dented car hub-cap containing several coins. I threw him a cursory glance and a one rand coin that clattered into the hub-cap.

'Dankie, baas, baie dankie,' he either mumbled or shouted his thanks. It was difficult to tell one way or another in that wind.

Our hire car was parked close to the terminal building and within minutes we were clambering thankfully inside, leaving the wind to howl in frustration as it tried in vain to get at us through the tightly shut windows.

As Paul drove out of the car park a police car sat on our tail. Before we could even think about feeling nervous it overtook us and tore off in the direction of the black township of Nyanga with its lights flashing and its siren blaring.

By the time I had cursed myself for the elementary mistake of forgetting to fasten my seatbelt and risking being pulled over by an overzealous cop, the police car was already out of sight. By the time we reached Settlers Way, the motorway into Cape Town, the police car was a distant memory; and by the time we reached the King David Golf Club I had managed finally to tune the radio into an English speaking station.

Not long after that I found the grubby envelope in the glove compartment. It was addressed to Mr D. Stratton and smelled strongly of fish. I forgave the sender the misspelling of my surname because all my life people had insisted on adding the extra letter "r" to it.

I tore open the envelope and pulled out an oblong slip of paper with a message printed with a purple crayon. It was short and to the point. It read: 827199. Johan Carlse.

'Our contact?' Paul asked.

'It looks like it,' I replied, impressed at how quickly Robert

Dyakala had acted after our meeting the previous day. I said a silent prayer hoping that the rest of his organisation was equally efficient. With that I settled back to enjoy the beauty of the Cape scenery.

We were nearing the outskirts of Cape Town and the magnificent mountains that surround the city loomed large in the background. To the right Lions Head, tall and pointed like a pyramid, to the left the craggy outline of Devil's Peak and centre stage, the most spectacular of them all, Table Mountain.

Over three and a half thousand feet high its flat summit dominates the Cape Town vista, while its lower slopes cradle the city in its folds. I could see a cable car inching its way to the top of the mountain. It looked so fragile against the granite cliffs and I did not envy the passengers their swaying journey with that southeasterly wind blowing.

Table Mountain is at the northern end of a mountain range that forms the backbone of the Cape Peninsular. A hook of land, it stretches thirty odd miles from Cape Town in the north, to the Cape of Good Hope in the south.

Ranging along the eastern coast of the peninsular, facing the wide expanse of False Bay, were several small villages. One of these was little more than a hamlet called Clovelly. It was into the heart of this tiny community, which nestled unpretentiously into Kalk Bay Mountain that Paul and I arrived just over an hour later.

We had already visited the estate agent in Fish Hoek and handed him a bundle of used ten rand notes. In return, he gave us a very warm smile and the keys to our temporary home. He did not give us a receipt, but that lapse was between him and the South African tax authorities.

The house we were renting from the estate agent was hewn into the side of the mountain and the forecourt on which we drew to a halt sloped steeply up towards a triple garage.

'This is it, Dave,' Paul said as he cut the engine of the hire car.

Once out of the car, I helped the big South African to open one of the tall wooden doors. We entered the garage, which turned out to be massive with a high, wood beamed roof and a concrete floor wide enough to park three cars side by side easily, perhaps four at a pinch. I was pleased because we were going to need plenty of space in which to store our equipment.

The garage was long also, allowing plenty of room, even with cars parked inside, for somebody to work at the sturdy wooden bench that ran the length of the back wall. Above the bench hung a pair of eight feet long fluorescent tubes, the only source of light once the garage doors were closed.

'It's perfect,' I said.

Paul grinned. 'Coming from you, Dave, that is praise indeed.'

'Are you suggesting I'm difficult to please?'

His grin widened. 'Well, now you come to mention it... But don't be upset, it's an important trait for a leader.'

'Then I'll accept your comments as a compliment,' I said with a smile. 'Come on let me see if the house is as good.'

We left the garage through a side door and made our way out onto a long path that wound its way up the side of the mountain through a series of tiered gardens. The crazy-paved path joined with half a dozen sets of steps to connect one tier to the next as they led up through a profusion of trees, shrubs, plants and lawns to a large white bricked bungalow.

The building was surrounded by patios and was bedecked with colourful yellow and black striped window canopies. I was less concerned about the bungalow's appearance, more its non-appearance. It was splendidly secluded, being concealed behind a number of screens. For a start the building was well protected from the rear, with the sheer face of the mountain preventing any observation from that quarter, in addition there were two other barriers to thwart prying eyes. The first was a high, white fence that encircled the whole plot and the second was a row of tall, bushy pines that ran down both sides of the garden.

The front lounge of the bungalow was just visible from the road on which the garage was situated, but it was too far away to be any real risk from prying eyes. Besides which, the lounge windows had heavy curtains that could be drawn should we want to protect our privacy further.

The lounge was large and was of split level design. It overlooked the garden and gave an unrestricted view of the only access to the property. If we were vigilant, nobody would be able to enter the garden without our knowledge. The house was as secure as anything I could ever hope to find. Paul had done well.

I looked down the garden. I could see the garage, the boundary fence and short stretch of the road. A bottle green Mercedes-Benz 300D rolled slowly up the road and as it passed the house I fancied it slowed down, but I decided it was just my imagination.

In addition to the lounge, there was a dining room, a kitchen, five bedrooms, each with its own en-suite bathrooms, and a games room, complete with dartboard and pool table. The bungalow had a lot of space, but a group of healthy active men forced to live together for a few weeks needs space if any risk of conflict is to be minimised. As it happens I would be recruiting only the best mercenaries to join my team, real professionals, so such a problem was very unlikely to arise, but it was better to be safe than sorry.

Outside in the backyard there was a disused building that had at one time been the servant's quarters, but had been converted into a woodshed. The room was filled with a pine fragrance that came from the pile of logs that filled half the floor space. Except for the logs the room was bare apart from a moth-eaten lampshade that decorated the single ceiling light and a faded poster of Louis Armstrong that was stuck with adhesive tape to one of the grimy whitewashed walls.

Paul and I spent some time in the room, tossing ideas about until we decided how best to hide the weapons and munitions we would be procuring for use during the operation. When we were satisfied with our hiding place, we went back inside the house.

Adjoining the front door was a long hallway with a square lobby adjoining. In the lobby stood a table and chair. I picked up the receiver of the telephone that stood on the table. I raised an eyebrow at Paul when I heard the dialling tone.

'The estate agent organised a line for me,' he explained. 'I said we needed a phone in order to liaise with the university and he pulled a few strings and arranged for it to be connected in record time.'

'Which university?' I asked.

Paul smiled. 'He didn't ask, so I didn't tell him.'

'Good move,' I said as I sat down at the table and dialled the number I had found in the car. The phone rang several times before it was answered.

'Ja?'

'Meneer Carlse, asseblief,' I said.

'Wat wil jy van hom hê?' He replied, stretching my limited Afrikaans vocabulary.

'Ekskuus? Praat stadig, asseblief,' I asked him to speak slower.

'Is jy Engels?' He asked.

'Yes. Do you speak English? Praat Engels?'

'Miskien. Wat hom wil?' He asked who I was.

I ignored his question and instead asked in English: 'Is that Johan Carlse?'

'As I said before, meneer. Who wants him?'

'Statton.'

There was a pause. 'We have a mutual friend,' Carlse said eventually. 'What are his initials?'

'R.D,' I replied.

'Okay, this is Carlse' he said, but still sounding cautious. 'We should not talk on the telephone. You understand?'

I understood. 'When can we meet?' I asked.

'Tonight. Come late, come alone and be careful you are not followed.'

I shook my head and raised my eyebrows at Paul. Johan Carlse was starting to sound overly melodramatic.

'Where shall we meet?'

Again there was a lengthy pause. 'Do you know Ocean View?'

I covered the mouthpiece of the receiver. 'Have you heard of Ocean View?' I asked Paul.

He shook his head.

'No,' I replied to Carlse.

'Okay. It's easy to find. From where you are in Clovelly, go into Fish Hoek and then take the Kommetjie road. Ocean View is just outside Kommetjie. You can't miss it.'

'But what is Ocean View? Is it a hotel or something?'

'Nie, man,' Carlse said, laughing at my ignorance. 'It's a coloured township.'

'So how do I find you?'

'When you enter Ocean View, keep straight on and then take the third turning on the right. That is Third Avenue. You want number forty.'

'Four-zero?'

'Ja. I'll see you tonight. Totsiens, meneer.'

'Goodbye…' I started, but the phone was already dead.

'So far, so good,' Paul said.

I nodded my agreement, although I already had deep reservations about Mr Johan Carlse. I feared he was going to prove more of a liability than a help. However, I was more worried about something he had said. How the hell did he know we were staying in Clovelly?

Ocean View, Cape Peninsula

The highway from Fish Hoek to Kommetjie was deserted. There were no street lights and I was several yards past the signpost to Ocean View before I realised my error. I slammed on my brakes and reversed back up the road until I reached the side turning that led into the township.

The houses in the road were small and compact identical buildings whose only attempt at individuality could be found in the degrees of tidiness to be found on the small gardens that separated each house from the road. Number Forty, Third Avenue had solved the problem of competing with other gardens by cementing over the garden to make a parking space for a battered old Volkswagen van.

I knocked on the door and in response I heard a chair scrape across a wooden floor. Through a crack in the cheap curtains that covered the front window of the house I could see a small hearth with smouldering logs filling the grate. There was the sound of a chain and locks being unfastened. The door opened to reveal a scrawny figure who carried a glowing cigarette in one hand and a bottle of Lion lager in the other.

'Ja?' He demanded, filling the crisp night air in front of my face with beer fumes.

'Johan Carlse?'

'Wat wil jy van hom hê? He said before collapsing into drunken laughter. 'Wat wil jy van hom hê?' He repeated.

I gripped his two scrawny shoulders and eased him gently backwards before moving into the house and closing the door behind me. 'You know who wants him,' I said. 'Now let's stop playing silly buggers shall we?'

Carlse admonished me with a finger stained with nicotine and grime. 'Veiligheidshalwe, meneer, ja? For safety sakes, or as you English say, better safe than sorry. Is that not so, Mister Stratton?' There then followed another bout of drunken laughter.

Carlse was short and skinny and the dirty fisherman's jumper he wore above stained blue trousers was far too large for him. He had a dark skinned, heavily lined face that puckered in at the mouth betraying his lack of teeth. Even through his drunken state his black eyes had a shifty, watchful quality. He had tufts of white hair on his head and chin, giving his face the look of a pickled walnut that has started to go mouldy.

He stopped laughing and waved me towards the fire. As I edged past him and headed towards one of the two armchairs in the room, I noticed for the first time that beneath the smell of beer he reeked of fish.

I lowered myself into the armchair and Carlse sat opposite me. He lifted the bottle of lager to his lips and drained it in one gulp before tossing it into an overflowing cardboard box that stood at his side.

He clambered to his feet and stumbled out of the room, returning several minutes later with a fresh six-pack. He pulled a bottle of lager free and threw it to me. 'Have a beer, meneer,' he said with a smile on his lips and a sly look in his eye.

Carefully I pointed the top of the bottle away from me and unscrewed the cap. Foaming beer spewed from the neck of the bottle onto the wooden floor, missing me, but nonetheless provoking another drunken laugh from Carlse. I couldn't imagine I was going to achieve much that evening and with a sigh I realised my earlier reservations about the little man were probably justified. Silently I cursed Robert Dyakala for lumbering us with him.

Carlse must have sensed my feelings because suddenly he became more serious and seemed to sober up.

'So what can Johan Carlse do for you, Mister Stratton? Why have you come to see me? You want guns?' He did not wait for an answer, instead he jumped drunkenly to his feet and pushed aside a sideboard that stood in the corner of the room. Taking a lethal looking knife from his trouser pocket he used it to lever up one of the floorboards.

He bent down and pulled a bundle of rags from under the floor. Clutching the package to his chest Carlse sidled across to the window, pulled aside the curtain and looked outside. Satisfied, he drew the curtain and turned to face me. He discarded the rags to reveal a gleaming Kalashnikov rifle and it was pointing at me.

I said nothing, instead I stared at the AK47 and sat very still.

'Well. Is this what you have come for?' He asked waving the gun at me. 'Do you want guns?' He said it in a whisper as if frightened he would be overheard.

I shook my head and only relaxed when Carlse re-wrapped the AK47 and stowed it away in its hiding place. 'No,' I said. 'I don't want guns. All I want from you is information and possibly advice.'

Carlse looked at me keenly before sitting down again and

opening yet another Lion. 'Advice is it, Mister Stratton?' He winked at me. 'Well, Johan Carlse is the man for that. Ja, meneer, you have certainly come to the right man for advice.'

I did not share his confidence.

'So, what advice is it you seek?'

'I have nothing specific, at the moment,' I replied. This was a lie, but I was determined to share as little information as possible with him. 'Once I have completed my plan I will contact you again.'

'What are you planning?' Carlse asked.

'You know I cannot tell you that.'

'Okay, but don't forget you only need ask if there is anything I can do to help.' Carlse busied himself lighting a cigarette. For the tenth time that evening he offered me one and for the tenth time I told him I did not smoke.

I took a swig of my lager and when we next spoke it was together.

'I don't think I should come back here again,' I said.

'It might be better if you did not come here again,' he said at the same time.

I smiled and nodded.

'In fact,' he went on, 'it would be better if you and I do not meet at all.'

I looked at him questioningly.

'I am well known to the polisie. Verstaan? 'N knik is 'n goed soos 'n knipoog na 'n blinde man! A nod is as good as a wink to a blind man! Is that not what you say?'

It's not what I say, but I knew what he meant.

'There's always the possibility I'm being watched,' he continued. 'It is better you are not put at risk. I promised our mutual friend that I would look out for you.'

'Then how shall I contact you?' I asked. 'By telephone?'

He shook his head. 'No, that could be dangerous. My line might be tapped.'

'Then how?'

He smiled at me and gently touched the side of his nose a couple of times. 'It will be safest if you contact Freddie.'

'Who is Freddie?' I asked sharply. I was not happy about involving yet another person in the operation, particularly if he was anything like Carlse.

The little man drained his bottle of Lion, allowing the liquid to dribble down his chin to add yet another stain to his jumper. He levered himself upright and walked unsteadily to the door to the room from which he had brought the beer earlier.

He opened the door and motioned with his hand. 'Dit is my dogter Freddie,' Carlse explained, slipping back into Afrikaans as he ushered a young girl into the room. 'This is my daughter Freddie,' he repeated in English. 'You will contact her and she will act as our... what do you say?' He turned to the girl. 'Go-tussen?'

'Go-between, Papa,' the girl said quietly.

'Ja!' Carlse exclaimed before allowing a loud burp to escape his lips. 'Freddie will be our go-between.'

I had risen to my feet when the girl entered the room but now I resumed my seat. 'Has she been out there all the time?' I asked Carlse.

The little man nodded and swayed slightly as his daughter studied me with bright, intelligent eyes.

She smiled at me, although I detected a trace of scorn in the curve of her full lips. 'Don't worry, Mr Stratton,' she said in the soft sing-song that was distinctive of the Cape Coloureds. 'I am quite safe. I am committed to the struggle for justice. I fight for the Cause.'

'I'm sure your commitment is very commendable,' I commented drily. 'But I fight for no "Cause". I'm a mercenary. I fight for money.'

'That may well be true, Mr Stratton, but those whose help you seek, like my papa, cannot be so sanguine. They have a simpler choice. It is between life and death.' This time she did not try to hide her scorn behind a smile. She paused and helped the swaying Carlse to his seat. He slumped into his armchair with a groan and reached for another beer.

'Anyway,' she went on, 'I'm sure that even you do not offer your services to just anybody.' She raised an eyebrow at me, but I did not rise to the bait. 'I would like to think that sometimes even mercenaries are troubled enough by their consciences to have sympathy for those less fortunate than themselves. Do you?'

Deliberately ignoring the girl's question, I looked across at her father. 'Is it wise to involve your daughter in our business?' I asked. 'It could be dangerous.'

Carlse looked up at me through bleary and half hooded eyes. 'Freddie is a good girl,' he said.

'But she's still only a girl.' I pointed out, turning to face his daughter, wondering what reaction my words would provoke.

The girl's eyes flashed and her face flushed red as she glared at me. 'My, God! Who the hell do you think you are?' She snapped angrily, pointing a long nailed finger at me. 'Listen, mister, I may be "only a girl" but I'm already involved. Let me tell you why. In South Africa you become involved when you are a kid trying to get an education with fifty other pupils in one classroom, with no blackboard and no glass in the windows.

'You become involved when you and your friends are beaten with sticks and then locked up for taking part in a peaceful protest. And you become involved when you are forced to carry identity documents saying you are coloured, when you are whiter than most of the rooineks who come over here from England.' She paused and glared at me again. 'So you see, Mr Stratton, I have been involved all my damn life,' she went on, with the anger in her voice replaced by bitterness. 'Can you say the same? Of course not, but then it's easy for your kind, isn't it? When you've finished your dirty work, whatever that might be, you simply take your blood money and run? My people? We have to be involved simply to survive in this bloody country.'

I was satisfied with the girl's reaction to my deliberate provocation. I held my hands up in submission, palms facing her. 'Your daughter will do just fine, Mister Carlse.' I said to her father before turning back to the girl with what I hoped was a winning smile. I held out a hand to her. 'It'll be good, working with you, Freddie.'

She stood there with her hands on her hips, staring at my hand suspiciously, perhaps deciding whether to accept my olive branch. Her eyes were extraordinary; they were a strangely flecked green and looked out from behind a huge pair of spectacles with a vitality that lit up her whole face.

She was smaller even than her father, no more than five feet tall, and she wore tight fitting denim jeans that showed off a pair of shapely legs. The top half of her body was covered by a baggy maroon sweatshirt that showed off nothing except the legend UCT that was printed in large gold letters across her chest. Her long, dark hair had fallen across her face when she became angry with me, now she used both hands to pull it back as if opening curtains and tucked it behind her ears. Finished, she stuck out a hand and took my own. 'So I passed the test, did I, Mister Stratton?' She asked with a wry smile as we shook hands.

I smiled back. 'I needed to be sure you could cope if things get rough.'

'Oh, don't worry about me, Mister Stratton,' she assured me. 'I can look after myself.' I looked at the steely glint in those green eyes and I believed her.

'Ja! My Freddie can look after herself alright, meneer, but it will not be necessary. The polisie have no interest in her. She has always been very careful.' Carlse spoke hesitantly, his words slurred by the beer. 'Trust me the cops have nothing on her. She has never been in trouble.' He patted his daughter's leg proudly and then tugged her towards him. 'She is a good girl.' Freddie perched on the arm of Carlse chair and he rested his head against her. He closed his eyes and was soon snoring.

'Come on, Papa,' the girl said, gently shaking her father's shoulder. 'Let me get you to bed.'

Carlse awoke with a start. 'Hè? Nè? Wat het gebeur?'

'Hush, Papa, nothing has happened. I'm taking you to bed.'

'Nee, Freddie, nee.' Carlse shook his head emphatically. 'I promised to take you home. Belofte maak skuld, ja?' He tried to get to his feet but he never made it, his legs buckled under him.'

The girl made a clucking sound with her tongue as she scolded her father. 'Nee, Papa, no way! It's off to bed with you. Mr Stratton will see me home.' She turned to me. 'Won't you?' Although it was a question, the tone of her voice left me no choice.

'Of course,' I said. 'But only on condition that you call me by my proper name, which is Statton. That is S-T-A-double T-O-N. Statton. There is no R.'

'I'll try to remember,' she said.

'If you struggle that much with your memory you could always call me Dave.'

She grinned at me. 'It's a deal!'

I helped Freddie get her father up the narrow staircase to his bed, then I went outside and waited in the car for her while she turned off the house lights and collected her coat.

'Where to?' I asked when she joined me.

'Wynberg,' she replied. 'I have a flat there.' She sensed my unasked question. 'I work in a local building society and Thursday is my afternoon off. I come home most weeks to see my father. Usually I would have left earlier to catch my train, but today my father asked me to stay on so that I could meet you. He said that he would run me to Fish Hoek station, but... well you saw what state he was in.'

'I saw.'

I tried to keep my voice neutral but she must have sensed my feeling towards her father because she said: 'You mustn't blame him, Mr Statton, Dave. He has not always been like that you know.'

I shrugged and thought she was going to elaborate but she changed the subject, as if talking about her father was painful. She pulled a pen and notepad from her handbag.

'Here are my telephone numbers,' she said as she passed a slip of paper to me. 'Home and work. If you need to contact me you can ring me at any time, although it would be better if you only use the work number in an emergency. I will pass on any messages to my father and get a reply straight back to you.'

We drove on in silence for a while, until I asked: 'Why Freddie?'

'My name is Brigette Frederika,' she explained. 'It was papa who started calling me Freddie. It's a long story.'

'I prefer Brigette,' I said. 'It suits your femininity.'

She looked at me sharply and her eyes flashed again.

'Don't be so sensitive,' I said. 'It was meant as a compliment.'

'I'm sorry. It is difficult to accept compliments when you have grown up believing you are a second class citizen,' she said bitterly. 'It makes it very difficult for me to trust people, particularly white men.'

'But you are white,' I pointed out.

She snorted angrily. 'In South Africa you are not white unless the Boers say you are white and then give you a document to prove it. The book of life with which they issued me classifies me as coloured, so coloured I am.'

'But that is just the rotten system,' I pointed out, 'and the rotten people who uphold the system. It's not all the people and certainly not all white people. The colour of your persecutors is irrelevant. In Uganda it would be black people discriminating against you because you aren't black enough.'

She was silent again for several more minutes and when she next spoke there was no bitterness left in her voice: 'You're not such a bastard after all,' she said. 'And I'm sorry for what I said about you back there. I suppose being a mercenary is just another job.'

'You're right,' I said. 'But you asked me earlier whether I

would offer my services to anybody, well the answer is no. I do have some principles.'

'I'm glad, Dave,' she said and stared at me intently for a while. 'Tell me,' she asked eventually, 'Have you come to help our struggle?'

'Not exactly,' I replied honestly.

'Have you come to harm us?'

'Definitely not.'

She seemed satisfied with my assurance as she lapsed into another long silence. She did not speak again until we were travelling along Boyes Drive. 'Dave, I want you to know something. I don't expect you to tell me anything that might compromise your mission and I won't ask you any questions.'

'That's good,' I said. 'Because that way you won't be disappointed.

'But you will have to tell me certain things about whatever it is you are planning, how else will I be able to pass messages between you and papa?'

I nodded, but said nothing. The girl was smart.

'And for that reason it's important you know that you can trust me. Do you understand?'

'I understand.'

'And you can trust my father as well,' she insisted passionately, but not very convincingly.

It was my turn to change the subject. 'I'll take your contact numbers, however, it is best that we do not discuss anything of importance over the phone,' I said. 'It'll be better to meet up whenever I need you to pass on anything to your father, unless you have any objections?'

'No. Ring me when you have something to pass on and we can agree a meeting place.' Suddenly she touched my arm. 'Can you pull in over there, Dave?' She pointed to a layby a hundred yards or so ahead.

I pulled off the road and cut the engine.

Freddie got out of the car, crossed the road and sat down on a wall.

I followed and sat next to her. I had taken the scenic route back along the coast and Boyes Drive ran along the mountainside high above Kalk Bay. She was staring down at the harbour with a distant look in her eye.

'Papa is a fisherman,' she said quietly.

'I guessed that.'

Kalk Bay was beautiful in the dark. There seemed to be lights everywhere: coloured lights along the sea-front; car headlights and tail lights; bright amber lights on the pedestrian crossing and bright lights outside the harbour. The harbour itself was dark except for red and green signal lights to direct incoming fishing boats.

'He used to have his own boat called the Von Riebeck. She was a lovely little thing. She had a white hull with red paintwork on the wheelhouse.' Freddie hugged her knees as she spoke, rocking backwards and forwards on the wall. 'My mama often used to bring us up here to wait for Papa to come home from a day's fishing.' She looked out to sea. 'It was a better view from up here and we could see the Von Riebeck coming from miles away.' She pointed out into the darkness where in the distance a boat's navigation lights headed our way.

'And when the British navy ships used to come here you could see all the fishing boats over there.' Now she pointed towards the twinkling lights of Simon's Town, the naval base some four or five miles further down the coast. 'They used to sail up to the ships and sell fresh fish to the sailors.' She looked sad. 'But the British ships have all gone, and so has Papa's fishing boat.' She lapsed into silence. She shivered and that made me realise how cold it had become.

Tentatively I put my arm round her to keep her warm. At first, she stiffened, but slowly she relaxed and snuggled into my side. I felt a spot of rain on my hand, but when I looked up it was into a cloudless sky. That's when I realised it was a teardrop that had fallen onto my hand. I lifted the girl's face and turned it towards me. Her eyes were glistening and tears ran down her cheeks. I pulled a handkerchief from my pocket, took off her spectacles and gently wiped each eye.

'Don't be sad,' I said with a smile. 'It spoils the image.'

Freddie's faced cleared and she smiled impishly. 'What image?'

'That super confident, anything you can do I can do better, I know what I want and I know how to get it, image.'

'Oh, I see. You mean this image?' Suddenly she twisted her body, reached up, grabbed my head, pulled me towards her and crushed her lips against mine in a passionate kiss. Then just as suddenly she broke away, snatched back her spectacles, jumped to her feet. 'Come on.' she said with a laugh. 'Let's go before we're seen by somebody and get arrested for having an inter-racial relationship.' She laughed again as if she had cracked a joke, but of course under the South African Apartheid system, it was no joke.

When I dropped her off at her flat she kissed me briefly again, pressing her body against mine as she did so. Then she was gone.

I stood staring at her door for a few moments and listened as a security chain rattled into position and a key was turned in the lock, then I went back to my car. As I drove back to Clovelly, I mulled over the evening's events.

I thought about the drunken Johan Carlse and how I was going to get the best out of him. I thought about his daughter, Freddie, and the way her sparkling green eyes lit up her face. I thought about the sweet taste of her mouth as she kissed me. I thought about the feel of her full breasts against my body under her baggy UTC sweatshirt. I thought and I wondered.

I wondered why a smart, attractive young girl should want to kiss a hard-bitten old mercenary like me. I wondered what would happen if I pushed her further and I wondered how somebody like Carlse had managed to father such an intelligent, beautiful daughter.

It was truly one of life's mysteries.

Friday April 23rd 1982: Western Cape Province

The following morning the weather conditions were perfect for an expedition to Table Mountain. The southeasterly had blown itself out and had been replaced by what South African weather forecasters call bergwind conditions.

A gentle breeze blew down from the Karoo Desert and caressed Cape Town with its warm touch after flirting briefly with the Hottentot Hollands Mountains. The sky was clear and light blue with not a cloud to be seen. It felt good to be alive.

I stared out across False Bay where a few early morning surfers braved the chilly waters astride their boards. In their shiny black wetsuits they looked like a colony of playful seals as they paddled around in search of a breaker to ride. They were destined to be disappointed because the slate grey sea was as calm as a mill-pond, with little more than a frill of white at its edge where it lapped against the shore.

Further out into the bay a layer of mist lay across the water's surface like a fluffy white wig. It stretched to the very northern reaches of the bay, and then some, rolling across the Cape Flats until it licked at the outer limits of Cape Town's southern suburbs.

In the distance, far away across the other side of False Bay, the Hottentot Hollands and Blousteenberge mountain ranges rose dark and sombre in the early morning sun. In a few weeks' time they would be capped with winter snow, but now they were a jagged black silhouette.

They extended down to Cape Hangklip like a row of rotting crocodile teeth forming one half of a gigantic jaw - with the mountains of the Cape Peninsular as the other half - that bites into and rips apart the swirling green waters off Cape Point. This mammoth granite mouth gulps in enough sea to replenish False Bay and leaves the remainder to separate into the Indian Ocean and the Atlantic Ocean.

Paul and I made good time into Cape Town. It was just after eight thirty when we drew into the Tafelberg Road car park at the foot of Table Mountain and we caught one of the first cable cars of the day up to the mountain's summit.

The cars were designed to carry 28 passengers, but apart from us and a morose car attendant, there was only another group of four people. It consisted of three men and a pretty young girl, whose job seemed to be to look after the colourful canvas bag that accompanied them.

There was little wind to rock the yellow cable car, but it still swayed alarmingly on the four minute journey up the twelve hundred metre long cable. The attendant noticed the look of alarm on the young girl's face. He cheered up sufficiently to smile at her and tried to reassure her by explaining that this always happened on the early morning journeys because of the lack of passengers.

With so few of us aboard you would have thought the attendant might have found time to reassure the rest of his passengers, but he ignored us. Perhaps he thought we were big enough to look after ourselves. He was probably right, after all what was there to worry about?

Risk is relative, I thought to myself as I stared out of the car's window at several climbers who were making their way up the sheer face of the mountain. Each wore a brightly coloured helmet, but they were daft if they thought their headwear would do much to save their lives should they lose their grip and fall. One of the climbers looked up at the cable car and waved. He certainly didn't seem worried about the way the car was swaying.

By the time we arrived on the mountain's flat summit the ground mist that covered the Cape Flats and surrounding sea was rapidly being burned off by an increasingly hot sun. Within fifteen minutes the mist had cleared completely, leaving us with a panoramic view, with the whole of Cape Town laid out before us like a model village.

The Samlam Centre, Shell House, the BP Centre and the Heerengracht Hotel, all of them sky-scrapers, looked no larger than upended match boxes amidst the other surrounding buildings, some of which had been there for three hundred years.

The city's reservoirs, each containing millions of litres of water, were like puddles left by a rainstorm and the numerous swimming pools dotted about in the gardens of the suburbs were mere droplets of aqua blue.

The ships anchored in the harbour looked no larger than the plastic toys that used to be given away in packets of cereals. District Six, once the thriving coloured quarter of the city, but now bulldozed to extinction as a sacrifice to the god that the Nationalist Party Government called Separate Development, resembled little more than a dusty, shed dotted allotment.

The group who had shared our cable car had unpacked their canvas bag and strewn about them now was an assortment of metal rods, leather straps, wire and coloured canvass sheets.

Paul and I stood on one of the telescope observation platforms that were positioned along the leading edge of Table Mountain's summit. Unfortunately the lens of the telescope was covered on the inside with a thick layer of condensation caused by the clouds that often shrouded the mountain top.

Because Paul knew this was a common problem, he had taken the precaution of packing a powerful pair of binoculars in the knapsack that was slung over my back.

From our position we could see the full sweep of Table Bay, from the Foreshore, round through the sprawling Paarden Eiland Industrial Estate and on to Cape Town's northern most suburbs of Blouberg and Milnerton. And there, out in the bay, five and a half miles north-west of Cape Town and four and a half miles due west of Bloubergstrand, was Robben Island.

'What are they building?' Paul asked, pointing to the group that had shared our cable car. 'It's not what I think, is it?'

'That depends what you think.'

'I think it looks like a hang-glider.'

'Then it probably is.'

'Sies, man! Are you telling me that one of those domkops is crazy enough to jump off this bloody mountain top on a hang-glider? They must have a death wish!'

I looked over at the group. 'Don't knock it, Paul, unless we can find a better way of getting onto the island we might have to use hang-gliders.'

He looked at me sharply with his blue eyes narrowed, trying to decide if I was serious.

I smiled to show I was joking. 'Don't worry,' I said. 'It's out of the question for at least three reasons. One, the distance is too great; two, we would be spotted a mile away; and three we wouldn't be able to get back from the island using hang-gliders, with or without Zamyatin.'

I used the binoculars to study Cape Bay and considered the challenges we faced. The most likely way of reaching Robben Island was by sea, but I was sure that whichever mode of transport we used, getting onto Robben Island was not going to be a picnic. Gut instinct told me that getting back off would be even harder. As I stared out across the sea at the island, I mulled over what I knew about it.

Just two miles long and a mile wide, at one time the island had been home to thousands of penguins and seals. Then in the 17th century a Dutch sea-captain, by the name of Cornelius Maletief, landed on the island with his crew in search of relief from the boredom that afflicted them. They set about clubbing to death the harmless beasts they found and in the process almost wiped out the entire animal population. It was an unintentional irony that the sailors named their refuge Robben Island, after the Dutch name for seal.

From those early savage days the island went on to have a chequered and tragic history. In the early 18th century the first few in a long line of political prisoners were incarcerated on the island.

Those unfortunates were transported from the Malay Peninsula and Indonesia to be taught a lesson because they had the temerity to rebel against the Dutch who had invaded their countries. It was a harsh lesson because in those days, imprisonment was considered by many a fate worse than death.

By the 19th century the prison camp was flourishing as more

and more prisoners were sent to the island. Since none could escape, and none was released because the authorities chose to forget that the inmates ever existed, the population rose dramatically.

In 1806 an entrepreneur by the name of John Murray was given permission to open a whaling station on the east coast of the island. He built a harbour in the only suitable bay, which was later named after him. Unfortunately for Murray, but perhaps fortunately for the whale population in the area, the authorities eventually decided the whaling station must close because too many of the prisoners used his boats in unsuccessful attempts to escape.

But even with the closure of the station the attempts to escape continued, with prisoners ignoring the treacherous currents and the shark infested waters to try to swim to freedom. Sadly for the prisoners their ignorance resulted in a great many deaths and not a single successful escape.

Eventually the administration decided that if the prisoners wanted so badly to commit suicide then they should be given an opportunity to do so usefully, by working themselves to death. The inmates were transferred to the mainland and were put to work in chain gangs to build the roads on which the country's subsequent prosperity was founded.

Robben Island was turned into a leper colony and soon became a dumping ground for all the other misfits in the country, the lunatics, the chronically sick, paupers. Of course, any criminal who was too weak to work on road construction was sent there.

Towards the end of the 19th century the authorities, in a rare fit of compassion, moved all the female paupers off the island. Over the next few years homes were found on the mainland for most of the other island-bound undesirables until finally, during the early part of the 20th century, even the lunatics were found more congenial quarters. Only the lepers remained and they had to wait another twenty years, until the 1930s, before they were found a sanctuary in Pretoria and their home on Robben Island was razed to the ground.

This presented the South African government with a problem. What to do with the island? Obligingly an uncertified Austrian lunatic, by the name of Adolph Hitler, solved the problem by attempting to colonise the world. Robben Island was handed over to the tiny South African army as a base.

The island remained in army hands until 1950 when the

South African Navy inherited the base and it was renamed S.A.S Robben, a name it retained for fifteen years. Then a full circle was completed when the Nationalist Government decided to convert the base into a prison where it sent all those found guilty of opposing its racial policies.

All of this interesting, but mainly useless, information flashed through my mind as I studied the island through my binoculars. Unfortunately, the reference books from which I had gleaned these facts were unable to provide me with the information I most wanted. I needed to know about the tiny section of the island's coastline that had interested me when I first studied the aerial photographs given me by Rogers.

There was a stretch of sand that seemed to offer at least the possibility of a seaborne landing and it had planted in my mind the plan I was slowly developing. However, the photograph was not very clear so I needed to undertake further research to make sure the beach was suitable.

The books I had found in Fish Hoek library were of no help and nor was our trip to Table Mountain. However, it had been a useful visit, because the opportunity to view the southern coastline of the island had ruled out its use as a landing place. We would need a different location to get a clearer view of the eastern coastline of the island and at Paul's suggestion we had already decided on the ideal spot.

'I've seen all I want here,' I said. 'Let's head for Bloubergstrand.'

'OK, boss,' Paul replied, but he made no move to leave. 'But let's hang on a minute. Before we go, I'd like to watch that stupid oke kill himself.'

The hang-glider was fully assembled and one of the men was already strapped in and his companions were helping to manoeuvre it towards the edge of the plateau. The little group stood motionless for a few minutes as they waited for the right moment. Slowly the man in the hang-glider rocked back on his heels then with a loud shout he tore towards the edge and hurled himself into space. The glider dropped several feet and then its wings caught a thermal and soared higher into the air before settling into a slow zigzag descent towards Green Point.

Having seen their companion safely airborne, the rest of the hang-glider group headed towards the cable car station, with the pretty girl carrying the now empty canvas bag. We tagged along and made the station just as a cable car spilled a load of passengers. The mountain top was filling fast with camera laden tourists looking for dassies to film and alabaster plaques inscribed with "I've been up Table Mountain" to buy.

I was pleased to escape.

Bloubergstrand was one of several small seaside resorts situated along the northern coast of Table Bay. Similar in nature to most of the neighbouring communities it boasted several clusters of houses, some of which were holiday homes. There were a handful of bars, a couple of café-cum-supermarkets, a garage and very little else except a wonderful view of Table Mountain.

However, Bloubergstrand did have something shared by few of its sister resorts. Built close to the beach, and looking completely out of place amongst the bungalows that surrounded it, was a tall block of flats. It was to this building that Paul drove us.

On one side of the block of flats, and set back from the approach road, was an area of dusty wasteland on which stood a row of shabby lock up garages. Somebody had nailed a handwritten sign to the wooden up and over door of one of the garages. It read simply: For Rent. Tel 262462.

The writing on the sign was faded and looked as if it had been there for some time. Looking at the state of the garage I was not surprised. Assuming nobody was using the garage we parked in front of its door and headed for the tall building in whose shadow it lay.

The block of flats was serviced by two lifts, but we ignored them and instead headed for the flight of stairs situated at the rear of the building. Unlike the lifts, the stairs went all the way to the flat windswept roof. From there I was able to use my binoculars to get an unrestricted view of the eastern coastline of Robben Island, including the small sandy beach in which I was interested.

I smiled to myself with satisfaction. It was as I had hoped and my idea of a sea-borne landing began to look possible. If I was right, then the rough plan I had started to formulate became much more plausible. I handed the binoculars to Paul.

'What do you reckon, big feller?' I asked as the South African studied the stretch of coastline.

'It looks lekker to me. It's certainly a possibility, but I'm no expert of these waters.'

'Nor me, but I think I know a man who is.'

113

'Our friend Carlse?'

'The very same,' I acknowledged without enthusiasm. Relying on Johan Carlse did not fill me with great confidence. 'Come on, let's get back to the house.' I took my binoculars from Paul, stored them in my knapsack and slung it over my shoulder.

'I suppose that means you will have to meet his daughter again.' Paul said when we reached the car.

'Yes. It's a tough life.'

'You still haven't told me what she's like,' he said with twinkle in his eye.

'Well she isn't going to win any beauty contests in the near future, that's for sure.' I was pretty confident this was the truth. Paul looked as me sceptically, but didn't ask any more questions.

We left Bloubergstrand and drove up the coast. We eventually found a stretch of isolated beach that would make a perfect rendezvous place to hand Zamyatin over to Rogers should we succeed in actually getting him off Robben Island. Satisfied with our day's work we drove back to Clovelly in companionable silence.

It gave me time to think about something that had been worrying me since our descent from Table Mountain's summit earlier that day.

When we had returned to the car park, it was already three quarters full. At the other end of the line in which our Chevrolet was parked was a bottle green Mercedes 300D. It looked like the car I had seen cruising past the bottom of our garden on my first day in Clovelly.

I suppose seeing the car again could have been a coincidence, but I have learnt in my life that believing in coincidences can seriously damage your health.

Saturday April 24th 1982: Wynberg, Cape Town

Freddie and I met at her flat in Wynberg. She wore her hair in a ponytail that made her look about sixteen, which was in contrast to her tight white blouse and navy pleated skirt that made her look mature and alluring. The smile with which she greeted me sent out similar mixed messages; it was friendly without being inviting.

'Please excuse my appearance,' she said as she led me through to a small but neat lounge-diner. 'But I've just arrived home from work.' She was brisk and slightly aloof as she manoeuvred me away from the invitingly plush sofa and onto one of the straight backed chairs that stood alongside a table at the dining end of the room. 'I was about to get myself a cup of tea. Would you like one?' She asked as she disappeared into the kitchen.

'Thank you. That would be nice.' I said, sounding like a vicar.

'I only have rooibos tea. Is that okay?'

'Rooibos is fine with me.' I looked around the room while Freddie clattered around in the kitchen. The lounge-diner was tastefully decorated and well furnished. In addition to the sofa and the dining set there was a smoked glass fronted bookcase, a matching coffee table and a sideboard on which stood a modern music centre. Standing next to the sideboard was a wooden rack full of long playing records. I wandered across and pulled out an album. It was Double Fantasy by John Lennon.

'That was a Christmas present from my papa,' Freddie explained as she came back into the room carrying a tray containing two mugs, a sugar bowl and a small milk jug. She put the tray on the table and sat down opposite me.

'It's a great LP,' I said as I slipped the record back into the rack and joined her at the table. 'I'm seriously impressed.'

'Milk and sugar?' She asked.

I shook my head. 'As it comes.'

'Now, I'm seriously impressed,' she said with a smile as she pushed a mug towards me. 'A rooinek who knows the proper way to drink rooibos tea!'

I pulled an envelope from my pocket and slipped an aerial photograph of Robben Island from it and pushed it across the table in the opposite direction to the mug. 'I need your father's help,' I said.

'Yeah,' she said. If she was surprised at the subject of the photograph, she did not show it.

I pointed to a tiny speck of white on the north-east coast of the island. 'I need to know if it is possible to land a boat on this beach.

She stared intently at the photograph, putting her head on one side as if trying to get a better look at it. 'Have you seen the beach?' She asked.

'Only through binoculars.'

'It's just along the coast from Murray's Bay Harbour.'

'That's right.' I pointed to the photo again. 'As you can see there is a longer beach stretching south from the harbour, but I don't want to use that because it looks too exposed and we would be easily seen.' I explained. 'Which is why I plumped for the smaller beach.'

She took a sip of her tea, then shook her head. 'It will be difficult for you to land there.'

'You know it?'

'Yeah, I know it well. It's called Rock Cove. It's only a narrow strip of sand, but quite safe to beach a small boat on...'

'But you said...' I interrupted her.

'I know what I said, but please be patient and hear me out,' her voice trailed off and she frowned at me.

'I'm sorry, go ahead.'

'As I was saying; it's quite safe to get a boat onto the beach at that point, however, it will be impossible to reach Rock Cove unless you overcome an obstacle out here.' She tapped the photograph with a well-manicured fingernail painted with bright red varnish and ran it down the length of the island in an arc. 'The problem is that about fifty metres from the shore there are rocks that make the cove almost inaccessible. It's those rocks that give the cove its name.'

I stared down at the photograph.

'But that's not your only problem,' Freddie went on. 'Even if you reach the cove you would then need to contend with…'

'I know what you are going to say.' I interrupted her again. This time she did not complain. 'You're talking about the slope, aren't you?'

'You know about the slope?'

I nodded and explained about my trip to Bloubergstrand. 'I could see that the beach is bordered by a slope. However, I was too far away to see clearly. Is it steep?'

'Yeah, very steep and very treacherous. There are often landslides at that point. That is how the cove was formed.'

I nodded thoughtfully as I sipped my tea. 'To be honest the slope is the least of my worries,' I said eventually. 'With the right equipment, we can overcome any potential hazards. I am more concerned about how to navigate through the rocks.'

'Can't you land somewhere else?'

'I want to land on the east side of the island. Can you suggest anywhere else?'

Freddie looked up and shook her head again. 'On the east coast it's either Rock Cove or the harbour beach. There is no other suitable landing place.'

'That's what I thought.' We sat in silence for a few moments and then I said: 'Okay, so it has to be Rock Cove. Is there no way through the rocks? You said it was "almost inaccessible". Does that mean it is possible?'

'Yeah,' she said. 'There's a narrow channel through the rocks that can be navigated by a small shallow-draft boat,' she tapped the photo again. 'But you'll never make it on your own. You'll need somebody to pilot you in.'

'Can you suggest anybody?'

'Yeah, my father knows those waters like the back of his hand.'

'Will he do it?' I asked without much enthusiasm. I was not particular happy about using Johan Carlse.

She shrugged. 'I'll ask him, but I think he will agree when he finds out what you intend. I'm sorry. I'm assuming too much.' She finished her tea and stared across the table at me.

I stared back at her, but said nothing.

She stood up and wandered over took a record from the rack. Soon the smooth golden voice of Barry White filled the apartment. She turned to me and held out her hands. 'Dance with me.' It was not a request.

She did not have to invite me more than once. I held her close and we shuffled around the lounge carpet. I could feel the heat of her body as pressed it against mine. She buried her head in my chest and sighed. I lifted her face and bent to kiss her, but she bowed her head.

'Be patient,' she whispered.

'I don't understand,' I said quietly.

She sighed again and shook her head. She pulled me towards the sofa. 'Nor me. It's all happening so fast.' She said as we sat down.

'I always was a fast worker,' I joked.

'I really don't believe you,' she said in a serious voice.

'And I really don't understand.' I took her hand. 'How old are you?' I asked.

'Twenty-two.'

'I am thirty-nine years old. Almost twice your age.'

'Your maths aren't up to much are they?' She smiled.

'I said almost, in the same way that I am almost old enough to be your father. It was a turn of phrase.'

'It's not almost. You are as old as my father. So what?'

'So why did you come on to me last night?'

'Did I come on to you?'

'You kissed me twice.'

'You've obviously lived a sheltered life if you think that's coming on to you.

'Okay let me rephrase my question. Why did you kiss me?'

'I like you.'

'That's reassuring.'

'You're laughing at me.'

'You must excuse my cynicism. It comes with age.'

'Your age is one of the reasons I like you. The truth is that I am attracted to older men.' She blushed and I guessed she was being honest.

'So why did you pull away when I went to kiss you just now?

She did not answer for a while then eventually she stood up. 'Wait here,' she said.

I watched as she walked to the electric fire that was set into the wall. It was one of those with a couple of heating bars and some imitation coal that lit up. She switched on the light, but not the bars. She then turned off the light so that the room was lit only by the fire. She came back, sat next to me on the sofa and pulled her knees up so that they were under her. I tried not to look at the expanse of smooth white thigh she revealed.

'I prefer to talk in the dark,' she said. 'I find it easier to express myself.'

'Express away.'

'It is difficult to explain how I feel because I am not sure I know myself. I suppose I'm pretty mixed up. You see I have spent all my life being conditioned to hate white people in one way or another. What that does to you eventually is make you one of them. It makes you believe all the propaganda. Makes you believe that we are all different. Whites, Blacks, Indians, Chinese and Coloureds. You begin to believe that we are all better off separated and that it's wrong for us to mix.' She stared over at the fire.

'You know, some of my friends have been thrown out by their parents because they went out on a date with a white boy. That sort of attitude begins to rub off on all of us. It becomes ingrained in our psyche. It comes as a shock when you wake up one day and realise that you are deeply attracted to a white man. It seems almost immoral. But then the law under which I have been brought up tells me that such thoughts are depraved.'

Gently I took hold of her hand and lifted it up with the palm facing her face. 'What colour is your palm?' I asked.

I felt her shrug.

'What colour is it?' I repeated.

'White,' she replied.

I held up my own hand, again palm towards her. 'And mine?'

'White.'

'How do you know?' I asked.

She shrugged again before replying. 'Well I just know. I can see you're white.'

'But can you?' I insisted. 'Can you? Here and now? Here in this darkened room? Can you honestly see that our hands are white? Look!' I turned my hand round so that the hairy back was now towards her. It looked black in the glow of the fire. 'What colour now?'

She was silent.

'Listen, Freddie. How can it be immoral if you only base your judgement on the colour of a person's skin? Supposing you were blind and couldn't see my colour? How would that be immoral? What would make you decide whether you wanted anything to do with me? Shall I tell you? It would be whether I felt good. Whether I was gentle with you. Whether you felt you could trust me. Am I right?'

I felt her fingers caressing the side of my face. I turned to her and saw that she had her eyes closed.

'Mmmm,' she murmured, 'you feel good.' She opened her eyes. 'Of course you're right and if you have a little patience with me perhaps I might even get my sub-conscience to believe that as well. Do you understand what I am saying?'

I nodded. I understood, or thought I did. I looked at her in silence and then changed the subject. 'There is something that puzzles me. How do you know so much about Rock Cove?'

She laughed lightly. 'Papa has been visiting that cove for years. He catches crayfish and perlemoen off the rocks there. Of course, he has to go there at night when he can't be seen because it's a restricted area and it's illegal in this country to catch them without a licence.'

'Which he doesn't have?'

'Which he doesn't have,' she agreed. 'But both fetch a good price in the local restaurants and chefs never ask to see your permit.

Anyway, ever since we were small kids Papa took us along to help. If I had a Kruggerrand for every time we've dived for crayfish with Papa off Rock Cove I'd be a wealthy woman.'

'You said we,' I pointed out, 'and that's a number of times you've done it. How many other children are there in the family?'

She did not answer immediately and when she did, her voice was thick with emotion. 'There's only me now,' she said. 'But I had a twin brother. He died three years ago.'

'I'm sorry.'

'It's okay, Dave, you weren't to know. His name was Frederick, but we called him Frikkie.' she broke down and started to sob.

I cuddled her. 'Don't talk about it anymore.'

'But I want to talk,' she insisted through her tears. 'I need to. It's the first time I've allowed myself to think about it since it happened and it's the first time I've cried.' She pulled away and took off her spectacles.

'How did it happen?' I asked, taking a handkerchief from my pocket and handing it to her.

She blew her nose and took a deep breath.

'It happened in the summer of nineteen-seventy-nine. We were protesting in the Golden Acre, that's the shopping mall in Adderley Street. There were only about twenty of us and it was a silent demonstration. There were no chants, no songs and no banners.

'We stood in a group, each with a small placard hung round our neck demanding equal education facilities for all students. Frikkie and I were at university at the time, but most of the other protesters were high-school kids.

'We had been there about an hour, with no fuss and no problems, when suddenly a riot truck pulled up at the front doors and policemen in camouflage uniforms lined up inside the doors leading to the shopping mall.

'An officer using a loud-hailer instructed all the shoppers to leave the mall and soon only our group was left. Then the officer told us in Afrikaans that we had sixty seconds in which to disperse. We didn't move, although we probably would have obeyed if he had spoken to us in English.'

'But you come from an Afrikaans speaking family,' I pointed out.

'I know, so did most of the other members of our group that

day, but that is not the point. It has been a long standing principle that we do not use the language of our oppressors. I rarely use Afrikaans at home and never outside the house.

'Anyway, none of us was looking for trouble so if that cop had spoken English we would have been more inclined to disperse. Speaking in Afrikaans he had no chance of us obeying him and he knew it.

'There was no second warning. No attempt at conciliation. When the sixty seconds was up the cops came at us with batons flailing and boots kicking. The group split up and we ran for the exits.

'That was when we found the doors had been locked on the orders of the police. We didn't stand a chance. We were rounded up and carted off to Cape Town Central. That was the last time I saw Frikkie alive.

'Most of us were released the same day, but Frikkie and two other boys were detained. We heard nothing of him for two months and then Papa was told that Frikkie had committed suicide in his cell. The police alleged he hung himself with a strip torn from a bed-sheet.

'Those bastards murdered my brother and in doing so killed my mother. She was distraught and threw herself under a train outside Plumstead railway station. And papa? Well you have seen what it did to him. He never touched alcohol until Frikkie died.'

She cried on and off for some time after she finished her story, but then the flow of tears finally dried up and she was cleansed.

I stood up and looked down at her. 'I must go,' I said.

'You can stay here the night if you want,' she said quietly. 'I would welcome your company.'

So okay, I admit it. I was tempted. I hesitated and then shook my head, once again trying hard to avoid looking at her shapely exposed thighs. 'I have to get back to Clovelly. I have a colleague waiting for me. We have much to discuss.'

She slipped from the sofa and pulled her skirt down over her legs.

I gave her my telephone number and asked her to contact me as soon as possible with an answer from her father. 'It would be helpful if you could ring me with his answer tomorrow,' I said as she escorted me to her front door, 'because I am going away on Monday.' The look of disappointment on her face when she heard this news softened even my cynical heart.

At the door she stood close to me and went to hand me back my handkerchief.

I shook my head and smiled down at her. 'Keep it. You can return it when next we meet.'

'You are coming back, then?'

'Oh, yes. I'll be back. That's a promise.'

'How long will you be gone?'

'A few days.'

I half expected her to ask me where I was going, but she asked no more questions and that impressed me. Instead, she reached up and pulled my head down so that she could kiss me.

'Thank you,' she said.

'For what?'

'Well, for a start thank you for listening to me.'

'No problem. It was easy.'

'And thank you for understanding.'

'That was slightly more difficult. You're one pretty mixed up girlie.' I grinned at her.

She grinned back briefly and then said with a serious face: 'But most of all, thank you for not taking advantage of me when I was at my most vulnerable.'

'That was definitely the most difficult part.' I kissed her one last time and left.

Sunday April 25th 1982: Clovelly, Cape Peninsula

Early on Sunday morning Freddie rang to tell me that her father was willing to guide us to Rock Cove and that good news provided me with another important piece in our jigsaw. By that evening all our preliminary planning was complete and, after sharing a bottle of whisky with Paul, even I began to believe it might work.

We had drawn up a list of all the equipment that could be bought legally on the open market. There was a second list of more specialist items that if found in our possession on South African soil would land us in jail quicker than a call for black majority rule. None of these latter items could be bought legally and would have to be purchased through Robert Dyakala.

It was Paul's responsibility to source the items on both lists. I had another task.

We had drawn up a third list, which, in many ways, was the

most important. It consisted of the men I wanted to recruit for our team. It was the shortest list, containing just three names. It would be my job to locate those men and persuade them to join us.

My first destination was the United States of America.

Recruitment

The first thing I did when I reached my suite in the Jefferson Hotel, was to strip off my clothes. Five minutes spent under the powerful spray of the shower beat the travel weariness out of me.

As soon as I got out of the shower I rang room service and ordered a bottle of Jack Daniels. It was just before noon local time, but, what the hell? My body still thought it was in Cape Town, where it was early evening.

I sipped from my glass of bourbon as I dressed in a clean Ben Sherman shirt and a pair of slacks. Only then did I feel able to face Gavin Rogers II. I telephoned his number and we arranged to meet in my room in an hour.

Rogers was on time, cool, smart and unruffled. He was accompanied by a goon I had never seen before, but Hank Graham and Joe Welensky were nowhere to be seen. Rogers' companion was tall with the physique of a gorilla. He had a bald head, light coloured eyebrows and a large black curly beard that made his face look as if it was upside down.

Rogers introduced the man as Agent Sam Potter and then dismissed him with a regal wave of his wrist. Potter hesitated, as if worried about leaving the CIA deputy director on his own with me. Perhaps he thought I was going to shoot his boss, or maybe try to seduce him. He needn't have worried, because I wasn't carrying a gun and I preferred my lovers to wear skirts.

Evidently Potter decided I was harmless because he left the room and closed the door quietly behind him.

'Bourbon?' I asked Rogers as he sat down in one of the two tasteful armchairs that stood on the expensive looking rug in the middle of the room.

He stood his briefcase on the floor beside his chair and made a point of studying his watch. He shook his head and frowned disapprovingly as I topped up my own glass, but that frown was wasted on me. I did not give a stuff what he thought. It was my JD and my liver.

With the preliminaries out of the way we got down to business. I began by telling Rogers how much I estimated it would cost to buy the equipment needed for the operation and gave him the number of the bank account I had set up in Cape Town. 'Can you have the money cabled to that account immediately?' I asked. 'I've left somebody in South Africa to start procuring the equipment and he's going to need access to money fairly quickly.'

I had half expected the CIA man to quibble about the amount for which I had asked and I had prepared myself by bringing along details of our estimates to justify the expenditure. To my surprise Rogers accepted my request with another wave of his elegant hand.

'It will be transferred this afternoon,' he said.

'That figure does not take into account manpower,' I explained.

'How many men are you proposing to use?'

'It will be five man team, plus me, so I'll need quarter of a million paid directly into my Swiss bank account so that I can pay them.' I had lumped Johan Carlse into the total. If we managed to get Zamyatin off the island then Freddie's dad would have earned his money and be able to buy himself a second hand fishing boat.

Rogers shrugged off this news in the same nonchalant fashion. 'Their deal is the same as yours. Fifty percent paid up front; the rest payable once we get Zamyatin. Let me have your estimates and I will give them the once over later.' He smiled as he saw the surprise on my face. 'I told you Statton, this is the big one. Now, when do we get our man?'

'First things, first,' I said as I handed over a sheet setting out my calculations for the operation's costs. 'You promised to find out exactly where in the prison the South Africans are holding Zamyatin.'

'I have. As I suggested, he is definitely being held in Section B of the isolation block, currently cell number sixteen but there is a possibility that he will be transferred to a better cell in the near future. If that happens, I will let you know.'

I looked at him quizzically. 'How do you know all this?'

He smiled. 'We have a top level informer in the South African Justice Department. That is who supplied us with details of the layout of the prison. It cost us a bomb, as you limeys might say.' He smiled again, perhaps at his own pun. 'Now,' he went on, repeating his question: 'When do we get the Ruskie?'

'May fifteenth,' I replied.

He did not look happy. 'Are you not able to get him out earlier?' He asked.

I shook my head. 'No, it's not possible for a couple of reasons. One; as I told you when I agreed to take this job, it takes time to prepare for an operation like this. It's not something that can be rushed. Rush means risk and risk is something I want to minimise. Remember it's my neck in the noose if this operation goes tits up.

'Two; I want to hit the island at high tide and in the middle of the night. May fourteenth is the only suitable date that will allow sufficient preparation time and offer the right tide conditions.' I smiled at him and added: 'You should be grateful. I would have preferred to leave it for another couple of weeks when there's a new moon. I'm just keeping my fingers crossed there is some cloud cover on the fourteenth.'

Rogers did not return my smile, nor did he thank me for bringing forward the operation by two weeks, instead he grumbled: 'But you said you would get Zamyatin out within a month.'

'No. I said I'd try,' I pointed out. 'Anyway, it will only be marginally over a month. A few hours in fact. In fact, if everything goes according to plan, we will hand him over at 0230 hrs. The rendezvous point will be here…' I handed Rogers the map co-ordinates, which he put into his briefcase without even glancing at the slip of paper. '… it's a deserted part of the coast some fifteen miles north of Cape Town and a couple of miles from Bloubergstrand.'

Rogers seem to accept the logic of my proposal. 'Okay,' he said. 'But don't be late. We won't sit around on our butts waiting for you. The submarine will have to be in and out of South African waters as quickly as possible. I have no say in that matter. The navy won't take any chance on being compromised. If you don't make the rendezvous on time you will be on your own and you will have to get Zamyatin out of the country as best you can.'

'You said we won't sit around waiting. Does that mean you will be on the sub?'

The CIA deputy director shook his head. 'No, but I will be at the rendezvous point, because I want to check out Zamyatin and make sure he's in one piece.'

'So when are you coming to Cape Town?' I asked suspiciously. The last thing I wanted was Rogers interfering in our Operation.

'I plan to arrive in South Africa a few days before you are due to deliver Zamyatin. When I arrive I want to meet you for a final briefing.'

'No problem. When and where?'

'Let's say Wednesday, May twelfth at nineteen hundred hours. We can meet at my hotel. I'll be staying at the Mount Nelson Hotel.'

'Of course you will,' I said, not surprised at his choice. The Mount Nelson was the best hotel in Cape Town.

Rogers stared at me, weighing up whether to take offence at my sarcasm. He obviously decided to ignore my comment because he went on: 'At our meeting I will confirm availability of the submarine and at the same time we can iron out details of the handover. I don't want any last minute screw ups.'

'There won't be any last minute screw ups,' I assured him, with my fingers firmly crossed. 'But don't forget to bring our money with you to the handover. That way you get Zamyatin and we get the rest of our fees. It will avoid any misunderstanding or embarrassment later.'

'You don't trust me?' Now Rogers did sound offended.

'Does it show?'

'Don't worry, Statton. You deliver the Red and you'll get your money.' He stood up, walked to the door and opened it. He stopped and turned to face me. 'Oh, and for my own selfish reasons, Good luck!' With that he was gone.

I wandered across to the window and looked down onto a busy 16th Street. Five storeys below I saw Rogers emerge onto the sidewalk and wave. At first I thought he was hailing a cab and then I saw an open topped sports car pull into the kerbside. Rogers climbed in and the car sped away in the direction of the White House.

I had lunch and was still able to catch a late afternoon flight out of Dulles Airport. The destination on my ticket said Los Angeles International Airport.

As soon as I was on board the aircraft I settled down in my seat and wrapped a blanket round me. The flight was due to take just over six hours and my eyes were heavy. Jetlag had caught up with me and my body still thought it was back in Cape Town, where the clocks had recently struck midnight to herald in April 28th.

I wanted to sleep but my mind was still mulling over the relaxed way in which Rogers had accepted my estimates for the funds I needed for the operation. I wondered why that was. It was not like him to be so laissez faire about financial matters.

I wondered also why Rogers had not been particularly interested in the co-ordinates I gave him. It was almost as if he knew the location of our rendezvous place already. First it had been Johan Carlse who knew where we were staying in Clovelly, when I had not mentioned it to him, now it appeared that Rogers might also be one step ahead of me.

Finally I wondered about the significance of Rogers getting into a sports-car driven by Major Percival Carsons (Rtd). This seemed to confirm that Carsons was working for the CIA in some capacity. I wondered if he was a private detective hired by Rogers to follow me. Was this possible or was I just being paranoid?

Paranoid or not, I sensed there were things going on behind the scenes of which I was unaware and that always makes me nervous. I decided it was time to start watching my back.

Thursday April 29th 1982: Hollywood, California, USA

The two cars hit the ton as they sped down the final stretch of the mountain road. It was only when the vehicles reached the flat coastal highway that the needles of their speedometers dropped back below the 100 mph mark.

The leading car was a vivid green Chevrolet. It weaved across the road in an attempt to stop the second car from overtaking. The tyres of the Chevy squealed horribly as it skidded from side to side, sending puffs of smoke up into the morning air.

The pursuing vehicle was a black and white police highway-patrol car and its strident siren combined with the noise from the leading vehicle's tyres to produce a nerve jangling screech.

The distance between the two cars constantly changed. Sometimes the gap widened to several car lengths. Then, with a sudden burst of extra speed, the chasing patrol car would narrow the gap again until it seemed the two vehicles must collide. Always, just in time, the driver of the police car would touch his brakes and a crash was averted.

The only person in the Chevy was its driver, who was crouched low over the steering wheel. His head was barely visible above the dashboard as he made himself as small as possible a target for the cop who was firing his pistol out of the passenger window of the highway patrol car. A number of bullets struck the careering green car and its rear window was starred and frosted.

The two cars screamed into a sharp bend, then, as soon as

they came out the other side, the cars started accelerating up the next stretch of straight road. Suddenly the drivers of both cars slammed on the brakes as they were confronted by a barrier of brightly coloured oil drums strung across the road, behind which were parked a number of police cars.

The cops who manned the road block stood with shotguns raised and muzzles pointing at the fast approaching Chevrolet. When the end came everything happened at the same time and was over in seconds.

A barrage of fire was directed at the still speeding Chevy, the driver of which spun his steering wheel to send the car swerving violently off the highway. The patrol car accelerated yet again and this time made contact, clipping the Chevrolet's rear fender. Already unbalanced from its swerve the green car spun out of control. It swayed, rocked and then reared up in the air, before somersaulting over to land on its roof.

The car's big engine roared madly as its wheels found nothing more substantial to grip on than the dust filled air. The momentum of the upturned car carried it forward on its roof for several yards, leaving a bright green streak on the hard packed sand. The petrol tank did not blow until the Chevy came to rest, but when it did go up it was in a spectacular explosion of flames and black swirling smoke.

'Cut!' The film director shouted through a megaphone. 'OK. That's a wrap. For Christ sake get those goddamn flames out.' Even as the director spoke, a team of fire-fighters dashed towards the Chevrolet and smothered the car's rear end in thick foam.

A man wearing a fawn gabardine raincoat eased himself from the wreckage of the car and levered himself upright. He stood motionless for a short while and examined his hands closely as if making sure his fingers were all in place. Then, as if answering the call of some invisible drill-sergeant, he stamped his feet several times in a marching on the spot routine. As he marched the man flexed his upper torso and arms. Finally, satisfied he was still in one piece, he looked over towards the camera truck where I was standing and waved.

I waved back. The man's name was John Brandon. He was a stuntman and he was the second member of my team.

John walked towards me, shrugging off his raincoat as he came. 'How did it look, boss?' He asked when he reached me.

'Spectacular.'

'That's what I like to hear,' he said as he dropped the raincoat on the ground in front of me and stripped away the protective body suit that the coat had concealed. 'Jeez! This junk is damned hot,' he complained as he piled the heavy flame resistant clothing on top of the coat. 'Goddammit. I need a cold drink.'

I took a beer from the metal ice-box that stood on the back of the camera truck, removed the cap and handed it to him. I pointed at the crashed Chevrolet from which the fire fighters were cleaning the foam used to douse the flames.

'Aren't you scared something might go wrong with your stunts?' I asked. 'For instance, if that fire had spread quicker no protective clothing on earth would have saved you.'

He didn't reply at first, instead he took a long swig from his beer bottle. 'Yeah, I'm often scared, my friend,' he said eventually, before letting out a loud burp. 'In fact, scared shitless and d'ya know why?' He took another swig of beer.

I didn't answer him, deciding it was probably a rhetorical question.

'It's because despite all the precautions we take, and all the safety regulations we have to observe, being a stuntman is a damn dangerous occupation. I've seen lots of my colleagues end up dead or spending the rest of their lives paralysed. But I suppose that's why the studio pays me megabucks.'

He finished off the beer with a third long gulp before reaching for a replacement. 'But I have to admit that particular stunt ain't as dangerous as it looks, Dave.' He paused as he took a sip from his fresh beer bottle.

We watched as the fire fighters sprinkled pink liquid over the upended green car.

'That explosion when the Chevy crashed?' He said eventually. 'That wasn't the gas tank blowing.' He smiled. 'No way, Jose! When I started that stunt there was just enough gas in the tank to get the car from up there' he pointed up the mountain road, 'to down there.' He pointed to where the upturned car lay shining in the hot sun.

'By the time I put that baby into a spin the gas tank was completely empty. As dry as a bone. The biggest risk to my safety was getting trapped in the cab and being engulfed by flames before I could be rescued and that was highly unlikely.'

He paused again as a man emerged from one of the gigantic motor homes that were parked by the roadside and headed in our direction. He staggered as he walked, as if the half empty bottle of whisky he clutched in one hand was affecting his balance.

John looked at his watch and shook his head slowly. 'A quarter after ten and he's drunk already. Jesus Christ, he gets earlier each day.' He turned to me again. 'Where was I?'

'Getting blown up.'

'Ah, but that's the point, Dave. The car couldn't blow up without my help.'

I raised an eyebrow at him.

'Let me explain,' he said with an amiable smile. 'That explosion you saw was an electronically operated charge that was fitted into the trunk of the Chevy. It was connected to a can containing just enough gas to produce some dramatic flames, but little risk to me.

'More importantly, it ensured we actually got a damn explosion. When a car is crashed deliberately, you can't always guarantee the gas tank will explode. So, when the car flipped I simply hit the detonation button and, "Pow!"'

The man with the whisky bottle had reached us. 'Howya doing, Johnnie-ol'-buddy?' He asked, greeting the stuntman with a slap on the back and a wave of his bottle. He swayed as he spoke.

'I'm real cool, man, how about you?' John replied.

The man sucked a lungful of air through melodramatically pursed lips before exhaling with a whistle. 'Me? I'm as high as a kite and lovin' it. But, listen up Johnnie, I bring you news of heap big shit. I've just left Vanessa.' He crossed himself with a theatrical wave of his spare hand. 'Beware our resident pincushion on legs, ol' buddy. Boy, oh, boy, is she steaming. She really has the knife out for you, man, and that bitch can wipe a guy out at a hundred paces. If she sees you, watch out, because you are dead, dead, dead.' He demonstrated John's likely fate by drawing a shaking forefinger across his own Adam's apple.

'Dave, meet Carlo Pullini. Carlo, this is my limey friend, Dave Statton.'

Pullini hit me with the same expansive smile that had stolen the hearts of females around the world. It was that smile, combined with his husky voice, smoky eyes, manly physique and natural acting ability that had won him fame and fortune as one of Hollywood's superstars.

The image of Carlo Pullini promoted by his studio was that of a virile Latin colossus. Seeing him now, swaying on his feet in

131

front of me, I could see that he was less muscular than he appeared on the big screen and much shorter than John or me. However, he was a good deal drunker than both of us.

The actor bent down and tried to put on the protective suit that John had discarded. He found it difficult because his ability to dress was restricted by the tight grip with which he held onto his whisky bottle.

Gently John eased the bottle from the actor's grasp.

'Yeah! Thanks, ol' buddy.' Pullini grinned drunkenly at the stuntman. Eventually, between them, they managed to get the actor into the suit, then John helped him into the raincoat.

'Come on, Carlo. We're waiting for you.' The director called across the set, then in exasperation he shouted: 'Carlo! Pleeeese!'

'Screw you!' the actor shouted back. He grinned at us. With a last longing look at the whisky bottle, he shrugged, turned away and staggered to the side of the overturned Chevrolet.

'Shit, Carlo! Have you been on the juice already?'

In answer Pullini waved his middle finger in the air.

'He ain't gonna last much longer,' John said. 'He's on the way out and he knows it. Trouble is, he's past caring. It's a shame, because Carlo's a nice guy when he's sober.'

Pullini crouched down beside the open driver's door. A fire fighter carefully poured liquid from a red can down the back of the actor's raincoat.

'Okay, let's get ready to roll,' the director shouted.

The fire fighter struck a match and threw it at the Chevrolet. With a roar the car burst into flames. Quickly, he struck another match and set fire to the actor's coat then ran out of camera shot.

'And action!'

Pullini came out of his crouch, his back a mass of flames, and ran towards the camera looking for all the world as if he had escaped from the blazing car behind him. Two policemen rushed up to the human torch that was Carlo Pullini and pushed him to the ground. Not too gently they rolled him over and over in the sand until the flames were extinguished. Pulling him to his feet one of the policemen roughly snapped a pair of handcuffs on the struggling actor's wrists.

'Bastards!' Pullini screamed with real venom.

'Cut! Good, we'll print it.' The director said. 'Okay, Carlo, you can get back to your bottle now. Just try to turn up sober tomorrow.'

But Pullini was not listening. 'Bastards!' He shouted again at the grinning actor-policemen who had manhandled him so roughly. With a final obscene gesture at them he turned tail and made a bee-line for John and the whisky he was holding.

The actor relieved John of the bottle and took a long swig. The golden fluid gurgled another inch or so nearer extinction. He smacked his lips in appreciation. 'I needed that Johnnie,' he said. He was about to raise the bottle to his lips again when he glanced over John's shoulder. 'Oh, shit! Here comes trouble,' he hissed before intoning: 'O! Beware, my lord of jealousy; It is the green-ey'd monster which doth mock the meat it feeds on.' He forked two fingers at John's eyes then looked at me. 'Othello, Act Three, Scene Three,' he said proudly.

'I know, Carlo.'

'And so, with that, my friends, methinks it time for our hero to exit stage left.' He grinned drunkenly and ambled off, no doubt to find a quiet corner in which to finish his bottle in peace.

'John Brandon! Where the fuck did you get to last night?' A woman's voice shrilled out from behind us. 'You said you would come to my motor-home last night. Where the hell were you, you son-of-a-bitch? I really had the hots and needed you.'

I recognised the woman at once. She was Vanessa Penn, the cinema-going husbands' answer to Carlo Pullini. The ultimate in sex symbols. She bore down on us now, all uplifted breast and silky skinned thigh.

She stood in front of John, hands on hip, her famous, heavily insured legs spread aggressively apart, exposed in all their glory by the long splits that sliced up both sides of her black silk skirt.

'Good morning, Vanessa,' John said pleasantly.

'Fuck good morning, you arsehole, where were you last night?'

'Let's get one thing straight, Vanessa. I never said I'd see you last night. If you remember, you told me to come see you.' John looked at her with ill-disguised distaste. 'And as it happens, although it's none of your goddam business, I was with a real woman.'

I knew John was lying because he had spent the previous evening with me, during which we drank plenty of beer, reminisced and discussed the operation in which I wanted him to take part. When we parted in the small hours of the morning, there was not a woman to be seen.

John turned to me. 'Remember Carlo called this babe a pincushion on legs? Well that's because of the number of pricks she's had in her. She's been screwed by every straight guy on the set, from the director down to the tea-boy. Well every straight guy with one exception. Me. And that's why she's so mad, Dave. It really gets to her that anybody could resist her beautiful body, and there is no getting away from it, she does have a beautiful body. Don't you agree?'

I looked down at her lustrous raven hair, long tanned legs, unfettered firm breasts and classically beautiful face and found it difficult to disagree.

'But the day has yet to arrive when I let myself become just another slat in Vanessa Penn's sexual conveyor belt.'

The actress said nothing while John was speaking, she just glared at him as her fury increased. Her face gradually tightened and whitened, becoming a ghastly parody of the screen beauty so many cinema going men had lusted after.

I thought she was going to stab John's eye out with half an inch of painted nail, but the finger that flew through the air towards his face stopped an inch short and stabbed the air instead.

'You arrogant son-of-a-bitch!' She hissed. 'I wouldn't fuck you anyway, Brandon. You're nothing but a faggot and I'll make you regret those words. God damn you! I'll see you never stunt on another picture in this country.'

John smiled benignly at her then tipped up the bottle he held in his hand and deposited the remainder of his beer on her small feet.

Vanessa leapt backwards and then stabbed the air with her finger nail again. 'Never!' She screamed with a venom that was accentuated by the spittle that clung to her full lips.

She spun on her heel and strode away across the film lot. We watched her go, both staring at her swaying hips, her tight backside and her long, slender legs.

John shook his head sadly. 'What a body,' he sighed.

'I've seen worse,' I said. 'How did you resist the temptation?'

'I have principles, Dave,' he said, although his voice was tinged with regret.

'Will she do it?' I asked. 'Have you blacklisted by the studios?'

He shrugged. 'She'll try,' he said. 'She might even screw enough producers to persuade them not to use me, but I ain't

134

worried. All the time there are actors like Carlo Pullini around to funk the dangerous work, then there will be a job for the likes of me. Don't worry, boss. In the words of Gloria Gaynor; I will survive.'

I looked at him. A hard, confident American who would not know what panic was if it jumped up and bit him on the end of his nose. A cool, competent man with swarthy good looks, a strong jutting jaw, wide shoulders and a pair of strong hands. He could locate and repair an automobile engine fault in less time than it takes to get through on the phone to some motoring rescue organisations I know. I looked at him and knew he was right. There would always be work for men like John Brandon.

At one time he had worked as a motor mechanic in his father's garage in Des Moines and by the time he was twenty he could strip an engine with his eyes closed. He enjoyed working with cars, but it lacked the one element he needed more than any other: excitement.

He wanted adventure and the chance to do something out of the ordinary. So he threw in his spanner and joined the US Marines, where he served with distinction and became both a master sergeant and an explosives expert. After leaving the marines, he headed for Laos to become a mercenary. That's where I met him.

As with Paul Helsdon, I came to know John Brandon well and I appreciated his fearlessness, technical expertise and reliability.

The last campaign we fought together was in Angola and after we extracted ourselves from that ill-fated debacle John decided to return to America. I didn't see him again until the day before his stunt with the Chevrolet, but I had kept track of him through mutual friends.

I knew that when he arrived back in Iowa he was unable to settle down in the mundane routine offered by the family auto business and he soon packed his bags again. He worked the motor racing circuit for a time as a mechanic, then, still unsettled and still searching for excitement, he became a film stuntman where he put to good use his expertise in explosives.

It didn't take much legwork on my part to track John down. Everybody in Hollywood seemed to know the dare-devil stuntman, and when, over drinks, I offered him a chance to join the team I was putting together, he accepted without hesitation or a single question.

His only request was that he be allowed to honour his current contract and complete the final stunt, which was the car crash scene. I agreed, after all waiting a day would not hold up my schedule and I would have waited a week to secure his talents as a mechanic, driver, explosives expert and all round reliable ally.

I had recruited half my team, but I still had a couple more men to track down. My next destination was London.

Mr Mac

Bismarck Road was dark and lined with the type of house that was described by up-market estate agents based in Kensington as "a desirable town cottage with fantastic development potential". However, it was only "a terraced house in need of renovation" to those estate agents who plied their trade in that part of South London in which a growing number of dysfunctional families kept the capital city's social workers busy.

Mr Mac studied with practiced eyes the rundown street, which epitomised the depressing urban decay that was widespread in the area.

On one side of the road a crumbling row of houses ended abruptly in a jagged edge of loose bricks and flaking wallpaper. Two upper floor fireplaces had been exposed by the demolition hammer that had reduced the rest of the row of houses to rubble. They looked out from their faded floral wallpaper surrounds like two burnt out eyes, patiently waiting for the housing development that was promised for the site.

So far the only sign of construction work was the erection of a high corrugated iron fence covered in old and torn posters advertising local performances by obscure black singers and the meetings of various revolutionary protest groups.

On the other side of the street the row of houses was complete, saved from destruction, like the remaining houses opposite, by the lack of council funds to complete the development.

Mr Mac had done his homework well. He knew that at one end of the street was the Continental and Indian Delicatessen Emporium, a somewhat grandiose name for the tiny, one windowed shop owned by an exiled Ugandan Asian. At one time the other end of the street had been connected to the main Tooting to Stockwell road, but it had been turned into a cul-de-sac by the erection of the poster covered fence.

With no through traffic and no police presence, Bismarck Road had become a no-go zone for everybody other than vandals, drug dealers and local gang members. The youths who

137

congregated at the end of the street could be all three.

The windows of the houses in the street had been broken so many times that the occupiers, mostly squatters, no longer bothered to have them repaired. Instead, the holes that regularly appeared in the glass were stuffed with newspapers or dirty cloth, which offered the illegal tenants at least some protection from the elements.

The Electricity Board had also given up trying to keep the lamp posts in good repair. Not content with merely breaking the globes in the lamps, the local hooligans had wrenched the metal base plates loose and had systematically pulled the wiring out until it was left to hang in the gutter like multi-coloured spaghetti.

However, now the sun had set and the squalid scene was covered in a veil of darkness, it could be seen that at least one of the street-lights was working. It was positioned at the enclosed end of the street and it shone out like a beacon in the sea of destruction.

In the street-lamp's soft yellow light the youths straggled across the pavement. A couple of gang members lounged against the fence. Somewhere in their midst a ghetto-blaster was pumping out reggae music. Occasionally one of the group would perform a little bobbing solo dance in time to the pounding rhythmic beat.

Flat, unevenly rolled cigarettes were passed from one eager mouth to another and as the marijuana began to take effect the gang members became more boisterous and their laughter louder.

Two of the youths began pushing each other in a semi-aggressive manner that gradually grew more heated and serious. Egged on by their mates, who formed a yelping circle round them, the two protagonists were soon rolling round on the ground in a clumsy tussle.

'Excuse me,' Mr Mac said, too quietly it seemed to be heard above the cries and jeers.

But one of the gang did hear him, or maybe the youth sensed the presence of a stranger. He spun round and slowly the noise subsided as the rest of the group became aware there was an intruder in their midst.

The two youths who had been fighting sprang to their feet, their rivalry forgotten in the face of a potential common enemy. The gang members viewed the stranger with hostile eyes.

Mr Mac was a short, wiry man with sparse grey hair swept sidewards across the dome of his head. He wore a crumpled and baggy suit, the jacket of which was fastened by a single button and below which hung several inches of bright yellow cardigan. His tartan necktie was thin, dirty and was loose at his neck and showed the fastened top button of his shirt. In his hand he carried a rolled up newspaper with which he fidgeted nervously.

Mr Mac coughed hesitantly and when he eventually spoke again it was in a voice with a distinct Scottish accent. 'Excuse me,' he repeated. 'I'm sorry to bother ye, but I'm looking for Alvin Smith. D'ye ken?'

A tall black youth, dressed in an ankle length leather coat and a colourful Rastafarian woollen hat, pushed his way to the front of the group.

'Who wants him, honkey?' The youth asked.

Mr Mac peered at the youth through round, wire framed spectacles. 'Are ye Alvin Smith?' He asked.

'What's it to you, whitey?'

'Please, I'm nae here looking for trouble. Are ye Alvin Smith? If ye are, there is something I'd like to discuss with ye, so I would.' There was a nervous tremor in Mr Mac's voice as he spoke.

'Yeah, man. I'm Alvin Smith,' the black youth admitted with a swagger. 'So whatcha want?'

'And your brother, Winston. Is he here too?' Mr Mac peered through his spectacles at the youths who now crowded behind Smith.

'Winston? Whatcha want him for, man?' Smith asked suspiciously. 'You ain't the filth, are you?' He laughed out loud at what he obviously believed was a ludicrous suggestion.

Mr Mac shook his head. 'I'm nae the police.'

'Hey Winston, this honkey is looking for you,' Alvin Smith called over his shoulder. 'D'ya reckon he's looking for bother?' He laughed again and his friends joined in.

Another youth, shorter than the first, pushed his way forward and joined Smith. He wore an identical Rasta hat to his brother. 'No way, man,' he said. 'He ain't dangerous.' He took a step towards Mr Mac. 'You ain't looking for trouble, are you whitey?'

Mr Mac looked nervously at the youth, who was younger than his taller brother. 'Are ye Winston Smith?' He asked.

'Yeah, I'm Winston?'

'Okay, honkey,' the older Smith said. 'So now you've found us, what gives?'

Mr Mac blinked as his glasses caught the light from in the streetlamp. He stared up at the two youths. 'I've come to talk with ye about Beverley Martin.'

The two brothers glanced at each other. 'Who she, man?' The taller brother asked with a sneer. 'I don't know no Beverley Muffin.' He grinned.

'Martin,' Mr Mac said quietly. 'Beverley Martin. D'ye nae remember her?'

'Nah!' The younger one insisted.

'Beverley is the wee lassie ye beat up and raped two weeks ago,' Mr Mac said.

The youths fell silent and looked at each other again. 'Who says so?' Alvin finally said. 'Are you her old man?'

'I hardly think so,' Mr Mac replied. 'She was a wee black lassie as ye well know.'

'Listen you honkey prick, you ain't got no proof we done it so why dontcha just piss off?' The older youth said and he and his brother stepped menacingly towards the little man. 'Scram!'

'No, no!' Mr Mac put up his hand in self-defence. 'I told ye, I'm not here to cause trouble, ye ken. I just wanted to give ye a message from her pa. He knows there's no proof and the poor wee lassie cannae talk because she was so badly beaten. That's why he hasnae contacted the police.' He took a stepped closer to the youths. 'Look, I'm only the messenger. Dinnae take it out on me. I told Mister Martin it was probably Beverley's own fault, the way she goes around dressed like a strumpet. It's disgusting, so it is. I bet she asked for it.'

The two brothers laughed. 'She was gagging for it, man,' Alvin said. 'She's been coming on to Winston for months, but when he finally wanted to give her some, she went all innocent on him. Know what I mean, man? So he decided to teach her a lesson and I wanted a bit of the action, you dig? Okay, so we had to knock her about a bit to make her see sense, but she deserved it.' Alvin paused as his brother chipped in.

'Listen, honkey, don't let that slag tell you she didn't enjoy it. She loved it. She took us both at the same time, didn't she Al?'

'So it was ye boys?' Mr Mac asked.

'Yeah, but howdja know it was us. You said the bitch couldn't talk.'

'Aye, the poor wee lassie cannae speak, but she can write.' Mr Mac explained. As he spoke he took a step forward and shoved the rolled up newspaper into Alvin Smith's groin. As it struck home he twisted his wrist and the newspaper fell away to reveal the handle of a six inch razor sharp knife. There was a sucking sound

140

as he pulled the knife out.

Winston Smith froze as he stared at the dark red patch that spread across the front of his brother's trousers. He barely moved as Mr Mac pivoted on his heel, lunged forward again and with a deft stab and flick of his wrist castrated him. He fell to join his brother, who was already on the ground holding his groin and whimpering in agony.

Even before Winston Smith had hit the ground Mr Mac had melted into the gloom and disappeared.

David Statton

I heard the sound of running feet and turned the ignition key of the hire car. The engine roared into life as the passenger door was flung open and a man threw himself onto the seat. I flicked on the headlights and let out the clutch. With a squeal of tyres I accelerated away towards Tooting.

'You were a long time,' I said. 'I was about to come find you.'

'Och, it was nae a problem, Mister Statton. I had to be sure. I dinnae want to get the wrong two laddies, ye ken. He took a couple of deep breaths. 'Thanks for waiting anyhow. Now, perhaps ye'd be good enough to take me to the airport.'

My passenger's name was Andrew Hamish Macmillan, but I had never heard anyone call him by his full name. It was always Mr Mac. In his turn, the little Scotsman only ever used formal titles and surnames when addressing other people. It was 'Mr This' and 'Mrs That'.

If a psychologist had analysed Mr Mac, they would no doubt have concluded that his insistence on formality was a device to prevent the formation of close relationships. They would probably have been right. He was a very private man who rarely showed his true feelings. Indeed, I sometimes wondered if he had any feelings.

I suppose I know as much about Mr Mac as anybody else in our line of work.

Born in Glasgow to poor, but strict parents, Mr Mac had spent the whole of his working life dealing in death. In common with many other Glaswegian boys who sought an early escape from the deprivation that life in post-war Maryhill offered, Mr Mac joined the British Army straight from school.

After basic training, he transferred to the Seaforth

Highlanders, the regiment in which his father, grandfather and great-grandfather had served, but when he was 18 he applied for a transfer to the Special Air Service.

When the short, wiry, untidy youth from the slums of Glasgow subsequently presented himself to the SAS selection board he was almost assessed as unsuitable, simply because of his appearance. However, he was given a chance to prove himself and by the end two weeks of tough physical and mental tests Private Andrew Macmillan was top of the class.

He was phenomenal. In unarmed combat the little Scotsman was silent, lightning quick and deadly. He was lethal with a knife and the equal of men twice his size. His instructors found that although he was quiet and unassuming, with a polite demeanour, he could be utterly ruthless when the need arose. Intellectually he had a natural cunning that more than made up for his lack of academic qualifications. Temperamentally he was as cold as ice when he was under pressure.

So Private Macmillan was accepted into the elite SAS and for the next 22 years he served the regiment with dedication and distinction. He saw active service in Malaya, Oman, Borneo, Yemen and Northern Island. He retired from the service when he was 40 years of age, with three stripes and a reputation for toughness. He could have transferred to another regiment, but he decided to make a clean break and return to Civvy Street.

Mr Mac took a job in a warehouse, but after so many years of adventure and action he was like a fish out of water. It was simply not for him, so he left and once again he became a soldier, only this time he sold his considerable talents and loyalty to anybody who offered to pay his wages. He became a mercenary.

Mr Mac made only one stipulation when considering offers of work. That was that the assignment, whatever it was, would not harm his country, which, despite being a proud Scotsman, he considered to be the United Kingdom of Great Britain and Northern Ireland.

When there were no foreign wars to fight, Mr Mac did freelance work for anybody who could make use of his special skills. He accepted work anywhere. As long as the assignment fitted in with his own high standards of loyalty, honour and morality, then he would carry out his task with a single mindedness that bordered on the unnatural.

Such was Mr Mac's integrity that when I finally tracked him

down the previous day and invited him to join my team he refused. He was not able to commit himself until he had successfully completed the work for which he was contracted.

In his book there were few sins greater than committing to a contract and then reneging on that agreement. Mr Mac's attitude reflected that of John Brandon and convinced me that I had made the right decision in recruiting both men.

'I appreciate your invitation, Mister Statton,' he had said the previous day. 'But fulfilling my current contract successfully might prove a might tricky, ye ken. I couldnae look at myself in the mirror if I agreed to join ye and then had to let ye down because I suffered some mishap tomorrow.'

'The offer will still be valid tomorrow night, Mister Mac,' I assured him. 'You can give me the answer then. Now is there anything I can do to help?'

There was and now his task had been completed, Mr Mac was sitting in the passenger seat of my car, unscathed, his request to be taken to the airport was his answer to my offer.

Two hours later I saw him safely aboard a South African Airways flight to Cape Town. I set off for France happy in the knowledge that the little Scotsman was now an integral part of my almost fully recruited team and his deadly skills would be at my sole disposal for the next two weeks.

Sunday May 2nd 1982: Juan Les Pins, France.

I first met Charlie Le Roux in the Algerian prison where I was being held following my arrest on a trumped up charge of gun-running. I was locked up because I was unlucky enough to be in the wrong place at the wrong time, set up by the man who actually organised the shipment of arms. They were discovered in the hold of the tramp steamer on which I happened to have secured a berth.

Most times the Algerian authorities would probably have turned a blind eye to such a shipment, particularly if their good eye was able to see a sufficiently large wad of bank notes. On this occasion the arms were destined for the Polisario Front, the rebel force that, although it operated mainly in the Western Sahara, was considered a threat by the Algerians.

Of course I protested my innocence, but the gun-runner who pointed the finger at me was the youngest brother of the local police chief, so my arrest was a foregone conclusion. A week after my arrest both the cop and his brother were found dead in an alley. The cop was carrying a briefcase containing documents that clearly implicated his brother in the gun-running operation.

Although the documents exonerated me, the authorities, used the old maxim that there is no smoke without fire. They decided that I must be guilty of something and kept me in prison pending deportation from the country with the status "persona non grata" stamped on my passport.

Charlie Le Roux's arrival in the same prison was as a result of him putting to good use his circus training when he climbed the side of the Algiers Hilton as if using a ladder. He entered the hotel through a half open window on the tenth floor and removed from a bedroom safe incriminating photographs that could have been embarrassing for a senior member of the Algerian government.

Twenty minutes after stealing the photographs Charlie was back in the smelly alley that ran along the back of the hotel and shortly after that he was in the city centre mingling with the late night crowds.

Charlie's troubles began when he delivered the photographs to the very grateful government minister. As soon as the evidence of his indiscretion with a Bedouin rent-boy was burning brightly in his fireplace, the politician calmly announced that he had no money with which to pay the Frenchman for his services.

That admission resulted in the minister ending up in hospital and Charlie being thrown into what passes as a prison in Algeria. Luckily for him the politician recovered quickly. On his discharge from hospital he insisted that the charges against his assailant be dropped, no doubt to avoid a trial in which the Frenchman would be able to have his say.

In the few days that Charlie and I shared the same dingy cell in that hell-hole of a prison I came both to like and respect him. For a couple of years after our release we kept in touch, visiting each other on a number of occasions, during which time I got to know him well.

"The Human Fly" is how Charlie Le Roux was billed in circuses and theatres across Europe. It was an apt, if somewhat hackneyed, name for a man who could climb the side of a multi storey building as easily as you or I could climb a flight of stairs. The truth was that Charlie's act contradicted the laws of gravity.

The central prop in his act was a thirty foot high wall made from a clear sheet of thick Perspex that was held rigid in its own purpose built frame. To a fanfare Charlie would enter the ring and throw off his cape with a flourish. Without the apparent use of any mechanical aids he would then inch his way up the side of that perfectly smooth and impossible sheer wall. It was magic and the crowds loved it.

But of course it was not magic. I knew Charlie's secret and there was nothing supernatural about it, just incredible skill, strength, stamina, will-power and hard work. Yet although I knew how the Frenchman did his trick, or perhaps because of that knowledge, his incredible climb never ceased to amaze me.

Charlie had once persuaded me to try to climb the Perspex wall. He showed me how to use the tiny almost invisible suction pads that he attached to the tips of my fingers and toes. I tried to climb that damn wall, but it was impossible. I had climbed only four feet before I was in agony. The pain in my toes was not quite as intense as in my finger joints but it was a close run thing. So, with every muscle in my body protesting against the punishment with which it was being inflicted, I gave up.

It was then that I appreciated fully the phenomenal skill of Charlie Le Roux and realised that in his tiny frame he had muscles of steel.

During that couple of years we spent an enjoyable time drinking, whoring and playing cards, but gradually the visits became fewer. I went on to spend most of my time in various trouble spots in the Third World, while Charlie passed his days in the casinos of Europe.

Charlie had always been a lover of card games, but, typical of the man, he scorned the traditional games of chance. Instead he favoured a version of an obscure game of bluff called "cheat", which had been adapted to add elements of both skill and gambling to what otherwise would have been just another parlour game.

The Frenchman, who knew the game as "tricheur", played it with the same dedication and expertise as is shown by the world's finest bridge and poker players. So successful was he that he made more money at cards than he could ever hope to earn in a circus, with less effort and in infinitely more pleasurable surroundings. So he turned his back on the greasepaint and sawdust to become a professional gambler.

Consequently my search for Charlie led me to an imposing three storey building in the South of France. Its luxurious and tastefully decorated interior was home to a very exclusive casino that catered for those super-rich punters who could afford to lose in a night what most French people earn in a year.

The building's ground floor housed the main gaming tables at which wealthy, but casual, gamblers, with more money and unbeatable systems than good sense, helped keep the casino profitable.

The second floor was the domain of the serious high-rollers. It was sub-divided into a number of privately let rooms that allowed privacy and discretion for the privileged few who not only had the necessary pedigree, but also could afford the extortionately high hire charges.

In these rooms fortunes were won and lost in private games of poker, bridge and backgammon. Some sessions lasted days and there were several bedrooms on the third floor of the casino in which players could rest and recharge their batteries.

In one of those private gaming rooms two men were about to begin their game watched by a handful of expectant and silent spectators. I caught Charlie's eye and he excused himself from the table.

'David! What a wonderful surprise. It's been a long time since we last met.' He pronounced my name the French way, but otherwise he spoke perfectly, unaccented English. 'How long is it?'

'Too long, Charlie,' I said as we shook hands.

'So what brings you here to Juan les Pins?'

'You,' I replied with a smile.

'Me? I am intrigued. What can I do for you?'

I glanced over at the card table. 'I'll tell you later. I think your friend is waiting for you.'

'He's no friend of mine,' Charlie said quietly. 'He's just another sucker whose ambition is greater than his ability. Let him wait.'

'Are you still playing cheat?'

'Tricheur, David, please. It sounds so much better. Non?'

'And you are still finding mugs to play with you?' I said, lowering my voice to a whisper.

'The world is full of gullible people, David,' Charlie nodded towards his opponent, who was watching our whispered conversation with an impatient frown on his face. 'Easy come, easy go.'

'I think you'd better start your game,' I said. 'Your friend looks none too happy.'

'If you want to talk…' His voice tailed off as he looked at me with shrewd eyes. 'I can adjourn the game for a while if it is important.'

I shook my head. 'No,' I insisted. 'I'm happy to wait for you. You know how much I like watching a master at work.'

Charlie accepted the compliment with a smile and a Gallic shrug. 'Okay, David, this won't take long.' With that he returned to his seat.

I moved to stand in the shadows at the side of the table, a position that allowed me to see both players and, with a side step in either direction, their respective hands. I studied Charlie's opponent, who I recognised as a well-known German playboy, called Franz Schmidt. He had inherited from his industrialist father the fortune he had accumulated, but none of the old man's capacity for the hard work needed to generate that wealth.

If the many lines printed about the playboy in the gossip columns were right, then he was a weak, arrogant man. His only ambition in life appeared to be squandering his inheritance as quickly as possible while hurting as many people as possible in the process. So far his success rate was high.

As Charlie sat down Schmidt drummed his fingers on the table and stared irritably at him, clearly unaccustomed to being kept waiting.

'Pardon, Herr Schmidt,' the Frenchman apologised, showing no sign that he was intimidated by the hostile stare from the man on the other side of the table. Although Charlie smiled warmly at his opponent, I recognised a cold glint in his eyes that hinted at the ruthlessness that I knew lay just beneath the surface.

Unless I was very much mistaken the German was about to get a real spanking and before the night was much older his family fortune would be weighing a little lighter on his well padded shoulders.

Schmidt balanced a large cigar between his thick lips and snapped his fingers. Immediately an anonymous hand carrying a spluttering match appeared from out of the darkness behind his head. A cloud of smoke billowed across the table towards Charlie's face. Having made his point the German removed the cigar from his mouth and reached for the large balloon glass that stood at his elbow.

The glass contained a good measure of amber coloured liquid, no doubt expensive cognac. As he lifted the glass to his lips the diamond studded links that held together the cuffs of his brilliant white dress-shirt sparkled in the light of the solitary, low-hanging, overhead light. 'Stakes?' The German asked when he had returned his glass to its position on the table.

Charlie shrugged. 'Would a five thousand franc entry suit you?' He asked.

Schmidt nodded his head once in agreement.

'Very well,' Charlie went on, 'five thousand francs to start, five hundred to challenge, five hundred penalty if the call is wrong and the loser of the game doubles the pot. Is that okay?'

Again the German gave a perfunctory nod.

The croupier unwrapped a brand new pack of cards, removed the two jokers, shuffled the cards expertly and placed the pack in front of Schmidt. The two players cut the pack of cards to decide who would lead. Charlie's king of clubs beat his opponent's knave of diamonds. I wondered if that was both symbolic and prophetic.

'Deal,' Schmidt ordered the croupier.

The croupier picked up the pack and quickly shuffled it again and then, almost in the same movement, began to deal. Cards slithered face down across the green baize and clicked into neat piles of thirteen cards in front of the players. The croupier put the remaining cards to one side and positioned the empty card box on top of them so they could not be touched.

In all games of bluff the best players keep an expressionless face in order that opponents get no clue as to the strength of their hand. That Charlie ignored this rule, yet very rarely lost, was testament to his skill. He picked up his cards and sorted them into numerical order in his hand, his lips twitched in a self-satisfied smile. His smile widened into a grin as he caught the eye of the German whose own face was immobile.

Charlie selected two cards from his hand and threw them face down into the centre of the table to nestle up against the two five thousand franc chips that already lay there. 'Two sixes,' he said quietly, staring straight at the cards that remained in his hand.

I looked at Charlie and tried to put myself in the position of Schmidt. Was the Frenchman likely to bluff on the first call of the game? Of course, it was a fifty-fifty chance, and it was highly likely that in the thirteen cards he had been dealt there would be at least one pair. But was he telling the truth or simply trying to get rid of a couple of unwanted cards? I decided the latter was probable, but then had second thoughts. Would that not be exactly what he would expect his opponent to think? I decided then that it was a double bluff. Charlie was hoping his opponent would call him and have to pay for the privilege.

I could see Schmidt weighing up the options. In addition to the 500 francs needed to make the call, he would have to stump up another 500 if he was wrong, and incorporate the two sixes into his own hand. He obviously came to the same conclusion as me because he did not make a challenge. Instead, he carefully withdrew a card from his hand and laid it on the two cards that were already face down on the table. 'One seven,' he said.

No sooner had the words left the German's lips than Charlie threw another two cards onto the pile of cards. 'Two sixes,' he repeated his first call and his sparkling eyes mocked the playboy for his mistake.

Schmidt laid a second card. 'One seven,' he called, confident that this time the Frenchman had laid his two sixes.

'One six,' Charlie said as he sent another card to join the growing pile. Now his expression was deadpan.

The German stared at Charlie, some of his arrogance already gone, replaced by confusion and irritation. His opponent had now claimed to have laid five sixes, which was obviously impossible, so he must have been tempted to challenge him, but again he resisted the temptation. I didn't blame him because if he was wrong he would have to pick up the seven cards already in the centre of the table.

'One five,' Schmidt said, forced by Charlie's tactics to move down the pack in the opposite direction to the one in which he probably wanted to go.

'One six.' The Frenchman responded immediately.

This was one six too many for the German. 'Tricheur!' He spat and reached for his opponent's card to see what he had just laid.

Charlie caught the man's outstretched hand and then smiled as Schmidt looked up him. 'Pardon, monsieur, but it will cost you 500 francs to look at that card.'

The German playboy glared at his opponent and threw a 500 franc chip onto the table to join the two larger chips.

Charlie nonchalantly flipped over the disputed card. It was the six of spades.

'That will cost you another 500 hundred francs, monsieur,' Charlie said softly.

Schmidt parted with another chip before sweeping up the pile of cards and incorporating them into his hand. He looked up and glared at the Frenchman when he discovered that the last card laid was the only six in the cards he had added to his hand.

'One five,' Charlie said as he restarted the game.

'Tricheur!' His opponent exclaimed, remembering how he had been tricked earlier. He irritably flung a chip onto the table only to find he was forced to pick up Charlie's five of diamonds and at the same time boost the pot by a further 500 francs.

'One four,' Charlie continued.

The German challenged again and this time he parted with another two 500 franc chips in exchange for the Charlie's four of clubs.

'Two threes,' the Frenchman said and the grin that accompanied his call challenged his opponent to part with even more of his money.

But Schmidt let the call ride. 'One two,' he called, a determined look had replaced his earlier arrogance on his face. That expression said it all. He was not going to let some jumped up Frenchman make a monkey out of him again.

He was wrong. He was not in the same league as Charlie. Even I could see that he had made a fundamental tactical error. One of the rules of the game was that a player has to declare a card either the same as the preceding card, one higher or one lower. Schmidt should have moved in the opposite direction to the one in which Charlie was heading by calling a four, whether or not he had one, and forced his opponent back up the pack.

'One two,' Charlie said.

The look on the German's face told his own story as he realised both his mistake and the realisation that Charlie had only two cards left in his hand. Now he had a real problem. Should he move back up to threes, and take the risk that the Frenchman had another two, or should he challenge and perhaps give his opponent an opportunity to move further down the scale. Eventually he made up his mind and it cost him another 1,000 francs. 'Tricheur,' he mumbled, already sensing that defeat was close.

I watched as Schmidt turned over Charlie's two of clubs. All that was needed was for the Frenchman to administer the coup-de-grace. Knowing my friend I guessed there would be a sting in the tail. I was not disappointed.

Charlie theatrically shuffled the two cards in his hand and

laid them both face down on the table in front of him. He tapped each in turn several times and then he shrugged and pushed one of the cards into the middle of the table. 'One ace,' his voice was resigned.

I tried not to smile.

The German stared at the table in desperation. He looked first at the card that lay in front of Charlie, then at the one in the centre of the table. Finally, he looked at the pile of chips in the pot. It totalled 14,000 francs. A line of perspiration dotted across his forehead. He took a handkerchief from his breast pocket and dabbed it away. Picking up a chip he weighed it carefully in his hand. Suddenly he tossed it to join with a clatter the other chips. 'Tricheur!' He said as he hurriedly turned over the Frenchman's card. It was the ace of hearts.

Schmidt threw another chip into the pot. But despite the loss a defiant smile flickered across his lips. He obviously thought he still had a chance. I took a step to my left and saw that he had all four kings in his hand and all four twos.

With his next call the Frenchman could not go up and he could not go down. If the German played his cards right he could make it very difficult, and very expensive, for his opponent to get rid of his last card.

I could see that Schmidt was calculating in which direction it was best to move when his turn to play came, as inevitably it must. Logic dictated that he should force the play back up through the twos, threes and fours that he now held in abundance. I could read all this in the German's face and he was still working out his options when Charlie picked up his last card and looked at it and stared at it intently.

The Frenchman's face was equally easy to read. He was wondering how best he could force Schmidt to head in the direction he wanted. With another expressive shrug Charlie flicked the card onto the table. 'One ace,' he said quietly.

That was the obvious call for the Frenchman to make in the circumstances and the German did not even look up as he threw a chip into the pot and said: 'Tricheur!' He was still studying his cards, still working out how best to get back into the game. Finally, he decided which way to move. He selected his four twos and was about to lay them on the table when with a shock he saw that Charlie's card was lying face up on the green baize. It was the ace of spades.

The Frenchman's smile was not without sympathy. 'I'm afraid you owe the pot another sixteen thousand five hundred francs, monsieur.'

Two hours later Charlie left the table 80,000 francs better off. He winked at me and smiled. 'Come on, David. Let's go down to the lounge where we can talk in private. We will order a bottle of champagne. It's on Franz!'

'How on earth do you get away with it, Charlie?' I asked when we were seated in the lounge.

'I don't know what you mean,' he replied with a grin as he poured us both a glass of Bollinger and replaced the bottle in the silver ice bucket that stood on the floor beside his chair.

'How do you manage to con people into playing that stupid game with you?'

'Stupid game?' He laughed. 'Do I detect a hint of jealousy in my friend's voice?'

'Yes.'

He laughed again. 'The answer is quite simple, David. It is a mixture of old fashioned boredom and competitiveness.' He raised his glass. 'And thank God for both!' He sipped his champagne before adding: 'The people who play me, David, are fed up with the traditional gambling games and are looking for new and different ways in which to amuse themselves. I willingly provide that alternative amusement.'

'Herr Schmidt did not find it very amusing.'

'Oh, he will get over it and I am no doubt he will want to play again. You see there is a race under way amongst the glitterati to see who can beat me first. That is where the competitiveness comes in. I understand one million US dollars have been wagered on the outcome.' Charlie preened himself as he spoke. 'One or two people have come close to beating me and no doubt someday it will happen, but I will not be beaten by poor old Franz.'

He drank more of his Champagne and smiled. 'He will never make a good tricheur player. His mind is too inflexible and is unable to adjust his strategy quickly. No, I think our German friend would be wiser sticking to baccarat or the roulette wheel, where he will not have to think too deeply.' He smiled and pulled the bottle of Bollinger from the ice bucket and topped up our glasses. 'So tell me, David, what do you want with me?'

'I have an operation lined up in South Africa,' I explained what we were planning, without mentioning the involvement of the

152

CIA.

'And what would be my role?' He asked.

'Are you still as fit as you were,' I asked, 'or has all this good living turned you soft?'

Charlie pretended to look hurt. 'Of course I'm fit, David. Don't be fooled by all this,' he waved at the expensive décor in the room. 'I can assure you that I visit the gym every day.'

'And what about your wall climbing?'

'I am still the best.'

I smiled. Charlie had never been short of confidence. 'Good, because it is climbing we want you to do.'

'Who is we?'

I told him the names of the other members of the team and he nodded in satisfaction.

'Good men,' he said and drained his glass. He stood up and held out his hand. 'Do you know, David, I think a break away from, what did you call it? The good living?'

I accepted his hand. 'Yes, that's what I called it.'

'Well, to tell the truth I am getting rather bored. I think a break away from the good living is just what I need, so, yes, I would like to join your team very much. When do we leave?'

I took an envelope from my jacket pocket and showed it to him. 'This is an airline ticket to South Africa.'

'In my name of course,' he said with a grin.

'Of course,' I handed the envelope to him. 'Your Air France flight leaves Charles De Gaulle at twenty-three hundred hours tomorrow.' I explained, as we walked to the casino's ornate front double doors. 'You fly to Johannesburg and then catch a connecting flight to Cape Town where Paul will be waiting for you at the airport. I'll join you on Wednesday.'

We shook hands again at the top of the marble steps that led down to the casino's forecourt. I watched as Charlie headed for the white convertible Rolls Royce that had just drawn up in the forecourt. A car park attendant got out and opened the driver's door for him. The discreet transfer of a tip from the Frenchman's hand to that of the attendant was as smooth and seamless as his slide into the driver's seat of the roller. With a semi-regal wave he gunned the engine and swept out of the forecourt. Classy.

I smiled to myself as I headed towards my own hotel. My team was complete. I had recruited a group of men I could trust with my life. That they reciprocated my trust was highlighted by the fact that not one of them had asked how much he would be paid. Each knew without asking that I would have obtained the best possible deal for them.

As I made my way out of the casino's front gate a tall figure staggered out of the shadows and bumped into me. I could smell cheap brandy on the balmy night air as the stranger tried to stop himself from collapsing by wrapping one of his arms round my shoulders and the other round my waist. I pushed him away and he stumbled off towards the sea.

'Sorry, pal,' I heard him mumble.

As I walked down the Chemin des Sables towards Avenue Sainte Valerie I did not once look back at the drunk. I had no need. I knew who he was because I had recognised his voice.

When I arrived back in my hotel room I pulled the curtains and switched on the light. I found Hank Graham's note in the right hand pocket of my jacket. It was short and to the point: *31 Allée des Mouettes. Come tonight.*

Allée des Mouettes was within walking distance of my hotel, but it still took half an hour to get there. It was gone midnight before I found the ground floor *pied-à-terre* that displayed a white metal sign with the number 31 on it in blue letters.

Parked in the road outside the house was a white Chrysler Cordoba with a green registration plate, on which the number 206 CD 601 was printed in yellow figures. The car belonged to a member of the US diplomatic corps.

31 Allée des Mouettes was in darkness and there was no sign of life. I tried the front door but it was locked. On the right hand side of the house was an archway that gave access to a dark alley. I slipped through the archway and waited until my eyes became accustomed to the lack of light.

Close by an owl hooted and I heard the gentle swishing sound of a car as it drove along the road behind me. About twenty feet up the alley on the left hand side I could see an oblong patch that was darker than the rest of the wall. I guessed it was a door.

I edged along the alley until I reached the door. It was open. I waited a full five minutes, listening for the slightest sound from inside the building, but I heard nothing. Cautiously I stepped into the house and found myself in a narrow corridor at the end of which I could see a second door. I gingerly tiptoed up the corridor, holding my breath in case one of the floorboards squeaked.

154

I pressed my ear against the door and listened, but there was no sound from the room beyond. I turned the handle silently and pushed the door open and found myself in a kitchen. Directly in front of me was a modern cooking range, while to my right was a table with a window above it through which the moon shone, providing what light there was in the kitchen. I looked through the window and saw a starlit sky and the outline of a tree. I wondered whether the owl was perched on one of the tree's branches.

On my left there were a couple of kitchen floor units, above which were matching wall cupboards. To the right of the units was another door. It was slightly ajar. I edged towards the door, but froze when I heard light footsteps on the other side and the sound of something being dragged across the floor.

Whatever it was, the "something" sounded heavy. Heavy enough to be a sack of potatoes or a dead body. The footsteps stopped and I heard the distinctive sound of a key being turned in a lock and a bolt being drawn across. Then I heard nothing more because a blow from behind knocked me senseless.

When I came to, I was stretched out on the tiled kitchen floor. I lay for a while with my eyes closed, playing dead, but listening. There was no sound of life in the house, although somewhere in the distance I could hear a police siren. I opened my eyes and could see that both kitchen doors were closed.

I staggered to my feet and lowered my head in the hope this would ease the pain that shot through the back of my skull as I stood up, but it did nothing to help. I opened the kitchen door through which I had come and made my way back to the outer door. It came as no surprise to find it was locked and there was no key in the lock. I returned to the kitchen, went to the window and closed the blinds. I found a light switch and turned it on.

At some time the walls of the kitchen had been painted brilliant white, but now they would need to be repainted. The wall by the window was splattered with red liquid, as was the kitchen table. I touched the discoloured table top with my finger and when I looked at the tip it was wet. The liquid was blood and it was fresh. Beneath the table was a pool of blood in which lay a man's left shoe.

Now the light was on I could see there was a streak of blood running across the length of the kitchen floor, leading from the table to the door that had been ajar. Cautiously I opened the door, although I was pretty sure I was alone in the house.

Beyond the door was a hallway that led to the front door, which I just knew would be locked and bolted. I was not disappointed. I quickly checked out the rest of the house, but there was no sign of anybody, not even a dead body.

The police siren was getting closer.

I returned to the back door and sized it up. The lock did not look very substantial. I went back to the kitchen and rummaged about in the drawers. I could have kicked the door down, but I decided it would be quieter to unscrew the lock with the screwdriver I found in one of the drawers. A couple of minutes later I was back in the alley and making my way towards the street beyond.

I stopped in the shadows of the archway and peered up Allée des Mouettes. A police car came tearing round the corner from Chemin du Crouton and raced, with its siren blaring and its blue light flashing, towards where I was hidden.

I moved further back into the alley and instinctively held my breath. I have no idea why I did that, because the cops were never going to hear me breathing.

The blue light went flashing past the entrance of the alley and the car disappeared in the direction of Avenue du Soleil Saramartel.

I let out a sigh of relief and stepped out onto the pavement of Allée des Mouettes and noticed that the white Chrysler Cordoba with the US diplomatic plates was gone.

I headed back to my hotel deep in thought. As appeared to be the norm these days, I had a number of questions to which I had no answers. For instance; I hadn't told anybody that I was going to Juan Les Pins to look for Charlie, so how did Hank Graham know where to find me?

Then there was the matter of the mystery person who had coshed me in the house in Allée des Mouettes and given me the headache that was currently making it difficult to concentrate on all these questions. Was my attacker Hank Graham and had it been him driving the US Government Cordoba that had been parked outside the house?

Another question I pondered over was what had happened to the owner of the expensive leather shoe with fashionable leather tassels that I had found in the pool of blood under the kitchen table? Had the man wearing that shoe been killed?

However, there was one thing of which I was pretty sure. The last time I had seen that particular shoe it was being worn by Joe Welensky on a lock bridge next to a pub on the River Medway in

Kent.

Monday May 3rd 1982: Allington

I had spent my journey from the South of France trying to make some sense out of what had happened in Juan Les Pain. I was still thinking about the left shoe with the leather tassels as I pulled off the M20 and headed towards the same pub by the river where I had last seen its owner.

When I arrived at the pub I found it closed, so I headed for the side door that led to Billy Neal's private quarters. I pressed the bell and did not have long to wait before the ex-boxer opened the door and ushered me up the stairs to his neat and tidy flat.

This was the second time I had visited him within the past few days. He had the same bottle of whisky perched on the coffee table that stood between the two armchairs in which we sat, although it was now only half full.

'Drink?' It was a rhetorical question because Billy didn't wait for an answer before tipping a generous measure of whisky into the two glasses that stood alongside the bottle.

I wondered whether the table ever saw any coffee. Probably not. 'Thanks,' I said and meant it. My head still ached and I hoped the whisky would help dull the pain.

'How did your trip to the smoke go?' Billy asked.

I had popped down to see Billy before my meeting with Mr Mac and had mentioned to him that I was visiting London. I smiled at him and picked up my glass. 'Cheers!' I said as we clinked glasses. 'You know better than to ask, Billy,' I added.

He grinned. 'Always worth trying, Dave.'

'Did you find out anything about Carsons?' I asked.

'Yeah, but I had to get my boy to pull a few strings,' he replied.

'Thank him for me. Tell him that someday I'll return the favour.'

'Kev don't want nothing, Dave, he knows what you done for me. My family owes you big time.'

I shrugged. I had done no more than ensure that the thug who raped and murdered Billy's wife received the death sentence he deserved. A punishment he would never have received if he had been dealt with by Britain's criminal justice system.

'You've already repaid that debt several times over, Billy,' I pointed out quietly. 'I'll ensure Kevin is rewarded in a way that will not embarrass him. I too have a number of powerful contacts who owe me a favour.'

He nodded his thanks.

'Major Percival Carsons?' I asked. 'Does he exist?'

'Oh, yes, he exists alright. Well he used to.'

'What do you mean?'

Billy stood up and walked over to a sideboard that stood against the wall. He opened a drawer and took out a black and white photograph. He sat back down and handed the photo to me. 'That's your Percy Carsons, Dave. What do you think?'

The man who looked up at me from the photograph with shrewd eyes was young and dark haired. He wore an army dress uniform with major's crowns on his shoulder epaulettes and his peaked cap carried the badge of the Royal Signals.

I had no doubt it was a photograph of Major Carsons, the problem was that the man in photo bore no resemblance to the Carsons to whom Billy had introduced me.

'That photo was taken about ten years ago,' Billy explained. 'Shortly afterwards Carsons disappeared in East Berlin.'

'East Berlin?'

'Yeah. Kev reckons Percy was working undercover. It appears he was helping to set up a communications network for an opposition group in East Germany.'

'He was a spy?'

'Seems that way.'

I looked at the photo again and tried to turn the face into the Percival Carsons I knew. 'Plastic surgery?' I asked, thinking out loud, but dismissing the suggestion immediately.

'Impossible,' Billy said, answering my question anyway. 'Not unless plastic surgeons, in addition to giving somebody a new face, have mastered the trick of resurrection.'

'You mean the real Percival Carsons is dead?'

'Yeah, as dead as a bleeding dodo. His body was handed back to the military a few months after he disappeared. The Stasis said that he committed suicide in his prison cell.' Billy finished off his drink. 'I understand the body weren't a pretty sight,' he added as he replenished his glass and then went to do the same to mine.

I put a hand over my glass to stop him. 'I'm driving,' I said.

'You can stay here if you like,' he offered. 'I've a spare room you can use.'

I thought about the drive back to London and the soulless hotel room into which I was booked. It was too good an offer to turn down. I took my hand away. 'Pour away,' I said.

We finished off the bottle of whisky chatting about old times and eventually I got to bed just after midnight. Late nights were becoming a habit, but at least my headache had eased, no doubt thanks to Mr Teacher.

Despite the effects of the whisky, which had increased my tiredness, it took me some time getting to sleep. I laid awake staring at the ceiling and wondered about the real identity of the fake Major Percival Carsons and how he had managed to wheedle himself into Rogers' team.

Carol Du Toit

Wednesday May 5th 1982: Mondeor, Johannesburg

Carol Du Toit moaned with ecstasy as she felt Robert's hands kneading her breasts. She enjoyed the way the black man treated her as his chattel, commanding her and taking her to heights of sensuality she had never reached with any other lover.

For instance, she relished the way he used his tongue on the inside of her thighs until she became so aroused she begged him to fill her. That was when he would finally take her, pushing himself inside her, slamming into her until she thought she would die from the ecstasy of it.

He took her in so many ways, using her body as his own sex tool, twisting her this way and that, finding all her erogenous zones. He did to her things that her husband would never even think of and she loved it. She looked up at Robert now and caressed his wet chest. 'Take me from behind,' she urged.

Robert rolled her over so that she was kneeling on his narrow bed. He poised over her and thrust into her. With a sharp intake of breath and another moan she climaxed immediately, but the man kept pounding into her until she climaxed again and again. With a final scream, she collapsed on her stomach with his weight bearing down on her back.

Carol stared down at the floor and in that state of semi-stupor that always followed these sex sessions she noticed that many of the floor tiles were cracked and stained. She made a mental note to get her husband to redecorate the room.

Gerald would be back from his latest business trip by the weekend and he was then due to be at home on holiday for a week. Decorating the room would keep him out of her way. It would also give Robert a nice surprise when he returned from wherever he was going.

Carol felt the gardener slide off her. She rolled over quickly and clung to him, not letting him leave her yet.

'You will come back, won't you?'

'Yes,' he assured her.

She looked into his eyes and she believed him.

Preparations

John Brandon met me at D.F. Malan Airport with the Avis hire car, a handshake and a lopsided grin. It had been thirteen days since my previous arrival in the Cape.

Thirteen days of travel during which time I had covered thirty thousand miles in eleven different planes while visiting three continents. I had stayed in five hotels, been body searched four times, and tipped half a dozen waitresses, three porters and sixteen cab drivers.

In addition, I was sworn at in Paris by one of the cabbies who was unhappy with the tip he was given. In Brixton it was by a glazed-eyed prostitute who was upset when I turned down her offer of a good time. In Los Angeles it was by a little old lady with a blue rinse who became abusive when I nudged her dog with the toe of my foot. She did not seem to understand that I did not like it cocking its leg to pee up my suitcase.

All in all I was pleased to be back in South Africa, despite the weather that greeted me at the airport. The southeasterly I faced when I arrived in the Cape a couple of weeks before had given way to a wind that gusted down from the northwest. It brought with it a driving rain that hammered onto the roofs of the parked cars with the sound of a demented steel band.

Before John and I reached our car we were both soaked through to the skin. He started the engine and warmed it up before heading out of the car park. He put the heater on full blast and soon the inside of the car was as hot and steamy as a sauna. It was not very comfortable but I was past caring. Shattered, and with my body clock thinking a spring had snapped, I settled back into my seat and relaxed.

I felt reasonably satisfied. Everything was on schedule and moving along nicely to plan. But I did not allow myself the luxury of complacency. There was still a long way to go and I had a great deal more to do. One of my first jobs would be to make contact with Freddie to get a message to her father. The thought of seeing her again was not unappealing, but first I had business in Clovelly.

I stared out of the windscreen and watched the rain pour down. It swept in from Table Bay and across the Cape Peninsula in a deluge. It was thickened into a blinding curtain of spray by the water splashing up from the wheels of the steady flow of cars that thundered along the R3 Motorway that led in and out of Cape Town.

The conditions were not conducive to speed so John kept our car to just under the legal 60km per hour. We were regularly overtaken by speeding vehicles driven by motorists with an apparent death wish. Indeed, the only other driver that night keeping to the speed limit was behind the wheel of the car I could see in the nearside wing mirror, which had settled into position a couple of hundred yards behind us.

It was a big car with large headlamps set wide apart, which the car's driver had switched on, no doubt to combat the gathering gloom. I had first noticed it as we joined the R3 at Mowbray, but I didn't make a song and dance about it. John didn't seem to notice the car, but why should he? After all, the driver had every right to be on the same road as us, moving in the same direction, at the same speed.

It was dark when we reached the end of the motorway that eventually would link up with the scenic drive that bypasses St James and along which I had driven with Freddie two weeks earlier. For now the unfinished motorway ended in a sudden profusion of metal barriers and giant boulders.

We turned onto the R5 and made our way through Lakeside, the first of False Bay's coastal communities. The yellow street lamps that lined the flooded road were distorted into kaleidoscope patterns across the car's windscreen as the wipers swish-swished rainwater across the glass.

At the junction with Boyes Drive we took the left hand fork along the lower road that runs parallel with the Simon's Town to Cape Town railway line. The mystery car took the right hand fork and disappeared from sight. I told myself its presence behind us for so long had been a coincidence, but I wasn't convinced. I couldn't get out of my mind the thought that Mercedes-Benz 300Ds are big cars with large headlamps set wide apart.

Soon we reached Kalk Bay. Through the lashing rain I could see the two warning lights at the mouth of the tiny harbour. They winked out their red and green message to any fisherman foolhardy enough to be still out at sea on such a night. Two minutes later we drew up outside the garage of our rented house in Clovelly.

Our friends must have been watching out for us because one of the doors swung open even before the car had stopped. Paul Helsdon stood in the shelter of the garage, his big frame silhouetted by the bright light thrown by the twin fluorescent tubes that hung from the ceiling, with his head almost touching the lintel of the door frame. Standing at his side was the diminutive figure of Charlie Le Roux.

John edged the car up onto the pavement and onto the plot of waste land that adjoined the garage. He parked next to a dirty-white Toyota pick-up truck, the open back of which was slowly collecting a pool of rain water.

I pushed open the car door and was immediately hit by the full force of the rain that pelted down. Behind us a car cruised up the road with a hiss of spray. It was a big Mercedes with dark paintwork. I couldn't see its actual colour because my eyes had difficulty seeing through the stinging rain that lashed my face, but I would not have bet a bent penny against the car being bottle-green.

I swore quietly to myself. Who the hell did the car belong to? My first thought was that it was the security police, but I dismissed that idea almost immediately. If the South African National Intelligence Service was onto us, we would have been picked up already. Those boys tended to act first and ask questions later.

Paul saw the car too and raised an eyebrow at me. I shook my head imperceptibly and shrugged. There was no point in making a big thing of it just yet. We would just have to be careful, try to find out who was following us and then, if necessary, do something about it.

John and I joined our two friends and shook hands with them. I was pleased to get into the shelter of the garage, which was no longer empty. One half of the building was taken up by a battered looking seven and a half ton Mercedes 407D box van.

The radiator of the van rested against the long wooden workbench and the rear bumper was almost flush with the garage door that Paul had now swung shut. It was a tight fit with the roof of the truck only around an inch away from the wooden ceiling beams, which with the wrong manoeuvre threatened to gouge even more scratches into its white paintwork.

'I decided on a second hand van,' Paul explained. 'I thought it would attract less attention than a new vehicle.'

'Second hand?' I peeled a flaking piece of paintwork away

from the side of the van's diver's cab. 'If that van has been owned by less than half a dozen people I'm a Dutch uncle.'

'But it was cheap,' Paul protested with a grin.

'I should hope so.'

'Look, it has four good tyres,' Paul said patting one of the wheels. 'They're almost new.'

'Great, we might break down on the motorway, but at least we won't get a puncture,' I said.

'Show him the engine, John,' Paul said.

The American vaulted up into the cab and pulled on the starter. With a rumble of exhaust pipe that rattled the garage door, the diesel engine fired first time and pounded into life.

I was satisfied. 'Okay, turn it off,' I shouted and slapped on the side of the van before we were all overcome by exhaust fumes. I turned to Paul as the engine spluttered and died. 'It'll do. What else have we got?'

'Well there's the bakkie outside,' the big South African replied as John jumped lightly from the cab of the van and re-joined us.

'That looks pretty beat up too. Did you buy it at the same place?'

'No. I thought it might be remembered if I bought both vehicles in the same place so I got the bakkie from a little garage in Plumstead.'

It made sense.

'I know the bakkie doesn't look much but it goes like a bomb.'

I nodded my approval. 'What about the motor cycles. Did you manage to get them?'

'Yeah. I found a dealer in Newlands.'

'Are they in the same condition as the van?'

'John's done them up a treat,' Paul said with a grin, sidestepping my question.

I turned to the American. 'Are they okay, John?' I asked. 'Those bikes have to get us a long way.'

'Don't worry, Dave. He's messing with you. Those goddamn machines are barely shop soiled. They could get you all the way from here to Cairo.'

'That's a relief,' I said, 'because they might have to.'

'As for the van and the pick-up truck,' John went on. 'Don't worry about their appearance. I was with Paul when he bought both and I checked them over real good. They're both as sound as a bell.'

'Where are the bikes?' I asked, looking round the garage.

'In here,' Paul replied, sliding the side door of the van across so that I could peer inside. He leaned across me and flicked a switch and immediately the interior of the van was lit up.

I could see the shiny chrome or three Kawasaki 500 motorcycles. The bikes were stood upright, each with its front wheel chained to a metal rack that had been bolted to the van's floor. The two outer bikes had been tied with heavy canvass straps to metal struts set into the sides of the van. John was right; all three bikes looked brand new.

I guessed that at some time the vehicle had been used as a small removal van. It was certainly large enough. Even allowing for the motorcycles there was still more than enough room for the rest of our equipment. It was obvious they had chosen the van with care. I would have expected nothing less. I was well satisfied.

The other half of the garage was taken up by something covered by a large tarpaulin sheet.

'Is that the boats?' I asked.

Paul didn't answer, instead he motioned for John to help him and between them they pulled back the tarpaulin to reveal two Suzuki ski-boats. Each one sat in a shiny black transporter, complete with tow-bar, and with an outboard motor attached to its stern.

Charlie stared at the boats and then at me. He did not look happy.

'You didn't mention we were using boats, David,' he said.

'Did I not?'

'No.'

'It must have slipped my mind,' I said with a smile. I knew he disliked sea travel, but I knew also that he would never let his dislike of water affect any operation in which he was involved. Charlie, like the rest of my team, was the consummate professional. 'I take it this is the first time you've seen the boats.' I remarked. 'I thought Paul might have shown them to you already.'

'Sorry, but I didn't think to do that and we've been pretty busy,' the South African said. 'Is there a problem, Charlie?'

'I'm not good with water,' the Frenchman explained. 'I get the mal de mer just crossing the Seine. Is there no other way we can reach the island?' He directed this last question at me.

'I'm afraid not,' I said.

'Can we not fly in?' He asked. 'I thought there was an airstrip on Robben Island.

'There is,' I confirmed, impressed that Charlie had done some research into the island. 'But a plane would be detected long before we landed and we'd lose the element of surprise we'll need if we are going to break into the prison with minimum resistance.'

'What about parachutes?' Charlie persisted.

I shook my head. 'Think about it. How would we get off the island?'

Silently Charlie nodded his acceptance of my logic, but he did not look any happier. He tapped the side of one boat with his knuckle. 'I hope these aren't second hand, Paul. I'd hate them to fall apart in the middle of the Atlantic Ocean.'

'We're not visiting the middle of any ocean, Charlie.' Paul said with a chuckle. 'We'll be taking a nice gentle trip across Table Bay.' He caressed the fibreglass side of the boat with the palm of one big hand. 'Relax, these boats are just like the bikes. Brand spanking new and a bargain to boot. The normal price for one of these beauties is plus or minus sixteen hundred bucks. I got the pair for two grand.'

'They're probably factory rejects,' Charlie said and then made a point of studying the boat's hull for cracks or defects.

'Not at all,' Paul assured the Frenchman. 'As it happens they were cheap because they were bankrupt stock.' He grinned at Charlie. 'Anyway,' he added, 'there's nothing to worry about because even if your boat sinks you won't drown.'

'Why?'

'Because the sharks will eat you first!'

We all laughed including Charlie, who had switched his attention to three large wooden crates that stood on the floor in the corner. 'And these?' He asked. 'What do they contain?'

'Go-karts,' John replied.

'Go-karts?' Charlie's face lit up. 'Can I open a crate?'

'Of course,' John said handing him a screwdriver. 'We haven't had chance to check them out yet,' he explained to me. 'Paul only collected them from the dealer this morning.'

'What's the fuel capacity of the boats?' I asked.

'Twenty five litres, which should be enough for our purpose,' he answered. He turned to John, 'As one colonial to another that's about five gallons,' he explained with a grin.

John grinned back. 'Listen, buddy. I might be a colonial, but I know what a litre is!'

'Perhaps we should put a spare jerry can full of petrol in each boat, just in case,' Charlie suggested as he worked the screwdriver under the lid of the crate.

'Good idea,' I said, before asking John: 'Did Paul explain about the need to muffle the sound of the motors?'

'Yeah. No hassle. See that cowl?' He pointed at the top of the outboard motor. ''It's made of insulated fibre-glass that's specially designed to deaden the sound of the motor. All I have to do is build a second cowl, large enough to fit over the original, like an overcoat. See?' He motioned with his hands.

I saw.

'By the time I've finished with those motors,' he went on. 'You won't be able to hear them until the boats are right on top of you. Of course, the downside is that we'll lose some power and speed because we'll have to cut back on the gas to avoid overheating.'

'That won't be a problem as long as we can get the cowls off quickly and easily,' I said. 'Speed won't be as importance as silence on the way over to the island, however, we'll need as much speed as possible on the way back when silence won't matter.'

'Don't worry,' John assured me. 'I'll fit the muffle-boxes on with a couple of metal clips. They'll slip off in a second.'

Charlie had finally prised open the lid of the crate. 'Wow!' He exclaimed, the sparkle in his eyes showed that the go-kart was more to his liking than the ski-boats. 'How many of these beauties do we have?'

'Three,' I replied. 'There's one in each crate. Here let me give you a hand.'

'Okay, so what are they for?' Charlie asked after I had helped him lift the Lynx go-kart out of the crate and onto the floor. 'Are we setting up a race circuit?'

'No, we'll be using them once we reach Robben Island. Don't worry, I'll explain all later.' I turned back to John. 'These karts need to be modified too. For a start I'd like a light aluminium frame fitted that stretches from this back strut here,' I pointed to the rear of the Lynx's sturdy chassis, 'arches up over the top of the kart, and joins to this strut at the front. Let me show you.' I picked up a pencil and a scrap of paper from the bench and drew a primitive diagram of my idea on it. 'Can you do it?'

The American studied the drawing for a couple of minutes. 'Yeah,' he said, 'but I'll need some aluminium tubing and a spot welding kit.'

'We can get the tubing from the electrical wholesaler in Cape Town,' Paul suggested.

I remembered something I had seen during our last visit to the city. 'And I know just the place to buy welding equipment. I think it was in Adderley Street. Do you remember, Paul? We took a short-cut to get to the bank.'

'Yes. It was in the OK Bazaars. There was a guy demonstrating a welding set. I think it was called Easiweld or something. But he might not still be there.'

'Well it's worth having a look,' I said. 'Why don't you and John check it out tomorrow?'

'That suits me fine,' Paul said. 'I have to go into Cape Town to collect the two rubber dinghies we need from the boat wholesaler.'

'Does the wholesaler stock covers to go with dinghies?' I asked.

'Ja, I already thought about that,' Paul confirmed. 'I ordered them at the same time as the dinghies.'

I turned back to John. 'There's something else,' I went on. 'I'd like a small platform fitted to the back of each kart.' I added a few more lines to my drawing. 'It needs to be strong enough for a man to stand on. Can you do that?'

The American ran the palm of his hand across jowls that were dark with stubble as he stared at the drawing. 'Yeah. That shouldn't be a problem. Anything else?'

'One last thing. Can you do something to silence the sound of the kart engines? Perhaps fit something similar to the muffle-boxes you're proposing for the outboard motors?'

'I can make a box to fit over the engine similar to those for the boats. In addition I can make a metal sheath with a pinched end to fit over the exhaust pipe. But remember, as with the outboard motors, we'll lose some power and speed.'

'That's not a problem. As with the boats, speed won't matter as long as the silencers are easily removable. It's just under a mile to the prison from the cove where we'll be landing. Using karts we should be able to cover that distance before the guards know what's hit them, just as long as they don't hear us coming.'

'No worries, Dave,' John said with a smile. 'Nobody within a few yards of us is going to hear the karts and the muffle-boxes and exhaust silencers will come off just like that.' He snapped his fingers. 'Now, what about a drink?'

Paul led us out of the garage and we made our way out into the pouring rain and up the tiered garden to the house. By the time we arrived I was wet through again.

Mr Mac was in the kitchen preparing a pot of bubbling soup. His face was flushed red by the heat from the stove. He stopped stirring long enough to shake my hand. 'Good evening, Mister Statton. Ye look a wee bit damp, so ye do. Away with ye to yon lounge where I've set a fire. I'll fetch through some broth in a wee while.'

'That sounds good, Mister Mac, but first Paul and I have a couple of jobs to do.' I turned to Charlie and John. 'You go through to the lounge. We'll join you later.'

Paul and I stepped outside into the wet blustery night and headed for the servant's quarters. He unlocked the door and switched on the light. The room was empty except for the pile of logs and the faded picture of Louis Armstrong.

'It worked out okay, then?' I asked.

In answer Paul made a circle with his thumb and forefinger.

'How many rows down?'

'Two.'

Without another word I helped Paul remove the top two layers of logs until a wooden lid was revealed some three feet above floor level. The lid was four foot six inches long and two foot six inches wide.

I knew these dimensions because I had helped design the wooden chest of which the lid was part. The double stack of logs had been carefully arranged to camouflage the chest. At each end of the lid was a coarse rope handle and with my help Paul easily lifted it and laid it on the floor.

I examined the inside of the chest, which eventually would be home to all the weapons, ammunition and explosives that we would need for our operation, but which was currently empty except for five small packages. I lifted one out and unwrapped it to reveal a waterproof holster containing a Star PD .45 automatic pistol.

'Good job with the chest,' I said as I weighed the pistol in my hand.

'It was nothing,' Paul said modestly.

'So when will the rest of the weapons and explosives arrive?'

I asked.

For the first time Paul's cheerful expression disappeared to be replaced by a frown. 'I'm not sure. When Dyakala delivered the pistols all he said was that he'd be in touch again when the other stuff was ready to be shipped. I wasn't happy, but I had to accept his word. I had no other option.'

'Did you pay him?' I asked.

'Ja. He insisted on cash up front for the whole shipment.' His frown deepened. 'Can we trust him, Dave?' He asked.

I thought about that for a while as I studied the pistol. Made in Spain from an aluminium alloy the Star .45 weighed just over 700 grams and was considerably lighter than the Colt .45 on which the Spanish had modelled their version. It was smaller too, which made it easier to conceal. 'Yes,' I said eventually. 'We can trust him. Robert will deliver. Did you tell him when we needed the shipment by?'

'Ja and he assured me that we would definitely get the goods in time.'

Suddenly the rain increased in intensity and we stood listening to it bouncing off the corrugated roof of the little building like hailstones. Perhaps it was hailstones. The racket highlighted our own silence.

I took the Star apart, laying its parts in a line on the oilskin packaging in which it had been wrapped and which now lay across the double row of logs that covered the front of the chest.

'So what do you reckon about our friend in the green Merc?' Paul asked lightly, as if it was not important, but the frown remained on his face.

'I don't know. Special Branch?' I suggested.

'I think not,' he said without hesitation.

'No? Why not?'

'Because, if Special Branch were on to us they wouldn't bother with a tail, they'd simply pick us up, proof or no proof.'

'That's what I think,' I agreed, pleased that Paul had come to the same conclusion. 'And the same goes for the NIS.'

'Too right, Dave. Those okes don't worry about the niceties of civil liberties, hey. If they had the slightest suspicion we were planning an operation, we would already be in Pollsmoor. So if it isn't Special Branch or NIS watching us, who the hell is it?'

I shook my head thoughtfully. 'A coincidence, perhaps?' I suggested.

'No, man. It's no coincidence. That bloody car turns up everywhere.'

'Did you see the car while I was away?'

'Well I think it tailed us when I took you to the airport for your flight to the States and I'm pretty sure I saw it the day I flew up to Jo'burg to meet your friend. That would have been April 29th. But I didn't see it again until yesterday.'

'You saw it yesterday?'

'Ja.'

'Did you see the driver?'

'No, he's far too clever for that. He never came close enough to get a good look at his face. Actually, yesterday I tried to catch him out.'

I raised an eyebrow at him.

'Ja, I know it was stupid of me, but that oke was really pissing me off, Dave. I was heading into Cape Town last night and the Merc was sitting on my tail. Just before Lakeside I diverted along the coast road, which was deserted except for the two of us.

'Just past Muizenberg I accelerated and opened up a wider gap, then suddenly I pulled the car round in a U-turn and headed back towards him.' He paused and shook his head. 'Dave, I swear to you that oke was no more than three or four hundred yards behind me, yet by the time I reached the spot where I had last seen his headlights the car had disappeared.'

'A professional?'

'Damn right.'

'He obviously pulled off the road.'

'Ja, probably into the sand dunes that line the road, but I didn't hang around to check.'

'So he knows we're on to him, whoever he is.'

'Ja, but it doesn't appear to have fazed him, because he was stalking us again today.'

'That's why I think he's a pro.'

'So what are we going to do about the son of a bitch?'

I didn't reply. Instead, I flexed my fingers and then quickly reassembled the Star. I slammed a magazine into the butt of the pistol and took up the marksman's classic two handed stance. I was ready to blast a hole in Louis Armstrong's head.

'Six seconds.' Paul said with a grin. 'You haven't lost your touch.'

I still said nothing, but I was pleased.

171

'So, do we take him out?' Paul asked.

'Of course, the driver could be a woman,' I pointed out.

'Is that really what you think?' He asked.

I shook my head. 'Instinct tells me that it's a man,' I replied. 'But instinct often lies.'

'So do we take him out?' Paul repeated.

'Not yet. He could be somebody sent by Rogers to keep an eye on his investment.' I said and immediately Percival Carsons sprang to mind.

'Or it could be the Reds,' Paul said.

I thought about that suggestion for a few minutes, but shrugged the idea aside, not because I did not consider Soviet involvement a possibility, but because the longer I thought about it, the more likely it became. It was not a comforting thought. 'I don't think it's the Russians,' I said eventually.

Paul looked about as unconvinced as I was. 'So we leave him alone?'

'Yes, for now anyway. But we'll keep a close eye on him and hope that he shows his hand. Meanwhile, we'll take extra care to ensure he witnesses nothing incriminating.'

'What if he becomes a threat to the operation?'

'Then that's when we take him out,' I replied with a grim smile. I squeezed the trigger of the Star and if it had been loaded Louis would have had a hole between his eyes. I pulled back the pistol's slide to reveal the chamber was empty and slipped on the safety catch to lock it into that position. I handed the weapon to Paul who unlocked it, eased the slide forward, re-holstered the pistol, wrapped it in the oilskin sheet and returned the package to the chest.

'What about the others? Do we tell them we're being watched?'

I bent to grab one of the handles of the lid. 'Yes, we'll tell them later,' I said.

Paul smiled and held up a hand in apology. 'Sorry, Dave. It was a silly question,' he acknowledged as he grabbed the other handle. 'Of course we have to tell them. They need to know about the bottle green Mercedes so they can be on the alert for it.'

Together we lifted the lid from the floor and lowered it back into position. We started putting the logs carefully back in place. When we had finished hiding the chest, we stood back to admire our work. Once again, our hiding place was just a pile of logs.

We locked up the servant's quarters and went back inside the house. It was time for some of Mr Mac's broth, but first I had a phone call to make.

A phone call to Freddie.

Thursday May 6th 1982: Wynberg

'You said you were only going away for a few days,' Freddie admonished me when she opened the door of her apartment.

'It was only a few days,' I said.

'Twelve days,' she said. 'But it felt like twelve weeks.' She pulled me inside, slammed the door behind me, reached up, pulled my head towards her and kissed me briefly, but fiercely. 'I missed you,' she said taking a step backwards. I thought I detected tears in her eyes. 'I thought you weren't coming back.' She moved towards me again, putting her arms about my waist and burying her face in my chest.

I hugged her tightly. 'Oh, ye of little faith,' I said.

'Men have never given me much cause to have faith in them,' she said quietly. She pulled away again and wiped her eyes with the sleeve of her dress.

'You look lovely,' I told her. It was the truth. She wore a short black silk dress with a low cut neck. On most women the dress would have looked slutty, but on her it looked sensational. I pulled her towards me again and ran my hands over her back. I could feel through the silk that she wore no underclothes.

Freddie knew what I was thinking. She looked up at me and smiled shyly. 'I'm ready now,' she said gently.

I looked at my watch. It was six o'clock. 'I still have a lot to do this evening. I can't stay long,' I said without conviction.

'You don't have to stay long,' she said with a smile as she took my hand and led me towards her bed. 'A couple of hours should be ample time.'

It was.

Afterwards we lay together, with me on my back and her nestled into the crook of my arm. We were still wet from the exertions of our lovemaking and the bed also was soaked with our perspiration. We were silent for a long time as we luxuriated in the sexual relief we had both just experienced.

It was me who eventually broke the silence. 'I need you to get another message to your father. I need his help.'

'That might be difficult, Dave,' she replied. 'Papa is away.'

'Away?'

'Yeah, he's on a fishing trip.'

'I thought he had lost his boat.'

'He has a new trawler,' she explained. 'Well, actually it belongs to somebody else,' she added quickly. 'A mutual friend of Papa and you.'

I could think of only one person who fitted into that category. 'Robert Dyakala?'

'Yeah.'

I considered her news for a while, weighing up the possibilities. I wondered whether my visit to Rock Cove could be postponed. I decided not. 'When is your father expected back?' I asked.

'I don't know. He said he was heading for the East Coast, but he didn't say exactly where. Sometimes he can be away for a week.'

'Any chance your father will be back by Saturday morning?'

She thought about that. 'That's the day after tomorrow? I suppose it's possible, but unlikely, because he only left yesterday.'

'Damn!' I swore quietly.

'What is it you wanted Papa to do, Dave?'

'I need to get a closer look at Rock Cove and I hoped he and I might take a little fishing trip of our own.'

'Do you have your own boat?' She asked as she ran her fingers through the hairs on my chest.

'Yes.'

'And rods?'

'I was going to buy some tomorrow.'

'Do you fish?' She asked. Her fingers had started a sensual journey down my body.

'No, but I can't imagine it's too difficult and I hoped you dad would be able to teach me. Anyway the fishing rods were only for show, in case we were spotted.'

Her hand crept slowly across my stomach, heading towards my groin area. 'I could take you to see Rock Cove on Saturday and teach you to fish at the same time,' she offered.

'I thought you worked Saturdays?'

'I have every third Saturday off.' She had reached my groin and was gently squeezing me.

I quickly became aroused again. 'I really do have to go,' I protested weakly, but I didn't push her hand away.

'Will you come again?' She asked.

'Yes,' I replied, missing the double meaning of her words.

She giggled and rolled on top of me. I felt her hard nipples pressing into my chest as she raised her bottom in the air. 'Then let me come with you,' she whispered in my ear as she lowered her pelvis and guided me into her.

Even as we began to make love half my mind was still thinking about Robert Dyakala and wondering why on earth he might need a trawler.

Clovelly

It was almost ten o'clock when I parked the Chevy outside the garage and made my way up the garden path to the house. The rain had abated but the howling wind still blew with the same bone chilling intensity.

The path was lit by a number of ornamental lampposts and by their yellow light I could see the pine trees that surrounded the garden being bent and buffeted. The gale force winds had been born somewhere out at sea, had funnelled up through Sun Valley and swept across Clovelly Golf Course before battering themselves to death against the mountain side.

My companions were sitting in front of the lounge fire. Five chairs were positioned in a semicircle, one of which was empty. On the floor in the middle of the semi-circle stood a bottle of Teachers whisky and a bottle of KWV brandy.

'Sorry I'm late,' I apologised as I sat in the empty chair. I held the palm of my hands towards the fire, which Mr Mac enhanced by taking another log from the wicker wood basket that stood next to the hearth and throwing it onto its burning embers.

'So how was Freddie?' Paul asked deadpan.

'Depressed,' I lied, knowing he had no idea what she looked like. 'She's finding it hard to get her weight down below twenty stone and the cream she uses for her acne has burnt holes in her face.' I poured myself a generous measure of Teachers and took a long swig. It hit my stomach within seconds and helped the now blazing fire drive the chill from my insides. 'Actually, she had bad news for me. It seems her father has gone away and is unlikely to be back in time for my trip to stake out Robben Island on Saturday.'

'Is that a problem?'

'It would have been, but Freddie has offered to come with me

175

instead. If she can squeeze herself into the boat.'

'Are you still taking fishing rods?' Paul asked.

I nodded. 'She is going to show me how to fish.'

'This Freddie of yours can fish?' John asked. 'She sounds quite a gal.'

'Several girls,' I said and turned to Paul again. 'Have you explained about Carlse's role?'

The big South African nodded.

'Did you manage to start modifying the go-karts?' I asked John.

'Yeah. It's a piece of cake. The welding kit we bought works like a dream.'

I replenished my glass and topped up those of Mr Mac and John, who were also drinking whisky. Paul poured himself and Charlie another brandy.

We sat in companionable silence until the little Scotsman said: 'D'ye ken. I thought that Mister Helsdon was joshing me when he told me ye cannae buy booze in yon toon.' He pointed in the general direction of Fish Hoek. 'It was only when I asked the lassie in the supermarket where I could buy a bottle of whisky that I discovered he was telling the truth.' He took a sip from his glass. 'The wee young thing looked at me as if my brains were addled, so she did,' he added. 'I had to drive along the coast to St James before I found a bottle store, that's what they call off-licences in this country according to Mister Helsdon.'

'Well, I say here's to St James!' John held his glass in the air and then sipped his whisky.

I moved the two liquor bottles aside and spread a large scale map across the floor. It depicted Robben Island and the adjacent mainland coastline. Alongside the map I laid a large sheet of white paper which contained a more detailed diagram of the island.

Paul knew what was coming because he had helped me put together our plan, and the rest of the team all had a rough idea of what lay ahead for us, but now it was time to brief them properly.

'Let's talk turkey,' I said looking round at my companions. I had their full attention. 'First things first, you will each be paid fifty thousand US dollars, half up front and half on completion of the operation.'

John whistled quietly. 'That's a nice pay day,' he said happily.

I smiled. 'If you each let me have details of your bank

176

accounts I will arrange for an immediate transfer of twenty five thousand into them.'

'Fifty thousand dollars, that's over thirty thousand pounds sterling,' Mr Mac quickly did the calculation. 'With what I have already saved I'll be able to retire, so I will,' he mused, then noticing our questioning looks, and realising he had spoken out aloud, he went on to explain. 'I'm not getting any younger, ye ken. I've been promising myself for some time that I would settle down. I've my eye on a wee place in the Highlands. It has more than enough land for me to be able to support myself and it's on the bank of a loch that's just brimming with fish.' As he spoke, the Scotsman's normally stern features softened.

I was surprised. This was a side of Mr Mac I had never seen before. 'It sounds wonderful,' I said.

'Aye, well, I've nae had quite enough put away, ye ken,' he said, his voice reverting to his usual gruffness. 'But with thirty thousand pounds I will be able to afford the cottage.' He paused and stared into the fire. 'So this is likely to be my last contract.'

The rest of us raised our glasses in a silent toast to Mr Mac and his dreams.

He acknowledged our toast. 'But first, we must finish this wee job,' he went on quickly. 'And I've a notion it will nae be easy. Am I right Mister Statton?'

'Yes, Mister Mac, you're right,' I agreed as I held out my glass and allowed the Scotsman to recharge it with another couple of fingers of whisky.

Paul threw another couple of logs on to the fire and they exploded in a shower of sparks that was quickly sucked up the chimney by the strong draught. I hoped the absent owner of the house had arranged to have the chimney swept in the not too distant past.

The logs, once part of the pile in the servant's room, and as dry as winter veld grass, spluttered and spat as they crackled into flames. One of the smouldering logs rolled slowly forward and rested precariously on the edge of the grate. I took a long blackened metal poker from the wicker basket and pushed the glowing log back into the fire before it toppled onto the stone floor.

'Okay,' I said. 'We hit the prison on Robben Island a week tomorrow. We leave Clovelly at twenty-three hundred hours and arrive here just before midnight, when it will be high tide.' I used the poker to point to a cross that was marked on the map. 'It's an isolated beach roughly two and a half miles north of Bloubergstrand and is situated on a deserted stretch of the coastline.'

'We're unlikely to be seen,' Paul added, 'because the beach is located behind high sand dunes and out of sight from the highway.'

'Which, of course, is one of the reasons why we chose it. Anyway, once we've launched the ski-boats we'll travel to the island, towing our equipment behind us in the rubber dinghies that Paul collected today, and will land here.' I touched the diagram with the tip of the poker and left a black soot mark on the white paper at a point where Rock Cove was located.

'It's only a small strip of sand, but it's more than large enough for us to land the boats on, so that shouldn't be a problem. However, there is a problem out here,' I pointed to the map again. 'Freddie tells me that there are lots of rocks in that area, which makes approaching the island treacherous. That's one of the reasons I want to visit the area on Saturday to see for myself what we're up against.'

I took a sip of my whisky. The wind had dropped and the only sound to be heard was the crackle of the fire and the steady tick-tick of the grandfather clock that stood in the hall.

'However, she reckons there's a channel through the rocks,' I went on to explain. 'But finding it could be tricky. However, we'll have Freddie's father with us and she assures me that he knows the waters round the island like the back of his hand. He will be in the first boat accompanied by Mister Mac and John, and will pilot us through the rocks.

'I'll follow in the second boat, with Paul and Charlie. When we reach the island we'll manhandle the boats and dinghies ashore. While we head to the prison Carlse will stay with the boats and ensure they are ready for a quick getaway on our return.'

'I hate getting wet,' Charlie said to nobody in particular.

'Don't worry, Charlie,' I assured him. 'You will have some protection from the water because we will all be wearing motorbike leathers.'

'Motorbike leathers?'

'Yes.'

'How so?'

'Three reasons. The first is to offer some protection from the elements. The second is because when we return to the mainland we will be making our escape on motorcycles and wearing leathers during the operation will save us valuable time. The third is that the leathers will act as a kind of uniform so that we don't shoot at each other. In addition, whilst we are actually on the island, we will be wearing crash helmets for the same reasons and to make identification of us by the other side more difficult.'

'It makes sense,' Charlie admitted.

'Now, let me tell you a little about where we are going.' I pointed at the diagram and stabbed the lower tip of the kidney shaped Robben Island with the poker. 'There's a lighthouse here.' I stabbed the kidney again. 'Round here, to the east is a small village. It comprises houses, a church, post office, primary school and several community buildings. It is where the white prison officers live. Further up the eastern coast, about here, is where members of the non-white staff live.'

The tip of the poker moved again.

'There is a police station about here and, just to the north of where we'll be landing, is Murray's Bay Harbour.'

By now the kidney's coastline was pockmarked with black dots.

'There is a tarred road that leads from the village to the prison, which is situated here, in the north-east of the island, close to the harbour. The only other access to the prison for vehicles is a dirt service track that branches off from the tarred road down here, just south of the prison.

'We'll use the go-karts to get from Rock Cove and we'll head for the dirt track and follow it round to the west and then north towards the top of the prison compound.' I moved the poker round the track as I spoke. I looked round at the faces of my companions. 'Okay?' I asked. They all nodded.

'Right, now for the prison itself.' I laid another diagram on the floor, it was the one given me by Rogers.

'The prison complex includes a number of buildings and has an outer compound that is surrounded by a sixteen foot high wire fence. There are then a number of internal walls that enclose the buildings and form an inner compound.

'At each corner of the outer compound there is a tall square shaped stone built watchtower. The observation posts at the top of the towers are pretty primitive affairs and provide only limited protection from the elements.'

'The guards get a wee bit cold then?' Mr Mac said thoughtfully.

'Yes, so they wear bulky greatcoats in an effort to keep

themselves warm.'

'Cold and unwieldy,' Mr Mac said with quiet satisfaction.

'The watchtowers are serviced by staircases that are accessed from the outer compound.' I pointed to the diagram. 'The main gate is situated here on the eastern side of the complex and is adjacent to this administration building, which includes the main guard room for the prison. Obviously one of our first challenges will be to neutralise the guards in that room.'

'How do you propose to do that, boss?' John asked.

'You'll create a diversion.'

'Of course I will.' He smiled wryly.

I pointed to a small structure that was situated just inside the outer fence in the northeast corner of the prison next to a watchtower. 'That's an electricity distribution substation. It supplies all the power to the prison. It's divided into two chambers, the larger of which contains control equipment, switches and transformers. The second smaller chamber houses two emergency generators, which are supplied with fuel from a large diesel tank that is positioned at the side of the building.'

'You want me to blow up the substation?' John looked thoughtful. 'How do I get to it?'

'That's where Charlie comes in. He will climb up the back of the watchtower.' I turned to the Frenchman. 'You'll need to be quick and silent.'

Charlie shrugged his shoulders expressively. 'But of course,' he said quietly.

'And you'll have to take a rope ladder up with you. Will its weight make any difference?'

'No, I am used to carrying such things as part of my act.'

'Good. So when you reach the top of the tower, you will attach the rope ladder to the parapet of the observation box with grapples that we will cover with foam to minimise any noise.'

'What if I am seen by the guards?'

'That's most unlikely, because the guards will be at the front of the box looking into the compound. Remember they are there to keep prisoners in, not intruders out. Anyway, Paul and I will be hiding in a clump of shrubs over here,' I pointed to a spot north of the prison. 'If the guards pose a danger to you then we will shoot them.'

'What happens once the ladder is in place?'

'Mister Mac will come up.' I replied. I turned to the

Scotsman. 'There probably will be two guards on duty in the box. It will be your job to take them both out before they can raise the alarm.' I turned back to the Frenchman. 'Charlie you will cover Mister Mac, but only fire if his life is in danger. Your pistol will have a sound suppressor, but it will still make some noise and we don't want to risk warning the guards in the other watchtowers.'

'He will nae have to fire,' the little Scotsman said with quiet confidence.

'I have every faith in you,' I assured him and I meant it. 'Once the guards are immobilised, you tie them up and gag them whilst Charlie joins you and signals the all clear.'

Charlie and Mr Mac nodded.

'John, it is then over to you. You join Charlie and Mister Mac in the watchtower before going down the internal stairs and out of the door, where you'll be almost dead opposite the substation. You force the door and attach delayed charges to the equipment. There's a connecting door to the second chamber and you'll need to attach charges also to the two emergency generators. Finally, you slip round the back of the building and do the same to the fuel tank.'

'How long a delay do you want on the charges?'

'Twenty minutes,' I said.

'Consider it done,' John said with a grin.

'Mister Mac, you go with John while he is placing the charges and cover him. Charlie, you remain in the tower and ensure that the guards in the other watchtowers aren't taking any undue interest in the substation. If they do, you'll have to shoot them, but that's a last resort.

'As soon as John and Mister Mac get back to the box they'll use the ladder. When they're safely on the ground you drop it to the ground and come back down the tower wall the same way you went up. We'll have the go-karts ticking over and waiting to go.'

'Where to?' The Frenchman asked.

'Back down the dirt track the way we came. It should only take us a few minutes to reach the southwest watchtower, where you go through the same exercise again. Once the guards are disabled by Mister Mac he will return to the karts leaving John and you to perform the next important task.'

I pointed to the diagram again. 'Here's the service gate I spoke about before. It leads to this area here, which as you can see is surrounded by a wall. There are four buildings in the enclosure. A storeroom, kitchens, a dining hall and this much smaller building, which is used as a guard room from which use of the gate is controlled. The gate is only used for service vehicles, such as the garbage van, and is only usually opened during daytime hours. Consequently, there are only ever a couple of guards on duty at night.

'It will be the job of John and you to relieve those guards of the keys for both the service gate and the internal gate up here.' I pointed to a point about half way along the wall that encircled the buildings. 'Once you have the keys John will return to the karts. Okay?'

'Okay,' John said.

'What do I do?' Charlie asked.

'As soon as you hear the explosions go off in the electricity substation you open the service gate and we'll drive the go-karts into the outer compound.'

'What are these buildings here?' Mr Mac asked, pointing to four large H-shaped buildings, each of which was surrounded by a wall that separated it from the others.

'They are the cell blocks. They are designated Sections D, E, F and G.'

'Do you know which section Zamyatin is in?'

'Yes, but it's not in one of the H-blocks.' I pointed at the buildings that adjoined the administration building. 'That is the prison hospital and this is the isolation block. It's divided into three sections; A, B and C. This is Section B,' I explained, pointing to the western wing of the block. 'It has thirty single cells and houses high profile political detainees such as Nelson Mandela and Walter Sisulu. Zamyatin is in cell number 16.'

'Howdya know?' John asked.

Rogers had told me to tell my team members as little as possible and then only on a need to know basis, but I trusted these men with my life so felt it only right they should know everything. 'Gavin Rogers told me,' I explained.

'Gavin Rogers? That CIA faggot?' John asked.

I nodded.

'I wouldn't trust that son-of-a-bitch as far as I could throw him,' he said. 'Where'd he get his information from?'

'He has an informant in the South African Department of Justice. Very high up, so he says. Listen. John, I share your mistrust of Rogers, but frankly it's the only information we have. We have no choice but to take it at face value.'

182

'What happens if he's wrong and the Ruskie ain't anywhere to be found in Section B?'

'Then we're out of that place rapido,' I assured him. 'We certainly won't be hanging around looking for the bastard.'

I went on to explain the rest of our plan and how I expected to be off the island within an hour of our arrival. 'When we get back to Rock Cove we'll dump the go-karts in the sea. On the return journey John, Charlie and Mister Mac will join Carlse in the first boat, while Paul and I will take the Russian in the other one.'

'What happens when we reach the mainland?' John asked. 'Do we join you at the rendezvous with Rogers?'

'No,' I replied. 'I'll go alone. We'll lock Zamyatin in the back of the Mercedes truck and I'll deliver him to Rogers while you guys head for Botswana on two of the motorbikes. When I've handed over the Russian and collected the rest of our money, I'll use the third bike to head north and join you in Gaborone.'

'Will you be alright on your own, boss?' John asked. 'Wouldn't it be better if we stay to cover you? I don't trust that…'

Charlie cut the American off by first putting his finger to his lips in warning and then pointing towards the patio door, which was covered by a drawn curtain.

'Carry on talking,' I mouthed silently and spun a forefinger. I rose quickly from my chair and headed for the side door with Mr Mac close behind me.

Luckily the bolt on the door was well oiled and slid across silently. I pulled the door open and stepped out into the yard. The rain clouds had vanished and a bright moon shone down from a star filled sky to light up the yard.

I let Mr Mac go first and watched as he edged along the side of the house until he could peer round the corner at the patio. He raised a hand in warning and then disappeared into the shadows.

I took his place at the corner of the house and knelt down so that I could peek round from a lower level. The patio was dark, as yet unlit by the moonbeams that shone on the yard behind me. In the shadows I could just make out the tall figure of a man standing close to the patio door with his ear pressed against the glass. Behind the figure was a smaller shape that moved closer as I watched.

Suddenly in a whirlwind of action the tall figure was whirled off his feet and was thrown to the ground. I leapt to my feet and ran onto the patio, where I found Mr Mac knelt on top him.

'Okay, Mister Mac, let him go,' I said gently. 'I know him.'

The Scotsman released his iron grip on the taller man's throat and sprang to his feet with the agility of a cat. The intruder took longer to get to his feet, perhaps because he was trying to regain his breath and rub his neck at the same time.

'Are all your friends so rough, David?' Robert Dyakala asked with a wry smile.

Friday May 7th 1982

The grandfather clock in the hall struck midnight and reminded me that we had one day less in which to prepare for our operation.

Charlie, John and Mr Mac had discreetly bid us goodnight and disappeared to their bedrooms. I was left sitting in front of the fire with Paul, Robert Dyakala and the bottle of brandy he had pulled from his pocket as soon as he recovered from his encounter with Mr Mac on the patio.

'I'm glad this didn't break when your friend threw me to the ground,' Robert had said with a chuckle as he produced the bottle after I introduced him to the Scotsman. 'I wanted to return your hospitality.' He handed the bottle to me. 'Perhaps now we can go inside and discuss the delivery of goods you are expecting.'

The bottle of brandy was now light the two generous measures that now swirled gently round the balloon glasses that Paul and Robert warmed in their hands. I stuck to whisky, being a firm believer in the old maxim of never mixing the grape with the grain.

Robert took a sip of his brandy and sighed with pleasure. 'Somehow it tastes better out of a glass than a cup,' he said.

'Better a cup than the bottle.'

'That is true, David. But it would not be the first time I have had to drink from a bottle.'

'Have you been watching us, Robert?' Paul asked without preamble.

Robert laughed. 'You certainly believe in coming straight to the point, Paul.'

'Life is too short for beating about the bush.'

'Okay, I put my hand up. Yes I have been watching you and tonight I eavesdropped on your discussions. But I make no apology. I needed to know for sure that what you are planning will not be a threat to my own operation.'

'How much did you hear?' I asked.

'Enough to know that you were being honest with me when you said the Boers will not be happy if your operation is successful.'

'A successful operation will be much more likely if we have the weapons we need,' I pointed out. 'What news is there on that score?'

Robert looked at me sombrely. 'I am afraid there is good and bad news, David.'

'I'm not sure I am in the mood for bad news.'

'In that case perhaps it would be wise to deliver the good news first.'

'Go ahead,' I said. 'I am all ears.'

'OK, most of the items you wanted have been acquired and can be delivered as soon as I give the order.'

'Most?'

'Yes, most but not all.'

'I seem to recall that Paul delivered to you all the money up front, not most of it, Robert. Don't you think it's fair that you should deliver all the weapons we ordered?'

'That is certainly my intention, however, I have a couple of problems.'

'What problems?'

'Well the first is we only have a limited supply of the Semtex you requested and I am not sure we can get any more as quickly as we would wish.'

'How much Semtex do you have?'

'Oh we have enough for you.'

'Then deliver it, Robert.'

'Sadly, David, it is not as easy as that.'

'Sies man, you found it easy enough to take our money,' Paul said angrily.

'I would dearly love to hand the explosive over to you, but you must understand that yours is not the only operation taking place here in the Cape.'

'Is that so?' I guessed this conversation was leading somewhere.

'Yes, I have an operation planned and also need a quantity of Semtex. A large quantity.'

'You said you had a couple of problems,' I pointed out. 'What's the second one?'

Robert finished off his brandy and held his glass out with a

185

smile and a raised eyebrow.

I picked up the bottle and poured him some more. 'Paul?' I asked.

'Why not,' the South African said. 'It might settle my stomach.'

I tipped another couple of fingers into both their glasses and then stared into my own glass, swirling the whisky thoughtfully. 'The other problem, Robert?' I asked eventually.

'Well actually it's another side of the same coin. It's about my operation.'

'What about your operation?'

'I am concerned that your plans might affect its outcome.'

'How so?'

'Well if the Special Branch heard about what you intend doing they would step up security and that would mean postponing my operation.'

'At least we would get our Semtex,' Paul said sardonically.

'And how would Special Branch get to hear, Robert?' I asked.

The African smiled at me again and shrugged. 'Who can tell, David? There are many traitors out there.'

'But not in my team.'

'I am sure that is true, but there are other people who have some knowledge of your plans, do they not? An anonymous telephone call here, or an unsigned letter there. You understand?'

'I understand, Robert.'

We lapsed into silence. Robert and I considered our next move, while Paul wondered what was going on.

'There is something else I must raise with you, David,' Robert said breaking the silence.

'What is that?'

'I have a favour to ask.'

I smiled to myself. Here was his move. 'Ask away,' I said.

'It is a simple request, David. When you rescue the Russian from Robben Island, I would like you to bring Madiba back with you.'

'Madiba?' I asked.

'Nelson Mandela,' Paul explained. 'Madiba is his tribal name.'

'I see. And what do we get in return, Robert?'

'Well, for a start I think I can guarantee that you will get

186

your Semtex.'

'And the Special Branch?'

He smiled. 'Oh, I am sure we can ensure that your plans remain a secret.'

'That's blackmail, you skollie!' Paul hissed.

'No, Paul.' Robert said. 'That's the politics of repression.'

'You're a sly, cynical bastard, Robert,' I said.

'It is to my shame that duty to my people forces me to take advantage of my friends.' He smiled at me and held out his hand. 'And I hope we are still friends.'

I took his hand and shook it the African way. 'Let's just say that your actions have not come as a complete surprise to me.'

He laughed at that. 'I don't know whether to be offended, or proud of myself.'

'Take your pick. Now, when do we get our shipment?'

'So you will do it? You will help Madiba escape?'

'Yes.'

'Sunday night. Go to Kalk Bay harbour at 10 pm, reverse down the long seawall to the very end and wait. There are no lights in the harbour and you should not be seen at that time of night, but can I suggest that you buy some matt black paint for your truck. White does rather stand out.'

'We were planning to do that anyway,' Paul said. 'We're going into Cape Town tomorrow to get some.'

'Today,' I pointed to my watch.

'I must go,' Robert said getting to his feet.

I let him out the door and walked with him down the garden to his car. It stood in the road outside and the moonlight highlighted the coat of thick grime that covered its paintwork.

'I am truly sorry I had to do that to you, David,' he said as he shook my hand again. 'I suppose we are now working towards the same objective, so please do not hesitate to contact me again if you need my help.'

'I won't,' I said and I meant it. I have never been too proud to ask for help. 'As a start, I don't suppose you know in which cell Mandela is being kept?'

'Oh, yes,' he said with a broad smile. 'Madiba is in cell number four. You can't miss him, his is the only cell with a desk.' He smiled again as he got into his car and started the engine.

I watched thoughtfully as Robert drove slowly away and I did not move until his car had disappeared from sight round the bend at the bottom of the road.

Paul was still sitting in front of the fire when I arrived back in the lounge.

'Can we get another go-kart?' I asked as I joined him.

'Ja, I think so,' Paul replied. 'I'll check it out when we're in Cape Town buying the paint.' He lapsed into silence, staring at the remnants of the brandy in his glass. Finally he looked up at me and smiled. 'I feel a little happier now,' he said. 'At least we know who has been following us.'

'Yes,' I said, not wanting to shatter his illusions. However, I was not convinced we had discovered our mystery stalker. Even covered in grime the white Audi that Robert Dyakala had been driving could not be mistaken for a bottle green Mercedes-Benz 300D.

Cape Town

We took two vehicles into Cape Town. Paul drove the pick-up, with Charlie and John in the cab for company. It was their job to buy the matt black paint we needed for the Mercedes truck and the rest of the equipment, including the extra go-kart, motorbike leathers and helmets.

I went in the hire car with Mr Mac. The little Scotsman had offered to join me on my visit to the post office. From there, I wanted to send a telegram authorising the transfer of twenty five thousand dollars into four different bank accounts and I readily accepted his offer.

As I watched my three friends clamber into the cab of the pick-up, with laughter and good natured banter, I realised how alike they were in many ways.

Physically they were poles apart; Paul, with his big, rugged South African frame, towered over John Brandon, who, at over six feet tall, dwarfed the tiny, lithe figure of Charlie Le Roux.

However, temperamentally they were stamped from the same mould. Good natured, even tempered and unruffled for the most part, each of them, when provoked, had the ability to explode into angry aggression. They were men who could look after themselves. Each had known fear at one time or another and had managed to overcome it.

On the other hand, to the best of my knowledge, Mr Mac had never experienced fear. He had on one occasion assured me that there was nothing on earth of which he was frightened. His fearlessness was based on a deeply held Christian faith. He believed that fright is just an extension of the fear of death. It was a fear he did not share because to him death was only the gateway to a better world.

While I understood Mr Mac's philosophy, it was not one I shared. I was often frightened.

When we reached Cape Town, I parked in the car park opposite Central Station. The parking attendant took my money with an air of indifference that he probably inherited with his official peaked cap.

All trace of the previous day's rain had disappeared. The sky was clear blue and the sun was warm. Mr Mac and I strolled unhurriedly from the car park and headed to the post office where I sent a telegram to my Swiss bank. We then headed for the world famous Flower Market, which was located opposite the post office.

As we walked through the market we savoured the sights and sounds that gave that part of Cape Town such a special atmosphere. The excited sing-song voices of the Cape Coloureds as they laughed and joked their way along the pavement. The flower sellers who stood on every corner thrusting forward bunches of sweet smelling blooms with their cries of: 'Arandabunch! Arandabunch!'

The Flower Market was actually located in what was little more than an extra wide alley that joined Adderley Street to Parliament Street and was named, somewhat grandly for an alley, Trafalgar Place.

At the Parliament Street end of the market was a tall needle shaped monument attached to which was a copper plate. It proclaimed that Thomas Fothergill Lightfoot, Archdeacon of the Cape, was born on 4th March1831 and died 73 years later on 12th November 1904. The plate had been corroded green by the sea air and looked as if it had last been cleaned in the same year as the Archdeacon's death.

The monument was surrounded by equally weather beaten railings and stood alongside a row of double sided wooden benches that were full of women dressed in gaily coloured overalls and head-scarves. On either side of the benches were positioned several concrete water troughs filled with an array of flowers, which the women were bundling into bunches for the flower sellers.

Mr Mac approached one plump, dusky skinned woman, whose missing front teeth were highlighted by the warm smile with which she greeted him, and asked the price of a single yellow rose. Satisfied with the answer he handed over a twenty cent coin and allowed her to fit the flower into the button hole of his blazer. It went well with the yellow lines that ran through the predominantly blue and green MacMillan hunting tartan tie he wore.

We walked through Trafalgar Place to Adderley Street where Mr Mac bought a Cape Times from the newsvendor who stood at the entrance to the Flower Market. I settled for a two day old edition of the Washington Post. Mr Mac put his change into the little leather purse that he always carried, but I dropped mine into the empty Coca-Cola can that was rattled in our direction by the wizened old beggar who squatted at the roadside.

We headed down Adderley Street towards the gardens that stood next to the Parliament buildings. On the way we chatted about Mr Mac's intended retirement. He was obviously relishing the prospect because his face lit up with pleasure as he spoke animatedly of the goats and chickens he would keep. His normally dour and serious manner disappeared to be replaced by a warm, natural friendliness that was usually kept well under wraps.

'After I've moved in ye must come and visit me in my new house, so ye must.'

'I will,' I promised. 'I envy you, Mister Mac. I love the Highlands.'

The gardens were quiet and peaceful and we had no problem finding a seat. We sat in silence for a while listening to the low hum of the traffic in Adderley Street. Busy yellow weaver birds made their basket shaped nests in the trees that shaded us from the midday hot sun.

I opened my Washington Post and my eyes were drawn immediately to a headline underneath which were two head and shoulders photographs. They were grainy and slightly indistinct, but there was no mistaking the identity of the two men depicted. It was Hank Graham and Joe Welensky.

The article itself was short:

US agent murdered

Côte d'Azur, France:

A CIA agent has been found dead in the South of France. The body of Joseph Welensky was discovered in a ditch this week in the town of Juan Les Pins He had been shot.

Agent Welensky was working in France with

a second agent, Henry (Hank) Graham, who is being sought by police in connection with the shooting.

The motive for the murder is unclear and no details have been released regarding the assignment the two agents were on.

However, there was speculation today that they were investigating a link between Unione Corse and drug smuggling into the US.

A deputy director of the CIA, Gavin Rogers II, announced the death of Agent Welensky in a short statement during which he said: "Joe will be a great loss to the Agency. We will use all our resources to hunt down his killer. We have no reason to believe that Agent Graham is guilty of this despicable crime, however, his disappearance is very worrying.

"I would urge anybody who sees Agent Graham to notify the police immediately. Under no circumstances should he be approached because he could be extremely dangerous."

SAPA REUTER.

So it appeared Hank Graham was not dead and the CIA was treating him as a suspect. My mind went back to the events in the house at Juan les Pins. I soon came to the conclusion that it was unlikely that it was Hank who had killed Welensky and dragged his body to the front door of the house.

I reasoned that if Hank had wanted to kill his partner he could have done it at any time and in any place. Why leave it until he was in the South of France and, more importantly, why invite me to the house that night and risk that I might witness the murder? It simply made no sense.

Another thing that puzzled me about the night of Welensky's murder was the US embassy car parked in the road outside 31 Allée des Mouettes. I had no doubt it was used to dump his body in the ditch in which he was eventually found. The use of that car seemed to indicate some involvement by at least one US government official. But who?

Now the newspaper article had posed a couple of other unanswered questions. The first being why was Rogers so keen to set Hank Graham up as Welensky's murderer? The second was that if Hank was still alive, where the hell was he?

Clovelly

When Mr Mac and I left the gardens we headed back up Adderley Street to a sports shop. There we bought half a dozen fishing rods and a rigid plastic box containing an assortment of saltwater fishing equipment, including lines and lures.

Satisfied with our purchases we headed back to Clovelly where we found our three companions hard at work in the garage.

'What kept you?' Paul asked good-naturedly as he walked from behind the battered white Mercedes van with a paint brush in his hand. It was now matt black. 'I suppose you've been sunning yourself,' he added with a grin as he put the brush in a glass jar of white spirit that stood on the floor next to the van.

'Well, we did have a wee sit down in the park,' Mr Mac admitted.

'Nice painting,' I said as I put the fishing equipment into the back of one of the ski-boats.

'Don't look too closely, man,' Paul said. 'My brushwork was never the best.'

'It will do. Did you get the other things we need?'

'Ja. No problem.'

'Including the extra go-kart,' John chipped in looking up from what he was doing on the workbench. Charlie was standing at his side holding in place the large box on which John was using a screwdriver to attach a long leather strap, identical to one that I could see already dangled from the side of the box.

'Excellent,' I said. 'I take it that's one of the muffle-boxes. How's it going?'

'We're cool, boss,' John replied. 'This first one is just about complete.' He finished tightening the screw, took the box from Charlie and handed it to me.

The muffle-box was bulky, but very light. It was made from sheet aluminium and had only three sides and when I turned it over I could see that it had been lined with several layers of thick polystyrene. On the opposite side of the box to the straps were positioned two buckles.

I handed the muffle-box back to John, who carried it over to the ski-boat into which I had put the fishing equipment.

'It fits on like this,' John said as he fitted the box over the cowling of the outboard motor.

I started counting and watched as John passed the straps underneath the motor and up the other side where he slipped them through the buckles and pulled them tight before fastening them.

'Five seconds,' I told him.

'It's even quicker coming off,' he responded, with a hint of pride in his voice.

'I'm impressed,' I told him. 'When will the rest of the boxes be finished?'

'Including those for the karts? Two days or three at the most.'

I was satisfied. 'OK. We'll test the boat boxes on Monday morning and the go-kart boxes as soon as they are finished, perhaps Tuesday, or Wednesday.'

'I'm cool with that,' John said. 'They'll definitely be finished by Monday.'

As Mr Mac and I were about to leave the garage Paul pulled me to one side.

'You go on,' I told the little Scotsman. 'Yes, Paul?'

'I think you ought to know that we were followed back from Cape Town.'

'The green Merc?'

'No, it was a white Audi.'

'Robert Dyakala drives a white Audi.'

'Sies man. So it wasn't Robert driving the Benz?'

'No.'

'Then who was it?'

'I don't know,' I admitted.

He stared at me silently. 'So why was Robert following us today?' He finally asked.

But I didn't know the answer to that question either.

Saturday May 8ᵗʰ 1982: Cape Bay, South Africa

Main Road in Wynberg was exactly that. Designated on official maps as the M4 it was the main road that pierced the heart of one of Cape Town's southern suburbs and ran north to the very outskirts of the city. There it changed its name to Victoria Road. In the opposite direction it headed for Diep Park and did not stop for twenty miles until it reached Simon's Town on the Cape Peninsula.

Freddie's apartment was located just off Main Road in Church Street, a side road in the central shopping area of Wynberg. On the corner of Church Street was a white painted shop across the side wall of which somebody had sprayed in red paint the legend:

Vry Mandela!

She was standing on the pavement already when I drew up at the kerb outside her apartment block. She leaped into the pick up's cab like an excited puppy, lunged towards me and planted a kiss on my cheek before settling back in her seat with a wide smile on her face.

'You were waiting for me,' I said.

'You seem surprised I was ready.'

'I am.' I let out the clutch and pulled away from the kerb.

'Why?'

'You're a woman.'

'Don't be sexist.'

'It's not sexist to tell the truth. In my experience women usually take longer to get ready than men. It's the natural state of the world.'

'Not all women are the same,' she said with a light laugh.

'No, but you're a rarity.' I glanced across at her. She was dressed in jeans, jumper and a waterproof jacket. On her feet she wore heavy duty boots. Her only concession to femininity was the pink frames of her spectacles, the diamante slide that pulled her dark hair from her face and the battered little handbag she had thrown on the seat between us.

There were lots of women I knew who would have turned up for today's trip late and dressed in unsuitably skimpy clothes. Freddie was my sort of woman all right.

'I was up early this morning,' she said. 'I was looking forward to a day with you,' she added shyly.

'It's good to have you along,' I responded non-committally, although her words touched me more than I was willing to admit. 'Now, make yourself useful. Can you find us some music?'

She turned on the car radio and found a station playing pop and the sound of John Lennon singing *Starting Over* filled the cab. Somehow it seemed right for the occasion.

She glanced over her shoulder through the rear window of the pickup. 'Nice boat,' she said. 'It looks new.'

'It's a Suzuki ski-boat and yes, it's new. You can launch her if you like.' I pointed to a large picnic hamper that stood on the floor of the cab between us. 'What you need is in there.'

With a squeal of excitement she undid the straps of the hamper and pulled open the lid. She pulled out a bottle of Moet & Chandon champagne and waved it in the air. 'You really mean it? I can launch the boat?'

'I really mean it,' I said. 'But not with that bottle. It would be a waste of good champers for such a small boat. Look again.'

She lifted the lid and looked inside again. She pulled out a half bottle of South African sparkling wine. 'This one?' She asked.

'Yes. You had better start thinking of a name for the boat.'

'I can name her also?' Freddie asked.

'Also would be a very odd name for a boat,' I said with a straight face.

She punched me lightly on the arm. 'You know what I mean.'

'Yes, you can name her,' I replied as I swung the pick-up onto the M5 northbound carriageway. By now John Lennon had given way to the distinctive voice of Mark Knopfler as Dire Straits performed *Romeo and Juliet*. 'If you'd like to,' I added.

'Yeah, I'd like to very much.' She leaned over and planted another kiss on my cheek. 'What other treats do you have in the hamper?' She asked.

'Mister Mac put together a few sandwiches and other snacks for us.'

'Mister Mac?'

'He's a member of my team. Perhaps you'll get to meet him someday soon,' I said.

Being a Saturday morning there was not much traffic on the roads and it took us just over half an hour to reach Bloubergstrand. I didn't stop when we hit the built up area. Instead, I kept on the M14 and drove two or three miles further along the deserted coastline that ran north as far as the newly built Koeberg Nuclear Power Station.

By the time we reached the place I was looking for, Freddie Mercury was belting out Queen's *Another One Bites The Dust*, which, as it turned out, was a most prophetic song.

I pulled into the side of the road and checked my rear view mirror but there were no vehicles coming up behind us. Quickly I drove off the road and across a narrow stretch of gorse and coarse brown grass covered land that separated the highway from high sand dunes. We were soon travelling along a narrow track through them.

I drove through the dunes until we reached our destination, where I turned round the pick-up and reversed the final fifty yards or so across the beach to the edge of the sea. I switched off the engine and jumped out onto a stretch of almost pure white sand. I glanced at the sea and saw that the tide was on its way in.

I walked round to the passenger door, from which Freddie's legs were already emerging. She jumped into my arms and I lowered her to the ground. I pulled the picnic hamper from the cab and took the bottle of sparkling wine from the hamper and handed it to her. 'Have you thought of a name?' I asked as I loaded the hamper into the back of the boat.

'Yeah. It was easy.'

'Then let's do it. Smash the bottle against her side and name her.'

Freddie looked at the pristine white sand and shook her head. 'I think not. What about the glass fragments? Can't we just pull the cork and tip it over the bow?'

'Of course,' I said. 'It was thoughtless of me. Can you pop the cap of the bottle, or do you want me to do it?'

She looked at me scornfully and said nothing. She ripped the foil and retaining wire from the neck of the bottle and skilfully twisted the cork, keeping her hand pressed hard against the bottom of the bottle as she did so. There was a loud pop and the wine was open without any spillage.

'You've done that before,' I said.

'Many times. When we were at university Frikkie and I worked weekends in a restaurant. It helped us pay our way.' She stared moodily out to sea as she remembered her brother and I could see tears welling in her eyes. But she soon snapped out of it and the tears never materialised. She smiled at me. 'Now?' She asked.

'Now,' I agreed.

We stood side by side alongside the boat and trailer. Freddie raised the wine bottle above her head. 'I name this boat the Spirit of Freedom, may God bless her and all who sail in her,' she said in a cut-glass English accent she had probably picked up from the television. With that she jerked her arm forward several times so that all the sparkling wine sprayed out across the boat's bow.

When the bottle was empty, she handed it to me. 'Wait here,' she said and went back to the cab. When she returned she was carrying her handbag, opening it as she walked. She rummaged around in the bag and eventually pulled out a lipstick. Carefully she wrote on the white hull of the boat in large, bright-pink letters: Spirit of Freedom. 'There you are, now everybody knows her name.'

'Nice colour lipstick,' I said. 'I hope the fish round here wear shades.'

Freddie punched me lightly on the arm, before throwing her handbag into the boat. 'You ain't seen nothing yet, feller,' she said as she removed her boots and started to strip off her clothes to reveal a swimsuit in a shade of pink even more vivid than her lipstick.

'I see what you mean,' I said as I watched her put her clothes in the boat with her handbag.

'Now it's your turn,' she said. 'Or are you going into the water fully dressed?'

I quickly removed my own clothes to reveal a pair of somewhat less flamboyant swimming trunks. I took a black plastic bag from the back of the pick-up. 'Towels,' I explained when Freddie raised an eyebrow. I put it in the back of the ski-boat with the fishing equipment.

I uncoupled the trailer from the back of the truck and together we pushed it into the ocean until the water was lapping at the bottom of the boat's stern. The sun was high in the sky now and was warm on our bodies, but that only served to increase the shock as we entered the ice cold waters of the Atlantic Ocean. I quickly unfastened the straps that held the boat in place and Freddie helped me guide it off the trailer until it was floating.

'Jump in,' I told her through chattering teeth.

She did not need telling twice. She pulled herself up and into the boat. Her wet limbs were covered in goose bumps and her nipples stood proud against her swimsuit. Several seconds later she was turning the ignition key of the Suzuki outboard motors, which sprang into life.

I made my way out of the water towards the front of the trailer and pulled it up onto the beach and reconnected it to the pick-up. I jumped into the truck and parked it behind the sand dunes, out of sight to anybody driving along the highway.

I attached a crook-lock and wheel clamp that were stored in the back of the pick-up. I locked up the pick-up and put the small bunch of keys carefully into the pocket of my trunks. Round my neck I carried a waterproof case containing a pair of binoculars.

By the time I joined Freddie in the boat she had dried herself, slipped on her clothes and was already sitting in the plastic white seat setting a course for Robben Island. I grabbed a dry towel from the plastic sack and rubbed myself vigorously to get my circulation going again.

Once dry I dressed and laid my towel alongside Freddie's on the deck to dry out in the sun. Soon I was sitting in the passenger seat next to her as she pushed the Suzuki outboard motor up to about half its maximum power.

I settled back, enjoying the warm sunshine and the gentle throb of the outboard motor. We were heading due west and to my left I could see Table Mountain climbing majestically into the sky. A thin layer of fluffy cloud rolled over the edge of its flat top to form the table cloth for which the mountain was famous. The clouds would deter visitors from visiting the summit and there certainly would be no hang-glider enthusiasts using the cable cars that day.

It took us about twenty minutes to reach the crescent of rocks that guarded entry to Rock Cove. As we approached where the water was roiling against the rocks in a white foam, Freddie changed course to a southerly direction and slowed the boat to idling speed.

I took out the binoculars and was able to get a better look at the beach on which we planned to land. I was pleased to see that the rock barrier formed a tranquil lagoon in which the water looked calm as it washed against the sand. I saw no problem in beaching the boats and dinghies once we were through the rocks.

'Where is the channel?' I asked.

'Over there,' she replied pointing to a point in the ocean that to me looked no different to the rest of the foaming water.

'You are joking.'

'I tell you, man. That's where the channel is. Use your binoculars and look more carefully.'

I did as she suggested and this time I detected a slightly less turbulent area of the sea's surface, which I guessed was no wider than a dozen feet.

'Can you see it now?' She asked.

'I think so, but it's not very wide. Are you sure your father can get a boat this size through the rocks?'

'Yeah, I'm absolutely sure,' she replied without hesitation. 'I told you before, we've visited the cove lots of times to dive for crayfish and perlemoen.'

'What about when it's dark?'

'That won't be a problem. We only ever dive for crayfish at night anyway, because we don't want to be seen. Don't worry, you'll be fine as long as you follow papa carefully.'

'We'll need a powerful torch,' I said thoughtfully. 'The problem is using a torch will risk our boat being seen from the island.'

'Not if the torch is fixed to the back of Papa's boat and its beam is pointing away from land. You can then simply follow the light.'

I looked at her steadily. 'Why didn't I think of that?'

'Because you are a man,' she said with a wicked grin.

'Touché!' I said and looked again at the channel entrance. 'Not a torch,' I said. 'Two rear bicycle lights. One on either side of the stern. That will make it easier to gauge the width of the channel.'

'Now, that is good thinking, Dave. Obviously not all men are the same.'

'Get us out of here, wench! Before we're seen.'

She increased speed and we continued our journey in a southerly direction towards Cape Town. We had been idling by the rocks for no more than a couple of minutes and if we had been seen it would have looked simply as if we had stopped to gawp at the island. That probably happened all time.

When we had travelled about a mile Freddie eased the boat towards the west and we headed back towards Blouberg Heights. Half a mile off shore she cut back power and dropped anchor.

We got out the fishing rods and Freddie showed me how to load the line, attach bait and cast. She did it with the expertise that I suppose was something else she learned from her fisherman father. I eventually managed to cast a line successfully but I was not optimistic about catching anything. In that respect I was not to be disappointed.

We propped the fishing rods against the side of the boat and Freddie secured them with brackets that she found in the box of equipment, while I moved the picnic hamper onto the now dry towels opposite the rods.

The noon sun was really beating down now and we stripped off our clothes again and settled down to eat our picnic, sitting on the deck with our backs against the side of the boat. In the near distance, to our right, Robben Island rose from the sea like a great humpback whale. To our left a small ship steamed slowly north across our sight line.

'She's heading for Murray's Bay Harbour,' Freddie said as she watched me open the bottle of Moet & Chandon. 'She's either carrying provisions, or new prisoners.'

I took two champagne glasses from the hamper and handed them to her. She held them up to let me fill them.

'Have you heard from your father?' I asked.

Her face clouded over. 'Yeah, he came to my home in the early hours of this morning.'

'He's back from his fishing trip?'

'Yeah,' she replied.

'What did he want?' I asked. 'I thought he was trying to avoid drawing attention to you?'

'He does. That's why he left it until two o'clock to visit me.'

'Does he think the cops all go off duty at night?'

'He had been drinking,' she said as if that was an explanation. 'But he was careful.'

'So what was so urgent that he felt the need to put you at risk?'

She looked at me silently for a moment and then said: 'I'm touched you care about my safety.'

'I care about my operation and any involvement by the police could jeopardise its success,' I said, not wanting to admit that she was right, but the happy smile on her lips showed that she was not deceived. 'So why did your dad come to see you at such an unearthly hour?' I added hastily.

'He wanted me to ask you how much he would be getting for guiding you to the island.'

'Fifty thousand American dollars.'

She stared at me open mouthed. 'How much?'

'Fifty thousand. Half up front and the balance on completion of the job. If he lets me have his bank account number I will arrange for the first twenty five K to be transferred immediately.'

She shook her head. 'Papa doesn't have a bank account. Can he have it in cash?'

'That can be arranged, but I won't be able to get it to him until the middle of next week.'

'That will be fine. If you give me the money I will look after it and give it to Papa when he gets back.'

'Back from where?'

'He's off on another trip on Wednesday.'

'Where to this time?' I tried to keep concern from my voice, but I must have failed because she said.

'Don't worry, Dave, Papa said he would be back in time to

meet you on Thursday night.'

'I'm not worried,' I lied. 'But you look as if something is worrying you. What is it?'

She did not answer straight away, instead she rummaged around in the hamper and brought out a large Tupperware container and a couple of plastic plates, one of which she handed to me.

'Yeah, I'm worried,' she admitted as she pulled the lid from the container and took out a smoked salmon sandwich before passing the container to me.

I loaded my plate with sandwiches. I was hungry. 'Worried about your father?' I asked before demolishing half a sandwich in two bites.

'Yeah.'

'What's the problem?'

She fell silent again and nibbled delicately at her sandwich. 'Papa lied to me,' she eventually said. 'He hasn't been fishing. He's working with Robert Dyakala. He was boasting they had a big operation planned.' She fell silent and her face clouded over again.

News of a big operation came as no surprise, after all Robert had told me as much only a couple of days before. However, I was surprised that Carlse was as heavily involved as Freddie was suggesting. 'I wonder why Robert needs the services of a fisherman.' I said.

'Papa is not just a fisherman, Dave. He's also a master seaman who knows the Cape waters better than anybody else I know. Remember, that's why you need him.'

'And you are worried about him?'

'Yeah. I think he's getting out of his depth.'

'You have an idea what they are planning, don't you?'

'Yeah,' she said quietly. 'I think they're going to plant a bomb somewhere.'

'What makes you say that?' I kept my voice neutral.

'Because I asked Papa what they were planning.'

'And?'

'And he stood in front of me, clapped his hands together and went "boom".'

There was little more that I could say after that and we finished our lunch in silence, each preoccupied with our own thoughts and worries.

Freddie's suspicions about Robert Dyakala planning to plant a bomb came as no surprise because he had told me himself they needed Semtex for their operation. But who or what were they out to destroy?

They needed an expert seaman so the odds were they were planning a seaborne attack. But when and, more importantly, where would that attack take place? I knew it was in the Cape somewhere, because once again Robert had told me. But what was the target?

I mulled over that question as we headed back to Bloubergstrand, with me at the wheel. It was good to feel the boat's surge of speed as I pushed the Suzuki outboard motor to full power. We reached our destination at about the same time that I made up my mind what Robert's target would be.

'They're going to blow up the Koeberg Nuclear Power Station,' Freddie said suddenly, not only breaking into my thoughts but mirroring them.

'What makes you say that?' I asked as I manoeuvred the boat closer to the beach. I knew the answer, but I was interested to see how she had arrived at the same conclusion as me.

'It's the only logical target.'

'Because?'

'Because their target needs to be large. Its destruction needs to hit the Government hard. It has to be reachable from the sea. It has to be in the Cape and finally, it must be in a location that minimises collateral damage to our people.' She looked at me steadily, the eyes behind the spectacles challenging me to deny her logic.

'John was right,' I said. 'You really are quite a girl.' I rose from my seat to make way for her. 'Take over,' I told her. 'I'll go get the trailer.'

'Who's John?' She asked as she slipped behind the wheel and I clambered over the side of the boat to brave the cold surf.

'Another member of my team,' I said as I waded for the shore.

'I like the sound of John,' she called after me. 'It sounds as if he has good judgement.'

By the time I reached the beach I was shivering from the cold, but the afternoon sun was still hot and I soon warmed up as I ran to where the pick-up truck and trailer were parked. I quickly removed the wheel clamp and was putting it in the back of the pick-up when I noticed a shoe print in the soft sand next to the passenger door.

When I looked more carefully I saw several more prints,

some more distinct than others. I put my bare foot into one of the print and found there was plenty of room to spare. Whoever had been snooping round the pick-up was taller than me, which narrowed his identity down to only several million people.

I followed the footprints round the bonnet of the pick-up to the driver's door, on past the rear side of the trailer and along the edge of the sand dunes. A couple of hundred yards further along the beach another track bisected the dunes and went off in a north-easterly direction towards the main road. A few yards on the landward side of the dunes I saw a set of tyre marks in the sandy track.

The tyre prints were noticeably wider than those made by either the pickup truck or the boat trailer. I could not help thinking the Mercedes-Benz that had been following us since we arrived in South Africa was large enough to have wheels wide enough to need those tyres. Momentarily I asked myself whether I was being paranoid, but it was difficult to contradict my instincts, which on this occasion I thought were probably sending me justified warning signals.

I reversed the pickup truck closer to the sea and then disconnected the trailer and pushed it into the water. Together Freddie and I manoeuvred the boat onto the trailer and strapped it securely into place. We dried ourselves and then unselfconsciously we stripped off our swimsuits before putting our clothes back on.

The late afternoon sun was lower in the sky, but still hot, so Freddie left off her jumper and now she wore only a tight, silk vest top that accentuated her shapely breasts.

'I need to pop into the Bloubergstrand,' I said once we were settled in the cab of the pick-up truck and heading back down the M14. 'I have an appointment with somebody at half past four.'

We were a few minutes late when we drew up outside the garage on which I had seen the For Rent sign two weeks before when I had visited the block of flats with Paul. But when we got out of the pick-up truck the man who greeted us didn't seem all that fussed about the time. He took more interest in Freddie than he did the expensive watch he wore on his wrist.

The garage door was open and he stood in the shade offered by the garage's interior. He was tall and slim with long wavy black hair that touched his narrow shoulders. He wore a colourful Hawaiian shirt and had the look of an Italian gigolo about him, but perhaps I was just biased because of the way he was ogling

Freddie's chest.

I resisted the urge to punch Mr Gigolo on the nose and instead started pacing out the size of the garage. The man watched me as I worked, but I could see that he still studied Freddie out of the corner of his eyes. She must have felt his eyes on her breasts because she turned her back on him and stared out towards the sea, but he seemed to find the rear view of her equally appealing.

When I had finished measuring the garage, I decided that it would suit our needs perfectly. I handed over six month's rent and the garage owner dragged his eyes away from Freddie's backside long enough to concentrate on counting the bundle of notes I had given him. Then, satisfied I hadn't short-changed him, he handed over a set of keys.

I locked up the garage and we headed back to the pick-up. I didn't have to look over my shoulder to know that Mr Gigolo was still staring at Freddie as she walked.

'What a slime ball,' she muttered as she climbed up into the cab.

I didn't respond, but I wasn't inclined to disagree with her.

Gavin Rogers II

Gavin loved the Mount Nelson Hotel because its historic provenance mirrored his position as the scion of a Rogers' line going back to the Pilgrim Fathers. The subtle pink colour of its exterior reflected the feminine-softness that lay at the core of his personality; and the indulgent grandeur of its interior décor suited his love of luxury.

But he was not happy. Staying in the hotel was expensive. Damned expensive. Too expensive to be covered by the paltry levels of travel allowance that had been imposed on the CIA by its new Director, William J Casey, who was well known for his own frugal tastes.

So Gavin had been forced to subsidise from his own pocket his stay in Cape Town's finest hotel. It was something that rankled, not least because since the estrangement from his father, who had never been able to accept that his only son was gay, he could no longer fall back on his family's wealth. Instead, he had to fund his lifestyle from his own salary and it was not easy.

He silently cursed his father for cutting him off from the inheritance to which he felt entitled. He was just as bitter about the bean counters in the accounts department at Langley for being so meticulous in the way in which they checked his expense claims.

Gavin was sitting on the terrace taking afternoon tea. The sun was starting to lose its heat and the shadows from the surrounding trees were lengthening, but it was still pleasantly warm sitting in the shelter of the bougainvillea covered outer wall of the lounge. From his position he was able to look out across the hotel's gardens towards the towering Table Mountain, but even this magnificent vista was not enough to raise his spirits.

Moodily he poured himself another cup of Earl Grey tea and then took another tiny triangular cucumber sandwich from the three tiered silver cake stand that stood on the table in front of him. He nibbled delicately at the sandwich and sipped from the fine bone china tea cup.

There was another reason for Gavin's unhappiness. He was

sure his time at the Firm was coming to an end. Rumours had been circulating for months that the staunchly Republican Bill Casey was about to launch a cull of staff with overtly Democrat sympathies and Gavin had never hidden his liberal views. He felt particularly vulnerable because there was a culture of institutionalised homophobia at Langley, which had been reinforced by the new Director, who was devoutly catholic.

But Gavin was determined to go out on his own terms and he was already working on an exit strategy. He was sure he could cut a deal with Casey that would see him walk away with a decent financial settlement. In addition, as and when he was forced out from the Firm, he had taken steps to supplement any pay-out he received.

In the shady world in which he had worked for so long there were always ways and means to turn a buck. Gavin was confident that he would be able to continue living in the manner to which he had become accustomed. He was still dispirited though because he would miss the status invested in him as a deputy director of the CIA.

A man coughed at his side and Gavin realised he had been day dreaming.

'What is it?' He asked as he stared up at the imposing figure of Agent Sam Potter. His right hand fluttered briefly in the air as he indicated that his subordinate should join him at the table.

'We've tracked down Hank, sir,' Potter said quietly as he sat down in the chair opposite Gavin. He said nothing more as a waiter wearing white gloves appeared from thin air and gently placed a cup and saucer on the table in front of him.

The waiter tipped more hot water into the teapot then disappeared just as quickly as he had arrived.

'Help yourself,' Gavin said, nodding towards the teapot.

Potter poured himself a cup of tea and added a dash of milk.

Gavin shook his head and pursed his lips in disapproval. 'With tea you always put milk into the cup first, Sam,' he said and demonstrated by putting a little milk into his own empty cup before pouring himself more tea.

Potter sipped his tea and then grimaced. He put his cup down.

'Don't you like the tea?' Gavin asked.

'It tastes of perfume.'

'It is Earl Grey,' Gavin explained with a superior smile.

'Don't they do coffee round here?'

'I'm sure we can arrange that,' Gavin said. 'But first tell me about Graham. Where is he?'

'He's shacked up in a piss-ant little hotel down on the coast.'

'Is he alone?'

'It looks that way. I gave his room a going over when he was out today and there was no sign of anybody else staying with him.'

'How did you find him?'

'Pure luck. It was our friends in NIS who stumbled across him. A couple of days ago they carried out a series of raids at addresses across the Cape looking for a terrorist suspect and one of the agents was Hendrick Vorster.'

'Henny?' Rogers asked. He knew the NIS agent and had worked with him on a number of occasions.

'Yeah. One of the addresses they raided was a hotel in a little place called St James. They checked out the passports of all the guests and Vorster recognised Hank's photograph straight away, although he appears to be travelling on a passport in the name of Gerry Fisher.'

Gavin nodded his head in quiet satisfaction. At last some good news.

'Do you want me to bring him in or carry on tailing him?'

Gavin stared off into the distance, thinking it through. 'Neither,' he said eventually. 'I want you to neutralise him.'

'Neutralise him? But Hank is one of us.'

'He was, but he's not now. Graham crossed the line when he killed Joe Welensky. So that's why I want you to neutralise him.' Gavin looked hard at his subordinate. 'Do you have a problem obeying that order, Sam?' He asked quietly.

Potter shook his head. 'No, sir,' he mumbled. 'I can handle it.'

David Statton

Wynberg

Freddie had told me in her usual unabashed way that her sexual experience was very limited. She admitted that she had lost her virginity on the back seat of a car to a university lecturer with whom she was infatuated, following a drunken end of term party.

Apparently the sex itself was as short lived as it was unsatisfying. She had only been tempted into his bed on a couple of other occasions, neither of which was any more satisfying for her, and soon the affair fizzled out. She claimed to have had no other lovers until she met me. I was inclined to believe her. After all, she was only twenty-two.

Freddie seemed determined to change her inexperienced status as quickly as possible and she proved to be an enthusiastic and energetic lover. No sooner had we arrived at her flat than she led me through to the bathroom where we shared a shower. She used her hands to wash the salt and sand from my body with soap and then insisted I did the same for her. She didn't have to twist my arm.

By the time I turned off the powerful spray we were both fully aroused. I lifted her from the shower cubicle and carried her through to the bed where she lay spread-eagled, lips swollen, nipples standing proud and with her pubic hairs moist from our recent shower.

She held out her arms in invitation and I went to her. No sooner had our damp bodies come together than she rolled me over onto my back and sat astride me. She stared into my eyes with an intensity that seemed to probe my very soul. She must have liked what she found because she smiled and started to move gently up and down on me.

After a few minutes of gentle rhythm she started to speed up, but I gripped her firmly by the hips and made her slow down. She closed her eyes and groaned in frustration as I held her back, raising and lowering her pelvis in a controlled lifting action. Then, as I sensed she was about to reach the point of no return, I raised and lowered her faster until finally I let go of her hips and let her take control. The pace of her movements increased until suddenly she threw back her head and with a loud scream she climaxed, as at the same time my own world exploded in ecstasy.

Afterwards she collapsed onto my chest and clung to me as if frightened I was going to escape. She had no reason to worry. I was going nowhere. Not yet anyway.

'My God!' She panted. 'That was incredible. I had no idea it could be like that. Mister Du Plessis might be a brilliant lecturer, but he has sure got a lot to learn about satisfying women. At the very least you deserve a master's degree.'

'It's easy to please yourself, but it takes two to ensure you satisfy somebody else.'

'Well, I was satisfied. Were you?'

'No,' I lied.

She nipped my chest with her teeth. 'Then why did you scream?'

'I did not scream.'

'You did so.'

'Cramp.'

'My mama warned me about men who lie.'

'She was a very wise lady.'

'She was also a very beautiful lady,' she said quietly. 'Would you like to see a photograph of her?' She did not wait for my answer, instead she pulled away from me, flicked on the bedside lamp, recovered her spectacles from the top of the bedside table and slid out of bed. She ran lightly across the floor to a dresser that stood against the far wall, opened the top drawer and took out a small photograph album.

She soon returned to my side and passed the album to me. 'This is my mama,' she said proudly, opening the album to reveal a full figure portrait of a young woman. Freddie was right. Her mother was beautiful, with pale skin, long thick hair, a pretty face and an hour glass figure. Like mother like daughter. I wondered how someone with such stunning good looks could have been attracted to Johan Carlse.

Freddie must have read my mind. 'Papa was not always like he is today,' she said turning over a couple of pages of the album before pointing to another photograph. 'That was taken on their wedding day.'

The photograph showed Freddie's mother with a young, good looking man who bore no resemblance to the Johan Carlse I had met only recently.

The man in the photo wore a smart suit and a wide smile, with a full set of teeth that shone whitely in the sun. He had a full head of black hair that was slicked back with pomade of some sort and the eyes that stared assuredly into the camera sparkled with humour and vitality. The man in the photograph was no pickled walnut.

'Is that your father?' I was astounded at the transformation.

She nodded. 'The death of Frikkie and my mama hit Papa hard,' she said, reading my mind again. 'He has never been the same since.'

I stared down at the photograph and for the first time since I had met Johan Carlse I felt sorry for him. 'They made a good looking couple,' I said quietly.

Freddie turned the page again to reveal a photograph of two children dressed in school uniform. Facially they looked identical and they wore identical blazers, but one of the children wore trousers and the other a skirt. 'That is Frikkie and me,' she said. 'We were ten years old when that photo was taken.'

Slowly she turned the next few pages to reveal a succession of pictures showing the twins growing up, ending in one depicting two serious looking young people carrying matching placards carrying the slogan: *No To Afrikaans!*

'That was taken three years ago at the start of the school boycotts,' Freddie explained. She turned the page again to reveal a group photo. The men all had black faces except one young man who was lighter skinned. It was Freddie's brother. The group stood in front of a metal Nissan hut. Frikkie stood in the front row and was shaking the hand of a tall African who I recognised immediately as Robert Dyakala.

'That photo was taken in Lusaka at an ANC Youth convention. Robert Dyakala presented Frikkie with an award for his dedication to the Cause.'

'You must have been proud of him.'

'I was,' she stared down at the photo and a tear welled from her eye.

'Weren't you at the camp?' I asked as I studied the photograph carefully.

'Yeah. It was me who took the photograph.'

Behind the group could be seen one of the long oblong windows of the Nissan hut. The sun was shining on its glass, but despite the glare I could just make out the ghostly white face of a man standing behind the window. I tapped the photograph. 'Who's that?' I asked.

Freddie frowned and shook her head. 'I don't know. I've never noticed him before.' She cocked her head and stared hard at the photo. 'Actually, I do vaguely remember him. He arrived at the camp the day before Frikkie and I left, but I never met him.'

She slammed the album closed. 'That photo was taken only two months before the Boers shot Frikkie,' she said bitterly as she laid the album on the bedside table and took off her glasses again. She reached for me. 'Please help me forget, David.'

So I did, which meant it was another late night and I did not get back to Clovelly until the early hours of the morning. I was tired and ready for sleep.

As I undressed, I caught a sight of myself in the full length mirror. When you're my age, having a 22 year old lover concentrates your mind. You become more conscious of changes to your body you have chosen to ignore. As I studied my body I decided that for somebody who was approaching 40 I was doing alright, except that some of my muscle was running to fat and it seemed to run faster with each passing year.

Despite my tiredness it took me some time to get to sleep. I kept remembering the group photograph in Freddie's album and the window in the Nissan hut through which could just be seen the ghostly white face of a man.

I had recognised the man immediately. He now called himself Major Percival Carsons, but I still didn't know his real identity and why, only three years before, he had been attending an ANC youth conference in Lusaka.

Sunday May 9th 1982: Kalk Bay, Cape Peninsula

Originally we had intended to use the Toyota pick-up truck to make our short journey from Clovelly to Kalk Bay, but in the event it was raining in the evening so we decided to take the Mercedes van instead. I drove and was joined in the cab by Paul and John.

It was just under a mile and a half from our house to the harbour and at that hour on a wet and miserable Sunday evening the local roads were deserted. Our journey took only a couple of minutes and we reached our destination with plenty of time to spare.

I parked outside the harbour gate and peered through the pouring rain into the harbour. It was as deserted as the road in which we sat and much darker because it did not have the luxury of the street lights that shone down on the van.

The harbour consisted of two walls, the longer one of which was L shaped. The shorter, left hand wall was straight and its far end formed the harbour entrance on either side of which were the red and green warning lights I had seen before. In the middle of the harbour and parallel to the longer harbour wall was a long pontoon alongside which were moored a couple of dozen small boats. There was no sign of life on any of the vessels.

We sat for a few minutes listening to the rain beating down on the roof of the van and saw no vehicles travelling on Main Road in either direction. There were only a couple of buildings opposite the harbour gate and they were in darkness.

Satisfied we were not being observed I reversed along the jetty, making sure to keep close to the harbour wall and well away from the seaward side. Most days the jetty would be full of trawlers, but that night there were only a handful and they were moored closer to the shore.

'There's a boat out there, boss,' John said, pointing out beyond the harbour entrance to where the glow from a single yellow navigation light managed to penetrate the driving rain.

I glanced at my watch. It was five minutes to ten. 'How big is it?' I asked.

'Not sure,' John said. 'It's hard to tell in the dark.'

'It doesn't appear to be moving,' Paul added.

'Is it anchored up?'

'Possibly,' John replied. 'Although I'm sure the light was moving when I first spotted it.'

'Do you think it's our shipment, Dave?' Paul asked.

'Who knows?' I said. 'Dyakala didn't actually say the shipment would be coming by sea. For all I know it could be coming by road.'

As I spoke, a pair of headlights came along the coast road from the direction of Muizenberg. It looked like a truck and I tensed as the vehicle slowed down as it reached the harbour gate, but I relaxed as it speeded up again. I realised it had simply slowed to check nothing was exiting from Boyes Drive onto Main Road.

'Over there,' Paul hissed and pointed across the harbour.

I saw nothing. 'What?'

'Another light. It came from the end boat moored by the pontoon.'

I saw it then. A couple of quick flashes, followed by a slight pause and then a longer burst of flashes. Then the night was black again, before the same sequence was repeated.

'It's Morse code,' John said.

'Did you catch it?' I asked as the message blinked briefly again. It was over in a couple of seconds and invisible from the land.

'Yeah. It's just two letters.' John said. 'A.C.'

'A.C?' Paul repeated.

'All clear?' John suggested.

I looked out to sea and saw the navigation light begin to move towards us. Soon a trawler made its way through the entrance of the harbour and chugged slowly towards the wall on which we were parked. The boat did not take long to reach us and was soon alongside.

We jumped out of the sanctuary of our van cab and stood on the rain lashed harbour wall as the trawler manoeuvred into position. It was a modern craft with a forward wheelhouse and an aft working deck with a gantry for winching a net aboard. Attached to the gantry was an inflatable dinghy, complete with outboard motor.

A man emerged from the wheelhouse. He was wearing a bright yellow sou'wester hat and a matching oilskin coat, the collar of which was pulled up to protect him from the rain. Despite his attire the man eased himself nimbly past the side of the boat's superstructure and along the forward deck to the bow.

The man picked up a thick rope that lay in a coil on the deck next to a large object that was covered by a tarpaulin. He threw the rope to Paul who tied it quickly to one of the large metal mooring posts that were set in a row along the length of the harbour wall. The man made his way quickly to the stern and threw a second rope to John. Soon the trawler was secured.

Finished the man looked up at me. 'Goeienaand, meneer Stratton,' he said. 'Hoe gaan dit?'

'I'll tell you how it goes,' I replied. 'I'm cold and wet.' I made a point of looking at my watch. 'You're late, Mister Carlse.'

'Johan, please,' he insisted with an amiable, toothless smile.

'You're late, Johan.'

'Ja, ek is laat. Ek is jammer, meneer.' His eyes twinkled as he repeated his apology in English. 'I'm sorry, but I was told to be careful.'

This was the first time I had seen Carlse sober and I recognised in him something of the young man I had seen in the photo. I began to warm to him, but perhaps my feelings for his daughter had something to do with that.

'Veiligheidshalwe, ja?' He asked.

'Yes, Johan, better safe than sorry.'

'If you would like to come aboard we can unload your shipment.'

I jumped onto the trawler and Carlse led me towards the working deck and down into the hold where a fish catch would usually be stored. I had been aboard a number of trawlers in my time. They had been of different shapes, sizes and technical sophistication, but the one thing they had in common, whatever their design, was a strong fishy smell. That was inevitable because after all a trawler is a trawler. Full stop. But the boat on which I stood lacked that smell and I suspected it had never been used for fishing.

In the hold Carlse pulled back a tarpaulin to reveal a number of wooden crates. Together we lifted the first crate out of the hold and carried it along the deck past the wheelhouse to the harbour wall where we passed it up to the waiting Paul and John. The crate was heavy, but the little man raised his end to shoulder height with no difficulty.

The remaining crates were smaller and lighter than the first and we were able to carry one each from the hold to the wall, by which time our two colleagues had stored the first crate in the van. This left four crates, which was two trips each, and when we arrived back in the hold to collect the last crates Carlse touched my shoulder. 'Meneer Stratton...' he started.

I stopped him. 'It is Statton,' I said with a resigned sigh. 'There is no "R".' I smiled at him. 'Perhaps you should call me David. It might be easier for you to remember.'

'Dankie, David,' he said with a wide grin, before becoming serious again. 'I would have words with you about Freddie.'

'Freddie?' I asked cautiously

'She is my dogter,' he said.

'I know who she is.'

He stared at me, his eyes troubled. 'Freddie is all the family I have left in the world.'

I nodded. 'So I understand.'

'David, my dogter is a very loving girl.' He paused and

214

looked uncomfortable before adding quietly: 'I suppose you know that my dogter is very fond of you?'

'She is a lovely girl,' I said, neatly side stepping his question.

He nodded. 'Ja, she is beautiful like her mama.' He paused and I could see that he was struggling to find the right words. 'There is a question I would ask you, David.'

'You can ask.'

'But will you answer me honestly?'

'If I can.'

He stared at me intently. 'Do you promise not to hurt my dogter?' He asked eventually.

I returned his stare and thought about his question. I had already tried to analyse my relationship with Freddie, but shied away from admitting she was anything other than my current lover. But I knew my reticence was a cop-out and probably far from the truth. Being confronted by her father forced me to come to terms with my true feelings for her.

'I'll happily promise not to intentionally hurt Freddie,' I said. 'However, don't forget that mercenaries have an unpredictable life span.'

'I'm happy with that,' Carlse said. 'I understand your circumstances and can expect no more. However, there is a second promise I want you to make.'

'I'm not sure I can cope with two promises in the same day, but ask away.'

Carlse looked at me intently. 'David, you should understand that I am all the family my dogter has,' he paused, as if to let that fact sink. 'I am about to undertake a dangerous mission with our mutual friend. Freddie probably mentioned this to you.'

'She mentioned it,' I acknowledged. 'But not the details.'

'That is because she doesn't know the details and I want to keep it that way.' He paused again, perhaps not knowing how to translate what he was feeling into words.

I knew how the little man felt, because I had the same difficulty.

'If something goes wrong with our operation, but you survive yours, will you promise to look after Freddie for me?'

I batted away his question as best I could. 'I hope nothing goes wrong with your operation, Johan, because we need you to help us next Friday night.'

He smiled. 'Don't worry, I'll be there. I want to be there to see you rescue Nelson Mandela from the Boers.'

I stared at him coldly. 'Who told you that?'

He shrugged and returned my stare. 'I might be a drunk, David, but I am not a stupid drunk. I worked it out for myself. It wasn't hard. For a start I was with our friend when he bought the arms you wanted in Beirut and I overheard him talking to our comrade from Hezbollah.

'Our friend told him the shipment was for a group of European mercenaries who were mounting an operation in the Cape. You recruited me to pilot you to Robben Island. There can only be one reason why you would want to attack the Island and that is to get somebody out of the prison. There is only one person I know in that prison who warrants such an effort. Mandela.'

'Have you discussed this with anybody else?' I asked.

'Nee,' he said with a shake of his head.

'Good. Well don't discuss it, not even with Robert.'

He nodded his agreement.

'And, Johan. I meant what I said. We need you on Friday and we need you sober.'

'Don't worry, David, I will be sober,' he paused again. 'Look, don't worry about me. I'm confident that nothing will go wrong with our operation. We're well prepared and well protected.' He tilted his head in the direction of the trawler's bow and lowered his voice. 'Did you notice the tarpaulin as we came aboard?'

I nodded.

'It's hiding a Soviet built 2M-7 14.5 calibre heavy machine gun. If we are detected the Boers will get the shock of their lives,' he said with another grin. 'But if the worst comes to the worst and I am caught, Freddie will be in real danger. All I ask of you, David, is that if I do not return on Thursday that you promise to get her out of South Africa somehow?'

'I promise,' I said simply.

'Dankie,' he said and squeezed my shoulder again before bending down to pick up his last crate.

I stopped him. 'So you return on Thursday?' I asked.

He looked up at me. 'In the early hours, God willing.'

'Then I will arrange to see Freddie on Tuesday and give her the final details for our rendezvous on Friday.'

'Do you want me to meet you at your house in Clovelly?' He asked.

I raised an eyebrow.

'I know everything that happens on the Peninsula,' he boasted.

'I haven't decided on a meeting place yet?' I lied. I might have been warming to him, but I still did not trust him fully, particularly if he got drunk. 'Do you have transport?'

'Ja. I have a car. What time do we meet?'

'I'm not sure,' I lied again. 'I'll give Freddie all the details when I see her. One other thing; I understand you want Freddie to look after your money?'

He nodded. 'Ja, she is a good girl. She will stop me squandering it on drink.'

'I'll give her the money on Tuesday.'

I bent down and lifted my last wooden crate.

'Dankie,' he said as he picked up his own crate and carried it to the harbour wall without another word.

Once all the crates were loaded in the van John jumped up into the driver's seat and started the engine. I shook hands with Johan Carlse, climbed up onto the harbour wall and untied the trawler's forward mooring rope while Paul undid the aft rope. Slowly the trawler pulled away from the wall.

As Carlse swung the bow towards the harbour entrance he poked his head round the wheelhouse door. 'Totsiens, David!' He shouted with a cheery wave. 'Ek sal u sien Vrydag!'

'Yes. See you on Friday,' I called back, but my words were whipped out of my mouth by the strengthening wind and were scattered unheard over the sea like a sailor's funeral ashes.

Hank Graham

Cape Peninsula

Hank Graham looked through his Zeiss night vision binoculars as crates were unloaded from the trawler and transferred into a black van that stood at the far end of the harbour wall. When the last crate was loaded into the van he saw the limey shake hands with the coloured fisherman and clamber up onto the quay.

As Hank watched Statton untie the trawler's mooring rope he smiled to himself, replaced the field glasses in their case and returned quickly to his auto, which was parked in a lay-by on Boyes Drive.

He started the engine and drove slowly along the road with his lights switched off. Periodically he glanced in his rear view mirror to check that he was not being followed and did not turn on his headlights until he reached the junction with Main Road. There he turned right and headed back along the coast towards the small hotel in St. James in which he was staying.

The hotel's parking lot was situated at the rear of the building and was lit by only a single floodlight attached to the back wall of the hotel. However, the light was directed only on the pathway leading from the parking lot to the front entrance, so only the autos parked closest to the path were covered by its yellow beam.

Hank headed for a part of the parking lot furthest from the light and parked in the dark shadows that lay there. He turned off his lights and waited patiently in his locked auto for ten minutes. He sat motionless in the dark, with only his eyes moving from side to side, checking the lot for any sign of life.

Except for the floodlit path the rear of the hotel was in darkness. Standing in a line along the back wall was a row of dumpsters. One, closest to the emergency fire exit, was overflowing and trash from it was starting to pile up on the asphalt surface of the parking lot.

Next to the dumpsters was a stack of Coca-Cola crates. The beam from the floodlight shone into the side window of a parked auto and its miniature reflection was mirrored in each of the narrow glass necks of the empty bottles that were stored in the top crate.

Something moved near the dumpsters and Hank saw that it was the hotel's resident ginger tom cat. He watched as the animal clawed its way through the pile of trash, no doubt looking for scraps. The cat obviously found something of interest because it crouched down and then crawled backwards on its haunches dragging something with it. Before the cat disappeared beneath a dumpster it raised its head and stared over at Hank's auto, alert and watchful. Then it was gone, swallowed by the black shadow under the bin.

Once again the night was still and silent, but Hank waited another five minutes before leaving the auto. He slipped silently out of the driver's door, locked it and headed for the hotel's emergency fire exit.

When Hank reached the door he grunted in satisfaction when he found the wedge of cardboard still in place. He had used it earlier that evening to keep the door slightly ajar and allow him access to and from the hotel without being seen by the receptionist.

He glanced over his shoulder but the parking lot still looked deserted.

Suddenly the fire exit was flung open from the inside, smashing into the side of Hank's head and throwing him off balance. A large dark figure leaped from the darkness of the open doorway and lunged towards him, pushing him to the ground.

As he hit the ground Hank rolled instinctively to one side, but in doing so he kicked the stack of Coca-Cola bottles and it toppled over with a crash of breaking glass. Even before the last bottle smashed onto the ground Hank had recovered and scrambled quickly to his knees.

But he was not quick enough. His assailant, who was dressed all in black and wore a ski-mask launched himself at Hank, landing on top of him with a crunch that spread-eagled him on the ground and knocked the breath from his body.

Hank's attacker was a heavily built man and easily pinned him to the ground in a way that made it difficult for him to prevent the man's hands from encircling his neck in a vice like grip. He stared up into his attacker's eyes, which were just visible through the narrow slits in his ski-mask. He felt his vision swim as a lack of air to his lungs pushed him closer to the edge of unconsciousness. He tried to struggle, but had no strength in his body and could do nothing to loosen the ever tightening grip on his throat.

Then, just as Hank began to black out, panic generated adrenalin kicked in and he managed to find enough energy to twist his torso and at the same time push upwards with his legs. He threw his assailant off balance for just long enough to loosen the grip on his throat.

The man quickly recovered his balance and rolled back on top of Hank, reaching again for his throat. Hank had won himself a few precious seconds, during which time he managed to fill his lungs with much needed air. With the surge of oxygen into his blood stream came renewed strength and he bucked again, throwing his assailant off balance again.

Hank managed to twist away with a half roll before his attacker once again grabbed him. As he was pulled violently onto his back, with his outstretched arms being slammed against the floor, Hank's right hand landed in a jumble of glass. He felt a searing pain in the back of his hand as it connected with the neck of a broken bottle.

The man was back on top of Hank and had resumed the murderous grip on his throat and once again he felt himself weaken as the flow of air was cut off from his tortured lungs. Hank's hand tightened on the broken bottle and with a supreme effort he twisted his body again and plunged the jagged glass through his attacker's black ski-mask and into the side of his neck.

The man immediately released his grip and slid off Hank, slumping back on the ground with his back against the hotel wall. Now his hands clasped his own throat as he fought to stem the blood that spurted in a dark fountain from his severed carotid artery.

Hank rose gasping to his knees, his lungs burning with the lack of oxygen, but by the time he had recovered sufficiently to go to his attacker's aid it was too late. The man's eyes glazed over and his hands dropped to his side. As the man's heart stopped pumping the fountain of blood stopped spurting and instead slowly oozed down the front of his black leather jacket.

Hank pulled off the man's ski-mask and was stunned as he recognised the bearded face of his CIA colleague, Sam Potter, who stared up at him with lifeless, accusing eyes. 'Shit!' Hank swore quietly as his mind grappled with the significance of Potter's attempt to kill him.

He clambered quickly to his feet as the two and two he added together in his mind came to a warning total of four. It was very clear to him that he needed to get the hell away from the hotel as quickly as possible.

Hank pushed the dead man behind one of the dumpsters, but could do nothing about the pool of blood that lay on the ground and would soon be discovered in the light of day. Taking care not to walk in the blood, he slipped through the fire door and made his way silently to his room. He quickly cleaned the wound on the back of his right hand and put a Band-Aid over it. He checked he had no blood on his clothes, threw his few possessions into a sea bag and headed back to the parking lot.

Five minutes later he was driving along Main Road towards the Cape Flats.

Clovelly

David Statton

'Bang!' Charlie pretended to shoot Louis Armstrong in the same spot on his forehead at which I had aimed only four days before. But the little Frenchman was not holding a Star pistol, he was pointing a Kalashnikov AK47 at the singer's black face.

'It's been a long time since I held one of these in my hands,' he said as he lowered the assault rifle and handed it back to me.

I balanced the Soviet made weapon in my hand. I knew it weighed ten pounds, but it felt lighter. The metal parts of the rifle were lightly greased and the wooden grips were clean and smelled strongly of linseed oil. I rubbed my hand across the curved magazine. When full, the magazine held 30 rounds of 7.62 mm ammunition. The wooden crate that stood on the floor at my feet contained another five AK47s. Next to it was a second crate in which were packed a couple of dozen spare magazines and enough ammunition to fight a small scale war.

I removed the magazine from the Kalashnikov I held and handed it to Paul before replacing the weapon in the crate. 'It might be a good idea to load all the magazines with bullets before we store them away,' I suggested. 'It will save time later.'

'Och! I'll do that, so I will,' Mr Mac said as he relieved Paul of the magazine. With the help of the big South African he dragged the two crates to a corner of the outhouse and settled down on the floor. He opened one of the cardboard boxes full of ammunition and deftly started loading one of the magazines.

Meanwhile John and I prised the lid off another crate to reveal a row of hand grenades. Each was decorated with white markings written in a language that I recognised, not least because I knew in which country they had been manufactured. It was Hebrew.

John picked up one of the grenades and looked at it with an expert eye. 'An Israeli smoke grenade,' he said before passing it to Charlie to look at. 'How many?' He asked.

Four crates of twelve grenades,' I replied.

'That should create plenty of smoke,' Charlie said as he returned the grenade to the crate and replaced the lid.

Paul picked up the crate effortlessly and lowered it into the hidden compartment in the wood pile. It was quickly followed by the other three crates.

'There are more smoke grenades,' I explained, pointing to a smaller crate. 'But a different type.'

John knelt beside the crate and levered open the lid. He whistled when he saw what was inside. 'Now that's what I call a smokie!' He picked a grenade up and showed it to Paul and Charlie. 'That, my friends, is a German made DM Twenty-Four. It's called a blend-brand-hand-grenade, otherwise known as a brandy.'

'Like the Israeli grenade it throws out a cloud of dense choking smoke, but there the similarity ends. The smoke from this mother burns for about five minutes and reaches temperatures of twelve hundred degrees Celsius. It ignites any combustible material with which it comes in contact, including human flesh and bone. In short, it's frigging lethal.'

'Very frigging lethal,' I emphasised. 'Which is why we will use them only as a last resort. I want to avoid any fatalities if we can.'

John gave me a questioning look.

'Don't worry I haven't gone soft,' I told him. 'My motive is completely tactical. If we succeed in getting Mandela and Zamyatin off Robben Island the South Africans will obviously try to track us down, but, I think they are likely to keep any activity pretty low key. They will be pretty embarrassed about such a lapse in security and they won't want to publicise it too much. However, if we kill any of their men they are going to be seriously pissed off and will throw all their resources into capturing us.'

'So air shots where we can?' Paul asked.

'Yes, unless it is a matter of them or us.'

'How many brandies are there?' John asked, passing the grenade to Paul to look at.

'Just the one box of ten.'

'It's very light,' Paul commented.

'Yeah,' John replied. 'It's made of plastic, so whatever you do, don't drop the damn thing. The DM Twenty-Four has no explosive charge to detonate it. Instead, when it hits a hard surface, like the concrete floor we're standing on, the plastic case splits. The charge ignites when it comes into contact with the air. There's a blinding flash and if you drop that one, we're charcoal.'

'Jesus Christ!' Paul swore as he gingerly passed the grenade back to John.

'I've seen one of these mothers work,' John said, 'and it ain't something you wanna be close to when it explodes, pal.' He carefully returned the grenade to its crate, put the lid back on and hid it in the wood pile.

'Ye can have these back just now, Mister Brandon,' Mr Mac said getting to his feet. He pointed at the crates containing the AK47s and ammunition. 'The magazines are all filled.'

John helped Mr Mac drag the crates to the wood pile and the two men stored them away with the other crates.

There were two wooden crates left on the floor, one slightly larger than the other. John eyed them with the professional eye of the explosives expert he was. 'I can guess what's in this crate,' he said, gently patting the larger crate. 'Semtex?'

'Yes.'

'So what's in this other crate?' He began to prise off the lid.

'More grenades!' Charlie exclaimed when he saw the crate's contents.

'Yeah, but those ain't smokies,' John said. 'Unless I'm very much mistaken this little beauty is a stun grenade.' He held one up. It was black with similar white markings in Hebrew as the Israeli smoke grenade.

'So, where do you reckon Dyakala got all this stuff?' Paul asked as he hid the final two crates in the compartment and replaced the lid.

I thought about my earlier conversation with Johan Carlse. 'Hezbollah,' I said with certainty as I helped him cover the compartment lid with logs. 'Carlse told me he was with Robert in Beirut when he bought the goods. There was a guy from Hezbollah there and you know those boys are pretty chummy with the ANC.'

'In that case I hope he was very careful,' Paul said. 'From what I hear Hezbollah has been heavily infiltrated by the Israelis. If MOSSAD get wind of the shipment they will tip off NIS straight away and if that happens it really will be time to start worrying.'

I was one step ahead of him. The same thought had crossed my mind and I was already worried.

Monday May 10th 1982: Muizenberg, Cape Town

The northern coastline of False Bay sweeps majestically for several miles from Muizenberg in the west to Strandfontain in the east. On

Monday morning I drove the pickup truck along the coast road, with Paul and Charlie at my side, with one of the ski-boats in tow. Our job was to see whether the muffle-box for the outboard motor worked. We had left John behind to carry on making the rest of the boxes and Mr Mac had offered to stay and help him.

When we arrived at the spot from which we would be launching the ski-boat, we were surrounded by the thick grey mist that lay across False Bay like a wet blanket. Although the mist was cold and damp, it was actually a blessing in disguise because it shielded us from prying eyes. Our excursion out into the Bay would not draw unwanted attention to our presence, but as an additional precaution we had brought along the fishing equipment.

'OK, Charlie, we'll leave the muffle-box off the engine on the outward journey, but fit it on before we return,' I explained as we all changed into our motor-cycle leathers. 'We need to see how close we can get to the beach before you hear us.'

It had been agreed that the little Frenchman would wait for us on the beach, but he didn't complain about being left behind, neither did he shrink from helping us launch the ski-boat. We had decided to bring the second boat because it had not yet had a run out, but unlike the launching of the Spirit of Freedom, there was no naming ceremony on this occasion.

The water in False Bay feeds in from the Indian Ocean. It is a few degrees warmer than the Atlantic Ocean, the white capped breakers of which batter themselves to death against the rocky coastline on the opposite side of the Peninsula from Muizenberg. But in May the False Bay water is still chilly and we were pleased to be wearing our protective leathers as we waded into the water.

Once the boat was afloat, Paul clambered aboard, started the big outboard engine and edged the craft away from the shore. I helped Charlie pull the trailer up onto the beach before joining the big South African in the boat.

Paul sat behind the wheel and I slipped into the passenger seat next to him. Behind us on the deck lay the fishing equipment and the muffle-box that would be fitted over the cowl of the Suzuki engine before our return to land.

My friend took the boat up to full power and I smiled contentedly to myself as I heard the healthy roar of the engine. We headed through the clinging mist towards a small rocky island that rose out of the sea three miles or so off the Muizenberg beach.

Seal Island gets its name from the large colony of Cape Fur

Seals that inhabit the outcrop of Cape granite. The island at 800 metres in length and 50 metres wide is much smaller than its namesake in Cape Bay, which is better known by its Dutch name of Robben Island.

There is next to no vegetation, soil or sand on the island. As the low lying islet slowly appeared through the swirling mist all we could see was guano streaked rock that bore witness to the fact that, in addition to the seals, the islet was home to thousands of seabirds.

As Paul cut the engine I dropped the boat's anchor over the side and for a while we bobbed around on the late grey sea. We watched the seals as they engaged in an endless game of push and shove as each fought off the invasion of rivals into their own hard won space on the crowded island.

Suddenly there was a commotion in the sea at the other end of the narrow island as even more squealing seals flapped out of the sea onto the already congested rock. The sea opened up in a cascade of white water and the unmistakeable shape of a great white shark launched itself into the air with its jaws clamped firmly round the body of a thrashing fat seal. With a crash the shark hit the surface of the sea and disappeared beneath the surface.

Paul sprang up from his seat and made his way to the stern of the boat, picking up the muffle-box on his way. 'Come on, Dave,' he said hurriedly. 'Let's strap on this contraption and get the hell out of here.'

I joined Paul as he stood over the outboard motor. I began counting slowly in my mind as I knelt by his side and watched him position the muffle-box over the cowl of the outboard motor. I reached under the motor and pulled the two straps up the side and quickly thread each through its buckle and tightened them.

From the time when I knelt on the deck to when I secured the second buckle I counted exactly twelve seconds. Satisfied we would be able to remove the box just as quickly Paul made his way back to his seat as I double checked the fastenings, before pulling up the anchor.

'Start her up,' I told Paul as I settled back in the seat next to him.

'Already done,' Paul replied, looking over his shoulder to where the shark had disappeared into the ocean. 'Man, I hate those bastards,' he said with a shudder.

I looked over my own shoulder towards the stern of the boat and saw a froth of bubbles as the propeller spun silently beneath the surface. I concentrated and detected a hum that I now realised was the engine turning over. The hum became more noticeable as Paul increased power and the Suzuki picked up speed. 'I wonder how close we can get to land before Charlie hears us,' I said.

'Man, I hate those bastards,' Paul repeated, ignoring my own comment as he steered the speedboat as far away from Seal Island as quickly as possible.

Soon the rocky island was swallowed once again by the thick mist. Paul reduced the outboard motor to half power as we made our way back to Muizenberg, We sat in silence as we both concentrated on navigating our way back to the spot where we had left Charlie. The mist was disorientating and when we reached the beach there was no sign of the little Frenchman.

'Which way?' Paul asked.

'It doesn't matter,' I replied. 'Whichever way we head is bound to be wrong.'

Paul spun the boat's steering wheel to the left and we made our way slowly westwards along the coast for about half a mile.

'You were right,' Paul said. 'We must be heading in the wrong direction. There is no way our calculations were this far out.'

'I agree. Let's head back in the other direction.'

Paul turned the boat round and we made our way back along the coast. Eventually, several hundred yards east of where we had first hit land, we came across Charlie standing on the edge of the sand peering out to sea. At first, he was unaware of our approach and when finally he caught sight of the boat, only a couple of yards to his right, he grinned and clapped his hands in an applause that echoed eerily in the mist.

'John was right,' Charlie said as he came wading through the water to help us land the speedboat. 'I heard nothing until you were a few meters away from me. Unbelievable!'

When we had finished loading the boat onto the trailer, we connected it to the back of the truck. I was pleased to get out of my leathers and into warm dry clothes. Mr Mac had made up a flask of coffee and some bacon sandwiches. We had breakfast in the cab of the truck before heading in high spirits to Bloubergstrand where we stored the boat and trailer in the empty garage that I had rented the previous Saturday.

'Why are we leaving the boat in the garage?' Charlie asked as we headed back to the Cape Peninsula.

'It's just a precaution,' I explained. 'We'll be using both the pickup and the Mercedes on Friday night and two vehicles pulling boats travelling in convoy up the M4 at might attract attention from the police.'

'Better safe than sorry, Charlie,' Paul added. 'It's very unusual to see a van pulling a boat and it would set alarm bells ringing if the police saw it.'

'I'll be driving the Mercedes, with Mr Mac and Carlse as passengers,' I explained. 'We'll divert to the garage and pick up the boat, whilst Paul takes John and you in the pick-up. We'll meet up on the beach.'

By the time we were driving through Lakeside, the southern-most of Cape Town's suburbs, the mist had been burned off. On our left the deep blue waters of Marina Da Gama sparkled in the unseasonably hot early winter sun, which added to our general sense of wellbeing.

Our high spirits disappeared abruptly when at the junction of Main Road and Beach Road a cop waved us to the side of the road. He carried the triple stripes of a sergeant on the shoulder of his waving arm and an R4 assault rifle slung over the other.

The sergeant was accompanied by three constables, all of whom looked pretty young, but we were not inclined to underestimate them because of their age, because the assault rifles they were pointing menacingly at us didn't look very old either.

Paul pulled into the side of the kerb and turned off the engine.

The sergeant approached the driver's door and Paul wound down his window. One of the constables split from the little group and went to check out the back of the pickup. His two companions didn't move. Nor did the muzzles of their R4s.

'Goeiemore, meneer,' the sergeant said. 'Mag ek u identiteitsdokument sien, asseblief?'

Paul took a thin green covered identity document from his shirt pocket and handed it to the cop, who studied his face carefully and compared it with the photograph in the book. Satisfied the cop returned the document to him and looked at me and held out his hand.

'Mag ek u identiteitsdokument sien, meneer?'

'Hy het geen identiteitsdokument, sersant. Hy is uit Engeland,' Paul explained quickly.

'Do you have your passport with you, sir?' The sergeant asked me in English.

I slipped a British passport from my pocket and handed it to him.

The cop studied my passport carefully before handing it back. 'Thank you, Dr Boyd. I trust you are enjoying your stay in South Africa.'

'Very much indeed,' I said with a smile and a feeling of relief. Even with the best forged passport, and mine was the very best, it is always good to know that it passes muster.

'And why are you in South Africa? Are you here on holiday?'

'No, I am a marine biologist,' I explained. 'My team and I are investigating marine life in False Bay, but because of the mist we decided to take the day off and do a little fishing. We were heading for the west coast, but conditions have improved so we decided to head back to Fish Hoek.'

'Is that where you are staying?'

'Not exactly. We are renting a house close to Fish Hoek. In a little place called Clovelly. Do you know it?'

'Ja, I know it.' The sergeant nodded towards Charlie who sat at the far end of the cab. 'I take it your other friend is English also?' He asked Paul.

'No, he's French.'

'French is it?' He looked at Charlie as if he were an alien. 'Watter taal praat hy?' He asked Paul in Afrikaans.

'He asks what language you speak, Charlie,' Paul translated with a laugh.

'What language does he want me to speak?' The little Frenchman asked in English. 'Tell him I speak English, German, Spanish, Russian, Portuguese, Mandarin and Hindi, oh, and a little French.'

'English will do,' the cop said with a good natured smile. 'Do you have a passport?' He asked, but then saw that Charlie was already leaning across me holding out the document for him to take. He gave the French passport only a cursory look and handed it straight back.'

The constable who had been checking the back of the pickup returned and shook his head at the sergeant, who indicated that his men should raise the barrier at the road block. 'Good bye, gentlemen,' he said to us. 'I hope you enjoy the rest of your stay in South Africa.'

'Totsiens,' Paul said as he started up the truck's engine and drove slowly under the raised barrier. He did not speak again until we were well out of sight of the road block. 'What was that all

229

about?' He asked.

'I have no idea,' I deliberately kept my voice neutral.

'Do you think the cops are on to us?' Charlie asked.

'Almost certainly not,' I replied. 'If they suspected us in any way we would already be staring at the walls of a Pollsmoor cell.'

'I hope you're right, my friend,' Charlie said with a rueful smile. 'I do not relish sharing another prison cell with you.'

I smiled back at him with more confidence than I felt. The road block had unsettled me more than I wanted to admit. If the police were not looking for us, who were they looking for?

Clovelly

By early evening the weather had reverted to type and the earlier warmth had been replaced by a biting north-west wind. It swept across the Cape Flats bringing with it heavy pulses of rain that beat against the lounge windows and made us feel pleased to be indoors.

Paul and I sat in our favourite chairs in front of the hearth in which a crackling fire was just beginning to create enough heat to make the room cosy. We each had a glass of red wine balanced on the arm of our chairs. John was still working in the garage, finishing off the last of the muffle-boxes and Mr Mac was in the kitchen cooking supper. Charlie was slumped in a chair in front of the television that stood in the corner of the room, sipping from his own glass of red wine as he waited for the early evening programmes to start.

The little Frenchman was an avid television watcher and constantly bemoaned the fact that in South Africa broadcasting did not start until five pm and finished at ten thirty.

'This country needs to understand that we are now living in the twentieth century,' he complained for the umpteenth time. 'It's the age of technology.'

'Sies, man, you're lucky there is anything to watch at all,' Paul said with a chuckle. 'The National Party never wanted television, so they delayed its introduction for as long as possible. We've only had proper coverage in South Africa for about six years.'

'Why didn't they want TV?' Charlie asked.

'The Boers thought it was a creation of the devil that would undermine the Afrikaner way of life and promote immorality.'

'That's stupid,' Charlie muttered irritably.

Paul, who was an avowed supporter of South Africa's liberal Progressive Federal Party, led by Frederik van Zyl Slabbert, agreed. 'Well, "stupid" is a word that pretty well sums up the Nats and their policies,' he said. 'But getting back to the TV, public pressure eventually forced the Government to accept the inevitable and transmissions began in Jo'burg in nineteen seventy five and went nationwide a year later. But ministers insisted that English and Afrikaans received equal broadcasting time. That's why programmes are broadcast in one of the two official languages in the first half of the evening and in the other language in the second half, each taking a turn to be early on alternative days.'

'Well watching The Sweeney in Afrikaans is hard to swallow,' Charlie took his displeasure out on his wine glass by gulping down the remainder of his red wine.

'What's hard to swallow, Charlie?' John asked as he walked into the lounge wiping his wet head with a towel. 'Obviously not the red wine.' He pointed at the Frenchman's empty glass.

'The wine is excellent, it's the television service in this country that is crap,' Charlie said as he got to his feet and stomped over to the drinks cabinet.

'I thought you were bellyaching about the TV again,' John said with a laugh.

'With good cause,' Charlie poured himself another glass of wine. 'Drink?'

'Sounds good,' the American replied. 'It's damn cold and wet out there.'

'Have you finished?' I asked.

John stopped drying his hair. 'Did you hear me running the go-kart engine?' He asked.

I shook my head.

'Well I fitted a muffle-box over the engine and ran it at full revs for at least a minute with the back door of the garage open,' John explained and held up both his thumbs in a gesture of success.

'I heard nothing except the wind and the rain.' I said.

'Can't even blame the television for drowning out the sound,' Charlie observed sourly. As he spoke the test card disappeared from the screen and the South African Broadcasting Company logo heralded the first programme of the day, which was the early evening news in English.

'Good work, John,' I said and raised my glass at him. 'We'll put the karts into the inflatable dinghies tomorrow with the rest of the equipment and load them into the back of the van.'

Mr Mac poked his head round the lounge door frame. 'The braised steak will be ready soon, gentlemen,' he announced.

'Do I have time to grab a shower before we eat,' John asked.

'Aye, as long as ye're quick, Mister Brandon,' the little Scotsman replied. 'Dinner will be ready in about fifteen minutes, so it will.'

'OK, I'm on my way. You might as well have this, Mr Mac,' John said handing him his glass of red wine. 'I'll get a fresh one later.'

'I don't mind if I do,' Mr Mac said as he sniffed the wine. 'Pinotage,' he said appreciatively. 'Ma favourite.'

I finished my glass of wine and went to uncork another bottle, with half an ear on the news. The third item featured was a report from the Cape Peninsula and it grabbed my full attention immediately.

'Police in Cape Town are investigating the brutal murder of an American tourist,' the female news reader announced, with a suitably solemn expression on her pretty young face. 'Early this morning the man was discovered dead in the car park of a hotel in St James on the Cape Peninsula. His body was discovered behind a rubbish bin by a kitchen worker. The police have not yet revealed how the man died, but an SABC source alleges that his throat was cut.'

The news item cut to a film showing a group of policemen standing round a car.

'In an effort to catch the culprit the police set up a number of road blocks in the area,' the news reader explained in a voice over, 'but as yet nobody has been apprehended.'

Judging from the background to the road block in the film it didn't look as if it was the same location as the one at which we had been stopped earlier that day. Neither were they the same cops, although they carried similar lethal looking weapons.

'The murdered man has not been named, however, the police have issued a photograph of the victim and are asking for anybody who recognises him to come forward with any information they might have.'

I stared at the photograph that filled the small television screen. It showed a white man with a bald head and a thick black beard.

I recognised immediately the upside down face of CIA agent

Sam Potter, but decided the police would have to press on with their investigation without any information from me.

Gerald Du Toit

Tuesday May 11th 1982
Mondeor

Gerald Du Toit hated decorating and had put off starting on the gardener's room for as long as he could. But constant badgering from his wife finally forced his hand and he was now on hands and knees about to remove what he considered to be perfectly good floor tiles.

'They're good enough for a kaffir anyway,' he mumbled to himself irritably. 'That nagging old cow must think money grows on trees. Doesn't she realise how many kilometres I have to travel and the amount of goods I have to sell to give her the lifestyle she enjoys?'

Gerald pushed the point of a cold-chisel under a floor tile closest to the door and hit it with a vicious blow of a heavy mallet. The tile was poorly cemented to the floor and flew through the air and landed with a satisfying crash against the distempered side wall on which hung a picture of a black football team. He quickly tackled another tile and then another and within a few minutes had removed the first row of tiles.

It took Gerald only half an hour to reach that part of the floor on which stood the table, chair and orange boxes. He got to his feet and stretched, then he dragged the primitive bed onto the part of the floor from which he had removed tiles and piled onto it the table, chairs and orange boxes.

Soon Gerald was on his hands and knees again continuing with his task. The floor tiles in this part of the room were looser than those he had just raised and he was able to prise them up easily without using the mallet.

As he lifted one of the tiles that had been covered by an orange box, he discovered a cavity in the floor. At first, he thought it was a rat hole and his heart leapt, but then logic took over and he realised that the cavity was oblong and could not have been dug by a rodent. He prised up a second tile and the rest of the hole was revealed.

Gerald inspected the edges of the hole more closely and he realised that it had been carefully cut out with a chisel. He frowned as he realised he would have to fill in the hole with concrete before he could re-tile the floor, which was a nuisance because he was not sure he had any sand and cement in the garage. He was just about to get to his feet and go check when he noticed something in the hole that was slightly lighter than its surroundings.

Still slightly nervous about the possibility of a rat living under the floor, Gerald very cautiously put two fingers into the hole to investigate. He touched something solid and realised immediately it was no rat.

Using his two fingers Gerald gently pulled a small leather bound book from the hole. Puzzled he opened the book and found it was filled with handwritten notes. It was obviously a diary of some kind. He flicked through and found the most recent entry was dated only a week before. As he read the single short, but descriptive sentence that was written in a neat hand beneath the date: Wednesday 5th May 1982, his face went white and his hands began to shake with anger.

'The filthy bitch!' He whispered to himself as he flicked back in the diary to see if there were similar entries. There were several. 'The dirty, sluttish bitch!' He swore as he scrambled to his feet and headed for the door.

Gerald found his wife in the lounge where she was sitting on the sofa reading a magazine. He walked up behind her and without warning grabbed her by the hair and dragged her off the sofa onto the floor. He pulled the magazine from her hand and threw it across the room

'Why you reading that crap?' he shouted. 'Read this instead, you slut.' He threw the gardener's diary at her face.

Carol dodged the book and stared up at her husband with wide frightened eyes. 'What are you talking about, Gerald.' She wailed.

'It's the kaffir's diary,' he screamed. 'He has listed every time you screwed him, you filthy whore.'

Carol's face went white as she stared at the book that lay on the floor next to her. She edged away as if it was poisonous and began to cry. 'It wasn't my fault, Gerald,' she sobbed. 'He forced me to have sex with him.'

'You mean the black bastard raped you?' Gerald asked, wanting to believe it was true, because the alternative was simply too awful to contemplate.

'Yes,' she said, her eyes wide and fearful. 'The first time

anyway. I went to his room to ask him to wash the windows and he pushed me onto his bed. I tried to resist but he was too strong for me.'

'What about the other times?'

She shook her head miserably. 'Not exactly,' she said.

'Not exactly?' Gerald screamed in rage. 'What the fuck do you mean by "not exactly"?'

'Well it was almost like rape,' Carol insisted pleadingly. 'He threatened to tell you I had slept with him willingly unless I let him have sex again, so I did. After that I had no choice but to give him what he wanted whenever he wanted it.'

'Why didn't you tell me he raped you when it first happened?'

'Because...' she mumbled quietly before falling silent.

'Because what?'

'Because he threatened to kill me if I told anybody.'

'Listen, you stupid cow. I'll kill you myself if I find out you're lying to me,' Gerald hissed as he leaned over her and retrieved the gardener's diary. 'Meanwhile, we are going to the police so you can tell them your story. Get your coat.'

Captain Alan Pienaar

Tuesday May 11th 1982: John Vorster Square, Johannesburg

Captain Alan Pienaar slowly read the entry in the diary and then looked up at the couple who sat in front of him on the other side of the interview desk. 'What I am reading doesn't sound like a description of forced sex, mevrou,' he said in an even voice, trying to keep disapproval from his voice.

The woman refused to make eye contact with him when he looked at her. Gut instinct and twenty years of service as a policeman convinced him he was looking at a white woman who liked a bit of black. It happened, but it made the situation no more palatable, nor legal.

'But I told you, Robert blackmailed me into having sex with him,' Carol du Toit insisted and started to weep again.

The woman had called her alleged assailant "Robert", Alan noted. Not, "my gardener" or "the kaffir". *Why was that?* He wondered.

'What is this nonsense, Captain?' Gerald du Toit snapped. 'My wife was raped and then threatened with death if she told anybody. You're talking as if she's the criminal and not the black bastard who attacked her.'

'Inter-racial sex is a crime, meneer,' Alan pointed out in a calm, even voice, despite really wanting to shout at the deluded idiot and tell him that he thought the woman sitting next to him was a lying whore. Instead he bit his tongue and added diplomatically: 'Not that I am saying your wife was a willing party to the sex.'

'I should think not! That would be a disgusting suggestion.'

But true, Alan wanted to say, but once again kept his thoughts to himself. The problem was he could never prove the woman was lying, and anyway in such cases it was often better to accept a lie. He knew his superiors would not be pleased if he managed to prove that the country's morality laws had yet again been ignored so blatantly by a white woman.

So he would go along with the Du Toit woman's story and charge Dyakala with rape and intimidation. Alan had long accepted that trumped up charges against blacks were a fact of police life in South Africa. However, he was not proud about the way he sometimes swallowed his own misgivings.

'Thank you, mevrou. Constable Malan here will take a written statement from you,' Pienaar nodded to the uniformed policeman who hovered in the background. 'Meanwhile I will issue an arrest warrant for Robert Dyakala.'

Alan stood up and left the interview room clutching Dyakala's diary in his hand. As he strode down the corridor towards the wing of the building that housed Special Branch, his pulse raced with excitement. There was another recent entry in the book that was far more significant than the gentle boastings of a black gardener who was servicing his white madam on the side.

Brigadier Kobus Coetzee

Kobus muttered quietly to himself as he read the cryptic entry in the diary that followed Dyakala's somewhat more graphic description of his sexual encounter with the Du Toit woman...

Leaving town today. Everything is arranged. The team is lined up. The boat is ready. The goods are on their way. The Boers are in for one hell of a surprise!

Kobus laid the diary on his desk and picked up a file that was marked Secret and bore the seal of the South African National Intelligence Service. He pulled out the single sheet contained in the file and reread the message from the Israeli intelligence service, MOSSAD, with whom NIS worked closely.

The ANC had been buying weapons and explosives from Hezbollah and instinct told Kobus that these were the "goods" referred to in the diary entry. 'What are they up to?' He mumbled.

'Sir?' Pienaar asked.

'Just thinking out loud, Captain,' Kobus replied.

'Does the entry in the gardener's diary mean anything to you?' Pienaar asked.

'Yes, Pienaar. It means trouble.' Kobus looked up and smiled grimly. 'Leave the diary with me. I need to study it in more depth.'

'But, sir, the diary is the only evidence I have in the Du Toit rape case,' Pienaar pointed out.

'Do you honestly think it was rape, Pienaar?' Kobus asked with a knowing smile.

'That will be for the court to decide,' the captain neatly side stepped the question.

'Look, Captain, I appreciate your concern about the Du Toit woman, but on this occasion I believe my need for the diary is greater than yours. This is a matter of national security. I am sure you understand my position.'

Pienaar nodded.

'Good. In that case, I would be grateful if you would put this rape nonsense on the back burner until we in Special Branch can find out exactly what Dyakala is up to.'

'You know him?'

'Ja, we know him alright. We believe he is a terrorist

sympathiser, but we have never been able to prove he is personally involved in criminal acts. This could be the breakthrough for which we have been waiting a very long time. Drawing the diary to my attention was good work on your part, Pienaar. Well done.'

'Thank you, Brigadier. Please be assured that I understand fully the importance of what you are doing and of course you must keep the diary. I can delay issuing Dyakala's arrest warrant for a time. However, I can't sit on it for too long. I am sure you understand my position.'

'Yes, I understand, Captain,' Kobus said with a smile. Just then his telephone rang. 'If you would excuse me,' he said and picked up the receiver, but he covered the mouthpiece and did not speak until Pienaar had taken the hint and left his office.

'Coetzee,' he said eventually.

'Goeienaand, Brigadier,' a voice said.

'Goeienaand. Wie is dit?' Kobus asked automatically in Afrikaans, but then realised that the voice on the other end of the telephone had what sounded like an English accent so he repeated his question in that language. 'Who is this?'

'Well, the last time I looked in the mirror I was Ma Brody's boy.'

'Dermot?'

'The very same, Kobus, me boyo.'

'I heard they made you Colonel,' Kobus said with a smile. 'Not bad for a rooinek.'

'A rooinek, is it. Well, I suppose that's marginally better than being called an Englishman.'

Kobus laughed. 'So what can I do for you, Dermot?'

'It's more what I can do for you, Kobus. We have somebody down here who is interested in talking to you.'

Experience had taught Kobus that detecting crime is often more about gut instinct and unexplained coincidences than raw policing. As he listened to Dermot Brody, he had a very strong feeling that this phone call was important. The Irishman was head of CID in Cape Town and Kobus sensed that the phone call was somehow connected to Robert Dyakala.

'Name?' Kobus asked.

'Johannes Smit.'

It was not a name that Kobus recognised. 'What does he want to talk to me about?'

'He says he has information about a terrorist incident that is being planned.'

'Why does he want to speak to me?' Kobus asked casually, but a worm of excitement was beginning to wriggle in his belly.

'Because my pay grade is not authorised to stump up the sort of money he is talking about,' Brody explained.

'He wants to sell information?'

'To be sure, boyo.'

'Lock him up and keep him safe, Dermot. I'll catch the next flight down to Cape Town.' Jumping to his feet, Kobus threw Dyakala's diary into his briefcase and ran from his office.

Central Police Station, Cape Town

It was almost midnight before Kobus reached Cape Town's Central Police Station where he was met by Dermot Brody who shook his hand and ushered him through to his office.

'It's a foul night, to be sure,' Brody said as he watched Kobus slip out of a wet raincoat that had already deposited water on his office floor. He nodded towards the rain lashed window through which the trees in the police station's courtyard could be seen being buffeted as they were picked out by the bright arc lights attached to the side of the building.

'Can I tempt you to a warming tipple?' Brody asked as he took a bottle of Bushmills and two glasses from a drawer and put them on his desk.

Kobus smiled. 'I'm always tempted by Irish Whiskey, Dermot,' he said, 'but I'll enjoy it better after I've had a word with this Smit fellow. Has he said anything more to you?'

Brody shook his head. 'I tried to wheedle something out of him, but he's kept his mouth closed as tight as a virgin's fanny.'

'Where is he now?'

'I've had him transferred to an interview room. He is under guard, but I've ensured he has been provided with a steady supply of beer.'

'Good work. That should loosen his tongue nicely,' Kobus said.

'I'm not so sure. He seems to have the constitution of an ox. I suspect the only thing that'll get him talking will be seeing the colour of your money. Let's go see if I'm right, shall we Brigadier?'

David Statton

The same Main Road that bisects Wynberg runs south through the town of Fish Hoek on its journey towards a sudden end in Simon's Town. Located in one of the side roads off the Fish Hoek stretch of Main Road was the Galleon Grill, a restaurant that specialised in steaks and seafood. It was everything I loved in an eatery; it was intimate, relaxed and unpretentious. A bonus was that it served wonderful food.

'What a cosy place,' Freddie said as we sat down at a window table.

'Have you not been here before?' I asked as I slid a briefcase under the table and stood it out of sight against the wall. The briefcase was heavy, but then it did contain twenty-five thousand rand in ten-rand notes.

'No, but I've been meaning to come for ages. It has a good reputation.' She looked at me and smiled. 'Although, technically it's a whites' only restaurant.'

I looked around the restaurant and saw a couple of brown faces at one of the tables. 'They don't look white,' I pointed out.

'I did say technically,' she said. 'The owner is more liberal than some of the Cape's other restaurateurs.' She smiled at me. 'You've obviously been here before.'

'A couple of times. The food is fantastic. I can recommend the Crayfish Thermidor.'

'I love crayfish.'

A pretty waitress approached our table wearing a narrow black skirt and a wide white smile. In her hand she carried a couple of menus. 'Good evening, Mr Statton,' she said.

'You remember my name? I'm impressed,' I said and I was. 'Sadly your memory is better than mine. Your name is...'

'Hayley.'

'Hayley, of course. Please excuse me. This is my friend Freddie.'

The waitress nodded amiably at Freddie and handed her a menu. She was about to hand me the other but I waved it away.

'I've made my mind up already,' I said.

Freddie handed her menu back. 'Me too.'

'Crayfish Thermidor for two I take it?' Hayley's smile widened slightly.

'You were eavesdropping.' I returned her smile.

'It's my job to eavesdrop so that I know what our customers want, Mr Statton. Can I get you guys a drink?'

'Do you have any special Appletisers?' I asked.

'I'll check,' Hayley said before sauntering off towards the front of the restaurant. She whispered something in the ear of a middle aged man who stood behind the counter that divided the eating area from the grill area.

The man glanced over at me then nodded.

'What's a special Appletiser?' Freddie asked.

'You know what Appletiser is?'

'Of course I do. It's a non-alcoholic apple juice.'

'Well the special version is the same thing.' I lowered my voice to a whisper. 'Except it contains no apple, is alcoholic and tastes like Sauvignon Blanc.'

'It's wine?' She whispered the question.

I nodded. 'Yes, but because they are not allowed to sell alcohol in Fish Hoek they pretend it's apple juice.'

'That's naughty,' she giggled.

'So you don't want one?'

'Don't be silly, of course I do.'

'We do have special Appletisers in stock, Mr Statton,' the waitress said on her return.

'Excellent, we'll both have one,' I said.

We were sitting next to a window in one of the side booths that lined the restaurant. The shop that was located on the opposite side of the street was in darkness. Standing in front of the shop and looking into its window was a man. He was tall with broad shoulders. He wore a trench coat with its collar turned up and had a wide brimmed hat pulled down over his ears. His face was nothing more than a shadow reflection and yet there was something familiar about the man. If I was right, the last time I had seen him was in Juan Les Pins

'Wait here and look after the briefcase,' I told Freddie as I slipped out of my seat and headed for the door. By the time I reached the pavement the man was disappearing round the corner into Main Road. I wandered across the road to see what the man had been looking at so intently.

The shop was empty and its shelves had been completely stripped of goods. The only thing that I could see was the reflected window of the restaurant through which I could see Freddie staring at my back. I did not need to be a rocket scientist to work out that the mystery man had been watching us.

'Who was that?' Freddie asked when I re-joined her at the table.

'Just somebody I thought I knew.'

'And was it?'

'I don't know, I didn't get to see his face.'

'Judging by the speed he disappeared, that was his intention,' she said with a smile. She didn't miss a thing that girl.

The waitress turned up carrying two large plates, each of which contained a shiny pink crayfish shell that had been split in two and filled with claw and tail meat covered in a steaming mustard and parmesan cheese sauce.

'Thank you, Hayley,' I said as the girl put my plate in front of me. 'Do you have any more special Appletisers?'

'Of course,' she replied with a smile before heading towards the bar.

My mouth watered as the smell of Crayfish Thermidor wafted up from the plate. I hadn't realised how hungry I was.

Freddie was hungry too and was already tucking into her meal. 'This is wonderful,' she said through a mouthful of food.

I forked some tender, sweet mustard-flavoured crayfish into my mouth and could not but agree with her.

'I need you to pass some information onto your father when you see him,' I said quietly when we had both finished our meal. 'When do you expect to see him again?'

She shrugged. 'He said he would contact me tomorrow morning. I told him not to come to my flat again, but I expect that's what he will do.' She frowned. 'What should I tell him?'

'Tell him that we'll meet him at this address at twenty-three-thirty hours on Friday night.' I slipped a piece of paper across the table on which I had written the address of the garage in Bloubergstrand. I had decided it was better to keep Carlse as far away from the house in Clovelly as possible.

'Twenty-three-thirty hours?' Freddie looked puzzled.

'Half past eleven in the evening,' I explained and then lowered my voice. 'Are you OK having all that money in your apartment?'

244

She smiled and replied in a whisper: 'I'll be fine. I have a special hiding place and it is only until the weekend when I can take it to papa's home.'

I hoped she was right.

Later that night, after dropping Freddie off at her apartment in Wynberg, I made my way back to Clovelly in a thoughtful mood.

I thought about the young girl who had elbowed herself into my life and wondered if the money would be safe hidden in the secret compartment set into the bottom of her wardrobe.

I thought about Johan Carlse and tried to second guess what he and Robert Dyakala were planning. If they really were intending to blow up the Koeberg Nuclear Power Station I wondered what impact it would have on my own operation.

I thought about my meeting the following day with Gavin Rogers II and wondered whether he would tell me what Sam Potter was doing in St James before he died.

Finally, I thought about the man who had been spying on me earlier that evening as I sat with Freddie in the Fish Hoek restaurant and wondered if Rogers knew that CIA agent Hank Graham was in town.

Wednesday, May 12th 1982

When I arrived at the Mount Nelson Hotel, I found Gavin Rogers sitting in the lounge sipping champagne. He was dressed in immaculately cut grey flannel trousers; a blazer with gold buttons; and a white button-down shirt that had a couple of top buttons undone to show off his dark blue paisley silk cravat. On his feet he wore black Oxford brogues that had been polished to a shine that would have passed any parade ground muster.

The CIA deputy director held his champagne glass in one hand with his pinkie sticking out at right angles as he raised it slowly to his pouting lips sipping the wine delicately. He placed the glass carefully on the table in front of him, making sure it sat centrally on one of the round, white coasters that were used to protect the surface of the table's heavy oak top.

Rogers made a point of gently pushing up the cuff of his shirt to look at the heavy Rolex watch on his wrist. He was reminding me that I was five minutes late for our seven o'clock meeting.

I ignored him and allowed a waiter to take my rain soaked coat from me. I sat down in the seat opposite Rogers and I poured myself a glass of champagne from the half empty bottle of Bollinger that stood on a silver tray on the table. I looked around the luxuriously decorated room. 'Very nice,' I said. 'I bet staying here doesn't come cheap. Who signs off your expense account?'

'My expense allowance only covers part of the cost of staying here,' Rogers complained, 'I have to make up the difference from my own pocket.' He stared moodily at his shoes. 'My trip to Cape Town is a very costly exercise,' he added unhappily.

'You could always stay at the Holiday Inn,' I pointed out.

'The Holiday Inn?' Rogers sounded shocked that I would imagine him ever staying in a budget hotel. 'I think not.'

'Of course, if you want to save money, you could always drink local sparkling wine rather than Bolly,'

Rogers shook his head sadly at my lack of taste and poured himself more champagne. He did not offer to refill my glass.

Rogers raised the champagne and instead of drinking he sniffed it with his perfectly proportioned nose. He closed his eyes and smiled his enjoyment at the wine's aroma. I took the opportunity to knock back the rest of my own drink and replenish my glass.

When Rogers opened his eyes he sipped his Bollinger and stared at me as if challenging me to deny his pleasure. If he noticed that I had refilled my glass he didn't mention my impertinence, instead he quietly changed the subject: 'Have you seen Hank Graham?'

'I saw him in the South of France when he set up a meeting with me.'

'Ah yes, Juan Les Pins,' he said rolling the French name round his mouth like the fine wine he was drinking. 'I am afraid that whole business was a bit of a fiasco. What happened hurt me.'

'Not as much as it hurt me,' I said. 'Who hit me over the head?'

'I'm afraid that was Potter. He was a little too enthusiastic.'

'You mean the dead Potter?'

'Yes. Sam's death was very distressing,' Rogers replied, although he didn't look particularly distressed.

'So, who killed him?'

'The same person who killed Welensky.'

'And who would that be?'

'Hank Graham.'

'Why would Hank kill Welensky?'

Rogers took another sip of his champagne before answering. 'Because he's been turned by the Russians and I think Joe Welensky was onto him. I suspect that Graham set up the meeting with you at Juan Les Pins so that he could pump you for information about the operation to rescue Zamyatin.

'I think the Reds plan to snatch Zamyatin once you have him off Robben Island and Graham was tasked with finding out when and where you were handing him over. Joe found out about your meeting with Graham and confronted him. That's when Graham wasted him.'

'And you think Hank killed Potter too?'

'Yes.'

'Why?'

'Because Graham knew we were onto him.'

'So Hank is here in South Africa?'

'Yes. Sam Potter tracked him down to a hotel on the Cape Peninsula.' He nodded his head slowly, as if to emphasise his words. 'Graham killed Potter in cold blood. He crept up behind him and slit his throat.' Rogers shuddered slightly and sipped some more Champagne, swilling it around briefly in his mouth as if trying to wash away words that were distasteful to him. 'Now, I would be grateful if you would give me a progress report on the operation. Is everything going according to plan?'

So I spent the next half an hour explaining what we had achieved so far, going over the final details of our plans for getting Zamyatin off Robben Island and delivering him to Rogers. When I had finished I asked if he had any questions, but he had none so I left him with his empty Bollinger bottle and headed back to Clovelly.

Me? I had plenty of questions, for instance, if Hank Graham had turned rogue, why was he hanging around Cape Town, what was he up to and did his presence compromise my operation?

Attack on Koeberg

Hout Bay is tucked away in a valley on the western seaboard of the Cape Peninsula and is surrounded on three sides by mountains. To the east Chapman's Peak Drive winds steeply up the mountainside towards False Bay, which lies on the other side of the Peninsula. In May the water in the bay is usually dark blue and cold, but on that afternoon the Atlantic Ocean reflected the grey sky above, where rain clouds were gathering and lowering.

Robert stood on the quayside and stared first at the sea and then the sky. It looked as if the early morning weather forecast he had heard on the radio might turn out to be right. Rain was due in the area soon after they set sail and during the afternoon would spread across the whole Western Cape region, become heavier and turn increasingly blustery. The conditions would be at their worst at about the time they were scheduled to arrive at their destination that evening. The adverse weather conditions would make their journey uncomfortable, but at least it would help them escape detection.

It was a good omen.

Tied up alongside the quay lay a trawler. Four men sat on its deck repairing a fishing net. Like him they were dressed as fishermen. Robert frowned as he clambered aboard because there should have been five men waiting on the boat.

'Where is Smitty?' He asked in a quiet voice, looking at each of the men in turn.

It was Johan Carlse who eventually responded. 'No idea, baas,' he replied hesitantly. 'I've not seen or heard from him since Sunday night.'

'Didn't you try to contact him?' Robert asked, his voice rising in anger.

Carlse looked at the African and in his nervousness he reverted to using his natural language to answer him. 'Ja, ek het na sy huis, maar hy was nie daar nie.'

'Speak English,' Robert demanded sternly.

'Sorry, meneer. Ja, I went to his house, but he was not

there.'

Robert glared at the other three men. 'Have any of you seen or heard from Smitty?'

One of the men had a face almost as black as the angry African who confronted them, but his eyes were startling blue like a European. His name was Big Jannie Swartz and he looked across at his son, Little Jannie, who sat at the other side of the net they were working on, and raised an eyebrow.

The young man, whose skin colour was much lighter than his father, coughed nervously. 'Me and Frikkie had a few drinks with Smitty on Monday night,' he said nervously. 'Didn't we, Frikkie?' He directed this question at the man who sat next to him on the deck.

Frikkie Pienaar nodded his head, but refused to make eye contact with the angry Robert who stood over him.

'What happened to him?' Robert demanded of Little Jannie.

'I don't know, baas. We last saw him heading for a shebeen in Nayanga, although he was already babalas when he left us.'

'Damn him! If he's gone on another of his benders I'll kill him with my own hands,' Robert warned darkly. He glanced at his watch. 'We can't wait any longer. We must leave or we'll miss the tide. We'll have to manage with one man short.' He turned to Carlse. 'You will have to take Smitty's place and make sure the boat's ready for us on our return from placing the bombs.'

Carlse nodded his acceptance of this new role without comment and made his way to the wheelhouse. Soon Robert heard the big diesel engines start up.

'OK,' Robert shouted above the noise of the engines. 'Let's go!'

The crew jumped into action. Big Jannie uncoupled the mooring ropes, while his son and Frikkie Pienaar stowed away the fishing net. Soon the trawler was steaming out of Hout Bay and heading north towards Koeberg.

Twenty minutes after the trawler carrying Robert Dyakala and his team left Hout Bay on a northerly course towards Koeberg, a police patrol boat rounded the Chapman's Peak headland and headed in the same direction.

By that time the trawler had disappeared over the horizon and Dyakala had no idea he was being followed by the police, who were monitoring progress of his vessel using the patrol boat's state-

249

of-the-art radar equipment.

Thursday May 13th 1982
Koeberg Nuclear Power Station, Western Cape

Robert Dyakala sat with his back against a tree trunk and waited to die.

He looked around and surveyed the carnage with which he was surrounded. In front of him two members of the South African Defence Force lay on the ground nestling against each other like sleeping lovers. The top of one soldier's head had been blown away and the other man had a row of blood stained bullet holes stitched across his chest. Both were dead, killed by Robert with the same prolonged burst from his AK47.

To Robert's right was scattered the remains of Frikkie Pienaar who had taken the full force of the grenade he was about to throw when a bullet entered the right side of his temple before vaporising his brains. It flew through his skull and exited through his left temple with a wound that tore away the side of his face. In the end it was a merciful death because Frikkie never felt the subsequent blast that decapitated both arms and what was left of his shattered head.

Robert heard a noise to his left and as he turned his body to look in that direction a terrible pain tore through his belly. He closed his eyes and managed to stifle the scream that bubbled up his throat. His body was on fire from the stomach wound inflicted on him by the bullets that the scalped SADF soldier had managed to fire at him before he died.

Robert opened his eyes again and saw a man emerge from the darkness and walk part way towards him before stopping and examining two figures that lay huddled against the power station's perimeter fence.

Little Jannie Swartz was the first to die. It was his task to cut through the wire perimeter fence and make a hole large enough for the rest of the team to climb through. Robert had chosen a spot furthest away from the main administration building, because the intelligence report he had received maintained that most of the security at the Koeberg Nuclear Power Station was concentrated in that area. The report also showed that the stretch of fence he had chosen through which to gain access to the site was not covered by any of the arc lights that were dotted around the site.

They had made good time getting to the power station from the beach and it appeared the intelligence report had been right. The perimeter fence was in darkness and there was no sign of any security guards.

Members of Robert's team were nervous, but in good spirits, as they stood in a silent group and surveyed their target from the edge of a clump of trees that grew a hundred metres or so from the fence.

'Go boy,' Robert said as he touched the younger Swartz on the shoulder. He watched as the youngster headed for the wire fence and was soon lost in the shadows. Suddenly the gloom was lit by a bright flash which highlighted Little Jannie as he clung to the perimeter fence with his arms outstretched in the imitation of a crucifixion.

The wire fence glowed in the night as it threw out blue and yellow electrical flashes that added to the sparks jumping from every part of the youngster's smoking and twitching body.

Robert watched in disbelief and horror. The intelligence report had made no mention of the perimeter fence being electrified and, unwittingly, by sending Little Jannie to cut the wire fence, he had sentenced him to a horrifying death.

Big Jannie ran to rescue his son, but he was far too late because Little Jannie was already dead. Without thinking he reached out a hand, but before he could touch his son, and risk electrocution himself, Little Jannie slithered down the fence and landed in a smouldering heap on the ground.

Suddenly a floodlight came on and the gory scene was brought into sharp relief. Big Jannie stood staring down at his son's dead body, with his shoulders hunched and a Kalashnikov slung across his back.

A shot rang out and Big Jannie was hurled forward towards the fence, but before he touched the wire mesh he managed to regain his balance. He spun round, facing in the direction from which the shot had come and pulled the Kalashnikov to his front, but for the second time that night he was too late. A sustained burst of bullets thudded into him and threw him in a heap on top of his son.

Robert and Frikkie Pienaar, both of whom had followed Big Jannie towards the fence, turned to face the attackers. Frikkie screamed in outrage as a bullet hit him in the leg. He pulled a grenade from his belt, pulled the pin and was about to throw it when he was shot through the head.

Robert dived to his left and was saved from immediate death because Frikkie took all the force of the explosion from the grenade. He struggled to his knees and pointed his AK47 in the direction of the attacking fire. He saw two soldiers running towards him and felt bullets tear into his body, but there was no pain, just a surreal numbness. He fired his gun at the two men and saw them both drop to the ground.

Despite his wounds Robert stood up, then, driven forward by a surge of adrenalin, he headed towards the clump of trees in which they had hidden earlier. However, he ran only a handful of paces before pain and shock hit him like an express train. He staggered to a halt, dropped his AK47 and fell to his knees.

He looked down and saw that his stomach had been ripped open and part of his intestines had been pushed out by his exertions and now hung down almost to his groin. He gritted his teeth and managed to pull himself to a nearby tree where he slumped against its trunk waiting for his own death to arrive.

He looked over at what remained of the decapitated body of Frikkie Pienaar, several metres to his right where it had been thrown by the blast from the grenade. Then he stared silently at the bodies of his other two comrades, which, although they lay nearer to the metal chain perimeter fence, were close enough for him to see clearly from where he sat against the tree trunk.

Big Jannie Swartz lay face down with tendrils of smoke rising from the back of his jacket. His son lay on his back with his face uppermost. Robert could see that the boy's eyes were open and staring sightlessly at a moon that had just escaped from the clouds that scudded across the sky on a north-westerly wind that was strengthening by the minute.

Another SADF soldier emerged from the darkness at the far end of the fence and walked towards him, before stopping and staring down at the bodies of Robert's two comrades. The soldier aimed carefully and spat into Little Jannie's face. He smiled as his spittle splattered across the young man's blood stained cheek. Turning on his heel he walked over and looked down at his own two dead colleagues. He shook his head with a sad expression on his face.

Then the soldier looked over at Robert and his lips tightened. He removed the magazine from his carbine and replaced it with a new one. There was murder in his steely eyes as he approached Robert, who tried to lift his own weapon but the excruciating pain from his stomach wound had sapped his strength. He was able only to raise the muzzle of the AK47 half a dozen inches in the air before it fell back against his leg.

Pain and tiredness forced Robert to close his eyes and when he reopened them the soldier was towering over him. Now he could see the two stripes of a corporal on the man's tunic. He stood, legs apart with his weapon trained steadily at Robert's chest.

'Sterf jy kaffir hond,' the soldier whispered as he squeezed the trigger of his gun.

Robert was still translating the Afrikaans words into the English 'Die you kaffir dog,' when he saw the flashes of light as the bullets left the muzzle. As they thudded into his body he was wracked by a pain even greater than the one he already experienced. Then death embraced him and his pain was no more.

Table Bay, South Africa
Johan Carlse

Johan swayed on his feet as the trawler rolled in the heaving waves of the Atlantic Ocean. The storm that had lashed the boat with rain for most of the day had grown steadily worse. He tugged hard on the wheel as he fought to keep the bow of the vessel pointing into the face of a powerful north-westerly wind that was forecast to turn into a gale during the next 24 hours.

Johan could hear nothing but the wind's roar as it buffeted the boat on its journey across the surface of the sea towards Koeberg and had no way of knowing what was going on at the power station.

For perhaps the hundredth time he glanced nervously at his watch and frowned. His companions should have been back at the beach by now. Yet again he looked into the night sky hoping to see the bright distress flare that would be the signal for him to head the trawler towards the shore to pick up Robert Dyakala and his team.

There was nothing.

Johan stared towards the shore where the blackness of the land set it apart from the slightly less black sky. It was far too still and quiet and he had a premonition of disaster. He would have expected some activity by now. Of course, the wind's direction would have carried away to the south-east any sound of the explosions when his companions hit their target, but the fires would have lit up the night sky. Again, there was nothing.

He decided to give Robert another five minutes and then he would head back to Hout Bay. It was a decision he would regret for the rest of his life.

Johan was just giving his clock yet another quick glance, which told him that another two minutes had elapsed, when the deck of the trawler suddenly was awash with bright light. He glanced over his left shoulder and saw a police launch bearing down on him from the south. It must have crept up on him using the strengthening wind to cover the sound of its engines.

Momentarily Johan was tempted to make a dash for it, but he quickly realised that he would never be able to outrun the fast police launch, so decided to simply try to brazen it out. Of course there was the small matter of the heavy machine gun that was erected on a stand in the bow of the trawler. However, the weapon was still covered with its tarpaulin and he could always deny knowing it was there. He managed to convince himself that, as long as he stuck to his story of simply being an unwitting crew member, the police would be able to charge him with nothing more serious than aiding and abetting.

The launch drew level and a figure in a yellow sou'wester came to the bow deck railing of the launch. He carried a rope and signalling to Johan to catch it when it was thrown.

Johan waved his hand to show he understood and would obey. He caught the rope and quickly hitched it to a deck post. Then he watched as the yellow clad figure made his way to the stern of the police launch where they repeated the operation with a stern line. Slowly the launch's winch pulled the two vessels together until they lay alongside each other.

The man who had thrown the rope jumped aboard the trawler and pulled open his sou'wester to reveal a policeman's uniform. The cop drew a pistol from his leather holster and pointed it at Johan who raised his hands in surrender. He really had no other choice.

Friday May 14th 1982: D.F. Malan International Airport
Kobus Coetzee

Kobus sat in the departure lounge of D.F. Malan Airport and smiled contentedly to himself. It had been a good twenty-four hours. The information that he had wheedled out of Smit with the offer of five hundred rand. The result was, the foiling of an attempt to blow up the Koeberg Nuclear Power Station and the death of a leading member of the ANC, Robert Dyakala.

As a bonus they had wiped out all but one of Dyakala's co-conspirators, with the sole survivor safely locked up in a cell in Cape Town awaiting interrogation. Of course, the man, who claimed he was only a crew member on the attack boat to Koeberg, was relatively insignificant. However, he would still be brought to trial and no doubt be sentenced to a lengthy stay on Robben Island.

Kobus was catching the last flight of the day to Jo'burg, which was scheduled to leave at 19:45 hours. He glanced at his watch and saw that he had over an hour to wait before boarding began. He opened his briefcase and took out Dyakala's diary, which he had not looked at since flying down to Cape Town. He decided to while away the time he had to wait reading the diary. Maybe there were more incriminating entries that would lead to the capture of other ANC leaders.

Suddenly he stiffened as he read an entry dated Wednesday 21st April 1982. Dyakala detailed a meeting with two men who wanted to buy weapons for a proposed attack on the maximum security prison on Robben Island. Only one of the men was named, and then only by the Christian name of David, however, there was another name mentioned in the same diary entry and it was a name Kobus was sure he recognised.

Leaping to his feet, he hurried to the airport's security office. Commandeering a telephone, he rang Dermot Brody in Cape Town to ask the name of the suspect who had been arrested following the failed attack on the nuclear power station.

Brody confirmed the detained man's name as Johan Carlse and explained that he was loudly protesting his innocence and demanding to see a lawyer.

'Innocent, is it?' Kobus said grimly. 'Well we'll see about that. I'm on my way back to Cape Town. Keep the skollie under lock and key and whatever you do, don't let him see anybody before I arrive.'

'What about a lawyer.'

'Definitely not a lawyer, Dermot.'

Western Cape Province

David Statton

The storm that had been battering the Cape Peninsula for the last couple of days had not relented. The rain lashed across the roofs of the houses in Clovelly like a scourge. The wind, which was slowly increasing to gale force, buffeted the tall pine trees that surrounded our plot, bending them as if they were saplings. It was not a good evening to be out and about, which suited me because the poor weather conditions would help us reach Bloubergstrand unobserved.

We stood in a group at the rear of the garage and listened to the wind rattling the tyres of the garage. We were dressed in matching motorbike leathers and each of us had a holster strapped to his hip containing a pistol. On the opposite hip we carried a large waterproof pouch containing ammunition for the pistols and spare magazines for the Kalashnikovs that we wore across our backs.

I looked in turn at each member of my team and nodded my approval. None of them showed any sign of nerves. That was good. I threw a thumb at the pick-up that now stood inside the garage next to the Mercedes truck. 'OK, on your way,' I said to Paul.

In the back of the pick-up, covered by a tarpaulin, were a couple of jerry cans full of fuel and one of the rubber dinghies loaded with two go-karts and other equipment, including three of the crash helmets. The second rubber dinghy, similarly loaded, was in the back of the Mercedes truck along with the three motor cycles.

'We'll meet you on the beach after we've picked up the other boat,' I added as Paul and Charlie clambered into the cab of the pick-up, while Mr Mac opened the garage door for them. 'You have the map reference?' I asked John as he moved to join the other two.

'No problem boss,' the American said as he waved a map in the air and then levered himself into the pick-up. 'Don't worry, we won't get lost.'

I waved briefly as the pick-up drove out of the garage

pulling The Spirit of Freedom behind it. We hadn't bothered to remove the pink lipstick from the side of the ski-boat and the letters stood out brightly as it passed under the fluorescent light. Then vehicle and boat were swallowed by the darkness of the stormy night.

I slipped on my sheepskin coat, clambered up into the cab of the Mercedes truck and flicked the diesel switch. When the ready light came on I turned the key in the ignition and gunned the engine as it sprang into life. I drove the truck slowly out of the garage and immediately felt the full force of the storm as rain hammered against the windscreen.

Mr Mac turned off the garage lights closed the door and joined me in the cab. It would be the last time we saw the house in Clovelly.

As we drove up Main Road towards Kalk Bay the rain intensified into an almost impenetrable curtain, so at first I did not see the figure standing on the pavement opposite the harbour entrance.

It was only when the man waved his arms frantically that I slowed down to get a better look. He was wearing a bright yellow sou'wester and long waterproof coat, the collar of which was pulled up round his ears. I recognised the outfit immediately. 'That's Carlse,' I said irritably. 'He was supposed to meet us in Bloubergstrand. What the hell is he doing here?'

I brought the van to a stop and Mr Mac opened the passenger door. He helped the fisherman clamber up into the high cab and we watched as he removed his sou'wester. It was only then that we realised that our passenger was not Johan Carlse.

'It's a wee lassie,' Mr Mac observed without emotion.

'Freddie?' I asked weakly.

'Hi, Dave,' she said as she took a handkerchief from her pocket and wiped the rain from her cheeks. Mr Mac moved out of her way so that she could slide along the bench-seat so she was sitting between us.

'Why are you here? Where's your father?' I asked in a quiet measured voice that I hoped did not betray my deepening concern at this unexpected turn of events.

Freddie did not reply at first, instead she continued to dab her face with the handkerchief and it was only then that I realised the moisture on her cheeks was not rain, but tears.

'Freddie, where's your father?' I repeated.

Eventually she looked up at me. The tears in her eyes sparkled in the reflection of the instrument panel lights. When she spoke the words poured from her mouth in a gabbled stream. 'Oh, David, I was so worried. I didn't know what to do and I thought I would miss you. I was going to come to your house in Clovelly, but I didn't know the address. I knew where Papa was supposed to meet you in Bloubergstrand but I had no means of getting there so I caught a train to Kalk Bay in the hope of catching you on the way, but when I got off the train the heavens opened up and I couldn't see anything in the rain. I didn't even know whether it was you in this van and if it was, whether you would see me…'

I took her shoulders and shook her sharply. 'Pull yourself together, Freddie,' I said harshly, hating myself as I spoke. 'Now tell me what happened. Where's your father?'

She looked up at me with a shocked look on her face as if I had slapped her round the face. There was a flash of anger on her cheeks. It was what I wanted to see.

Eventually she nodded to show she understood why I had provoked her. 'Papa is dead,' she said quietly.

This news was even worse than I had imagined. 'How do you know?' I asked, keeping my voice as soft as my anxiety would allow.

'I have a friend, Marika,' Freddie explained. 'Her husband is a security guard who works at the Koeberg Nuclear Power Station. He was on duty last night and told Marika that freedom fighters attacked the site but were ambushed by the Defence Force. There was a fire fight during which a number of soldiers were killed and all the attackers.' She stared at me, her eyes still welling with tears. 'The attackers were led by Robert Dyakala.'

'And Robert was killed?' I asked. 'Is your friend certain?'

'He was certain,' she replied.

'But what about your father. How can you be sure he's dead?'

'We both know that Papa was a member of Robert's team,' Freddie said.

'That means nothing,' I tried to reassure her, but knew I was probably giving her false hope. 'Remember your dad was skippering the boat. He might well have stayed on board during the attack'

Freddie shook her head. She had recovered much of her usual self-composure. 'No, papa told me that it was Smitty's job to look after the boat. He wasn't happy, because he didn't want to take part in the attack himself, but Robert insisted because papa had experience with explosives.'

'Who is Smitty?' I asked.

'Johannes Smit,' Freddie replied.

'What happened to him?'

Freddie shook her head. 'I don't know. Marika told me that a man was arrested on board the trawler and I assume that was Smitty, but I have no idea where he is now.'

'What are we going to do now, Mister Statton?' Mr Mac asked quietly. 'Can we still go ahead without the lassie's pa?'

'You must be Mister Mac?' Freddie said, recognising his Scottish accent.

'Aye,' Mr Mac replied and held a hand towards her. 'And right pleased I am to meet ye, Miss Carlse, so I am.'

Freddie shook the Scotsman's hand. 'Don't worry Mister Mac, I'll take my papa's place. That's why I'm here.'

She looked at me and I could see that the tearful look in her eyes had been replaced with one of steely determination. She was challenging me to contradict her.

Mr Mac looked at me as well, an eyebrow raised in question.

I shrugged and put the van into gear and continued our journey along the Main Road. 'Freddie comes, Mister Mac. We have no choice. Anyway, she's as good as any man.' I was concentrating on navigating the vehicle through the driving rain so I could no longer see the girl's face, but I guessed there would be a smile on her lips.

Because of the rain, and the late hour, traffic was light on the road north to Bloubergstrand. On any other occasion I would have been tempted to put my foot down, but I kept my speed well within the 100 km per hour limit for the freeway. I did not want to attract the attention of any police patrol car that we might encounter. If an inquisitive cop had looked in the back of the Mercedes truck, it would have been difficult to explain away the presence of three motor cycles and a large rubber dinghy containing assorted equipment. Two go-karts, firearms and enough explosives to blow up half of Cape Town. Very difficult.

It took just under an hour to cover the distance between Kalk Bay and Bloubergstrand and by the time we arrived the rain had stopped. The sky was cloudless, with only the twinkling stars and a slither of a full moon that had risen slowly out of the blackness of the Atlantic Ocean just in time to witness events. The truck headed towards the black silhouette of the high block of flats from the top of which Paul and I had first reconnoitred the approach to Robben Island.

But although the sky was clear, the howling wind that had blown away the rainclouds still swept in from the northwest. It rocked the truck as I drove onto the area of wasteland on which the garages stood and which had been turned into a sea of mud by the last couple of days' rain. I brought the truck to a stop outside the lock-up garage that sat in the shadow of the block of flats and in which was stored the second ski-boat.

I jumped down from the cab and was quickly followed by Mr Mac who helped me open the up-and-over garage door, which, because of the howling wind, was a struggle, even with two of us. Eventually we heaved the door up and stepped gratefully into the shelter of the garage, where we were joined by Freddie.

I switched on the light and we pulled the boat trailer out of the garage through the mud and connected it to the back of the Mercedes. It took only a few minutes to complete the task and we were soon on our way to join our friends, leaving behind a locked and darkened garage.

I drove a couple of miles up the coast until the lights of Bloubergstrand were well behind me. When I was sure we were alone on the freeway I pulled the van off onto the sandy track that led to the secluded beach from which the previous Saturday, Freddie and I had launched The Spirit of Freedom.

I felt the wheels of the truck sink into the rain soaked sand and the engine roared in protest as I pushed hard on the accelerator. The wheels spun and the truck slid from side to side, but I managed to keep our impetus going and soon we were making our way through the sand-dunes to the beach, where John had parked the pick-up truck. The boat trailer had already been uncoupled and was now standing with frothing waters swirling round its wheels.

I parked alongside the pick-up, with the rear of the van facing seaward. I jumped down from the cab, slipped out of my sheepskin coat, threw it onto the seat and slammed the door closed. By the time Freddie and Mr Mac joined me I already had the second boat trailer uncoupled and John and Paul were helping me to wheel it towards the water's edge.

The moon was higher now and had almost risen fully above

the gale lashed seas. Across the bay the lighthouse on Robben Island winked out its monotonous warning message. Three seconds off – six seconds on – three seconds off.

The island was close enough to the mainland to be able to see lights shining from houses in the village. To some eyes the clearness of those lights might have made our task look easier, but I knew differently. The island was further away than it looked and its record of not having had a prisoner escape alive was a more realistic way of judging the difficulties we faced, than the illusionary closeness of the house lights.

That night the island's natural defences - its rocky shoreline and the mile or so of sea, with its treacherous currents, which separated it from the mainland - were bolstered by another ally; the wind. It roared so loudly in my ears that at first I did not hear Charlie's call.

He moved closer and shouted again. 'We're not going out there are we?' He pointed towards the seething sea. 'We'll never make it.'

I looked at the crashing surf. 'We'll make it,' I told him confidently, but he did not look convinced, which was hardly surprising because I was not entirely convinced myself.

I glanced down at my wrist watch just as the hands met at the top of the dial. It was midnight and Friday was about to give way to Saturday.

Saturday May 15th 1982

Freddie sat at the helm of the Spirit of Freedom. She still wore her yellow oilskin coat but had abandoned the sou'wester because it impeded her vision. Her head was already soaked from the spray created by the waves that hammered the side of the bucking ski-boat and her black hair was plastered against her skull like a plastic helmet.

I saw her look over her shoulder to watch us as we tried to manhandle the boat through the heaving breakers. Her face was a pale white oval in which a pair of large dark eyes peered out with increasing concern as she witnessed the struggle we were having fighting the strong current.

And we were struggling. We found it difficult to manoeuvre the boat through the pounding waves into a position that would allow Freddie to power up the outboard motor. It would be easier when she could edge out into the marginally smoother water that lay beyond the breakers. Our biggest problem was the rubber dinghy that was attached to the boat's stern with a thick hawser. Just as we thought we had the boat under control, it pitched and weaved unpredictably, regularly knocking one or other of us off balance with its heavy load.

Eventually we worked out that by three of us manoeuvring the ski-boat and two of us the dinghy we had better control of both. With one final mighty heave we pushed both vessels up and over a wave that rose almost as high as my shoulder.

As the two craft glided down the swell into the trough beyond, Freddie gunned the outboard motor, its propeller bit into the sea in an explosion of white bubbles and the boat immediately came under her control. She set the bow until it was parallel with the beach and ran a couple of dozen yards along the coast before expertly swinging into a tight U-turn that saw the Spirit of Freedom head back our way.

We immediately turned our attention to the second boat that was parked on its trailer at the edge of the roiling sea with its rubber dinghy alongside. Charlie jumped up into the boat, no doubt relieved he would not again have to go through the torturous exercise we had just performed. The rest of us pushed the trailer into the water until the boat floated off. That was the easy part.

Paul and John positioned themselves on either side of the boat and held it as steady as they could while Mr Mac and I manoeuvred the dinghy into position and secured it to the stern. I waved to Charlie and watched as he started the boat's outboard motor.

'Let's go!' I shouted, but the wind whipped my words from my lips and threw them back towards the darkened sand dunes behind which we had parked the vehicles. I wasn't sure anybody else heard me, but I needn't have worried because Paul and John read my body language and started pushing the boat up to the crest of the nearest wave. Mr Mac and I did the same to the dinghy.

For some reason we found it easier the second time round. Perhaps it was the new technique we were using, or perhaps the power of the breakers had diminished slightly. Whatever the reason we soon had the boat and its dinghy in water deep enough to allow Charlie to push the outboard motor to full power.

Paul and I scrambled aboard the boat and I took over the wheel from the Frenchman. I waved to Freddie and she manoeuvred the Spirit of Freedom closer to the shore to pick up Mr Mac and John.

We left the boat trailers where they were, on the edge of the beach, half submerged in the sea. We would not need them again. I stared at the trailers while I waited for Freddie to rejoin us. Something was nagging at my mind. I had a feeling that we had forgotten something, but I couldn't quite put my finger on what it was.

Freddie followed our boat out to sea and I let her overtake us. I saw John make his way to the stern of the Spirit of Freedom where he had fitted on twelve inch high brackets a red light on either side. Soon both lights flickered into life. Now it was up to me to follow Freddie to Robben Island and rely on her to pilot both boats safely through the channel that led through the rocks surrounding the entrance to Rock Cove.

I was under no illusions; it would be no easy task. Freddie had only ever travelled to Rock Cove with her father at the helm and, despite her confidence, I knew it would take enormous skill to navigate those treacherous rocks in the dark on a stormy night. However, despite my reservations about the journey ahead, I was pleased we were actually on our way.

As it happens our journey went almost without a hitch and we made good time. There was one alarm when a police launch came into sight briefly as it cruised across our path on its passage from Cape Town to Robben Island. Its navigation lights winked at a sky once again full of black clouds that had already blotted out the moon.

Freddie immediately cut the speed of her boat and I followed suit. Paul snatched up the AK47 that was lying in the bottom of the boat next to his seat and held it at the ready as we watched the police launch's lights move slowly northwards. Luckily, the wind and the mufflers on the motors ensured our boats remained undetected and soon the lights disappeared into the dark night.

Paul and I exhaled loudly and for the first time I realised that we had both been holding our breath.

'Alarm over,' Paul shouted above the wind as he put the Kalashnikov to one side.

I nodded without comment and pushed the power lever forward so that I could keep up with the Spirit of Freedom, which was once again ploughing through the heaving waves at a rate of knots. Twenty minutes later we reached the crescent of rocks that surrounded our destination and Freddie reduced her speed to a crawl.

As I watched her edge the boat into an invisible channel in the ocean, my stomach churned like the surface of the white water into which I pointed the bow of our own vessel. I gritted my teeth and concentrated on keeping the point of our bow in the middle of the two red lights on the back of the rocking craft in front.

Slowly we inched our way through the rocks and eventually reached the relatively tranquil water in the lagoon beyond. Freddie allowed me to overtake and ease my boat through the breakers that swept across the strip of sand on which we would be landing.

I reduced speed and what little sound had been coming from the muffled outboard motor disappeared and the surf carried the boat the rest of the way towards land in total silence.

As our hull scraped against the sand, Paul jumped into the surf. At the same time Charlie untied the rope that attached the inflatable raft to the boat and threw it to the big South African. Paul grabbed the rope and pulled the raft effortlessly through the water and dragged it up onto the beach. Charlie and I followed Paul into the water and together the three of us manoeuvred the ski-boat towards the narrowest part of the sand strip and pushed it ashore. Its stern was wedged at the base of the steep, boulder strewn hillock that bordered the beach, with its bow almost touching the lapping waves. We deliberately positioned the boat that way so that we could launch it as quickly as possible on our return from the prison.

On that particular section of the hillock a rocky outcrop rose up about twenty feet into the air and snaked outwards, jutting over the sand like the head and neck of a dinosaur. It would effectively hide the boats from any prying eyes that might look down on the beach from above. I was confident that it would make a perfect natural shield and I smiled with satisfaction at what I thought was a perfect berth. I should have known better.

By the time we had our boat secured safely on the strip of sand, and we were sure it could not drift away, Freddie had brought the Spirit of Freedom closer to the shore. John and Mr Mac were already in the water pulling the second dinghy towards the beach.

Paul and Charlie had stripped the tarpaulin off the first raft and were starting to unload the equipment it carried. First thing out were the crash helmets, each of which had been fitted with a small, but powerful, battery-powered torch that would be needed later during our mission, but which, for now, remained switched off to conserve the batteries. Instead, my friends used large rubber flashlights to see what they were doing as they worked.

I helped John drag the second inflatable up the beach and positioned it next to the first, where it could be unloaded by our friends once they had finished what they were doing. We then waded into the water to help Freddie and Mr Mac, who were already trying to manhandle the Spirit of Freedom towards the sand strip. With our help it took only a few minutes to complete the exercise and soon the two ski-boats were lying side by side in the shelter of the overhanging rock.

That's when I remembered what had been nagging me after we left the beach at Bloubergstrand. We had forgotten to load the two spare cans of petrol that were still sitting in the back of the pick-up. I cursed my stupidity for making such an elementary error, but there was nothing we could do about it now. We would just have to hope there was enough fuel in the tanks of the ski-boats to get us all the way back to the mainland.

As the last canvas rucksack of grenades was being lifted from the rubber dinghy, the rain started again. It was only a light drizzle, but in the distance I saw a bolt of lightning tear a hole in the northern night sky. A rumble of thunder rolled across the sea towards us as it hitched a lift on the back of the still howling north-westerly wind.

Another storm was on its way. If the gods of war were with us the thunder and lightning would arrive over Robben Island just as we were launching our attack on the prison and add to the confusion we planned to create.

I signalled with my hands to start getting the equipment up the side of the hillock to the manatoka trees that stood along its brow. Charlie, already wearing his crash helmet and carrying two coils of rope, went up the treacherous, rock strewn ground first. He was as nimble as a cat and made the climb look as easy as going up stairs. Soon he disappeared into the blackness of the trees.

Freddie helped me store the two empty dinghies into the unnamed ski-boat before I helped her climb into the Spirit of Freedom. She had wanted to come with us to the prison, but I told her it was important for somebody to stay and guard the boats. She accepted this without argument, but there was a look in her eyes that betrayed her true emotions. She was not happy about not getting her own way.

'Stay in the boat and keep your head down,' I shouted above

the wind. 'You'll be safe there.'

She nodded silently and shouted something back, but the wind took her words and blew them out to sea before they reached my ears. I thought she said: 'I love you. Come back safely,' but that could have been wishful thinking on my part.

By the time I returned to where the equipment was stacked at the foot of the hillock Charlie had tied the end of rope round the trunk of a manatoka tree and it dangled down the rocky slope. Soon the first rope was joined by another rope, which had been tied to another tree. Paul was already using the first rope to help him climb the hillock, and was almost at the top, whilst John and Mr Mac started tying one of the go-karts to the second rope.

I put on my crash helmet and once I was happy the go-kart was securely tied I tugged on the rope and immediately Charlie and Paul began to pull the kart upwards. I grabbed with my right hand the rope Paul had used to climb the hillock and I followed the kart up, using my left hand to ease it over the rocky surface so that it did not get damaged.

Soon I was over the brow of the hillock and found myself in the temporary shelter of a wooded area in which Charlie and Paul were already untying the rope from the go-kart.

The trees that surrounded us creaked and groaned in protest at the battering they were receiving from the gale force wind that whistled across the island. One tree had been snapped already, broken in two like a giant matchstick. Several others looked in danger of a similar fate, which made it imperative that we get the rest of the equipment up from the beach as quickly as possible.

I made my way back down the hill to the beach and ten minutes later all four karts were safely hidden in the trees. Five minutes after that the rest of the equipment had been transferred from the beach, at which time we were joined by John and Mr Mac who helped load the knapsacks full of explosives onto the modified go-karts. Mr Mac's kart also carried the rope ladder Charlie would be using.

We left the ropes tied to the trees for use on our return and clambered aboard the heavily loaded karts. Each of us had a Kalashnikov AK47 slung across our back, a pistol on one hip and a pouch on the other containing plenty of ammunition.

The engines of the karts started first time. Fitted as they were with soundproof boxes, it was difficult to detect any noise, the only sign that the engines were running came from the muffled exhaust pipes. They pulsated quietly emitting tiny puffs of smoke that showed grey against the blackness of the surrounding trees.

Mr Mac drove one of the karts while Charlie stood on the metal plate that John had welded to its chassis. He supported himself with one of the struts that formed part of the sturdy aluminium frame that arched from front to back of the vehicle. Strapped to the frame was a bulging canvas rucksack, against which the little Frenchman rested his upper body.

The remaining three karts had been similarly modified and were driven by Paul, John and me. Because we carried no passengers, our machines each had two of the heavy canvas rucksacks strapped to their frames.

The wooded area stretched southwards from Murray's Bay Harbour to just beyond Rock Cove, where it petered out into individual clumps of trees. It filled part of the area between the coastline and the tarred road that led from the Robben Island village in the south, to the Maximum Security Prison in the north.

We were surrounded by manatoka trees that grew so close together it should have been impossible to navigate our way safely. Luckily a narrow track wound its way in a series of tight bends and with care, we managed to drive along in a slow convoy until we reached the tarred road.

The thunderstorm was very close now and the rain had increased in tempo, making it impossible for us to see any more than a hundred yards or so in either direction. That was good, because it meant it would be equally difficult for us to be seen by anybody foolish enough to venture out onto the road that night.

Somewhere behind us a bolt of lightning tore itself away from the black night sky and stabbed into the woods from where we had just emerged. Almost simultaneously a crash of thunder reverberated around our heads and I knew that the storm was upon us.

I led the go-kart convoy for a few hundred yards along the tarred road, then took a sharp turn left onto a dirt track that ran parallel with the prison's southern boundary fence.

Out of the corner of my eye I saw another bolt of lightning light up the island's coastline, but this time it took the sound of thunder a couple of seconds to reach us.

We drove down the dirt track until we came to a T-junction, the right-hand arm of which led to the prison's service gate. I took the left-hand arm and we found ourselves on another dirt track that curved slowly round until it headed in a northerly direction, effectively bypassing the southwest watchtower that was located close to the service gate.

This second track ran parallel to the prison compound and eventually led us to the aircraft landing strip that lay at the top of Robben Island. From there we arched round the northern side of the prison, ensuring that we avoided the northwest tower.

I saw yet another flash of lightning and began counting. I reached four seconds this time before I heard the clap of thunder, a sure sign that the storm was already moving across Cape Bay towards the mainland and with its departure the rain began to ease slightly.

We covered the rest of our journey in good time and soon the karts were parked in a patch of scrubland from where we could observe the northeast watchtower without being seen by the guards. As it happened, there was no sign of them and I guessed they were huddled at the front of the box, sheltering from the heavy rain driven by the gusting wind into the back of their tower.

Every member of the team was watching me, waiting for the order to move. I swung my arm in a circular motion, with my hand in a fist, as if cranking an engine. It was the army field signal that told them it was time to move. It was all that was needed. Each man knew exactly what they had to do and there was no need for further instructions from me.

Seconds later Charlie and Mr Mac were out of their go-kart and running silently towards the foot of the watchtower where they were soon swallowed up by the deep shadows that lay there.

John got out of his kart and unloaded the two canvass knapsacks containing the explosives he would need to blow up the electricity substation, emergency generators and fuel tank. He ran across the open ground to join our two comrades, carrying the two heavy bags as easily as if they were filled with cotton wool. Paul and I had our carbines at the ready, although I hoped very much that we would not need to use them.

As John reached the foot of the watchtower the moon broke through the clouds, flooding the ground with light. Now that the base of the tower was no longer hidden by dark shadows I could see the three members of my team looking up at the guard box.

I tightened my grip on the AK47 and held my breath. If a vehicle came along the dirt track from the direction of Murray's Bay Harbour it would be impossible for the driver to miss seeing my friends. If that happened I would have no option but to use my weapon.

Seconds later Charlie started climbing up the side of the tower with a rope ladder slung across his back. John and Mr Mac stood on the ground beneath him, weapons in hand, staring up at the little Frenchman as he climbed the wall with a dexterity that was almost superhuman.

I kept one eye on the approach road and at the same time watched Charlie's progress. He moved with the jerky mechanical action of a robot. Concentrating all his efforts on one limb at a time, he yanked away from the wall the attached suction pad before positioning it slightly higher up with a hard but silent blow.

The wind had dropped slightly but it still blew with a ferocity that cut through my leather motor cycle outfit as if it were made of gossamer. I began to regret not being able to bring with me the sheepskin jacket I had left in the cab of the Mercedes van on the beach at Bloubergstrand. Yet at the same time I welcomed the howling wind, because it would drown any noise that my comrades might make during their assault on the tower.

I watched Charlie's slow, steady ascent and tried to control the tension that was threatening to tie my stomach in knots. Pull right foot free. Kick and stick. Pull right hand free. Smack and stick. Pull left foot free. Kick and stick. Pull left hand free. Smack and stick.

Suddenly the regular, robotic rhythm was broken. As Charlie pulled his right foot free the suction pad on his left foot came loose, probably because of the rain that still lashed against the side of the watchtower, and momentarily he lost his grip. He dangled high above the ground, supported only by the pads that held his hands to the wall.

I held my breath as the Frenchman's left hand came unstuck too. For a split second, unbalanced by the weight of the rope ladder, he was held in place only by the single suction pad on his right hand. His body swayed away from the wall and for a moment it looked as if he would fall to the ground.

But with an incredible effort Charlie kicked the wall with the toes of both boots and, with a twist of his upper body, slapped his left hand against the tower. All three suction pads gripped and once again he was back in control. With barely a pause to regain his composure he resumed his climb.

The figure of a guard appeared in the open box above

Charlie's head. The man was silhouetted by the moonlight and I saw the glow of a cigarette in his hand. Oblivious to the close proximity of the guard the little Frenchman kept climbing. Slowly he moved closer to the dark figure until it seemed the man had only to lower his arm over the side of the box to touch his head.

I slipped my AK47 to single shot mode and aimed it at the guard's head, but, even as I flicked the safety catch to the off position, the guard threw his cigarette butt over the parapet. He disappeared from sight just as the Frenchman stopped climbing a few inches short of the guard box. I let out a sigh of relief, but kept the Kalashnikov trained on the empty space where the guard had been standing seconds before.

Charlie tugged his left arm from the wall and eased the rope ladder over his head and off his shoulder. He reached up and hitched the foam covered grapnels over the parapet and let the ladder itself flip-flop silently down the tower wall to where John and Mr Mac waited on the ground. The Scotsman wasted no time. He scrambled quickly up the ladder and within seconds was hauling himself over the guard box's wooden parapet before disappearing inside.

In one agile motion Charlie pulled himself free of the wall. He twisted himself onto the ladder, which he held with his left hand, removed the suction pad from his right hand, drew his pistol and covered Mr Mac as he disabled the guards.

I lowered my AK47 and glanced over at the north-west tower. If the guards in that box saw Mr Mac and Charlie they would soon raise the alarm, but there was no sign of movement, nor the sound of a siren.

I felt a touch on my arm. It was Paul who was pointing towards the guard box from where Charlie was giving a thumbs up signal to indicate that Mr Mac had succeeded in immobilising the guards.

John also saw the signal and needed no further urging. He made his way quickly up the ladder with a canvas bag slung across each broad shoulder and soon disappeared over the parapet to join Charlie and Mr Mac. The latter would escort him to the electricity substation where he would cover the American while he laid the explosive charges with delayed timers.

We gave our friends ten minutes and then Paul and I started up the four go-karts. No sooner were the engines of the karts ticking over than John and Mr Mac reappeared and made their way down the rope ladder. Once they were on the ground Charlie slipped the grapnels from the parapet and let the ladder drop to the ground. It was picked up by Mr Mac who then ran quickly to his go-kart, closely followed by John.

Charlie then used his suction pads to make his way back down the wall. He was quicker coming down than he had been going up and within minutes he clambered on the back of Mr Mac's go-cart.

I accelerated slowly away and led the karts in convoy as we headed cautiously back down the dirt track until we reached the southwest corner of the prison where we parked up just out of sight of the watchtower. The journey had taken only a few minutes, but we had less than fifteen minutes to complete the next phase of the operation before the electricity substation blew up. We had to move quickly.

Once again there was no need for instructions. Mr Mac and Charlie had left their kart and the little Frenchman, was already making his way up the side of the tower. This time, he found the climb easier, perhaps because he was now sheltered from the biting north-westerly wind. It took only a few minutes for him to reach the wooden parapet of the guard box and attach the rope ladder to it.

Mr Mac was ready for the ladder. He grabbed it before it hit the ground and clambered up. Within seconds, he was at the top and over the parapet to disappear into the guard box. Charlie once again, manoeuvred himself nimbly onto the ladder to cover him, and soon joined Mr Mac in the box. He was quickly followed by John, who took only seconds to climb up the ladder.

I looked at my watch and saw that time was running out before the first charge was due to explode. 'Come on boys!' I urged quietly. 'Go to it.' I continued to stare down at my watch and counted off the seconds as the hand swept round its luminous dial. Each time the second hand reached twelve I glanced up at the guard box to see if Mr Mac had reappeared.

One, two, three, four and then five minutes passed. I began to get nervous. I expected to hear an explosion at any time. On my sixth glance Mr Mac's silhouette appeared in the open guard box before climbing over the parapet and onto the ladder. Soon he was back on the ground and running towards his kart. As he slid into his seat he looked over at me and gave the thumbs up. A few moments later John climbed over the parapet, made his way down the ladder and was soon behind the steering wheel of his kart.

Without further delay we drove two abreast to the prison's

service entrance. As we reached the heavy wooden double gates an explosion rent the air, as loud as the thunder that had so recently buffeted the island. With luck, the prison guards would think it had returned. At the same time the lights that lit up the prison went off, but only for a few seconds because the emergency generator kicked in soon after.

Immediately the gates swung open and we drove into the outer compound where we slowed to a crawl briefly to allow Charlie to jump up behind Mr Mac. We headed straight for the gate that separated the outer compound from the middle section of the inner compound in which H-block D was situated.

As we approached the gate we slowed to allow the Frenchman to jump off again and run ahead of us to open the gate. It took a few seconds for him to find the right key - seconds that seemed like hours - but at last the gate swung open and we edged the karts through into the inner compound. Mr Mac once again carried Charlie, who had opened the canvas knapsack to remove a few of the smoke grenades it contained..

As we entered the inner compound a second loud explosion rolled through the night air from the northern end of the prison as the emergency generator was destroyed, once again plunging the compound into darkness. Moments later there was another, even louder explosion as the diesel tank blew up. Neither of the explosions sounded anything like thunder and I guessed the guards would by now have worked out they were under attack.

We had to move fast to counter any possible threat from the main guardroom so Mr Mac and Charlie headed quickly towards the barrack room where the reserve guards were housed. Their job was to create a diversion by confusing the guards with more explosions and smoke. However, I hoped that if they were forced to use their weapons, they would be able to deter the warders without resorting to lethal fire.

The go-kart disappeared into the dark and a few seconds later there was a series of explosions as Mr Mac and Charlie started throwing grenades. Soon a pall of smoke filled the night sky, where it blotted out the stars.

The wind took much of the smoke and blew it across the prison estate, reducing visibility in the compound to that of a thick fog. Somewhere in the distance I heard men shouting, first in obvious bewilderment and then in anger.

It was time to move.

Paul, John and I headed for the inner compound wall that separated H-block D from the isolation block in which Zamyatin and Mandela were imprisoned. Paul and I parked our karts alongside the building while John drove straight to the wall.

A siren started wailing loudly somewhere in the outer compound. The alarm had to be an old-fashioned, manually operated affair, probably a relic from the Second World War because we had knocked out all electricity to the prison. Manual or not, the siren made one hell of a noise, which added to the general racket coming from the direction of the administration block.

John set a Semtex charge against the inner compound wall before driving to join us in the shelter of the H-block building. Seconds later yet another loud explosion added to the rising noise levels in the compound, sending dust and bricks into the air and leaving a gap in the wall large enough for us to drive through.

Seconds later we had arrived at the western wing of the isolation block just as the external door swung open and a guard appeared. He stared north towards the administration block where Charlie and Mr Mac were laying down a steady flow of stun and smoke grenades. The guard did not see or hear us, which was hardly surprising considering the thick smoke screen and the siren that was still blaring out its warning of our attack. The first he knew of our arrival was when John chopped him across the side of his neck and felled him like a sapling.

Paul and I switched on our helmet lights and ran through the open door brandishing our AK47s. We found ourselves in a guard room confronted by five prison guards, but we were expecting them and they were not expecting us, so it was no contest.

We had them kneeling on the floor, facing the wall, with their hands behind their backs before any of them even thought about drawing the service revolvers they carried in holsters on their hips. Paul did that job for them, throwing the weapons one by one into the waste bin that stood in the corner of the room, before tying their wrists and ankles.

John appeared through the door with his helmet light blazing, carrying over his shoulder the guard he had knocked out earlier and who was soon lying on the floor next to his colleagues with his hands and feet tied.

On one wall of the guard room was a glass fronted cabinet fitted with a rack containing R1 FN assault rifles. Next to the cabinet was a rack from which hung a dozen batons and another holding leg manacles and handcuffs.

Fixed to a second wall was a large wooden board, much like those you see behind the reception desk of some hotels, on which numbered keys dangled from hooks.

I grabbed the key to Cell 16 and made my way out of an internal door, which stood opposite the entrance through which we had just entered. I found myself in a long corridor lined with wooden doors on which a number had been neatly painted. Set into the wall next to each door was a metal barred window.

Considering the noise in the compound outside it was remarkably quiet in the corridor. The siren had stopped now, but I could still hear the occasional dull thud of a grenade from the direction of the administration block and these explosions had been joined by a smattering of small arms fire. The noise was muffled, sounding like a distant firework display and did not appear to have woken up or alarmed any on the inmates of the cells. The strident sound of the siren would be carried on the wind towards the barracks in the south of the island and would alert any off duty warders who were billeted there. It would not be long until they came to investigate so time was of the essence.

I walked quickly down the silent corridor towards Cell 16. On my way I glanced through the window of Cell 4 and in the light from my helmet light I could see a man; upright and perfectly still, as if meditating, sitting on his bed. I recognised the familiar face of Nelson Mandela, but releasing him would have to wait. My priority was the Russian.

When I reached Cell 16 I discovered there was no lock on its wooden door, so I simply swung it back on its hinges until it was flush against the corridor wall. It revealed a second, steel barred door, which was locked. I unlocked the metal door, entered the cell, strode quickly to the side of the bed and shook the figure that lay there.

The sleeping man grunted once, pushed aside the thin blanket with which he was covered and sat up. He swung his legs onto the floor without further sound or comment and stared down at the floor. He did not complain, so I guessed that prisoners were probably regularly woken up in the middle of the night without warning by guards.

The man must have sensed that all was not as usual, because he glanced up at me with a sullen look and squinted as my helmet light shone in his eyes. A look of fear spread across his black face as he saw the weapon I was carrying.

I didn't want to alarm him, so I switched off the torch and raised my visor of my helmet. I smiled down at him. 'I mean you no harm, my friend,' I said in a quiet voice.

The man nodded and the tension left his face, but he said nothing.

'I am looking for the Russian.'

The man shrugged but remained silent.

'The white man?' I tried again.

In answer the man swung his legs back into his bed, pulled up his blanket and rolled over to turn his back on me. Our short interview was over.

I switched my torch back on and left the cell with my visor still raised, locking the door behind me, and made my way back down the corridor to the guardroom. 'Zamyatin is not in Cell Sixteen,' I said to Paul, hanging the key back on its hook as I spoke.

I walked over and looked down at the prison guards who still knelt on the floor. I used my Kalashnikov to prod in the back one of the guards who wore on his arm the three stripes of a sergeant. He turned his head to look at me, a nervous expression on his features.

'Where is the Russian?' I asked still pointing the AK47 at his back.

'In his cell,' the guard replied dumbly.

'Which cell?'

'Eighteen,' he offered quickly.

'Cover them,' I told John as I removed from the board the keys for cells 18 and 4, the latter I threw towards Paul. 'You get Mandela and I'll get Zamyatin,' I told him.

I headed out the door and back down the corridor. When I reached the door to cell 18, I realised how the mistake about Zamyatin's location had been made. The right hand line in the upper loop of the 8 had worn away over time and it now looked like a 6. I swung back the door and quickly unlocked the security door beyond.

I stepped into the cell and my stomach dropped when I saw the bed was empty, but then I saw the figure crouched in the corner. The prisoner looked up at me, but quickly turned his face away as the light from my helmet light shone in his eyes. In the short time his face was revealed I recognised him as the Russian in the photograph that Gavin Rogers had supplied. His face was unmistakeable. It had the look of a well-worn dartboard; round,

275

pock-marked and a little frayed at the edges.

I stepped towards Zamyatin, who whimpered and tried to squeeze himself further into the corner. I had no time to be gentle so I reached down and pulled him roughly to his feet.

The scientist looked at me with wild eyes and started jabbering away in what I took to be Russian.

'Shut up!' I demanded harshly, but my order did not stop the flow of words, although it did make him switch language to one I could understand.

'Please no kill me,' he said in broken English. 'You say you let me out of this place. You promise me. You say you no kill me if I tell you much I know. Please no kill me. Let me out. I tell you much you ask… anything… anything. Just let me go. No kill me.'

'I'm not going to kill you,' I said not unkindly. 'But you must come with me.'

Zamyatin backed away until his back was pressed against the cell wall. 'No,' he wailed. 'You lie! You try trick me by speak English. But I know you. You KGB…'

I glanced at my watch. We were running out of time. Warders from the barracks might already be on their way to find out why the siren had been sounded and would probably have reported the alarm to the authorities on the mainland. I wanted to be well away before reinforcements arrived on the Island.

'You take me and kill me. I know of you KGB people. Please you promise me. I will tell. I will tell anything.' Zamyatin was crying shamelessly now. Tears rolled down his ravaged face and onto his chin, where they hung in beads of water for a couple of seconds before dripping onto the prison uniform he wore.

I stared at him. He was either a good actor, a complete idiot or totally unhinged. I looked into his mad staring eyes and decided it might be the latter.

'Who shall I speak of?' He continued to babble. 'My wife? My mother? Yes, my mother. She often criticises the Party. I am sure she is a spy and…' He stopped in mid-sentence, before changing tack: 'I will not let you take me,' he shouted, then suddenly attacked me, lunging at me with both hands beating the air.

If I had any doubts about his sanity, that attack made up my mind. No sane man tackles somebody who is younger, fitter, taller and heavier than he is, particularly when that person is carrying an AK47. I swung the rifle through the air and brought its butt down

276

on the side of his head. I did not hit him hard, but there was sufficient force in the blow to reduce him to a whining heap on the floor.

I shook my head. In his present state Zamyatin was no use to anybody, but my orders were only to deliver him to Rogers alive. There was no clause in our unwritten contract that stipulated that the scientist must be sane on delivery.

I slung the AK47 across my back and pulled him to his feet and pushed him out of his cell and along the corridor towards the guardroom where John was holding the warders captive. As we passed Mandela's cell, Paul stuck his head out of the door. The visor of his helmet was up and he looked of concerned.

'What's up?' I asked.

'We have a problem.'

'OK, wait there and I'll be right back.' I pushed Zamyatin into the guardroom, where I grabbed two pairs of handcuffs from the rack on the wall, which luckily had keys already in their locks, before manhandling him through the door opposite and into the compound beyond.

When we reached my go-kart, Zamyatin realised what I intended. He tried to pull away from me, shaking his head vigorously. I had no time for nonsense. I took out my pistol from its holster and pushed the barrel against his thick lips. 'Either you co-operate,' I warned him, 'or I will blow your damn head off. My contract is to deliver you to the mainland, nowhere does it say you have to be alive,' I lied and then paused to let that message sink in. 'Now do as you're told.'

Zamyatin must have believed I was serious because he moved to the back of the go-kart and stepped up onto the platform.

'OK, now grab onto those two struts,' I said, pointing them out with one hand, while still training the pistol at his head.

Again he obeyed my command, however, he did so with little effort to disguise his hatred, which was ramped up a few notches when I used my free hand to secure him to the struts. I locked the handcuffs, removed the keys and stuffed them safely in my pocket.

Once I had the Russian in position on the go-kart and was certain he could neither escape nor pose a threat, I ran back inside the isolation block.

'So what's the problem?' I asked when I joined Paul in Mandela's cell.

The big South African nodded towards the prisoner. 'It's

him,' he said. 'He won't come with us.'

'Okay, I'll deal with it. You go and join John. Untie the warders so they can walk and take them to the cell Zamyatin was in and lock them up. I'll meet you outside.' I looked at the prisoner, who still sat in the same position on his bed. 'With or without Mister Mandela,' I added.

The African National Congress leader looked up at me and smiled. 'It will be without,' he said quietly in a deep husky voice.

'I gave my word to a friend that I would get you out of prison,' I said simply.

'Your friend or mine?' He asked.

'Both.'

'And who is this friend?'

'Robert Dyakala.'

Mandela looked at me steadily for a while and for the first time I felt the full force of his personality and charisma. I stared at him silently and understood why he was revered by so many of people.

'Robert was a very committed young man,' he said gently, 'but like many young men he let his enthusiasm blind him to the reality that sometimes we must lose a battle to win a war.'

I noticed his reference to Robert in the past tense. 'You know about Robert's death?' I asked.

'Yes, I heard of his sad passing,' he replied sombrely. 'He will be a great loss to our cause, but he will be remembered forever as a true martyr.' He looked at me again with those piercing eyes of his. 'You seem surprised that I knew of Robert's death,' he said gently.

I nodded. 'I heard you were banned from reading newspapers?'

Mandela smiled gently. 'I have ways of obtaining news, particularly when the subject is one in which I am interested. I get to hear about everything I need to know.'

I stared down at him and believed him. 'What did you mean about losing a battle to win a war?' I asked.

'It is a very old saying,' he replied.

'I know, but what did you mean in the context of Robert Dyakala?'

'Robert wanted you to rescue me from this prison, yes?'

I nodded. 'He made it a condition of supplying me with the weapons and explosives I needed for my operation.'

'And what was the object of your operation?' He asked.

'To rescue a Russian nuclear scientist who is a prisoner here,' I replied, not seeing any harm in telling the truth.

'I know of this man,' Mandela said. 'But I fear the Boers have destroyed his mind. Comrade Zamyatin will be of no use to those for whom you work.'

I agreed with Mandela's assessment of the Russian's mental state. Based on my own conversation with Zamyatin, even the CIA's interrogation experts would struggle to get any sensible information from him. I glanced at my watch. 'I must go,' I said. 'Are you sure you won't come with us?'

Mandela shook his head. 'No, I must stay here and that is what Robert did not understand. In some eyes my being imprisoned means that the oppressors of my people have beaten me. But I prefer to consider the wider picture. I know that I am more use to the Struggle as somebody who is being held prisoner. If I was free, then I would be just another rabble-rousing opponent of the hated Apartheid regime shouting abuse through a loudhailer in London's Trafalgar Square.

'The reality is that my imprisonment here on Robben Island might be a small battle lost, but it is the key to the success of our wider war against racial injustice. So you see, I cannot allow you to rescue me because being enclosed by these four walls,' he motioned with his hands, 'is part of the obstacle strewn path that will lead to me fulfilling my destiny.'

'Which is?'

'Helping my people win political freedom, Mister Statton.'

I was momentarily shaken into silence. 'You know my name?' I eventually managed to ask.

Mandela smiled again. 'I told you, I get to hear about everything I need to know.' He paused and looked at me intently for a few seconds. 'For instance,' he eventually said. 'I know that you are not an enemy of the Struggle. But I know also that you and your colleagues are being seriously misled.' He paused again until finally saying: 'You must be on your way, Mister Statton. You have your own destiny to meet. But remember this, if I know your identity, there are others, perhaps inclined to do you ill, who know your identity also. I will say no more.' He held out his hand. 'Goodbye, Mister Statton' he said, 'and good luck.'

I shook Mandela's hand and left his cell and trotted to join John and Paul who were sitting in their go-karts waiting for me surrounded by the still swirling smoke. John had already removed the soundproof boxes from all three engines and the pinched muffle tubes from the exhaust pipes.

I looked at Paul and pointed to the sky. He picked up a Very pistol from where it had been lying on the seat next to him and fired a flare into the smoke filled night sky. I clambered into my kart, ignoring the loud shouts of complaint from Zamyatin who was manacled to the frame that swept over my head. I gunned the accelerator and the machine surged forward and round the side of the isolation building towards the gap in the wall that led through to H-block D compound.

When we reached the far side of Section D we idled the karts and waited for Mr Mac and Charlie to join us. I heard the engine of their go-kart even before they appeared through the thick smoke that surrounded the administration building and I nodded in satisfaction that one or other of them had thought to remove the soundproof box. With a wave of my hand I drove forward, closely followed by John and Paul, just as Mr Mac reached us and tagged onto the end of our convoy.

My team had come through unscathed from our encounter with the prison guards, the most difficult part of our operation was behind us, Zamyatin was securely attached to my go-kart and I thought nothing could now go wrong.

The only concern I had was the warning from Nelson Mandela about somebody else knowing my identity. I had no idea what he meant, but I sensed it wasn't going to make my life any easier.

A few minutes later I raised my hand and brought the convoy to a halt. We had driven down the dirt track that led from the prison and had reached a clump of manatoka trees that grew alongside the tarred road that led to the village.

The wind was still blowing in from the north-west, but now it was only a blustery, rain soaked reminder of the cold weather front that had so recently buffeted the Island. It had moved south-east and was now sweeping across the distant Cape Flats, lightning up the sky with the ferocity that only an African storm can unleash.

Despite the sound of the wind, and the loud shouts of protest from Zamyatin, I heard clearly the wail of a siren. I slipped out of the seat of my kart and tore off one of the wide straps from the canvas bag, still fixed to the frame, and used it to gag him. Once I was sure he would not be able to raise the alarm, I signalled to my comrades to stay put. I made my way to the front of the clump of the manatoka grove where I peered out from behind a tree trunk.

I looked down the road and could see lights approaching from the direction of the village. One of the lights was blue and flashed in time with the wailing siren. Several seconds later a police car sped past my hiding place followed by two covered trucks, no doubt carrying reinforcements for the prison defenders. I smiled. They were much too late.

I returned to my go-kart and edged it towards the edge of the tarred road until I could see clearly in both ways. When I was satisfied the road was clear, I led the convoy out of the manatoka grove. We sped down the road towards the woods that stood above the beach on which our boats were moored and from which we had emerged less than an hour before.

With the go-karts now operating at full speed it took only seconds to reach the opening in the trees where the narrow track through the woods started. Once we were screened by the trees, we slowed down to navigate our way round the tight bends. Despite our reduced speed I was nearly caught out still when I went round one bend to be confronted by a tree that had been blown down by the wind and lay across the track. I braked and the kart swerved from side to side before coming to a halt no more than a couple of inches from the trunk. Luckily the reaction of the other drivers in the convoy was good and there were no nose to tail collisions.

I got out of the kart and Zamyatin twisted his head round to see what I was doing. His eyes were wide with fright and he had a sheen of perspiration on his face. He looked as if he was struggling to breathe so I removed the gag from his mouth. Mercifully he did not resume his shouting.

I inspected the tree trunk which proved to be neither particularly thick nor heavy. Paul, who was driving the kart directly behind mine, joined me and together we managed to lift the tree away from the track. Soon we were back on our way, but at an even slower, more cautious speed. There were no other obstacles in our way and soon we reached the two trees from which ropes still dangled down to the beach.

John and Paul trotted back down the track for a couple of hundred yards and took up a position to protect our rear in the event anyone approached us from the direction of the road.

I released Zamyatin from the kart and secured his arms

behind his back. Thinking ahead I used both pairs of handcuffs on his wrists. In addition to making it more difficult for him to escape the cuffs, I knew we would need both sets when we eventually got back to the beach at Bloubergstrand.

I pushed the Russian to the ground at the edge of the woods, where he sat staring up at me, sullen and silent. I ignored him and instead looked around to ensure it was all clear.

To the north floodlights shone out brightly from Murray's Bay Harbour, but there was little sign of activity. To the south-east a ship's navigation lights shone out brightly against the black of the sea as it travelled at a steady speed from the direction of Cape Town. From its size I guessed it was a ferry heading for the harbour. I followed the progress of the ship for a few moments, then I turned and looked south along the tree lined slope.

All was quiet in that direction, but an alarm bell rang in my mind as I stared thoughtfully at the hill top. Somehow the view was different from how I remembered it, but I couldn't work out what had changed.

Eventually I gave up. I raised the visor of my crash helmet and I turned to Charlie, who did the same so he could hear what I had to say. 'You go down first Charlie, but be careful,' I said. 'When you reach the beach use your torch to signal if it is all clear and Mister Mac will follow you down. You know the Morse code for OK?'

'Dash, dash, dash, pause, dash, dot, dash. Is that correct?'

'Correct,' I confirmed and touched him on the arm. 'Go!'

Charlie grabbed one of the ropes with one hand and, with a heavy duty rubber flashlight clutched in his other hand, he disappeared silently over the edge of the hill top and down the slope.

Mr Mac knelt at the very edge of the hill top and stared down into the darkness below waiting for Charlie's signal. Meanwhile I went to check on Zamyatin who now sat staring at the ground, with his arms cuffed behind his back and his chin in his chest.

I thanked whichever god was on duty that at least the Russian was quiet.

I turned round and looked out across the straits at the lights on the mainland. Starting at Bloubergstrand, almost opposite our position, the lights twinkled their way down the gentle sweep of Table Bay in tiny clusters until they linked into the single massed glare that was Cape Town.

Out of the corner of my eye I saw Mr Mac wave at me. I walked the short distance to him and knelt by his side. 'What's wrong?' I asked.

The Scotsman pointed towards the beach. I looked down the steep slope and saw Charlie's torch winking out a message, but it was not the one I wanted to see. Three short flashes, pause, three long flashes, pause, and three short flashes. The Morse code message spelt out the universal distress signal: S.O.S.

'What now?' I murmured in frustration as I peered into the blackness below. I could see nothing but the same message being repeated over and over again. 'I'm going down,' I turned back to Mr Mac just in time to see Zamyatin run towards the little Scotsman and kick him in the small of his back.

I put out a hand to grab my friend, but was too late. He went tumbling over the edge and out of sight into the blackness below, bouncing down the steep slope in a series of loud thuds and with a shower of rattling stones.

The Russian spun to face me with a loud scream. There was a look of pure hatred etched across his features and his eyes blazed with madness. He aimed a savage kick at my head and instinctively I flung myself backwards away from the slope. Because his arms were cuffed behind his back he was slightly off balance and so his foot did not connect properly, but he still caught me with a hard blow on the temple.

I hit the ground and a red curtain dropped over my eyes leaving me temporarily blind. I lay there stunned, cursing myself for my stupidity. The last time I checked Zamyatin he had looked dejected, the portrait of a defeated man. Now I realised his body language had been a clever ruse to convince me he was not a threat. I should have known better.

My sight slowly returned and I could see him standing over me with a look of triumph on his pock-marked face. He was hopping from one foot to the other in a gloating mad little jig. He stared down at me with those demented eyes of his for what seemed an age but I could not move. He let out another insane scream of rage, drew back his foot again and launched a kick at my unprotected groin.

I drew my legs up in an automatic reaction, seeking to protect my private parts from his attack, but the foot never reached me. As it shot forward, the leg to which it was connected seemed to shrink away from me as if it was a retracting telescope. Then his other leg was jerked from the ground and the pair of them were kicking in mid-air.

Yet again Paul had arrived just in time to save me.

Having heard the Russian's first scream, the big South African had trotted back to find out what was happening. He immediately weighed up the situation and acted. He seized Zamyatin with his big hands and yanked him into the air as if he was a rag doll. With the same ease he spun on his heel and slammed my attacker into the nearest tree with a satisfying crunch of his head, before letting him fall on the ground in an unconscious heap.

Still feeling groggy I staggered to my feet. After quickly explaining to Paul what had happened to Mr Mac, I stepped over to the rope that Charlie had used and made my way carefully down to the beach where I found my two friends.

They were at the bottom of the slope and were illuminated in a silent tableau by the beam of Charlie's powerful flashlight, which was wedged upright into the moist sand. The beam was pointed towards Mr Mac who lay against a pile of jagged rocks with his head set on one side at an unnatural angle. He barely moved as Charlie gently unfastened the strap of his helmet.

I touched the Frenchman's arm and shook my head. I pointed to the back of our injured friend's helmet, using the light from my own helmet torch to highlight my meaning. Charlie's hands clenched into fists at what he saw.

Mr Mac's head must have struck a razor sharp point on the large rock against which he was propped because there was a hole in the back of his helmet out of which oozed crimson blood. I guessed that part of the helmet was imbedded in the little man's head. If we tried to remove it we might pull away part his shattered skull at the same time.

Even knowing that risk, if I had felt that by removing his helmet we would save Mr Mac's life then I would have attempted it. However, it was obvious that our friend was dying and there was nothing we could do to save him. Mr Mac had very little time left to live and, judging from the way he screwed up his face, he was in such terrible agony death would be a merciful release.

I knelt at Mr Mac's side and gently lifted the visor of Mr Mac's helmet. He looked at me through pain filled eyes, reached up and gripped my arm. He grimaced again and opened his mouth in an effort to speak. A dribble of blood ran down his chin as he spoke. In addition to the wound to his head it looked as if he also had a serious chest injury.

Quickly I took off my own helmet and leaned closer to better hear his words.

'Mister Statton.' it was little more than a pain filled mumble, but it was clear enough. 'Promise me…'

I squeezed his shoulder in reply.

He shuddered and more crimson blood bubbled up from between his lips. 'My contract money… Mist… Statton… spend it… please…' He coughed painfully and blood sprayed onto the front of his leathers. 'Buy… wee house… dinnae forget…' he paused to cough again. 'Kirk…' he continued. 'Kirk… on hill…'

I squeezed his shoulder to show I understood. He had told me on more than one occasion the location of his dream home and I wanted him to know I remembered.

'Promise me…'

'I promise Mister Mac. Don't worry, I'll buy your house for you and have it ready for you when you recover and are well enough to move in.'

The Scotsman closed his eyes and tried to smile, but his face only contorted into a terrible mask of agony. I could see he was slipping away and went to stand up, but he opened his eyes again and pulled me back towards him and whispered something, but it was inaudible. I lowered my ear to his mouth and he repeated his words.

'Thank ye, David.' Momentarily his grip on my arm tightened and then slackened. It was the first and last time Mr Mac ever used my first name.

It was not much of a grave, but in the circumstances it was the best we could prepare. I was sure that Mr Mac would have understood. We scraped a shallow trench in the sand. After removing the dirk that our friend wore tucked into the top of his right boot we laid him to rest, covered him with sand and piled a few loose rocks on top of his grave.

I used his dirk to roughly chisel into one of the rocks a few words, then slipped the knife down the inside of my own boot. My simple message read: *R.I.P. Mr Mac*. It was the least I could do until I visited that Scottish hillside and gave my friend a more fitting epitaph.

Charlie and I stood next to Mr Mac's grave with our heads bowed, but it was for only a brief moment because the Frenchman touched my arm. 'David, we have a problem,' he said quietly.

The Interrogation

Friday May 14th 1982: *Central Police Station, Cape Town*
Kobus Coetzee

Kobus stared silently at the man who sat across the table from him and tried to dominate him with his personality, but he had been interrogating Carlse for two hours now. The little Cape coloured had so far refused to be intimidated into talking.

Kobus was getting frustrated. Although he didn't like using rough stuff unless there was no other choice, the time was fast approaching when he would have to take more direct action to make Carlse talk. Not that he had any moral or ethical objection to the use of torture as an interrogating tool, but he believed it should only ever be deployed as a last resort. In his experience, violence has a tendency to lose its effectiveness if used too frequently on a prisoner.

The digital clock on the wall of the room read 21:47 hours. Kobus stood up. He needed to visit the toilet. He decided to leave Carlse stewing in his own juices for a few minutes and then try again. If he had not broken the skollie by 22:30 hours he would have him transferred to a more discreet interrogation room in the cellar, where he would be wired up to the special machine that was kept there.

Johan Carlse

Johan had never experienced pain like it. He was naked and strapped to an upright chair. He had electrodes attached to his fingers, toes, nipples and testicles. When his interrogator twisted the knob on the control box of the machine his whole body convulsed in agony as the sensitive parts of his body were assailed by an electric shock.

In addition to the pain from the treatment with which he was being tortured, his body was covered in red bruises where he had been beaten repeatedly with the cosh that lay on the table beside the electricity control box.

Johan looked up at the kêrel. Brigadier Kobus Coetzee was

well known to him and he was not deceived by the benevolent smile on his face. All members of the South African Special Branch were feared by those who lived in the country's townships, but Coetzee was feared most because of his uncompromising style.

Beneath the kêrel's mild exterior was a hard and brutal thug and his treatment of Johan so far had done nothing to undermine that reputation. Now Coetzee's hand was resting gently on the control box as he waited for the right moment to twist the knob again.

'Listen, skollie, we know you were involved with the terrorist attack on Koeberg and we have enough evidence to see you swing on the end of a rope in Pollsmoor,' Coetzee said. 'But if you tell me the names of the two rooineks and what they are up to I think we can arrange to have your sentence commuted to life imprisonment.'

'I don't know what you are talking about,' Johan repeated the same response he had been giving for the past four hours.

He could see that Coetzee was trying to control his anger, but not for the first time the kêrel's frustration got the better of him. He picked up the cosh and whacked it across Johan's arm, creating yet another red weal. 'Praat my taal,' the kêrel shouted.

'Fuck off!' Johan said defiantly.

'Praat my taal,' Coetzee repeated his order and lashed out with the cosh again, this time across the side of Johan's head.

This second blow almost knocked Johan from his chair and at the same pushed him to the extreme edge of his resolve, so when he spoke again it was in the hated Afrikaans as demanded by the kêrel. 'Fokof!' He spat, hating himself for giving in to Coetzee's bullying, but finding himself no longer unable to fight against the constant pain being inflicted on his body.

'Dit is beter, skollie. Nou gee my die name van die rooineks,' the kêrel demanded.

Johan looked at his interrogator sullenly. Suddenly he felt very tired. He closed his eyes and he let his aching head drop onto his chest. He mumbled a repeat of his earlier denial, but this time, once again, he spoke in the language of his torturer: 'Ek weet nie wat jy praat.'

Kobus Coetzee

Kobus put down the cosh and nodded his head in satisfaction. The clock on the wall read 23:25 hours. It had taken almost an hour, but he was quietly pleased that finally he appeared to have broken the stubborn man's spirit sufficiently to force him to obey at least one order.

Getting the prisoner to speak in Afrikaans was a start, but now to confuse Carlse further Kobus spoke in English. 'Okay, skollie. Let me read the entry in Dyakala's diary to you again.' He picked up a small black book from the table, opened it to a marked page and began to read. 'The entry is dated Wednesday 21st April 1982…' he started and then paused.

He looked down at his prisoner, whose head was slumped on his chest. He put the diary back on the table, reached down and grabbed the man's tightly curled hair with the fingers of his left hand. He pulled his head up and at the same time slapped him sharply across the cheek with his right hand. 'Open your eyes and listen to what I am saying.'

Carlse cried out in pain, but his eyes flickered open and stayed that way.

'Good, now pay attention,' Kobus said as he picked up the diary again and opened it to the page headed Wednesday 21st April 1982. 'I had two visitors this evening.' he read out aloud, changing the text slightly to omit the single Christian name that was mentioned in the entry, 'They want me to get weapons for them.' In another entry, further on in the diary, the description of both weapons and explosives were detailed, but Kobus did not mention that.

'They would not tell me what they wanted the weapons for,' he continued. 'But when I mentioned Robben Island they did not deny it. I think they plan to attack the prison. They asked me to recommend somebody who knew the waters in Cape Bay well and I suggested Johan Carlse.' Kobus closed the diary and threw it onto the prisoner's lap, where it hit the wire that was attached to his genitals.

Carlse gasped and stared up at Kobus, who was pleased when he recognised fear in the prisoner's wide eyes. It would not be long now.

'And I suggested Johan Carlse,' Kobus repeated. 'So tell me, skollie, who were those two visitors and what are they up to?'

'Fuck off,' Carlse mumbled.

Kobus sighed and was just about to twist the knob on the electric shock control box when the door opened and Dermot Brody walked into the room. He looked worried.

'What is it?' Kobus asked.

'We have just received a report of explosions at the maximum security prison on Robben Island. The prison has been attacked by terrorists.'

'Attacked? Why attack the MSP?'

'They have broken into Section B of the isolation block and have helped a prisoner escape.'

'Mandela?'

Brody shook his head. 'I'm not sure. For some reason the boyos from the prison service are keeping pretty tight lipped about the identity of the prisoner who has escaped. Jesus Christ! The stupid bastards didn't even contact us.'

Kobus frowned his disapproval at his colleague's profanity.

'The local police only found out about the attack because they heard the explosions and contacted the prison authorities,' Brody went on, seemingly oblivious of Kobus's disapproving look. 'There is a police squad car on its way from the village to the MSP, so we might know more about the attack later.'

'Are the island police up to it?' Kobus asked.

'Probably not,' Brody replied, 'but the chief has sent reinforcements across to the island on a ferry and they should be arriving soon. In addition a navy boat is on its way to patrol the area in case the terrorists try to escape by sea.'

Kobus glanced at his prisoner, who, despite his obvious pain, had a slight smile on his lips. 'What's happening about the skollie's daughter?' He asked Brody in a loud voice and immediately saw the smile disappear from Carlse's face to be replaced by a look of concern.

'Don't worry,' Brody replied. 'A couple of my men are on their way to her apartment in Wynberg as we speak.'

'Good. I want her brought here as soon as you have her in custody,' Kobus said. 'I will interrogate that young lady personally.'

Johan Carlse

The pain being inflicted on his body was still excruciating, but Johan had found it easier because his senses were being anaesthetised by the increasing frequency of the electric shocks and beatings.

What also helped him cope with the agony inflicted on him by his torturer was the satisfaction of seeing the visible frustration on the face of Brigadier Coetzee, as he continued to resist the cop's efforts to force him into confessing his crime and incriminating his friends.

As Johan was preparing for the next round of questioning the wall phone rang. Coetzee picked up the receiver and listened, but said nothing.

Johan watched the cop for a few long seconds and then raised his eyes to stare at the clock that was set on the wall above the phone. The digital numbers clicked over to 00:00 hours. Soon it would be Saturday.

Finally the kêrel hung up the phone and went out of the room leaving Johan alone, with his naked, perspiration soaked body still wired up to the electric shock machine.

Johan closed his eyes as waves of tiredness washed over him, but any relief he felt was short-lived because the brigadier soon returned with a briefcase in his hand and a self-satisfied smile on his face.

That is when Johan's stomach turned to ice and he became scared. Very scared.

Saturday May 15th 1982
Kobus Coetzee

When Kobus Coetzee left the cellar in response to the phone call from Dermot Brody he was already planning his next move in the psychological chess game he was playing with Carlse, who, frustratingly, was showing far more resolve than he had expected.

'So the girl has disappeared?' Kobus said as he entered Brody's office.

'Yeah,' the Irishman replied.

'Any idea where she might be?'

Brody shook his head. 'My men took her flat apart and found no clues as to her whereabouts. Her wardrobe was full of clothes and there was an empty suitcase on top of it. It doesn't look as if she has gone far and is not expecting to be away for long, particularly since they discovered this in a hidden compartment in the bottom of the wardrobe.' Brody pointed to a large briefcase that lay on top of his desk.

'Is it locked?' Kobus asked as he reached for the case, which had a three-digit pin tumbler lock on either side of the handle.

'It was,' Brody said with a smile. 'But it didn't take our

locksmith long to break the code.'

Kobus flicked open the two locks and raised the lid of the briefcase to reveal that it was full of money. He whistled. 'How much?' He asked.

'Twenty-five thousand bucks,' Brody replied.

'Where would a young girl get that sort of money?'

'She could be on the game,' Brody suggested.

'Was there any sign of sexual activity in her apartment?'

'Nothing obvious, but she could be servicing punters in their cars or in alleys.'

'I think not,' Kobus said. 'No coloured girl amasses that much cash turning tricks in an alley. No, do you know what I think, Dermot?'

Brody shook his head again.

'I think the girl was looking after the money for our friend downstairs.'

'The money belongs to Carlse? Is that possible?' Brody asked.

'We'll soon find out,' Kobus said as he strode towards the door. 'Let's see what the skollie has to say about this,' he added as he raised the briefcase in the air.

Johan Carlse

So, skollie,' the kêrel said as he laid the briefcase on the table, 'I have news for you.' His self-satisfied smile widened to one of triumph.

Johan said nothing and his fear deepened as he stared at the briefcase. He did not recognise the case, but he sensed somehow that whatever it contained represented great danger for him.

'Are you not interested in my news, skollie?' Coetzee asked quietly.

Johan desperately wanted to hear the cop's news, but was never going to admit it. He shook his head sullenly.

Coetzee opened the briefcase and tipped it up so that Johan could see its contents. He guessed immediately what the money was and what was coming next. 'Soet Jesus,' he mumbled as the implications of what this meant to Freddie sunk in.

'Well, Jesus might well be sweet, skollie,' Coetzee said. 'But he is not here to help you.'

Johan closed his eyes in despair.

'That's right, my friend,' Coetzee said softly. 'It is all over. Half an hour ago your daughter was picked up in her Wynberg apartment and is currently in an interview room upstairs and is singing like the pretty little bird she is.' The cop smiled benevolently at Johan. 'She has told us everything she knows, including that this money is yours. So who gave it to you? Was it the rooinek?'

'My dogter is not involved in any of this stuff,' Johan protested desperately. He felt sick as a sense of helplessness gripped him.

'Perhaps you are telling the truth, skollie,' the kêrel told him, 'and perhaps you are lying. But whatever the truth of it, you can rest assured of one thing. If I wanted to implicate your daughter I could find enough evidence to send her to prison for a very long time, and that, my friend, is exactly what I will do if you continue with this nonsense.'

That's when Johan realised he was defeated, because he understood that the kêrel knew he would say and do anything to protect Freddie.

'So who gave you the money?' The brigadier asked again. 'Was it the rooinek?'

Johan nodded silently.

'Good. I assume he was one of the two visitors Dyakala mentions in his diary entry. Ja?'

Again Johan nodded.

'So what are their names and what are they up to?'

'I know only the name of the rooinek,' Johan said miserably. 'It is David Statton. I think he is from England.'

The cop nodded his head in obvious satisfaction. 'Are you sure you do not know the name of the other man?' He asked.

'Geen...' Johan started to speak in Afrikaans, then quickly corrected himself. 'Sorry, sir, I meant: no, I only know the name of the rooinek and that is the truth,' he insisted. 'I never met the other guy. We conducted all our business by telephone,' he paused and then added: 'But from his accent I would say he is a soutpiel.'

'An English speaking South African?'

Johan nodded.

'So what are these rooineks planning?'

With saving Freddie at the forefront of his mind Johan resigned himself to co-operating with the kêrel. He started talking and told Coetzee everything he knew, including the address where he was supposed to have met Statton the previous evening.

When Johan had finished his story, Coetzee removed the electrodes from his body and then walked over and opened the door. He called in two uniformed cops who were standing guard in the corridor outside. 'Get this piece of kak out of here,' he told them.

'Can I see my dogter?' Johan asked.

The kêrel looked at him coldly. 'Ja, as jy haar vind voor my.'

'What do you mean, sir, if I find her before you? I thought Freddie was upstairs.'

Cotzee shook his head and smiled grimly.

It was only then that Johan realised that he had been tricked by the cop into betraying the man he had entrusted with his daughter's life.

With that realisation, what remained of his fighting spirit died.

Escape from Robben Island

Saturday May 15th 1982: Robben Island

Where's Freddie?' I asked.

'She has been injured,' Charlie replied.

'Injured?' I asked anxiously.

'Don't worry, it's nothing serious. She's just slightly concussed.'

'Where is she?' I asked.

'She is with the boats and they are a bigger problem, David.' Charlie pointed his torch to the far side of the beach. 'Come on, I'll show you.'

What we found when we arrived made my stomach drop. Freddie sat huddled next to the front seat of the Spirit of Freedom with her yellow oilskin coat pulled over her head hiding her face.

She was surrounded by pieces of rock that must have fallen down with the huge rock that now straddled the sterns of both ski-boats. It had demolished not only the outboard motors but had taken a sizeable chunk out of each hull. The two boats would be taking us nowhere, nor would the inflatables, because both had been destroyed as well.

I looked up and realised what had been different about the view at the top of the hillock that had puzzled me earlier. The dinosaur head shaped rocky outcrop, which I thought had acted as such a natural shelter for the boats, had collapsed onto them.

I clambered into the boat and knelt down in front of Freddie and lifted the coat from her head. She looked up with a start. She had lost her glasses and squinted at me. 'Dave?' She asked. 'Is that you?'

'Yes, Freddie, it's me. What happened?'

She lunged forward and clasped me tightly. 'Oh, Dave, it was a nightmare.'

'What happened?' I asked again.

'It was the storm. It was horrible. There was thunder and lightning. I looked up and saw a bolt of lightning coming towards me. I thought it was going to hit me, but instead it hit that rock.' She pointed at the dinosaur's head.

'I saw the rock begin to fall and managed to get out of the

boat before it landed, but as I jumped onto the sand something hit me on the back of the head and I blacked out. When I recovered I climbed back into the front of the boat to get some shelter from the rain and must have passed out again, because the next thing I remember was Charlie shaking me.'

'Where are your glasses?'

'They came off when I fell on the sand and I couldn't find them because it was so dark.'

'OK wait here. I'll be back.' I told her and jumped down on the sand to join Charlie, who was already searching for Freddie's spectacles with his flashlight.

The little Frenchman bent over and picked something up from the beach. 'Here they are,' he said handing me a pair of glasses. 'They don't look damaged.'

'Thanks,' I said as I took them from him. 'So what are we going to do now, Charlie? Any suggestions?'

'I was rather hoping you would have some cunning alternative plan up your sleeve, mon ami,' he said in reply.

I shook my head. 'No alternative plan springs immediately to mind, cunning or otherwise.' I stared off into the distance, but even as the denial came out of my mouth the germ of an idea began to take root in my mind. 'But one thing is certain, Charlie. The only way off this island is by sea.'

'True,' he agreed.

'So we need a boat, yes?'

'True again.'

'And where do you find boats?' I pointed north.

Charlie smiled. 'A harbour!'

I smiled back at him. 'Come on, let's get Freddie up that slope and break the news to Paul and John.'

I climbed back into the boat and gave Freddie her glasses, which she took gratefully and slipped them on. 'That's better,' she smiled and reached up and took my face in her hands. 'I can see you properly now.' With that she pulled my head towards her and kissed me hard on the lips.

I didn't complain, but after a few seconds I pulled away. 'We have to go. Do you think you'll be able to climb up the hill?'

'Of course,' she replied.

'But it's very steep and you've had a knock on the head.'

I saw a warning flash in her eyes. 'Look, mister, you asked me a question and I gave you my answer. That should be enough.'

'It's enough,' I said with a smile, 'but will you at least do me a favour and wear my crash helmet in case you fall.'

She looked at me silently for a few moments and then nodded. 'Yes, I'll wear it as a favour to you.'

Suddenly I remembered that Mr Mac had been wearing a helmet when he fell and it had not protected him. At the same time I realised that Freddie would not know what happened to our friend. 'Mister Mac is dead,' I told her quietly.

'I don't believe it!' She said, as tears welled in her eyes. 'Not Mr Mac?'

'I'm afraid it's true,' I said, surprised at her show of emotion because she had only known the little Scotsman for a few short hours.

'Oh, David, I'm so sorry. He was such a gentleman. How did it happen?'

'I'll tell you later,' I said. 'First we must join the others and decide how we can get off this island without the ski-boats.'

'So what are we going to do?'

'I'm still thinking about it,' I replied truthfully.

'Quickly, mes amis,' Charlie shouted from where he stood on the sand. 'We have visitors…' He pointed towards the sea.

I saw what he meant immediately. The ferry I had seen earlier was now almost level with us and was heading at high speed towards Murray's Bay Harbour, but it was not the ferry to which Charlie pointed. His concern was provoked by a patrol boat that had emerged from the entrance to the harbour and was steaming down the length of the island toward us. As the boat cruised slowly towards Rock Cove, it probed the shoreline with a powerful searchlight. I didn't have to be a rocket scientist like Zamyatin to work out for whom the crew of that boat were searching.

I took Freddie's hand and pulled her to her feet. 'Come on,' I said urgently, 'we have to get up that slope and quickly.'

I removed my crash helmet and handed it to Freddie. She put it on and let me help her over the side of the boat. Charlie offered her his hand, but she waved him away and jumped nimbly down onto the sand. I smiled to myself as I recognised the hint of irritability that suggested she had almost recovered from her concussion. I joined them on the beach and together we ran quickly over to the ropes.

I signalled to the Frenchman that he should go first and he disappeared up the slope. Seconds later I felt him tug the rope to signal his arrival at the top. 'Your turn,' I said to Freddie. 'The slope is steep, but as long as you use the rope to steady yourself you should make it easily. Charlie will be there to help you. Now go!'

It took Freddie longer to climb the hillock than Charlie, but not so much longer that you would want to write a letter of complaint to The Times about it. There was another tug on the rope and I was on my way and soon had joined them at the top. As I got to my feet the Frenchman was already pulling up the two ropes, which he stored in one of the canvas bags.

We reached the hill top only just in time, because as I looked back, the patrol boat's bright white searchlight swept slowly across Rock Cove in a southerly direction.

'Get everybody under cover,' I told Charlie. 'Then go find John and get him to join us. I'll be with you shortly.'

Charlie ushered Freddie through the trees to where Paul watched over Zamyatin. I turned back to the beach and watched as the searchlight picked out the rocks that bordered the sand in the north of the bay. Without stopping, it swept over the spot where we had buried Mr Mac and crept slowly across the sand on which so recently we had been standing.

The light reached the far south of the beach and swept over the two destroyed ski-boats, luckily without stopping. It slipped off the beach and was picking out the white foaming water that crashed against the rocks that formed the bay when suddenly the crawling light came to an abrupt halt. It started edging back the way it had come, slower this time, until it settled once again on the speedboats.

I could imagine the operator of the light snatching up a pair of binoculars to see better what he was looking at and guessed he was trying to work out how long the boats had been on the beach. He obviously came to the conclusion they were a new addition to the scenery because he quickly trained the searchlight on the slope, moving it slowly as if looking for further clues of our whereabouts.

I heard a bosun's whistle from the launch and saw a dinghy being lowered into the water. A search party was being sent to the beach. It was my cue to leave.

I slipped into the trees and soon found the rest of my team standing in a group on the track next to the go-karts. They had taken off their crash helmets and I could see that Paul and John had sombre looks on their faces.

'Has Charlie told them about Mister Mac?' I asked, guessing

the answer.

'I told them,' the Frenchman confirmed.

'And he told us what happened to the boats also,' Paul said.

'What about the patrol boat?' I asked.

'That too,' John said.

'Well the crew have seen the ski-boats on the beach and there is a dinghy on its way to investigate.' I said.

As one, they looked in the direction of the sea, although any view was blocked by the trees with which we were surrounded.

'Don't worry,' I went on, 'they might have guessed we're still on the island, but they won't know where.'

'What sort of boat is it?' Paul asked.

'Not sure, but it didn't look very large.'

'It's probably one of the new Namacurra class boats built here in South Africa a couple of years ago,' Paul explained. 'They're used for harbour and coastal patrols.'

'How many in the crew?' I asked.

'Usually four, but it can be five.'

'Not many men then,' I mused.

'So what are we going to do, Dave?' John asked, cutting into my thoughts. 'Do we hit the harbour and take ourselves a boat?'

I looked back towards the beach and smiled. 'That was my original plan,' I said, 'but I think I have a better idea.'

Paul and I lay on top of the slope and looked down at the dinghy that was making slow progress towards the shore.

The helmsman kept the outboard motor at a low speed as he carefully navigated the narrow channel through the razor sharp crescent of rocks. He was no doubt conscious of the damage that would be inflicted on the rubber craft should it be pushed onto them by the still gusting wind. I know it had been something that worried me when we made the same journey earlier that night.

Because of the dark it was difficult to see how many men were in the dinghy, but I thought I counted three. 'How many men do you make it, Paul?' I asked.

'Three,' he confirmed without hesitation.

'So that leaves just one or two men on board the patrol boat.'

'Sies man, I wouldn't imagine it takes more than one oke to look after a vessel that size,' he pointed out.

I grunted my agreement. It made sense. I stood up and walked back into the trees where Charlie waited with John, who had his AK47 pointing at Zamyatin's stomach. 'Paul and I are going down now. You know what to do when you see our signal?'

'Yeah. We're cool,' John answered for both of them.

'Where's Freddie?' I asked.

'She needed to take a leak,' John replied without embarrassment. 'She went off to find a discreet tree to squat behind.'

'Let me have a rope,' I said to Charlie.

The Frenchman pulled one from the canvas bag that lay at his feet and handed it to me.

'Make sure you watch that bastard like a hawk,' I told John, slipping the rope over my shoulder. 'He is one tricky son of a bitch.' I turned to walk away but then paused and turned to Charlie. 'And look after Freddie for me. Make sure she wears my crash helmet and doesn't break anything when she comes down the slope.'

'Don't worry, David,' the Frenchman assured me. 'She will be fine.'

I re-joined Paul and we tied the rope to the same tree as before. 'Let's go,' I said.

I went down the slope and as soon as I reached the beach I signalled my arrival with my torch. Seconds later Paul was standing next to me.

The rope was several feet longer than the slope and a coil of it lay on the sand. Using Mr Mac's dirk I cut off four lengths from the rope and slipped the knife back into the top of my boot. The rope now hung three feet or so short of the beach, but I was sure it would not present a problem.

The beam from the patrol boat's searchlight was once again concentrated on the ruined ski-boats, leaving the rest of the beach in darkness. I hoped the men in the dinghy would not see us waiting in the shadows.

We waited in silence as the sound of the dinghy's motor grew louder as it approached the beach. When the craft was only a couple of yards from land we saw a couple of men jump into the sea and pull it closer to the shore. A third man joined them and together they dragged the dinghy up onto the dark sand. All three wore bright yellow oilskin jackets and black base-ball caps.

The three men walked up the beach in single file towards where the speedboats lay lit up by the searchlight. They were amateurs, those boys. As they trudged across the sand their heads were down and they looked neither right nor left. Perhaps they were made over confident by the carbine each carried, or maybe they were imbued with a sense of invincibility by the two words that were inscribed across the back of their yellow jackets in bold black letters: *Polisie Police*

As it happens, any confidence the cops felt was misplaced because we picked them off like sitting ducks. I took the back one with a single chop of my right hand at the same time that Paul grabbed the second man round the neck and throttled him. Both men fell soundlessly to the sand.

The remaining cop must have sensed something was wrong because he spun round and a look of shock froze his face as he saw that his two companions had been replaced by black leather clad figures. He raised his police carbine, but managed to lift it only an inch or two before he was felled by a punch on the chin from Paul.

It was all over in seconds.

While Paul removed the jackets from the three policemen and tied them up, I went back to the bottom of the hillock and signalled the all clear. I heard a movement at the top of the slope, followed by a shower of dirt and small pebbles as Freddie made her way down to the beach. I raised a hand to help her the final few feet where the shortened rope did not reach the sand, but she shrugged me off with an irritated shrug. That was my girl.

I looked up the slope and could only just about make out the figures of John and Charlie, so was pretty sure they would be invisible to whoever was left aboard the police patrol boat. At least that's what I hoped.

They came down together, with Zamyatin between them. Charlie had tied the second rope to a tree and he held it as he put one arm round the still handcuffed Russian and help guide him down the slope. John, who wore the bag containing our remaining grenades, took the other rope and linked his other arm in Charlie's so that they formed a cradle that supported Zamyatin as he edged backwards down the slope.

The Russian slipped on his way down. I tensed as Charlie struggled to keep his footing to stop them both sliding down the slope. John managed to yank the scientist to his feet with one mighty jerk of his arm and, with the nimble Frenchman's help, ensured Zamyatin made the rest of the descent without further mishap. Soon they joined us on the beach.

It was now time to execute the next part of my plan. Freddie, Paul and I put on the yellow jackets and caps that we had taken from the cops and headed for the rubber dinghy, leaving Charlie to guard our captives, whilst John took care of Zamyatin.

Freddie jumped into the dinghy as Paul and I pushed it out into the water. Despite the howling wind the little bay was relatively sheltered and it was easier launching the rubber craft than it had been the ski-boats from the beach at Bloubergstrand.

Freddie started the outboard motor at the first attempt and with the propeller churning the sea into white foam she slowly edged the dinghy towards the channel. A few feet from shore she cut back the motor and expertly kept the dinghy steady as Paul and I clambered aboard.

As soon as we settled ourselves into the bottom of the dinghy Freddie gunned the outboard motor and pointed the dinghy towards the patrol boat. She used her seamanship skills to guide us down the narrow channel through the rocks at a speed that would have shamed the captured policemen if they had been in a position to witness our progress.

As we left the channel, and chugged into the open sea, Freddie managed to avoid the beam from the searchlight, which was still trained on our abandoned ski-boats. She eased back the outboard motor so any noise from its exhaust was barely audible and steered the dinghy on a north-easterly course. We approached the twin hulled catamaran from its seaward side, so as not to be seen from any policemen left on board.

When the dinghy was a hundred feet or so from the patrol boat Freddie switched off the outboard motor and let the current push us slowly and silently towards our target.

Seconds later the dinghy bumped gently into the catamaran's portside hull, just forward of the two outboard motors that were attached to its stern. I stood up, and using the handrail that ran along the boat's bulwark to steady myself, I checked out how many cops had been left behind by the shore party.

Paul had been right. I could see only one cop on-board. He was clearly visible in the wheelhouse, with one arm raised as he controlled the searchlight that was attached by brackets to its roof. The bright beam was still aimed at the far end of Rock Cove beach, although what he hoped to see was beyond me.

I secured the dinghy to the deck-rail with its bow-line and gave Paul the thumbs up.

The big South African scrambled over the bulwark rail. So skilful and light-footed was he that despite being six foot six inches

302

tall, and over 250 pounds in weight, the catamaran barely bobbed as he gently landed on the deck.

He made his way silently across the fibreglass deck to the wheelhouse where he quickly immobilised the unsuspecting policeman, who was probably trying to work out what had happened to his colleagues. Whatever was going through the cop's mind, Paul took him completely by surprise. He grabbed the man from behind in a bear hug that squeezed all the breath from his body in seconds and any thought of resistance was crushed from him at the same time. Paul tied the man's hands behind his back and marched him over to the side of the boat.

Together we forced the policeman over the rail and into the dinghy where he huddled dejectedly against its rubber wall. He did not look inclined to try anything rash, but that might have been because I was sitting opposite him with my pistol aimed at his heart.

Paul untied the line that secured the dinghy to the patrol boat and dropped it into the waiting Freddie's hands. He gave us a wave and headed for the shelter of the wheelhouse from where he would guard the catamaran until our return.

Freddie steered the dinghy back to the beach. It took less time than our earlier journey because Paul had the foresight to move the beam of the searchlight away from the far edge of Rock Cove and train it on the channel through the rocks.

Not for the first time I thanked God that I had assembled such a competent team.

When we reached the beach I handed my pistol to Freddie, which somehow she managed to hold steadily pointing at the cop while at the same time controlling the bucking dinghy with her other hand. I jumped overboard, grabbed the bow-line in both hands and, using all my strength, pulled the rubber craft to the edge of the sand, where Charlie was waiting to give me a hand.

'Where are the cops?' I asked Charlie as I handed him the line.

'Tied hand and foot in one of the ski-boats,' the Frenchman replied.

'Good. Tie this round that rock over there.' I pointed at a small cone shaped rock that rose out of the sand. I reached up and took the pistol from Freddie. 'Out you get,' I said to the policeman as I indicated with my free hand that he should stand up. He didn't need telling twice. He jumped to his feet and clambered out of the dinghy onto the sand. 'OK, Charlie, take him to join his pals,' I said to the Frenchman when he had finished securing the line to the rock.

'Consider it done, mon ami,' he replied as he unslung his AK47 and used it to nudge the cop towards the dark shadows where the two destroyed ski-boats lay.

I ran across the sand to where I had left John guarding Zamyatin. They had not moved. John shone a torch in my face when he heard me coming, but switched it off quickly when he saw who it was.

'It's time to move out,' I said as I helped him get the Russian to his feet and then led them to the dinghy, where we waited until Charlie joined us before attempting to get Zamyatin aboard.

'You go first,' I told the Frenchman. 'We'll get Zamyatin into the boat once you're in position to cover him.' Then I added loud enough for the Russian to hear: 'And, Charlie, if he tries any tricks shoot the bastard through the head.'

'Why the head?'

'Because the bullets will go right through him and I don't want you puncturing the dinghy!'

'No problem. I hope he does try something, because it would give me immense pleasure to shoot him between the eyes,' the Frenchman said with feeling. 'I owe him for Mister Mac.' With that he pulled down the visor of his helmet and pulled himself nimbly aboard the dinghy.

John followed Charlie's lead and pulled down the visor, which would protect his face from the pounding waves. Sadly, Freddie still wore my helmet so I had to put up with the stinging water in my eyes as we manhandled the still manacled Zamyatin into position and heaved him over the side of the dinghy. John passed the canvas bag of grenades to Freddie, who placed it carefully on the floor of the boat, and then he returned to help me.

I untied the bow-line from the rock and together we pushed the dinghy through the waves until it was in deep enough water. Freddie started the outboard motor and used it to bring the rubber craft back under her control, but it was still shallow enough to enable us to scramble on board.

Once John and I were safely in the dinghy Freddie increased power and headed out to the police patrol boat. Zamyatin, who had been soaked through as we got him into the boat, was moaning loudly that he would catch pneumonia.

Charlie pushed his Kalashnikov closer to his face and raised the visor of his helmet. 'Shut up!' He ordered. 'It's difficult enough for me to resist the temptation to shoot you without your whinging. If you're not careful my finger might slip.'

Zamyatin, must have seen the warning light in the Frenchman's eyes because his mouth clamped tight like a mousetrap and he eased himself as far away from Charlie's weapon as the side of the dinghy would allow.

When we reached the patrol boat, Paul was waiting to help us on board. He had found a metal ladder somewhere and had fitted this over the bulwark rail, which made it easy for us to transfer from the dinghy. Within seconds, we were all aboard the catamaran and let the dinghy float off into the night, its job done.

Charlie maintained his watchful guard over Zamyatin, while John positioned himself behind the 12.7mm heavy machine gun, with which the patrol boat was equipped and which was mounted in the centre of the stern deck. Freddie and I joined Paul in the wheelhouse where we watched as he flicked the ignition switch that started up the two powerful Yamaha outboard motors. As the boat surged forward, he spun the wheel until the boat was set on an easterly course.

Freddie took off her crash helmet and set it down next to Paul's on the wide ledge that ran along one wall of the wheelhouse. 'It looks as if we pulled it off, Dave,' she said as she shook out her long hair in the way that only a woman can.

'Don't count our chickens yet,' I warned her. 'The job's not finished until we hand the Russian over to Rogers and collect the rest of our money.'

I was wise to be cautious because a few minutes later I felt Paul tap me on the arm and point to our right. A vessel was heading our way from the direction of Cape Town and it was moving very quickly.

'Any ideas?' I asked Paul.

'Yeah, but I'm not sure it's something you want to hear.'

'Try me.'

'Well, judging by its size and speed I'd guess it was one of the two navy Warrior class strike craft based in Simon's Town, probably the Frans Erasmus.'

'What armaments does she carry?'

'Two 76 mm guns and a few Scorpion missiles.'

'Is that all?' I asked sardonically.

'Oh, no,' he replied deadpan. 'The crew will also have a goodly supply of assault rifles and various side arms.'

'You're right, I don't want to hear.' I stared thoughtfully at the navigation lights that were all we could currently see of the approaching navy boat. It was approaching at an alarming rate.

'We don't want to be messing with those okes if we can help it,' Paul said increasing to full power the catamaran's outboard engines. 'They're nothing like the warders and cops we've been up against so far tonight. Those groentjies were amateurs compared to the crew of that navy boat.'

'How many in the crew?' I asked.

'45 officers and men.'

'Not good news, then?'

'Definitely not good news. Those navy boys are the real McCoy.'

'Can we outrun them?' Freddie asked.

Paul shrugged. 'Anything is possible, but it will be touch and go. Our boat is pretty nippy and at full power can do speeds of 32 knots. But that baby can do 34 knots without even trying. As you can see from their course they are trying to head us off before we reach land and that extra couple of knots will make all the difference.'

We stared in silence as the navy boat headed for a point midway between Robben Island and our destination on the mainland. It soon became obvious to me that at our current speeds the navy boat was going to easily head off our fibreglass patrol boat.

'It looks like we are going to have a fight on our hands,' I said softly. I turned to Freddie. 'Do you think you can drive this boat?' I asked.

'You mean steer the boat, landlubber,' she teased. 'Anyway, the answer is yes.'

I was quietly proud that she was so cool about the dangerous position in which we found ourselves. 'OK,' I said. 'Take over from Paul. When we get closer to the navy boat I expect they will hit us with their searchlight and signal for us to stop. Obey them and allow them to come in close to us. Don't do anything else until I tell you.'

'What if they start shooting?' She asked as she took the wheel from Paul.

'Oh, there will be shooting all right, so whatever you do,

keep your head down and keep the outboard motors ticking over.'

'Will do, skipper,' she said touching her forelock with a finger.

I smiled at her, but I never knew whether she was being serious or sarcastic.

Paul and I left the shelter of the wheelhouse and were immediately hit by the wind, which, if anything, was blowing even harder than before.

I picked up a coil of rope that was lying on the deck and handed it to Charlie. 'Tie him up,' I shouted over the howl of the wind and pointed towards Zamyatin. 'And make sure he can't move. We have a battle to fight and we don't need any nonsense from him.'

Charlie nodded his acknowledgment. He had seen the approaching naval vessel and read the situation straight away.

John too had seen the strike craft and was training the machine gun in its direction. He must have known though, that with the wind gusting so strongly there was very little chance of causing any significant damage to the boat. Of course, the same should apply in reverse, indeed, it would be worse for our opponents because they would be firing into the wind. Well that was my theory, but theories do not always work in practice.

'What munitions do we have left, John?' I shouted my question.

The American shook his head and tapped the side of his helmet to indicate that he could not hear properly. He took off his helmet and laid it in the deck next to the canvass bag that stood at his feet. I repeated my question, raising my voice.

He got it this time. 'Eight smoke grenades, a couple of stun grenades and a dozen magazines of ammunition for the AK47s.' he answered without hesitation, 'And, of course, all the brandies.'

I looked at the navy launch that was now close enough for me to be able to make out the white name that was emblazoned across its hull. Once again Paul had been right, it was the SAS Frans Erasmus. The ship was also close enough for me to see the menacing shape of the canvas covered 76mm guns that were located in the bow and stern of the boat. I could not see the Scorpion missile launcher, but I knew it was somewhere amongst the array of technology with which we were confronted. Suddenly the munitions at our disposal seemed puny by comparison.

I called the team together and told them my plan. It was not a particularly good plan, but it was the only one I had.

Bloubergstrand

Kobus Coetzee

It was one o'clock in the morning when Kobus and Dermot Brody reached the outskirts of Bloubergstrand. They had made good time from Cape Town in the police car and they soon found the block of flats for which they were looking.

Outside the flats was parked a police squad car, its roof light flashing on and off regularly. It sent pulses of distorted blue light through the rain soaked trees that lined the area of wasteland that stood alongside the building.

Brody parked behind the police car. He and Kobus got out of their own vehicle and were met by a young uniformed policeman with three chevrons on the sleeve of his greatcoat. The Colonel flashed his warrant card at the sergeant and introduced himself. 'And this is Brigadier Coetzee from the Special Branch,' he added.

The young policeman straightened up visibly at the mention of Coetzee's name and held out a hand. 'Sergeant Simeon Du Plessis,' he introduced himself, his eyes shining with pleasure. 'It's a real privilege to meet you, Brigadier,' he said with the hint of a pink tinge on his cheeks. 'What you are doing to defeat the communist terrorists is fantastic,' he added and then turned hurriedly towards Brody to hide his embarrassment. 'We've opened the garage as you asked, Colonel.' He pointed across to where a light shone out onto the wasteland.

Kobus could see another uniformed policeman standing in the garage doorway.

'Did you find anything?' Brody asked.

'Not in the garage itself,' Du Plessis said. 'But I did discover something outside that I found interesting.'

Just then the two-way radio in Brody's car trilled. 'I'd better get that,' he said and slid back into the driver's seat.

'Show me what you found,' Kobus told the young sergeant.

'OK, this way, sir,' Du Plessis said as he pulled a flashlight from his coat pocket and switched it on. 'But be careful of the mud.'

Kobus followed the sergeant, keeping to the firmer ground

wherever possible. They reached the garage where they were joined by the second uniformed policeman, whom Du Plessis introduced as Constable Maritz, then he pointed at the ground outside the up-and-over door and the clearly imprinted tyre tracks.

Du Plessis bent down and pointed the beam of his torch at the tracks. 'Looking at the size of the tyres, sir, I think they belonged to a trailer that was stored in the garage. My guess is that it was a boat trailer.'

Kobus leaned over, the better to see what the sergeant was talking about. He nodded. 'I agree with you, sergeant.'

Du Plessis trained the flashlight on the ground to the right of the garage door. Revealed by the powerful beam was another set of tyre tracks, but these were much wider.

'A van I think, sir, possibly one of those big Mercedes panel trucks,' Du Plessis suggested.

Again Kobus agreed, impressed with the young policeman's self-confidence. 'Do you have a local map in your car, sergeant?'

'Yes, sir.'

'Good,' Kobus said as he straightened up. 'Lead the way.'

When they arrived back where the two cars were parked, they found Brody leaning against their car staring out to sea with a thoughtful look on his face.

Du Plessis and Maritz went to their car to find a map while Kobus briefed the CID colonel.

'It looks as if a boat trailer was stored in the garage and was towed away on the back of a van,' Kobus explained. 'Sergeant Du Plessis believes it was a Mercedes.'

'He has the reputation of being a smart lad,' Brody said.

'I can believe it. What was the radio call about?'

'It was just confirmation that the reinforcements you requested are on their way from Cape Town.'

'Did they tell you anything about the navy boat that was sent to patrol round the island?'

'Yeah,' Brody replied. 'It seems there was a bit of a delay because the only available naval vessel was a strike craft called the Frans Erasmus. Trouble is, it was moored in Simon's Town, so to reach Cape Bay it had to come via Cape Point. The last progress report was that it was off Sea Point and steaming north as fast as it could.' Brody pointed out to sea. 'I think that's her now.'

Kobus screwed up his eyes to protect them from the wind and in the distance saw the navigation lights of a boat travelling at speed from the direction of Cape Town.

'There's something else,' Brody said.

'What now?' Kobus asked.

'They've just found Johan Carlse dead in his cell.'

'How did it happen?'

'He appears to have hanged himself with his trouser belt.'

Coetzee shrugged. 'Well that's one less terrorist to worry about,' he said. 'The skollie has saved us the job.'

'It's alright for you, Kobus, but I'm the one who has to sort out all the bloody paperwork,' moaned Brody, lowering his voice as the two junior officers re-joined them.

'Here's the map you wanted, sir,' Du Plessis said.

Kobus took the map and flattened it open across the bonnet of their car. To prevent it being blown away by the wind he held one side down while Brody and the two uniformed policemen held down another side each.

'Now tell me, son,' Kobus said to Du Plessis. 'If you were going to launch a boat round here somewhere, where would it be?'

The sergeant shone the beam of the flashlight onto the map and studied the shoreline carefully. He pointed to a spot on the map close to where the name "Bloubergstrand" was printed. 'Well, that's where we are, sir, so the easiest place from which to launch would be this beach here.' He slid his finger along the map and pointed to a long stretch of sand that lay directly to the east. 'However, if I wanted to launch without being seen by anyone, then that beach would be my last choice because it's visible from the windows of those apartments over there.' He pointed to the block of flats he said with the certainty of youth.

'So where would you choose?' Kobus asked.

'I am new to the area, sir,' Du Plessis said apologetically. 'Hennie here, that is Constable Maritz, knows this coast better than I do.'

Kobus looked at the constable and raised an eyebrow. 'What do you think, young man?'

'Sergeant Du Plessis is right, meneer,' Maritz said nervously, but without hesitation. 'I would choose somewhere more secluded.' He pointed at the map to a spot north of their position. 'If it was me, that's the beach I would use,' he said. 'It is surrounded by sand dunes so it's out of sight of the coast road.'

'How far is the beach?'

'Just over three kilometres, Brigadier,' Maritz replied.

'How does one reach the beach?' Kobus asked the constable. 'Is there an access road from the highway?'

'Ja, meneer, there is a track through the dunes.'

Kobus nodded in satisfaction. 'Then let's go see,' he said as he folded up the map and handed it to Du Plessis.

'The navy boat has stopped,' Brody said and pointed out to sea.

Kobus looked over his shoulder and saw that the navigation lights were no longer moving. He glanced at Brody and saw the Irishman had an apprehensive expression on his face. 'You look worried,' he said.

Brody stared at the navigation lights. 'To be sure I'm worried,' he admitted quietly. 'I've always had a touch of what my grannie called "The Gift". Psychic powers to you and me. For instance when I was a wee lad I lived on a farm in County Kildare,' he said. 'My da had a beautiful horse, a big bay mare called Bold Mary. He was a good jockey was my da and he used to ride Mary over the jumps in local national hunt competitions.

'When I was about ten, da was invited to ride at Punchestown. We were all excited for him, because it had always been his ambition to ride over the jumps at a proper racecourse. But the day before the big race I had a really bad feeling that Bold Mary would fall and be killed.' Brody fell silent.

'Did the horse fall?' Kobus asked.

'Aye,' Brody said. 'At the final hurdle.'

'And was it killed?'

'Aye, she broke her leg and had to be put down by the vet,' Brody lapsed into silence for a while before adding: 'But when Bold Mary fell she landed on my da and broke his neck. He died the next day.'

Kobus said nothing, there was nothing he could say.

It was Brody who broke the silence. 'And the thing is Kobus, my boyo,' he said, pointing again at the navigation lights. 'Is that when I look at that navy boat out there, I have the same bad feeling.'

Kobus Coetzee and Dermot Brody followed the police car being driven by Constable Maritz, who brought his vehicle to a halt on a dark and deserted stretch of the coast road a couple of kilometres north of Bloubergstrand.

Brody parked behind Maritz and Kobus opened the

passenger door. He got out and stood at the side of the highway facing the sand dunes that lined the coast road. He looked along the track that ran through the dunes, but it was unlit and he could see only for a couple of hundred metres. He heard the crunch of footsteps on the sand covered hard shoulder and soon the Irishman was standing at his side.

'While we're checking the beach here,' Kobus said to Brody. 'I think Sergeant Du Plessis should check further up the coast just in case Statton used a different bay.'

'I was thinking the same…' Brody started, but was interrupted by the sound of a loud explosion that lit up the sky somewhere in the distance to the west. 'Jesus, Mary and Joseph!' The Irishman intoned.

'The navy boat?' Kobus asked.

Brody shrugged 'I told you I had a bad feeling.' With that he walked over to the police car and spoke to Du Plessis through the open passenger window. He stepped away from the car as the sergeant wound up the window and watched as Constable Maritz eased the car out onto the highway and headed north.

Brody made his way back to his own car, where he found Kobus already sitting in the passenger seat waiting for him. The car's engine was still ticking over so he put it into gear and they made their way down the bumpy track through the sand dunes. They soon reached the beach beyond and immediately spotted two boat trailers parked close to the shoreline, just out of reach of the crashing surf.

They both stared out to sea where the bright glow of a fire lit up the night sky.

'The poor bastards,' Brody said.

'I suppose it could be the rooinek's boat,' Kobus said.

'I think not.'

'In that case turn off the headlights,' Kobus ordered. 'If Statton is on his way back we don't want to warn him of our presence.' He looked over his shoulder and saw two dark shapes standing in front of the sand dunes, one larger than the other. He guessed what they were straight away. 'Do we have a flashlight? He asked.

'I should think so,' Brody said. 'They are standard issue in police cars. Look in the glove compartment, that's where they usually keep them.'

Kobus opened the glove compartment and immediately found

what he wanted. He switched on the small rubber flashlight and the interior of the car was filled with a bright white light that he quickly dimmed with the palm of his hand. He grunted in satisfaction. He had half expected the batteries to be flat.

'I think the van they used is over there by the dunes and there is another vehicle parked next to it,' Kobus said as he opened the door. 'I'll go and check them out while you contact Central Station and see if they know what is happening out there.' He nodded towards the sea. 'And find out what has happened to the reinforcements we were promised.'

Kobus got out of the car and then ducked his head back inside. 'And Dermot,' he added as Brody picked up the two-way radio handset. 'Get control to contact Du Plessis and get him back here to help us.' With that he made his way to investigate the dark shapes on the edge of the sand dunes.

It only took a brief scan with the shielded flashlight to identify the large, panel-van and bakkie that were parked side by side on the sand. He smiled to himself as he saw that the van was indeed a Mercedes, as predicted by Sergeant Du Plessis.

Both vehicles were locked and Kobus was just deciding whether to break into the van when he heard the faint sound of an outboard motor out at sea. Quickly he returned to the car and clambered in. 'I think they are coming,' he said. 'Let's get out of here.'

Brody turned the car round and drove back up the track towards the highway with his lights off.

'Did you get any information?' Kobus asked.

'It's not good news,' Brody replied as he switched on the car's headlights once they were out of sight of the beach. 'The captain of the navy boat radioed in to report he had made contact with the terrorists and was about to send a boarding party to arrest them,' the Irishman went on. 'He followed that call up with a report that his boat was under fire from small arms fire.' He paused, perhaps to let the significance of his words sink in. 'There was no other communication until the boat sent out a May Day signal,' he said eventually. 'That was the last anybody heard from them.'

'Mag God ontferm U oor hulle siele,' Kobus whispered quietly, then said in a louder voice: 'What about our reinforcements, Dermot?'

'Two armoured personnel carriers are on their way. They reached Bloubergstrand five minutes ago, so should be with us very soon.' As he spoke two sets of headlights came up the highway towards them from the south. 'That looks like them now. How do you want them deployed?'

Kobus thought about that question for a minute or two. 'Get them to park here,' he said when they reached the highway. 'If we try to ambush the terrorists on the beach they are likely to see or hear us getting the carriers into position, so it will be better to set up a road block here.'

Cape Bay, South Africa
David Statton

The Frans Erasmus switched on its searchlight and pinned us against the black sky like a moth trapped in a porchlight on a summer's evening. There is no escape for the moth and there was no escape for us.

'Attention! Attention!' The voice that shouted across the water between the two boats was made mechanical by the loudhailer through which the message was sent. 'You are sailing in restricted waters. Reduce speed and identify yourselves.'

Freddie obeyed immediately, cutting power to the two outboard motors until they were only just ticking over, she brought the catamaran's speed down to a crawl,

'Ahoy daar!' Paul shouted from his position at the starboard rail of the boat. He was wearing one of the yellow police jackets and baseball caps. 'Ons is die polisie op soek na ontsnapte gevangenes van Robbeneiland.'

It was no more than a hopeful bluff for Paul to claim in Afrikaans that we were the police looking for escape prisoners from Robben Island, but it was worth trying. We might at least win ourselves a temporary delay while the captain of the navy strike boat checked out our story. However, any hope we had proved short lived.

'Thank you, sir,' the mechanical voice called back straight away. 'But I have been instructed to check out your identity. Please prepare to receive a boarding party.'

Out of the corner of my eye I saw Charlie make his way along the seaward side of the wheelhouse, well out of sight of anybody aboard the navy boat.

'He replied in English,' Paul hissed. 'The bastard knows who we are. If he believed we were really the police, he would have answered in Afrikaans.'

'I know,' I said. 'Get ready.'

Paul darted inside the wheelhouse to join Freddie, while behind me I heard John cock the deck-mounted machine gun

'Fire!' I shouted as I threw myself to the deck.

A line of bullets streaked through the air and the navy boat's searchlight exploded in a shower of broken glass and our vessel was plunged into darkness. At the same time Paul switched on our searchlight and immediately the naval craft was lit up, revealing a bustle of activity.

In the bow of the strike boat two sailors were stripping the canvas cover from a gun, while several other crew members were lined up along the railings that ran round the open platform above the bridge. Each carried an assault rifle that was pointing at us.

Several sailors on the upper deck were holding a hand to their foreheads as if they were saluting us. In fact they were trying to protect their eyes from the bright beam of light being directed their way from the wheelhouse of the catamaran.

A couple of sailors were already dismantling the damaged searchlight. I said a silent prayer that John had destroyed the light beyond repair.

Paul ran back from the wheelhouse and took up his position against the starboard rail of the stern deck. He was carrying half a dozen grenades in his big hands.

To my left I saw Charlie emerge from behind the catamaran's wheelhouse with his AK47 slung across his back. He made his way onto the bow deck with a stun-grenade held in one hand and in his other a crash helmet containing several smoke grenades.

Deftly Charlie pulled the pin out with his teeth and hurled a stun grenade in the general direction of the fore deck of the navy boat. As the grenade exploded with a deafening and disorientating bang the Frenchman threw a smoke grenade in the same direction, which, when it hit the deck, released a dense cloud of grey smoke.

A second, third and fourth smoke grenade followed in quick succession. The two sailors who had been in the process of uncovering the machine gun on the fore deck disappeared into a swirling cloud of smoke, coughing loudly as the acrid fumes attacked their lungs.

At the same time Paul was attacking the stern and soon the whole length of the strike boat was covered in clouds of thick smoke.

Suddenly I was momentarily blinded as a beam of white light shone into my eyes. I realised my prayer had not been answered and that our adversaries had been able to repair the damaged searchlight. Now both vessels were lit up and we were once again as exposed as the sailors on the navy boat, who took little time in opening fire at us.

Luckily the thick smoke surrounding the strike boat prevented the sailors from seeing us properly. Most of their shots went harmlessly above our heads, although bullets thudded into the side of the wheelhouse close to where I was standing.

John had joined Paul and the two of them were now flattened on the stern deck, resting their rifles on the railing and firing shots steadily at the smoke filled bridge platform. The shots from the Frans Erasmus slowly petered out until only the occasional bullet hit the catamaran.

I heard a cry from the bow of our boat and I turned round just in time to see Charlie collapse in a heap. I swung back in the direction of the navy boat, raising my Kalashnikov as I swivelled. I fired an extended burst at the bridge and then dived behind the wheelhouse. I edged towards where the Frenchman lay on the forward deck.

'You OK?' I asked when I reached him.

'I've been hit in my leg,' the little Frenchman replied with a painful grimace. 'But I'll live.'

I looked down and saw that just below the knee of his left leg a bullet had punched a hole through his leather trousers, through which I could see blood seeping. 'It doesn't look as if the bullet hit an artery,' I said.

'The blood is not spurting,' he said, reading my mind.

'Come on,' I said as I helped him to his feet. 'Let's get you out of the firing line.'

Charlie winced as he stood up and eased himself into the narrow gangway that ran between the wheelhouse and the portside bulwark. 'I think my bone has been smashed up pretty bad, David.'

'Can you make it to the wheelhouse door?' I asked once we were both behind the wheelhouse and out of sight of the navy sailors.

'I'll try,' he said.

We edged slowly along the bulwark. I tried to take as much weight as possible off Charlie's damaged leg, but it was difficult because we were constrained by the narrowness of the gangway and several times he gasped in pain. We managed to reach the stern and I helped him down onto the deck and through the door to the wheelhouse where we found Freddie slumped on the floor next to the boat's wheel.

At first, I thought she had been shot and my stomach dropped, but she turned her head, looked up at me and grinned. 'It's safer down here,' she said calmly.

I lowered Charlie onto the deck next to Freddie. 'He's been hit in the leg.' I explained and looked around the wheelhouse until I found for what I was looking. There was a large green first-aid box attached by a leather strap to a bracket on the wall. I undid the strap and lifted the box down. I pushed aside the helmets and laid the box on the ledge.

The box was well stocked with medical equipment. I found a field dressing, scissors, antiseptic cream, a packet of Oxycodone pain killers and a couple of safety pins. I handed Charlie two of the pills to take straight away and made him stuff the rest of the packet in the pocket of his leathers. I cut open his trouser leg as far as his knee and spread a liberal covering of antiseptic on his wound, before applying a field dressing.

'We need to get you to a hospital and have that bullet removed,' I told him. 'Hopefully this will stop the wound from festering until we get you there.' I stretched the leathers over the dressing and secured them at the back of his leg with safety pins. 'Stay here with Freddie,' I said as I made my way out of the wheelhouse. 'We'll be on our way soon,' I called over my shoulder, trying to sound confident. It was difficult.

I quickly covered the few paces to where John and Paul were still firing their automatics at the crew of the Frans Erasmus. On the portside of the deck a safely manacled Zamyatin was yelling blue murder, shouting insults about me, the South Africans, the KGB and the world in general. I ignored him, half hoping that a stray bullet would get him.

The smoke from the grenades was clearing noticeably, dispersed by the gusting wind, and the bullets being fired from the bridge platform of the navy boat had increased in number and were getting more accurate.

'I think we've just about reached the "them or us" time,' I said as I slid onto the deck next to my two friends. 'The only way of getting out of this mess is using the incendiary smoke grenades.'

'I agree,' Paul said.

'Do you want me to throw them?' John asked as he opened with one hand the canvas bag that lay on the deck next to him.

'No,' I said. 'I'll do it. You two cover me.' I grabbed the bag and crawled across the deck until I was again next to the wheelhouse.

When I was in position, Paul and John started firing more rapidly and immediately the fire from the Frans Erasmus petered out again. I leapt to my feet and hurled a blend-brand grenade at the navy vessel. The 'brandy' smashed against the side of the bridge and the result was spectacular. There was a blinding flash that made the searchlights look like birthday-cake candles and the non-metallic parts of the navy boat's superstructure started to glow and melt, including the rubber seals in the windows of the bridge.

The side window of the bridge blew out with a shower of broken glass. I threw a second blend-brand grenade and watched it fly through the open window. A second later the interior of the bridge was filled with white light as smoke burnt at 1000 degrees Celsius. My third brandy was already on its way towards the platform that was set above the bridge. It landed and in another blinding flash the sailors who had been firing at us were engulfed with smoke and simply evaporated with a chorus of screams that chilled an already cold night.

I watched and listened in horror. I had never seen or heard anything like it and was momentarily paralysed as my mind grappled with the death and destruction I had just inflicted on so many men.

Eventually, I snapped out of my self-induced paralysis and threw open the wheelhouse door. 'Go!' I shouted at Freddie.

She was ready and needed no more urging. She leapt to her feet and slammed the outboard motors control lever up to maximum speed. The engines roared and the catamaran surged forward and soon the navy boat was left behind, stranded and disabled by the fires that could be seen spreading rapidly through its superstructure.

We had only put a few hundred yards between us and the stricken vessel when I felt a rush of heat on the back of my neck as a massive explosion tore the navy boat apart. I guessed that the fire had reached the missile store. I wondered how many more men had been killed. I was not proud of the mounting tally of dead bodies we had left behind us.

Zamyatin was still shouting out his mad insults about all and sundry, but even his loud voice could not drown out the dreadful screams of the dying sailors. They were deeply ingrained in my sub-conscience and haunted me long after the navy boat was a silent burning funeral pyre.

Bloubergstrand, Western Cape

As we approached the beach in Bloubergstrand I looked behind us to see if we were being followed. The ocean was empty except for the wrecked Frans Erasmus, which was now just a small glowing dot in the dark sea.

I glanced at my watch. It was a 01:45. We had three quarters of an hour to beach the patrol boat, get Zamyatin loaded into the Mercedes van and reach my rendezvous with Gavin Rogers. It was going to be tight.

Freddie didn't do any fancy landing manoeuvres, she simply pointed the catamaran at the beach and steered straight at the sand. As the tips of the twin hulls approached land she spun the wheel sharply to starboard so that we covered the final couple of feet side-on. The vessel came to a juddering, crunching stop close to where we had left the two boat-trailers, which were now fully out of the water. As the portside hull slid up the beach the outboard motor on that side of the stern whined in protest as its propeller bit into sand rather than water.

Freddie quickly switched off the engines. The wind had finally dropped and suddenly the night was still and quiet except for the lapping of the waves and the occasional shouted insult from Zamyatin.

I moved quickly to where the Russian sat against the bulwark in a corner of the stern deck. Charlie had made a good job of tying him up and he had been unable to move. Ignoring the verbal abuse he hurled at me I removed the rope from his legs, but left the hand-cuffs on his wrists.

Free from the leg restraints Zamyatin leapt to his feet and tried to head-butt me. I stepped away and hit him once on the chin with my fist. It was one of the most satisfying punches I had ever thrown. His knees buckled and he slumped to the deck in a daze.

'Give me a hand,' I said to Paul who had joined me at Zamyatin's side. 'Hold his head. I don't want him drawing attention to us with all his noise.'

The South African grabbed the Zamyatin's head and clamped it with more force than was strictly necessary as I held a field dressing over his mouth without removing it from its outer packing.

The scientist struggled frantically, his eyes wide and shining with madness. He tried to shake his head to throw the dressing from his face, but Paul's big hands were far too strong and the Russian's head barely moved. I was able to easily bind the field dressing tightly into place with a bandage that I wrapped several times round the lower part of his face.

Paul helped me pull the struggling Zamyatin to his feet, lift him over the side of the boat and lower him down onto the beach where John already waited. If the Russian had any ideas about trying to escape, he would have been dissuaded by the Kalashnikov that was pointed at him by the American.

'Help John get him inside the back of the Mercedes,' I told Paul as I handed over the key to the vehicle. 'Cuff both his arms to the roof strut using the holes that John drilled in it.'

'No problem,' Paul said.

I also handed over the keys to the handcuffs. 'And, Paul,' I said as he prepared to jump over the side of the boat with his AK47 slung across his shoulder. 'Make sure the bastard is facing towards the back doors. I don't want to see his ugly face every time I look in the rear view mirror!'

I watched as Paul and John frogmarched Zamyatin up the beach towards where the van and truck were parked in the shelter of the sand dunes. I then made my way to the wheelhouse where Freddie was kneeling beside Charlie, who lay on the floor with his eyes closed.

'How's he doing?' I asked quietly.

Charlie's eyes fluttered open. 'I will survive, mon ami,' he assured me with a weak smile, but I could see from his pale pinched face that, despite the Oxycodone, he was in considerable pain.

'We have to go,' I said helping Freddie to her feet.

'He's lost a lot blood,' she whispered to me so that Charlie could not hear her. 'He says he's okay, but I'm worried about him.'

I looked down and saw that the field dressing was already soaked deep red and there was a pool of blood on the floor under his leg. 'I'll carry him,' I said and turned to the little man. 'Charlie, if we get you upright will you be able to climb on my back?'

'Of course. I have a second leg.' He eased himself into a sitting position. 'Come, help me to my feet.'

I reached down and took his hands in mine and slowly pulled him upright. Freddie stood behind him and supported him under his arm pits as he straightened first his right leg and then his shattered left.

I handed my AK47 to Freddie who slung it over one shoulder, she then picked up Charlie's weapon and put it over her other shoulder. I crouched down and let the Frenchman climb onto my back, holding himself in position by putting both arms round my neck, with me helping him with both my hands under his backside.

Freddie snatched up the two remaining crash helmets from the ledge and carrying them in one hand she held open the wheelhouse door to let us through with the other.

I carried Charlie to the side railing of the stern deck and was grateful to find that Paul was back alongside the catamaran.

'Where's John?' I asked as I helped Charlie over the side of the boat and into the arms of the big South African, who held him as easily as if he had been a ragdoll.

'He's unloading a couple of the motorbikes from the van and putting them in the back of the bakkie,' Paul replied. He saw the questioning look on my face. 'Yeah, I know we were going to get away on the bikes, but John and I don't reckon Napoleon here would make it, so we've decided to use the bakkie instead.

'We'll take him to see a doctor I know in Cape Town. He won't ask questions and once Charlie's patched up we'll get him out of the country, hopefully on the bikes, but if not, in the bakkie.'

'It's a good plan,' I said without much conviction.

Paul smiled up at me and then walked a few steps across the beach to one of the boat trailers so that Charlie had something to hold on to. He set the Frenchman gently down onto the sand, where he stood, using only his right leg to take his weight. Paul returned to the catamaran and helped Freddie as she jumped down onto the beach.

I grabbed John's canvas bag from where he had left it on the stern deck and went quickly back to the wheelhouse. I carefully stuffed the first aid box into the bag next to the remaining grenades and slung it across my back, then I joined my friends on the beach.

'Okay,' I said, 'let's get Charlie to the pick-up truck where we can change his dressing.'

With Paul and me on either side for support Charlie took a few hesitant steps forward, but it soon became obvious that he would never make it to the start of the sand dunes where the pick-up was parked.

'I'll carry him,' Paul said taking off his rifle and handing it to me. Without further ado he picked up Charlie carefully, positioned him over his shoulder in a fireman's lift and carried him quickly to the pick-up truck.

As Paul and I helped Charlie slide onto the passenger seat of the pick-up John came trotting out of the darkness from the direction of the track down which we had arrived. I could tell by his face that he was the bearer of bad news.

'What now?'

'There's a cop car and two armoured personnel carriers parked at the end of the track blocking our route to the highway.'

'Shit!' Paul swore. 'That's a real bummer. Those personnel carriers are probably Casspirs. They're new to the police and are the real deal.'

'Do the police know we're here?' I asked John.

'I assume so, otherwise they would have driven straight down to the beach. They must have heard our outboard motor.'

'Perhaps they're just being cautious,' I offered.

'But if that was the case, boss, at the very least they would have sent somebody through the dunes to check out the situation and there was no sign of anyone approaching on foot. No, I'm certain they plan to ambush us as we head out.'

'Looks like we're set for another fight then, Dave,' Paul said. He did not sound overly concerned by the prospect.

'Not necessarily,' I said. 'There is another track through the dunes a few hundred yards further up the beach to the north.'

John looked at me thoughtfully. 'How long will it take to get to the rendezvous with Rogers using the other track?' He asked.

'About fifteen minutes from when we reach the highway,' I replied. 'But it could take some time getting to the road through the dunes because we'll have to keep our lights off for a while.' I looked at my watch. It was 02:05. 'We're going to have to leave pretty soon,' I said.

John shook his head. 'Not we,' he said. 'You.' He started manoeuvring one of the motor cycles from the back of the pick-up. 'Give me a hand, Paul,' he said and the big South African responded immediately.

'What do you mean, "not we"?' I asked, grabbing John's arm.

John stopped what he was doing. He turned to face me, leaving Paul on his own to lift the bike effortlessly from the truck and hide it behind a clump of undergrowth that grew at the edge of the sand dunes.

'Think it through, boss,' the American said. 'The cops are bound to hear our engines when we start up and will wonder what has happened if we don't show up down the track they are blockading. It won't take them long to work out there's a second track.'

'John's right, Dave,' Paul said as he joined us after taking the second motor bike from the pick-up and hiding it alongside the first. 'You take Zamyatin out the back way in the Merc and get to the rendezvous. We'll take the heat off you by driving up the track and keeping the cops busy.'

I stared at him. I knew he was right, but that didn't mean I liked it. 'It will be suicide for whoever is driving that truck towards the blockade,' I pointed out. 'Those bastards will shoot the moment they see you. They won't take prisoners.'

'I think he's thought of that,' Paul said with a smile. 'That's why we've taken the bikes from the bakkie. Am I right, John?'

John nodded.

'You've lost me,' I said.

'We're not gonna drive the truck at the cops,' John said quietly. 'We're gonna reverse it halfway up the track, park up and then start firing.' He slapped the metal tailgate of the pick-up. 'This will give us far more protection than the glass windscreen ever could.'

'It makes sense,' I conceded.

'Can Charlie drive?' John asked Paul.

'I doubt it,' Paul replied. 'But he can still shoot, so if you do the driving there will be two of us to shoot up the cops.'

'There will be three of you shooting,' a voice said. 'I can drive the bakkie.'

We all stared at Freddie, who until she spoke had been watching the interchange in silence.

I shook my head. 'No way. You're coming with me.'

Freddie stared over at me, with a dangerous flash of her narrowed eyes. 'I stay,' she said with a hard expression on her face. 'Either I drive the bakkie or I shoot from the back of it. End of story.'

I doubted I would change her mind, but I tried anyway. 'I promised your father I would look after you.'

She softened slightly at mention of her father. 'Thank you for that. But Papa would understand that this is as much my battle as it is yours. In fact, more so.'

'What do you think, Paul?' I asked.

'It's cool. Don't worry, we'll take good care of Freddie. But you must go now. Time is running out.' He saw me hesitate. 'Look, Dave,' he went on. 'We came to do a job, let's finish it. We've come too far to lose it all now. If I'm going to end up in prison I'd like the satisfaction of knowing it was worth it and that I'll have a nice nest egg waiting for me on my release.'

I knew he was right. They had all known before we started out the risks that were involved. John and Paul had known and now they faced yet another fire fight. Charlie had known and he was sitting crippled in the front of the pick-up truck. Mr Mac had known and he was buried under a pile of rocks on a Robben Island beach and it was his memory that made up my mind for me.

We had to deliver Zamyatin to Rogers, if only to make the little Scotsman's sacrifice at least partly meaningful. Yet in my heart of hearts I knew that prison was the easy option. The truth was that I might be leaving the rest of them to perish like Mr Mac.

'You take Zamyatin, Paul,' I said. 'Let me stay and look after Freddie.'

'No, Dave. It's your contract and Rogers will be expecting you. He might not hand the dough over to anybody else.'

Once again, I knew the big South African was right. Rogers would find any excuse to renege on his deal.

I turned to the girl again. 'Do you promise to stay in the cab?' I asked, more in hope than expectation of an agreement.

'I promise nothing,' she said quietly. 'They are our friends and they might need my help.'

I shook my head in exasperation. 'Okay, well at least keep my rifle with you. I'll have my pistol if I need fire power.' I turned to my two friends. 'Make sure you look after her for me. Don't let her do anything stupid.' I said.

'Don't worry, boss,' John said. 'We'll give you time to get clear, then Paul will bring Freddie to join you on one of the bikes, while Charlie and I hightail it into Cape Town in the pick-up.' He spoke with such confidence that I almost believed him.

'Do you remember where the rendezvous is taking place?' I asked Paul.

'Sure, the details are up here,' Paul tapped his temple. 'Now, get the hell out of here. Rogers won't wait all day.'

I did not say goodbye, it somehow seemed inappropriate,

325

instead I said simply: 'Good luck, guys. I'll see you soon.' With that I turned on my heel and left them to get Charlie out of the cab and help him into the back of the pick-up truck.

When I reached the Mercedes van I glanced up at the back door and saw Zamyatin staring through the small window. The eyes that bulged above the bandage covering the bottom half of his face were full of hatred.

I ignored him and climbed up into the Mercedes van. Out of the corner of my eye I saw John and Paul jump into the back of the pick-up next to Charlie. The vehicle immediately started reversing across the beach towards the gap in the sand dunes with Freddie at the wheel. I wondered if I would ever see any of them again.

That is when I realised I still had the canvas bag on my back. I swore silently to myself. I had meant to leave the first aid box with Freddie. It was too late now so I took off the bag and put it on the passenger seat next to me.

By the time I had started the van's engine I could hear the unmistakeable sound of automatic weapon fire from somewhere behind me. It was time to leave.

Kobus Coetzee

Kobus and Dermot Brody stood in front of their squad car and stared up the dark track towards the beach. The car was parked side-on at the end of the track and behind them were positioned, nose to nose, two Casspir personnel carriers. Ranged in front of the armoured vehicles were policemen dressed in camouflage fatigues and carrying police carbines.

Together the three vehicles made an effective road block and Kobus was confident Statton and his team would not be able to pass them. The terrorists were trapped on the beach.

Kobus clearly heard two engines start up from the direction of the beach and shortly after a vehicle came into view with its engine revving loudly. 'Here they come,' he said.

'What the hell?' Brody exclaimed as he realised they were looking at the vehicle's reversing lights.

Kobus saw that the vehicle was the bakkie he had seen on the beach. The vehicle stopped a couple of hundred metres from the blockade and it was suddenly very quiet. All he could hear was the bakkie's engine ticking over and the rustle of clothing as the policemen behind him fidgeted nervously as they waited for something happen.

Suddenly there was a single spurt of light from the back of the pickup truck that Kobus recognised immediately as the flash from the muzzle of a weapon. Even as he registered this fact he heard a soft thud as a bullet hit Brody and with a gasp of pain the Irishman crumpled onto the sandy track next to him.

The uniformed policemen realised what was happening and Kobus heard a series of thumps and the clatter of weapons as they threw themselves to the ground and began firing at the pickup truck.

Luckily Dermot Brody was shorter than the six foot three tall Kobus and much lighter. He easily lifted the Irishman to his feet and bundled him into the front passenger seat of the squad car. He drew his pistol, pulled open the rear passenger door, threw himself inside, wound down the window and added his own fire to that of the prone policemen.

As Kobus fired his first shot the one thought that went through his mind was where the hell was the Mercedes van he had seen on the beach?

Paul Helsdon

Paul was impressed with the effortless way Freddie reversed the Toyota bakkie through the sand dunes. She used the vehicle's wing mirrors and reversing lights to navigate along the winding track with a skill of which even he would have been proud.

Charlie and John lay on their stomachs with their Kalashnikovs resting on the tailgate. Paul stood on the cargo bed of the open truck with his legs apart, holding onto the roof of the cab to balance himself as he peered up the track to see where they were going.

The police car was parked across the track with the two Casspirs positioned behind it, effectively blocking off their exit. Standing in front of the car were two men, neither of whom was in uniform, so Paul guessed they were plain clothes detectives. Fanned out in front of each armoured personnel carriers were half a dozen policemen dressed in fatigues. Each carried what looked like automatic weapons and they were all pointing at the bakkie.

Paul waited until the bakkie was about a couple of hundred metres from the police road-block and then rapped his knuckles on its roof. Immediately the vehicle came to a halt and he threw himself down on his stomach next to John.

Paul peered over the tailgate with his AK47 at the ready, aimed at the shorter of the two detectives and fired a single shot that hit the man in the leg. The cop fell to the ground and immediately all hell broke loose.

The uniformed cops who were in front of the Casspirs threw themselves to the ground and opened up a fierce fusillade. Bullets started thumping into the tailgate, but none pierced the thick metal.

The taller of the detectives bent over, picked up his injured colleague and helped him into the passenger seat of the police car. He slammed the door closed behind him, jumped into the back seat of the car, wound down the window and added pistol fire to that of the automatic weapons already being fired at the bakkie.

When the cops started firing at them Paul and John ducked down behind the tailgate to escape the murderous fire, but Charlie was not quick enough. Before he could get his head behind the metal shield he was shot through the temple with an explosion of bone and blood that splattered John's back. The Frenchman was dead long before his head slid down the inside of the tailgate and hit the cargo bed, where it rested in an expanding pool of blood.

Ignoring their dead friend, Paul and John took turns to raise their Kalashnikovs above the tailgate and direct a quick burst of automatic fire at the police blockade. This aggression inflicted little damage on the cops, but it did at least dissuade them from attempting a frontal assault on the bakkie.

They kept up this tactic for almost quarter of an hour before they decided it was time to move. John twisted his body and crawled the length of the bakkie's cargo bed. He eased himself to his knees in order to knock on the roof, which was the signal for Freddie to head back to the beach. As he raised his arm he let out a loud cry and his upper body smashed against the back of the cab.

Paul fired a long burst at the cops then slid along the cargo bed until he sat at the side of the American. 'Go, Freddie, go!' Paul shouted and immediately the bakkie surged forward and headed at speed back through the sand dunes.

When they reached the beach Paul turned John over and saw he had been hit by a bullet that had passed right through his body, leaving a gaping exit hole in his chest out of which blood bubbled. It was a bad wound but despite his injury the American managed to pull himself upright.

'Help me into the cab, Paul,' John said. 'I'm going back.'

'You'll never make it,' Paul replied.

'I'll make it, ol' buddy.'

'Then I'll come with you.'

'No you won't. You promised Dave you'd look after Freddie, and that's exactly what you're gonna do, pal,' John insisted. He must have seen something in Paul's face because he added: 'Don't worry, I have a plan. Help me into the cab and I'll explain.'

Paul saw that there would be no arguing with the American. 'Help me move John,' he told Freddie who was peering over the side of the bakkie with a worried look on her face.

'Is that wise?' She asked.

'Probably not,' Paul said, 'but you try telling that to this meathead.'

'Who you calling a meathead?' John said as he pulled himself to his feet, with a wince of pain twisting his ashen face into a horrible mask.

Together Paul and Freddie somehow managed to help John out of the cargo bed and into the driver's seat.

'Paul, bring me the two gas cans from the back of the pick-up,' John said before turning to Freddie who was standing on the beach looking up at him though the open door. 'Help me off with my boots and socks, babe,' he said, swinging his legs towards her.

When Paul returned with the petrol cans John told him to take off the caps and put the cans on the cab floor beside him. The American reached over and poked one of his socks into the neck of each can and then nodded in satisfaction as the socks quickly soaked up the petrol, turning them into rudimentary fuses.

'You're not planning what I think are you?' Paul asked.

John's face twisted into a grim, pain filled mockery of a smile. His brave attempt to downplay his condition was shown up for the deceit it was by a tiny trickle of blood that ran out of his mouth and onto his chin. 'I'm a stunt man, remember?' He said. 'I'm gonna drive at the police blockade, light the fuses and bang!' He looked at Paul's face and added: 'Don't worry, I'll jump out the cab well before the pick-up hits the cop car.'

Paul did not believe him and when he looked into John's eyes they could not deny the lie his friend had just told. 'Freddie and I will get the motorcycles ready and waiting for you,' Paul said. 'So you'd better come back, you stupid Yankee.'

'Listen, buddy,' John said. 'I've done loads of stunts like this. It'll be a cinch. I'll be back with you in no time at all.' He reached down and shook Paul's hand and said quietly. 'Now get that gal the hell outta here.' With those words he pulled the driver's door closed, engaged gears and headed back through the sand dunes.

Paul and Freddie climbed to the top of the nearest sand dune and had a perfect view of what happened next.

The bakkie sped down the track through the dunes and headed towards the police road block with its headlights blazing. The uniformed policemen were now on their feet, a small group of them were already heading down the track towards the beach, no doubt to find out where their attackers had gone. They scattered into the dunes as the bakkie raced towards them.

The rest of the policemen opened fire at the bakkie and Paul clearly heard the shattering of glass as bullets hit the truck's windscreen. Suddenly the cab of the vehicle glowed and he guessed that John had lit the fuses in the petrol cans.

As the careering vehicle drew closer to the police car its headlights picked out the faces of the two detectives who still sat in the car, although both men were now sitting in the front. Paul could see that the taller cop, who was sitting in the driver's seat, was holding a two way radio to his lips.

'Jump, you stupid Yankee,' Paul whispered. 'Jump!' But he knew his words were in vain and he swore bitterly to himself as the bakkie hit the police car square on, with the American still inside the cab.

Both vehicles burst in a single ball of flames as the two cans of petrol in the cab of the truck exploded. Seconds later an even louder explosion erupted as the fuel tanks of both bakkie and police car went up at the same time. This time the flames shot high in the night sky, engulfing the two Casspirs and the cops who found themselves trapped between the armoured vehicles and the sand dunes.

'Let's go,' Paul said to Freddie, who was staring in horror at the carnage that had unfolded before their eyes. Gently he took her hand and led her down to where the motorcycles were hidden on the edge of the dunes. By the time they had donned their crash helmets and climbed onto the bikes, the girl had recovered some of her composure and fighting spirit.

Paul drove the motorcycle slowly and carefully along the beach and up bumpy the northern track through the dunes, but once he reached the highway he took the powerful bike up to top speed and headed north.

They made good time and had only one minor mishap when

Paul kept tight to the inside curve as he navigated a sharp bend. With his mind concentrating less on the road and more on trying to remember the exact route to the rendezvous point, they were confronted by a burnt out car that was half on and half off the highway. The wreck was still glowing and as Paul steered into the middle of the highway to pass it a second car came speeding along in the opposite direction and almost hit the motorcycle.

Paul swerved away from the speeding car, which he recognised as a Mercedes saloon, and only just avoided a collision. He cursed both the driver of the car and his own lapse in concentration. Not long after their close escape he found the side turning that led to where Dave had arranged to meet Rogers.

The track they went down was very bumpy and he reduced speed again and navigated carefully round the many pot holes they encountered. Suddenly the beam of the bike's headlight illuminated a car parked in the middle of the track. It was not a car he recognised.

He braked and the motorcycle came to a stop. He felt Freddie jump from the pillion seat and move to his side. She carried her Kalashnikov pointed at the car. Paul raised his own weapon just as somebody emerged from a row of trees that lined the track.

It was a man and he had his hands in the air in a gesture of surrender.

The Rendezvous

Bloubergstrand, Western Cape
Simeon Du Plessis

Simeon was not surprised when he received the call from the night controller at Central Station in Cape Town ordering him to return to where he had left Brigadier Coetzee.

When the CID colonel, Brody, had passed him the order from Coetzee to head north, he had thought it was a waste of time to check out bays further along the coast. Instinct told him that the more southerly beach was the right location.

But Simeon was young and ambitious. He was the youngest sergeant in the South African Police Service and he wanted to become its youngest ever colonel. He was bright enough to know that you do not get promotion by questioning the orders of a superior, so he headed north without hesitation.

Now he was pleased they had been ordered to re-join Coetzee, which vindicated his intuition. He smiled to himself as the car headed back down the coast road.

'Where does that track lead to, Hennie?' he asked Constable Maritz as they drove past a narrow opening in the sand dunes.

'Sies, man, that goes to the same beach the big guys were checking out,' the driver replied.'

Immediately Simeon's instincts kicked in again. 'Stop!' He cried.

Maritz slammed on the brakes and the squad car came to a screeching halt.

'Turn round and go back,' Simeon said, ignoring his own dictum about disobeying orders. 'I have a feeling about that track.'

David Statton

With the sound of gun fire in my ears I let out the clutch of the Mercedes van and pressed hard on the accelerator. The van surged forward down the beach and in less than a minute I had reached the other gap in the sand dunes. I turned onto the northern track, which was narrower than the first track and much bumpier.

I drove in darkness, praying that I did not hit any deep potholes or patches of quicksand in the uneven surface. When I was far enough along the track to be certain that I could not be seen by the police, I switched on my headlights.

The track went through a narrow valley in the high sand dunes that ran in a northerly direction for several hundred yards. It then turned sharply to the east before petering out as they reached the dark and deserted M14, which was now close enough for me to see.

What I could see also, and what set my pulse racing, was the police car that was parked at the end of the track, just off the highway. Sitting in the car were two policemen, who looked startled as momentarily they were lit up by the van's headlights.

The police squad car did not quite fill the track, so I pushed the gear lever into second and aimed for the narrow gap that separated the vehicle from the gently sloping sand dune. The gap was never going to be wide enough for the van and it caught the car with a terrific clump that almost tore its front wing off.

The van rode up the sand dune and for a heart stopping moment I thought it was going to topple over, but it stayed upright. With a loud grating sound of metal against metal, which almost tore off the squad car's front wing, I just managed to squeeze past and reach the tarmac road beyond.

Once on the highway I turned left and quickly moved through the gears until the van was racing north along the coast. I glanced in my rear view mirror and saw the back of Zamyatin's head. It was moving up and down and from side to side as he tried to loosen the bandages that held the field dressing in place over his mouth.

More worryingly to me was that the Russian's head was silhouetted in a light that shined through the narrow rear window of the van. A glance in my offside wing mirror confirmed that the police car had managed to survive our collision and was following us and getting closer by the minute.

I could plainly see that the squad car's offside wing was flapping in the wind as it sped up the highway after us with its blue light flashing. I could hear no siren so I could only guess that it had somehow been damaged in the collision.

I heard a metallic twang and then another. I looked in my nearside wing mirror this time and was just in time to see a flash, closely followed by another twang. It was then I realised that the policeman in the passenger seat of the chasing car was firing at the van.

I accelerated and immediately opened up a larger gap between the two vehicles. It was obvious that the speed of the police car was being affected by the damaged wing panel, part of which was probably rubbing against its front wheel.

For a time I heard no more bullets hit the van, but, despite the cops having a disabled car, I was under no illusions about outrunning them over a longer distance. With that in mind I decided that I had no other option other than to put them out of the game entirely and I was running out of time to act.

I moved fast. Taking a DM24 blend-brand-hand grenade from the canvas bag that still lay on the passenger seat beside me, I waited until we were approaching a bend in the road and accelerated again.

The gap between van and car widened still further. Once round the bend I braked to a halt and jumped out of the van with the grenade in my hand. A few seconds later my pursuers came hurtling round the bend and now I could actually hear the high pitched whine as the car's offside wheel rubbed against the damaged wing.

The driver did not see the stationery black painted van until he was fifty or sixty feet away, then he slammed on his brakes with a squeal of tyres. The car swerved off onto the sand covered hard-shoulder and came to a stop no more than twenty feet away.

The cop in the passenger seat jumped from the car and started firing at me, but he must have been badly shaken because his shots hammered into the back of the van rather than into me. He looked very young and I hated myself for what I was going to do to him and his colleague.

I ignored the gun shots and instead took careful aim and hurled the brandy. It hit the windscreen of the police car with a flash of blinding white light, which spread rapidly to envelop the shooting policeman, who simply disappeared as if he had never existed.

I ran quickly back to the cab and climbed in and threw the van into gear. The Merc shot away, quickly opening up a gap between me and the police car. It was just as well because seconds later the car's petrol tank exploded, destroying what was left of the driver, which by then was probably not much.

For the second time that night I was appalled by the lethal power of the DM24 grenade and was upset I had been forced to use another one. But I had little time to dwell on the destruction I had wrought, or have too many guilty feelings about my actions, because shortly afterwards I reached the turn-off that led from the highway to the rendezvous spot.

Melkbosstrand, Western Cape

The rendezvous was due to take place on a wide expanse of scrubland that stood on the edge of a wide, sweeping bay. Once again I found myself driving down a bumpy, sandy track, but this time I was surrounded by trees and bushes rather than sand dunes.

As I neared the end of the track, my headlights picked out a flash of metal amongst the trees. I stopped the van, pulled on my sheepskin coat and went to investigate. I soon realised that what had caught my eye was the distinctive chrome hood emblem of a Mercedes Benz saloon.

The car was big and bottle green in colour and at first I thought it might belong to Rogers, but changed my mind when I discovered that the car was locked and its engine was stone cold. Obviously it had been parked in the trees for some time, so was unlikely to have been driven by the CIA deputy director, who was not renowned for arriving early for meetings. It was simply not his style. Clearly the Merc belonged to somebody else. But who?

I returned to the van and drove the rest of the way to the rendezvous spot, which was deserted. I looked at my watch and saw that it was 02:40 hours. Rogers was ten minutes late, which was definitely more his style.

I drove to the far edge of the scrubland where I reversed into position and parked the van so that I could see back up the track. I got out of the cab and made my way round to the back of the van.

Zamyatin had not moved and still stared out at me silently with mad unblinking eyes. I stared right back at him for a while, before opening the rear door and clambering up inside the van to join him. He had almost managed to push the gag away from his mouth so I removed it completely. I stared into his eyes one final time and returned to the comfort of the warm cab.

I waited.

The wind was getting up again. Still blowing in from the north-west it whipped across the bay, tearing gaping holes in the black churning sea and tossing water into the air in a hissing white spray. When the wind eventually reached land it swept up fine white sand as it raced across the beach and hurled it against the van in a tattoo of rasping sound.

I switched on my windscreen wipers and watched them slowly bulldoze their way across the sand encrusted glass, forming wedges at both ends of the screen and making my view of the approaching headlights much clearer.

I snapped my own headlights on and off a couple of times and almost immediately the oncoming vehicle winked back at me. It came to a halt on the opposite side of the scrubland, about ten yards or so from my position.

The main beams of the vehicle's headlights sliced through the swirling sand, filling the van's cab with bright light. I screwed up my eyes and not to be outdone I flicked on my own lights and switched them to full beam.

The car was a dark blue Cadillac Sedan de Ville with diplomatic plates. I could see it carried a driver and three passengers, which set alarm bells ringing in my head because I had assumed Rogers would be on his own.

The driver's door of the Caddy opened slowly and the CIA man emerged. He seemed surprised at the strength of the wind and huddled behind the open door for shelter. He thrust an arm high in the air as if testing the strength of the wind. It was only when he started flapping his hand back and forwards that I realised he was waving at me to join him.

I pushed open the cab door and jumped to the ground. The wind hit me as I moved from the cover of the van and tore at the buttons of my sheepskin coat, forcing me to lean forward to prevent myself from being blown over. The sand stung my face and within a short time my cheeks felt as if they had been rubbed with wet and dry paper. I pulled up the collar of my coat and thrust my hands deep into my pockets. Neither action helped much. I walked unsteadily, head bowed, towards the Caddy.

'That's far enough, Statton.'

I was halfway between van and car when I heard the shout. I stopped and looked up with narrowed eyes. Rogers was out in the open now and I could see that I had been wrong. He had not huddled behind the car door for protection from the wind, but had done so to conceal the sub-machine gun that he held in his hands and which was now pointing menacingly at me.

He moved towards me until he was close enough for us to be able to talk without having to shout, but far enough away to discourage me from even thinking about trying to grab his weapon.

He need not have worried. I was not that stupid. Now he was closer I could see the gun looked like a Smith & Wesson M76, but I might have been wrong. Whatever the weapon's design, it looked pretty lethal to me so I kept very still.

'Where's Zamyatin?' He asked. One side of his face was already covered in a thin film of sand and as he spoke he tilted his head to the side and tried to brush it off with the shoulder of his expensively tailored overcoat.

I nodded towards the Mercedes van. 'In the back,' I answered. 'Where's the money?'

Rogers opened his mouth and appeared to struggle for breath. For several seconds he wheezed like an asthmatic, but then stopped abruptly. It was only then that I realised he had been laughing. However, there was no sign of amusement in his face, but that could have been because there was no room alongside the hostility that was etched there.

The passenger door of the Cadillac opened and a man got out and headed towards where we stood. I recognised him immediately. It was Major Percival Carsons (Rtd). He was closely followed by the two men who had been sitting in the back passenger seat.

'There is no money for you, Statton,' Rogers said as Carsons joined us. 'There is only this.' He waved his M76 at me.

'Where is Comrade Zamyatin?' Carsons repeated the question that Rogers had asked, his voice edged with a trace of impatience.

I studied him. Somehow he had changed. In some respects he looked much the same as I remembered him; red face, white hair and bristling military moustache. But his overall appearance and attitude was different. He was no longer the bumbling caricature I had met the previous month. Gone was the blazer, cravat, slacks, deck shoes and sailor's hat, to be replaced by a cheap grey two piece suit, scuffed leather shoes, white shirt buttoned to the neck and a leather worker's cap.

His voice was different too; it had a timbre and hardness that changed his whole personality. No longer was he the opinionated blimpish ex-Indian Army officer with rheumy eyes, instead he had taken on the mantel of hard professionalism and carried about him an aura of authority and a cold eyed menace.

'I've just told him,' I nodded towards Rogers, making sure that I kept my hands in my coat pockets. 'He's in the back of the van.' I looked at Carsons hard for a few moments. 'So, who are you really?' I asked.

'Colonel Alexei Urinoff,' he replied with a slight bow. 'I am here to collect Comrade Scientist Zamyatin.'

That's when I noticed for the first time that in the button hole of his rumpled jacket he wore a small enamel badge depicting a hammer and sickle. 'On behalf of the KGB, I presume?'

Carsons/Urinoff smiled coldly but did not reply. He did not have to. It all began to fall into place. There was I, thinking that the just-too-good-to-be-true Major Percival Carsons was working for Rogers, but all along it was the CIA man who was working for the Russians.

'I suppose there is no submarine?' I asked Rogers.

'Oh, there most certainly is a submarine,' it was Carsons/Urinoff who answered. He glanced at his watch. 'And in about fifteen minutes its captain will fire a flare to confirm the sub is in position and waiting to pick us up. But, unfortunately for you, it will be flying the flag of the Soviet Socialist Republics.'

I turned to Rogers. 'And when he says "us", does that include you?'

The CIA agent shook his head. 'Of course not,' he said. 'My home is the US of A.'

'I bet Uncle Sam is delighted about that,' I said, but he did not rise to the bait.

I turned to Urinoff. 'How much are you paying him?' I asked.

The Russian smiled again and shook his head. 'The amount does not matter,' he said. 'Let's just say that he is being well rewarded for delivering Comrade Zamyatin safely to us.'

'Rewarded in Swiss francs, no doubt?'

Again Urinoff smiled coldly but said nothing.

I glared at Rogers. 'I have to hand it to you. You really stitched me up like a kipper. You were very clever and I made it easy for you by being very stupid. You set up the operation with the Agency footing an unlimited bill. That was neat and I would love to know exactly how much you managed to filter away for yourself.' I paused and tried to stare the CIA agent down, but failed. He had no shame that one. 'Then you got me to organize everything,' I went on eventually, 'and let my team and me do all the hard work and take all the risks.'

Rogers smiled and suddenly I felt very angry.

'Listen, you sanctimonious bastard! One of my team is dead and at least one other has been wounded. For all I know he might be dead now as well. But of course that doesn't concern you because all you have to do is sit back on your well protected arse and count the money that's paid into your Swiss bank account. And what now? I suppose you trot off back to Langley and tell Bill Casey that I double crossed you? Is that how the story goes? That I sold Zamyatin to the Russians?'

Rogers had another of his asthmatic laughter fits. When he composed himself he said: 'See, you're not stupid all the time, Statton. You got the deal in one.'

'So set out the whole deal for me,' I said.

'OK, you deserve that at least,' he said, although I suspect he was less interested in satisfying my curiosity than he was with showing me how clever he was.

'Okay, the story goes like this… I arrive at the rendezvous point to pick up Zamyatin and drive him north…' he paused when he saw the quizzical look I gave him. 'Yeah, there never was any US sub lined up to collect Zamyatin,' he went on to explain. 'The Firm thinks I was going to take him across the border into Botswana where he would have been met by somebody from the embassy.

'So, I'll tell Casey that when I arrived at the rendezvous point I discovered you in the process of handing Zamyatin over to the Russians. You started firing at me and during the ensuing gun fight you were killed. Unfortunately, your attack gave the Russians time to get Zamyatin aboard their submarine.'

'Neat,' I said. 'But what about the hundred and seventy five grand you were supposed to be handing over to me on completion of the job. Won't Casey wonder what happened to that?'

Rogers grinned. 'Oh, I'll give that back. I'm neither stupid nor greedy and our friends are being extremely generous.'

'But why Rogers? Why betray your country? I can't imagine you need the money.'

'We all need money,' the CIA agent replied sardonically. 'But it isn't all about money, Statton,' he added, before pausing. When he started talking again his voice rose until he was almost shrieking. 'You don't know what it's like working for the Firm,' he said with real venom. 'You have no idea how those bastards treated me. I have spent my whole adult working life with the Agency. I joined them when I was twenty-one and for the past twenty-three years I've given them everything.' He paused again, jabbing the sub-machine gun towards me as if to emphasise his point. 'Everything!'

339

He shouted and then fell silent.

When he spoke again, his tone was bitter. 'And now I'm to be phased out,' he said. 'Oh, nobody has told me that officially, but I have a couple of close friends on the top floor and they keep me well informed of what is going on. It seems it was decided that I'm to be quietly re-trenched. My belief is that Casey gave me this mission because he hoped I would fail. Well, now he'll get his wish and that will make it easier for him to get rid of me, but the irony is that I no longer care.'

Rogers stared at me for what seemed a long time. Despite the wind that was still blowing fine sand over the side of his face, his perfectly cut hair remained in place, which is more than could be said for my own.

Finally he asked: 'Do you know why Casey wants to get rid of me, Statton?' But he did not wait for a reply. 'The word from the top floor is that he thinks I'm a potential security risk and do you know why that is?'

'I think so,' I said, but he ignored me. Again his question had not really been a question at all. He just wanted to talk.

'It's because I'm gay,' he said and looked at me defiantly, perhaps expecting me to be shocked.

I shrugged my shoulders and said nothing.

'But, shit, Statton, that doesn't make me a goddamn security risk, not in this day and age,' again he stopped and stared at me as if I would disagree with him, but, when he realised I intended saying nothing, he continued. 'And the irony is that those bastards know I'm not a risk. Jesus Christ, if they rooted out all the queers from the Firm they would have more vacancies than they could fill. So why make an exception of me?'

'You're starting to sound paranoid, Rogers,' I said quietly.

'Paranoid?' He repeated and nodded slowly. 'I suppose that's possible, but being paranoid doesn't make me wrong. Look, I know the real reason Casey wants me out.'

'Why?' I asked. I thought I knew the reason, but I wanted to keep him talking.

'It's heat from above,' he said cryptically.

'Heat from above?'

'Yeah. I bedded the son of one of our illustrious senators. The old man found out and didn't like it one bit. But, Christ, Statton, the kid is over twenty-one and was as willing as hell. He came on to me, but the senator simply cannot accept that his son is gay and insists that I forced him into bed.

'Forced him? My God, the kid is well over six foot and I could never have forced him to do anything he didn't want to do. No, he wanted to do it all right, but daddy just won't admit the truth. He would sooner blame me, which is why he wants me fired. Trouble is that he has an awful lot of pull and has been friends with Casey for a long time. So there you have it, Statton, I'm on my way out and I am going to be taking a golden handshake with me, courtesy of Mister Zamyatin.'

'I'm afraid not, Rogers,' I said.

'What do you mean?' He asked suspiciously.

I looked at Urinoff, who stood a couple of paces behind Rogers, and who had been listening to our conversation without comment. 'How much are you willing to pay him for a stiff?' I asked.

The Russian's eyes narrowed and his mouth tightened.

Rogers stepped forward menacingly and now the muzzle of his gun nudged the front of my sheepskin coat. The layer of fine sand had spread across the whole of his face, covering it in a mask of white.

'Zamyatin is dead,' I said simply.

'No!' Rogers shouted at me. 'You're lying.'

'He's dead, Rogers,' I shouted back at him. 'D.E.A.D. Dead. He was hit by a stray bullet fired by a cop. Go look for yourself if you don't believe me.'

The American agent glared at me but didn't move. He refused to believe me. He thought I was trying to trick him.

'Check it out,' Urinoff said and waved forward the two men who stood behind him.

'You'll need these.' I slowly took my hand from the left pocket of my sheepskin and threw the handcuff keys to one of the men as the pair walked past me. He caught the keys deftly but didn't thank me. I wasn't surprised; that type of man doesn't do thanks.

While we waited for the men to return Rogers backed away from me until he was in line with the KGB colonel who had distanced himself from the American by edging several feet to his left. He was wise to be cautious.

Maybe Rogers moved away from me because he was worried I might change my mind about grabbing his weapon. I didn't want him getting the wrong impression, so carefully I put my left hand back into my pocket to show I had no intention of jumping him.

We stood in silence. Somewhere in the distance to the south there was an explosion, but before I could worry about what this might mean I heard the rear doors of the Mercedes van swing open. There was the sound of footsteps scrambling on the metal bumper as the men used it to clamber inside.

One of the men swore in Russian and then there was the distinctive sound of the metallic handcuffs being unlocked, followed by a loud thump. I guessed this was Zamyatin's body hitting the ground and my guess was confirmed when I heard something heavy being dragged across the sand behind me.

The two men reappeared and dumped Zamyatin's body on the ground in the bright arena created by the two sets of headlights. He lay there, the centrepiece of a triangle formed by the sub-machine gun wielding Rogers, the hard faced Urinoff, who was once again flanked by his two henchmen, and the very watchful me.

One of the police bullets had scored a double-top on the dead Russian's dartboard pitted face. High on his forehead was an ugly red bullet hole that already was slowly filling with white sand.

Behind Rogers in the dark night sky a red flare exploded. Urinoff saw the flare as well. He looked at me, nodded imperceptibly, then raised his arm and pointed above Rogers' head. 'Look,' he said.

Automatically Rogers glanced over his shoulder to see what the Russian was pointing at. It was all the time I needed.

The force of the shot took Rogers off his feet, but it did not kill him and as he fell to the ground he pulled the trigger of his M76.

Most of the bullets went high and wide, but I felt a jolt of pain as one hit me in the upper part of my right arm.

Somehow Rogers managed to stagger to his feet. He stood there swaying on his feet, staring incredulously at the smoking black hole that had been blasted in the front of my sheepskin coat when I fired my pistol from its right hand pocket.

He shook his head and I could tell from the expression on his face that he was cursing his own stupidity at not having searched me for weapons. As he moved his head from side to side, tiny globules of blood bubbled from his mouth and mingled with the white sand that covered his lips. The globules grew until they were large drops of red that slowly dribbled down his chin from where they were picked up by the wind and blown away into the night.

Rogers raised his sub-machine gun and with surprisingly steady hands aimed it at me.

I tried to fire my pistol, but it misfired. I tried again but the same thing happened. As I watched the muzzle of the M76 reach the level of my heart the thought ran through my mind that debris from my torn and burnt sheepskin coat must have become lodged under the hammer of the pistol.

Suddenly Rogers was lifted from his feet and was hurled forward as a gaping hole was torn out the front of his body in an explosion of blood. This time he was dead well before he hit the ground, where he lay alongside the body of Zamyatin.

A man walked out from behind the Cadillac. It was Hank Graham and in his hand he carried a .44 Magnum. He walked over to Rogers and nudged his body to make sure he was dead, but anyone shot in the back at point blank range by the heavy bullet fired by the revolver was unlikely to survive. Hank looked up at me and smiled briefly before disappearing back into the darkness.

I turned to meet any attack from the Russians, but Urinoff showed me the empty palms of both hands and shook his head. 'It's over,' he said simply. 'Killing him has saved me a job.' He pointed to his coat pocket and raised an eyebrow at me.

I nodded.

Slowly and carefully he pulled a Very pistol from his pocket. He looked at me enquiringly, and again I nodded. He aimed into the sky and fired a flare that would summons his transport back to Mother Russia.

'You will find the money Rogers owes you in the trunk of his car,' Urinoff said as he looked down at the dead scientist. 'With your permission we will take Comrade Zamyatin's body with us?'

'You're welcome to him,' I said.

'He will receive a burial befitting a hero of the Soviet Union,' the KGB man intoned without any apparent irony in his voice, but there was the hint of a smile on his lips. He moved his head in a silent order and his two companions stepped forward. Each grabbed an arm and together they dragged the body of the dead scientist across the sand towards the sea. They did not treat him like a hero.

Somewhere out in the darkness of the ocean I could hear the sound of an outboard motor approaching. It got louder very quickly. The boat was close. Without another word, Colonel Urinoff gave me a casual salute and headed off to join his companions.

Behind me I heard a revving engine. As I turned round a car

reversed out of the trees into the clearing and parked alongside the Cadillac. It was the bottle green Merc I had seen earlier parked in the trees. The driver's door opened and Hank Graham got out.

He walked over and looked down at Rogers again. He no longer carried the Magnum, but no doubt it was concealed somewhere handy. He looked up at me. 'Hi, Dave.'

'Hank.'

'You've been hit, old buddy,' he said, pointing to the patch of crimson that was spreading across the arm of my sheepskin coat.

'Yeah, there is a first aid box in the cab of the van if you're offering.'

'I'm offering,' he said and then made his way to the van, opened the driver's door and climbed up into the cab.

I followed him across the sand and looked up at him. 'It's in the canvas bag on the passenger seat,' I told him.

Hank opened the bag and whistled. He looked down at me. 'Are they what I think they are?' He asked.

'If you think they are blend-brand-hand grenades, then the answer is yes.'

'Jesus Christ! Those babies are lethal!'

'Don't I know it,' I agreed.

Very gently Hank eased the plastic first aid box from the bag, taking care not to disturb the grenades too much, and jumped back down to join me on the gravel.

I stripped off my coat and Hank used a pair of scissors to cut away the right sleeve of my leathers. My arm hurt like hell and blood was dripping down onto the sand.

Hank used the antiseptic to clean the wound. 'It's only a flesh wound,' he said.

I winced at the sting from the fiery liquid. 'Tell that to my arm,' I said, but I was pleased to hear the bullet had missed the bone.

Hank put a field dressing on the wound and wrapped it securely round my arm. 'Don't worry,' he said. 'The bullet went in one side of your arm and out the other.'

'I'll have that engraved on my headstone if I die of septicaemia,' I said as I put my sheepskin back on; thankful for the protection it offered from the wind.

'Don't be a pussy,' Hank said with a laugh. 'You'll be fine,' he added as he made his way back to where the body of Rogers lay on the ground slowly being covered by sand. 'Now help me dump this bastard in the trunk of my auto.'

I looked at the Merc. 'So it was you who has been following us?' I asked.

He nodded. 'Yeah, since you first arrived in South Africa.'

'Why?'

'Why?' Hank repeated.

'Yeah, why were you following us?'

'At the start I was checking up on you for Rogers, then after the business in Juan Les Pins it was to get him.'

'I don't understand, you could have got Rogers anywhere at any time.'

'That's true,' he agreed, 'but while I suspected he was working for the Reds, I didn't have enough evidence to nail the bastard. I wanted to catch him in the process of handing Zamyatin over to Urinoff. The problem was that Rogers kept all the details of the operation to himself. He told me nothing. The only way of getting to him was through you. That's why I set up the meeting with you in France.'

'What went wrong in Juan Les Pins?' I asked.

'Joe Welensky, went wrong, that's what.'

'How so?'

'It was Joe who first got wind of what Rogers was up to. He recognised Urinoff when first we saw him that day down by the river in Kent and when I saw Rogers visit him on his boat I started to smell a rat.

'We started digging and the stench got stronger. We discovered that Rogers was running a black operation that in some way implicated the Russians, but he wasn't sharing information with anyone. All we knew was that you were involved in the op somehow and that was confirmed when you started putting together a team.'

'So that's why you followed me to France?'

'Not exactly, it was coincidental that we were in Juan Les Plage at the same time as you. Joe and I were working on another assignment with Rogers in the South of France when I discovered you were in town as well. I decided to meet you covertly, explain about our suspicions and see what we could find out from you.'

'So what happened?'

'Welensky got greedy and for some reason tried to put the squeeze on Rogers. Joe must have let slip about our meeting with you because by the time I got back to the safe house in the Allée des

Mouettes he had been blown away.'

'Who killed him?' I asked.

'Urinoff,' he replied. 'And no doubt he would have wasted me as well if I hadn't seen him removing Joe's body from the kitchen. He saw me, but I was too quick for him and I managed to escape through the back door.'

'Was Sam Potter in the house?' I asked.

He shook his head. 'Why do you ask?'

'Because when I arrived at the house somebody hit me over the head. Rogers told me it was Potter.'

'I doubt that. I'm pretty sure that Sam wasn't even in France at that time. I suspect it would have been either Urinoff or one of his stooges who whacked you.'

I nodded. It made sense.

We both looked down at Rogers.

'Thanks, Hank,' I said. 'I'm sorry you weren't able to take him alive. Death is too good for him.'

'No problem, Dave. It was either him or you.' He smiled. 'Now help me.' He bent over to take one of Rogers' arms.

I did not move as a thought struck me. 'What are you going to do with the body, Hank?' I asked.

'Well I'm not taking him to the American embassy, if that's what you think. The Firm won't thank me for killing him and I could never prove his guilt anyway. No, it's better for everybody if he simply disappears. I thought I might bury him somewhere out on the Cape Flats.' He looked up at me sharply. 'Why d'you ask?

'Because, unless you have something in which to wrap the body, you're going to make one hell of a mess of your boot.'

'Go on,' he said.

'I have a better idea,' I said and explained what I had in mind.

Together we carried Rogers to the cab of the Mercedes van and lifted him up into the cab where we wedged him upright in the driver's seat. I picked up the canvas bag containing the smoke grenades, wound down the window on the passenger door and then jumped down onto the sand. I was closely followed by Hank who slammed shut the driver's door behind him.

I went to the back of the van and opened one of the doors. Hank looked inside and noticed the motorcycle that was strapped to the back wall.

'Are you leaving that there?' He asked.

'Yeah, I'm going to take Rogers' Cadillac.'

'Good move. Are you ready?'

'Are you?'

'I'm ready.'

'OK. On three… One… two… three…' With that I threw a brandy into the back of the van and before it hit the floor Hank had slammed the door shut. The inside of the van filled with a brilliant white light and the rear window blew out in an explosion of heat that singed my eyebrows.

I ran to the front of the van and threw a second grenade through the open passenger window to vaporise Roger's body, leaving nothing recognisable.

Hank and I ran to the other side of the clearing where the two cars were parked and moved them further away from the burning van.

I got out of the Caddy and went to join Hank who had parked his car in front of me on the track through the woods. He wound down the window of his car and held out his hand. He paused as he was about to shake my hand and cocked an ear, but I could hear nothing. 'Motorcycles,' he said. 'Coming our way.'

'Only one,' I said, as finally I picked up the distinctive sound of a single motorcycle. I was disappointed. I had hoped to hear two bikes.

'Yeah, only one,' he agreed. 'It could be the cops.' He stared up the track with his hand still extended. 'I'm going to make a move,' he said eventually.

We shook hands and he turned the ignition key and the Merc roared into life. 'It was good doing business with you again, Dave' he said as he gunned the engine. 'Perhaps we'll meet again someday.'

'Not someday soon, I hope,' I said with a smile.

'Ciao!' Hank shouted as he accelerated away and drove at speed down the track with the Merc's suspension taking a beating from the bumpy surface. Then he hit the highway and with a squeal of tyres turned sharply right and headed south towards Bloubergstrand.

I checked my pistol in the headlights of the Cadillac and saw immediately that the hammer was jammed half open with a scorched piece of material. I quickly cleaned the gun and put it back into the holster that was still strapped to my waist.

I leaned into the car and turned off its lights just in time to see the single headlight of a motorcycle turn off the highway. The light bounced and weaved from side to side as the bike came towards me as the cyclist navigated his way through the pot holes that littered the dirt track.

Deciding it was better to be safe than sorry I slipped into the trees and waited. I watched the motorcycle slow as its light picked out the parked Cadillac, then it stopped when it was within a dozen yards of the car.

I saw a small figure jump from the pillion seat of the motorcycle. It was Freddie and she was pointing a Kalashnikov at the car. She moved to stand next to the motorcyclist who already had a rifle at the ready. I recognised Paul immediately, but, because I did not want any accidents, when I walked out of the trees and into the bright beam from the motorcycle's headlight I had my hands high above my head.

When Freddie recognised me she dropped her AK47 onto the ground, came running down the track, raising the visor of her crash helmet as she ran, and threw her arms about my neck. 'Oh, David,' she sobbed, 'I was so worried I'd never see you again.'

I silently hugged her tightly to my chest. I didn't know what else to do or say.

Paul joined us. He took off his helmet and I could see that his grime smeared face was taut with tension. He tried to smile but managed little more than a grimace.

'Tough?' I asked him as I gently disentangled myself from Freddie's embrace.

He nodded silently.

'Charlie and John?'

'Both dead,' he said with a sad shake of his head. Quickly he explained what had happened after I left them on the beach.

'Are you sure that John didn't survive the crash?' I asked.

'He had no chance,' Paul said firmly. 'The bakkie turned into a fireball.'

I stared into the night and remembered the stunt that John was doing the day I saw him on the film set in Hollywood. 'It's how he'd have wanted to go,' I said sombrely.

'You've been shot,' Freddie said in alarm. She touched the blood stained arm of my coat gently.

'It's only a flesh wound,' I assured her.

'Who owns the lekker car?' Paul asked.

'It belonged to Rogers, but he won't be needing it any more

so I thought Freddie and I would use it to get to Botswana. Nobody will stop us in a car with diplomatic plates.'

'Good idea,' Paul said. 'Mind if I join you?'

'Of course not, but I thought you were taking the motorbike?'

'If it's the choice between two wheels or four there is no contest and anyway, flesh wound or not, that arm is going to tighten up pretty soon and it will be difficult for you to drive.'

'Freddie can drive,' I pointed out.

Paul looked at me as if I were mad. 'Sies, man,' he said. 'This is South Africa, remember, and Freddie is a coloured.'

'He's right, Dave,' Freddie chipped in. 'At a pinch I could drive a white man around in an expensive car like that in Cape Town, but we'll be travelling upcountry. I would stick out like a sore thumb if I was spotted driving a Caddy in somewhere like the Orange Free State, even with diplomatic plates. What we need is a male chauffeur.'

What they said made sense. 'You're right in more ways than one. An embassy car with a chauffeur will look even more authentic.'

'But it won't look authentic if we're dressed in motorcycle leathers,' Paul said. 'I need a chauffeur's uniform and you two need different clothes.' He paused and smiled, more like his old self. 'I know just the place to get them, but first we need to get you to my doctor friend in Cape Town.'

'What are your plans when we reach Gaborone?' I asked Paul as he took the wheel of the Cadillac and I helped Freddie slide onto the back seat.

'Oh, I thought I'd let the dust settle for a few days,' the big South African said as he watched me ease myself gently into the passenger seat. He started the car and drove up the track towards the highway, taking care to avoid any potholes. 'Then I'll head back across the border to Sun City,' he added, 'and spend some of my ill-gotten gains on wine, women and song. What about you guys?'

'I'll be flying straight back to the UK,' I said without hesitation. 'Mister Mac had his heart set on a croft he saw in the Scottish Highlands and I promised him I would use his money to buy it for him. I intend keeping that promise.'

'I have always wanted to go to Scotland,' Freddie chipped in quietly from the back seat.

Paul laughed. 'That sounds like an offer you can't refuse,

Dave!'

I smiled, but said nothing. Having Freddie accompany me back to Britain was not the worst prospect I could think of. Suddenly I felt desperately tired.

'So where is Rogers and what happened to Zamyatin?' Paul asked as we drove at speed towards Cape Town.

'It's a long story,' I said with a yawn. 'I'll tell you all about it later. I just need to rest my eyes for a few minutes.'

'No problem. We have plenty of time. It's a long drive to Botswana,' Paul said, but I did not hear him. I was sleeping like a baby.

ACKNOWLEDGEMENTS

I would like to thank the following:-_

My wife Louise and my good friend Jessica Drewery for proof reading my manuscript and drawing to my attention the many typos that I made.

I am thankful to Louise also for her encouragement during the process of getting *Operation Seal Island* published. She does not always appreciate my stories, so it was good to deliver something she enjoyed reading!

To James Apps and Peter Apps (no relation) for all their hard work in editing my manuscript and making sensible suggestions for improving the grammar and lay-out.

In addition, to James and Peter for the way in which they help and give advice not only to me, but many other local writers.

To TAUP UK for publishing *Operation Seal Island* and for showing faith in my ability.

And, finally, I would like to thank YOU for wanting to read my book. I hope you enjoy it.

Gordon Henderson

Gordon Henderson was born in Brompton Military Hospital in 1948 and is proud to be a true 'Man of Kent'. His early life was spent in the Medway Towns, where he grew up on a council estate in Chatham and went to Fort Luton Secondary Modern School.

Gordon left school at 16 to join Woolworths, where he worked his way up from being a 'stockroom boy' to senior store manager.

After spending some time in South Africa, where he had a restaurant, Gordon had a succession of jobs. They included being a political agent, a senior contracts officer in the Aerospace Industry and an operations manager for an international manufacturing company.

In 2010 he was elected as Member of Parliament for Sittingbourne and Sheppey.

Following this, his first novel, Gordon is working on a follow up book, which sees David Statton return to work for the British Intelligence Service.

www.ingramcontent.com/pod-product-compliance
Lightning Source LLC
Chambersburg PA
CBHW051229260626
47162CB00002B/341